OCTOBER DAWN

Other books in the Mysteries in Time series

Murder on the Titanic
Voices from the Titanic
Murder at Gettysburg
Murder at Pearl Harbor

OCTOBER DAWN

A NOVEL BASED ON THE CUBAN MISSILE CRISIS

Mysteries in Time Series

JIM WALKER

BROADMAN
& HOLMAN
PUBLISHERS

Nashville, Tennessee

Published by Broadman & Holman Publishers, Nashville, Tennessee

0-8054-2324-9

Dewey Decimal Classification: 813

Subject Heading: CUBAN MISSILE CRISIS, 1962—FICTION

Library of Congress Card Catalog Number: 00-059893

Published in association with the literary agency of Alive
Communications, Inc., 7680 Goddard Street, Suite 200,
Colorado Springs, CO 80920.

Library of Congress Cataloging-in-Publication Data

Walker, James, 1948–

October dawn : a novel / Jim Walker.

    p. cm.

    ISBN 0-8054-2324-9 (pb)

1. Cuban Missile Crisis, 1962—Fiction. I. Title.

PS3573.A425334 O28 2001

813'.54—dc21

00-059893

CIP

1 2 3 4 5   05 04 03 02 01

This book is dedicated to Pat and Carol Murphy. Real friends don't just offer correction, they give their love. At a time in my life when I should have received correction—all Pat and Carol did was offer their love.

MAIN CHARACTERS

*J*ohnny Pera. An ex-football star and war hero. After his conversion in the pacific during the heat of battle, he came home, renounced the family business and his ties to it, went to seminary, and then into the pastorate. Johnny is a recent widower.

Gina Cumo. Was raised in the Pera household and became the family lawyer.

Rocko Benedeto. A long-time soldier in the family's organized crime business.

Arturo Pera. The thoughtful older brother of the Pera clan. He runs much of the family business.

Baldassare Pera. The younger brother of Johnny. He is a hothead and very difficult to control.

"Junior" John Cumo. A young soldier in the family business who is a rising and trusted star.

Scott Gordon. A colonel in the Marine Corps who serves as a special assistant to the president, also a war buddy of Johnny Pera.

Maria Gonzales. Leads a band of anti-Castro guerrillas on the island of Cuba.

Lorenzo "The Crow" Pera. He is Johnny's 76-year-old father and the head of organized crime on the West coast. His main enterprise is the gambling interests in Las Vegas.

Pia Pera. Johnny's 70-year-old mother. Her problems with her son stem from his conversion from Catholicism.

Isabella Pera. The youngest child in the Pera clan, Johnny's 27-year-old sister. Isabella is a troubled artist with two failed marriages.

Dominico Pera. One of Johnny's older brothers, an operative in the family.

Anna Cumo. The Pera family cook and the mother of Gina.

Mitch Pera. Johnny Pera's 20-year-old son.

Nancy Pera. Johnny's 17-year-old daughter.

Santos Trafficante. Leads organized crime's operations in the Miami area. He also maintains close contacts with the Cuban exile community. Santos Trafficante is a historical figure.

Sam Giancana. Runs organized crime's interest in the labor unions and in Chicago. Sam Giancana is a historical figure.

Enzo "The Cat" Gatto. The head of the New York crime family. He also has contacts with politicians in Washington.

Javier Lage. The Cuban exile commander responsible for the training and development of anti-Castro forces.

Cliff Cox. A CIA operative responsible for American assistance to Cuban exiles in Florida.

Felix Gonzales. Serves in Castro's secret police, the DGI; also Maria Gonzales' ex-husband.

Ray Jeffers. The head of congressional security.

Frank Bass. An FBI agent in Miami Beach. Frank is an ex-Marine and one of Johnny Pera's wartime buddies.

Hurricane Nancy. A fictional storm which hits the Florida Keys.

PART 1
THE FAMILY

CHAPTER 1

Javier pushed aside several bodies that were gliding gently in the water. As he stumbled through the surf, he looked back toward the beach. Cuban tanks were slowly grinding down the sandy slope. Castro's army had beaten them. He lifted his gold cross from the opening in his sweat-soaked T-shirt and kissed it gently. His only hope was in God now, not the United States. He had been a fool to trust them. There was no air cover, nothing to protect his men.

The chatter of machine guns erupted from the hills.

He dragged his boots in the dark, sandy brine of the hip-deep water, lifting his carbine over his head with both hands. He was determined not to lose that. The Bay of Pigs had become a bay of death—death of his men and death of his dream. The free Cuba he wanted would now sink further into the quicksand of communism. His nation had become part of Fidel's ego; his nation had become a place where slaves lived to serve a new idealistic dictator.

He looked out to sea. Several rubber rafts were bobbing over the waves. At least some of his men had gotten away and were trying to make their way to American ships lying in wait, safely off shore. The Americans had gone to great lengths to stay safely uninvolved.

He caught a flash of light from the trees just at the edge of the beach. He moved toward it, slinging the M-1 carbine he was carrying over his shoulder. The gentle tide tugged against his legs. One of the things the brass had promised him was that thousands of volunteers would suddenly join their cause, pouring out of the villages and towns to take their country back by force. *Where are they?* he wondered.

When he hit shallow water, he ran in the direction of the flashing signal light, splashing through the gently lapping waves. The sea clung to him as he ran, a heavy oily brine trying its best to keep him and make him one of the floaters he had seen.

He kept his head low and ran toward the trees. They were the reason the decision had been made to land at the Bay of Pigs in the first place. The trees were supposed to provide cover while Brigade 2056 landed safely on the sandy beach. He could only hope that Castro's troops were not in the trees. The idea of spending the rest of his life in Morro Castle had no appeal to him. He would fight—fight and die—before he allowed that to happen.

Javier hit the soft sand, his water-soaked boots sloshing. He had to find cover. It was several hours before dawn, and he had to be away from this place of death when the sun crested the mountains.

Once again he saw the flashing light, a popping low beam in the trees up ahead. It was not accompanied by gunfire, and for that he was grateful.

He hit the first dune and flopped down on his belly, the sand clinging to his wet uniform. He slithered his way up, lifted his head, and peered over the sand. There it was again, the light.

Bracing his arms under him, he pushed himself up again. His arms quivered, muscles shaking. His elbows seemed to be giving way. Why did he feel so weak? Was it fatigue? Fright? Either way he knew he could not stay where he was. He had to move, move in the direction of the light.

He heard a bang and spotted a flare in the distance, back toward the beach. It popped and arced into the black sky, before descending, its quivering blue finger of light probing the darkness. The Cuban army would be looking for stragglers. They would be looking for him. If he got up and ran now, they might very well spot him. Of course he knew that to remain anywhere close to the beach was only an invitation to die. Men with searchlights would soon be on the beach, men with dogs. He had to be gone before that happened. He had to go to the mountains.

He scrambled to his feet and ran for the tree-covered hills. His boots felt like mukluks in the soft sand. Every step felt like it could be his last, and the blue light from the flare licked at his face. *Can they see me?* he wondered. *Will they be coming in my direction?*

He scrambled up the steep edge of the slope, his feet twisting and slipping as he grabbed for roots and plants, anything to help pull him up from the beach. Kicking at the sand, he dug his toes into it, pounding out a step-by-step climb.

It took him some time, and when at last he reached the top, he collapsed facedown into the sandy grass, panting. His lungs were heaving, and his heart was pounding. He could hear his heart even over the sound of the distant gunfire. He rubbed his eyes. *So this is war*, he thought. *One scared rat escaping from the maze.*

Suddenly, several pairs of hands snatched him and yanked him off the slope. He was dragged a few short yards and then dropped. "Are you wounded?" one of the voices asked in Spanish. It was a woman's voice.

Javier looked up and saw the outline of the woman, surrounded by several men. He shook his head. "No. I am fine. Who are you?"

"We are the troops of Free Cuba," the woman said. The men with her stepped over to him and pulled him to his feet.

"Where are the rest of you?" he asked.

"This is all of us left. Castro has thrown thousands into jail, many, many thousands. He knew you were coming. Where are the Marines, the Americans?"

Javier shook his head. "They are not coming."

"But Kennedy promised the Marines. Your landing was just to be a provocation, then the Marines were going to land."

Javier spit on the ground. "American promises are worthless."

A sudden explosion behind them jerked their heads around.

"Our men are blowing up the bridge, but it is too late." She shook her head. "They were supposed to blow that up many hours ago, before the tanks could come."

The men beside her nodded.

"We go," she said. "We go to the mountains."

Javier followed them through the trees. One by one they ran across the road beyond. They climbed the hill, then stopped to look back as they heard the roar of trucks speeding along the road, trucks filled with Cuban troops. Those same trucks would soon be filled with prisoners, Javier's men. They would all be taken to jail. Brigade 2056 would be no more.

Javier's mind raced. More than just the Americans had gone wrong. There were traitors in the exile group in Miami. He knew that.

Security could not protect them against men who decided to betray their country. Someone had told Castro's army their plans. Everybody in the bars and along the streets of Miami seemed to know the plans for the invasion. There were no secrets that sons could conceal from their mothers, and women talked.

Shortly after dawn they came to a small valley in the mountains. A farm sat in the middle of the valley. The house, which had once been sunshine yellow, now peeled blisters of paint over exposed gray and cracked wood. The front porch had lost its steps years ago and now sloped dangerously forward, making the front door something of a climb. Only a gray porch swing swayed straight from heavy chains in the roof. The red tin roof sparkled with the clean morning sun. A large, broken-down barn with half of its roof gone stood open in the field across from the house. Tobacco leaves were piled inside the barn. Chickens squawked and scratched the ground, pawing their way in search of a morning meal.

The men ran ahead, their rifles at the ready. One of the men ran up the stairs and into the house while the other men crept into the barn.

"Do you know this place?" Javier asked.

The woman nodded. "Yes. It is my house. I live here with my mother."

"And who are you?"

The woman held her head up high. "I am Maria, Maria Gonzales."

In the light of day Javier could see that she was strikingly beautiful with ravenlike black hair and dark eyes that looked like wells filled with ink. Her pouty lips and high cheekbones gave her an aristocratic air.

One of the men who had gone into the barn stepped back outside and waved for them to come forward. Maria nodded, and she and Javier walked down the hill.

They stepped into the morning shadows of the barn. Several men scrambled to their feet and saluted. Another man, a priest, stepped out of the darkness. He was wearing a dark robe with a silver cross around his neck. He was thin, with haunted eyes and hollow cheeks.

Maria nodded at the man. "Thank you for coming, Father Yago."

"How could I not come, my child? You will be in need of spiritual food."

Maria nodded. "Yes, Father."

"God has spoken, but He has more to say. This will not stand. It will take time, God's time."

"Who is in charge here?" Javier asked. "I must see the man in charge." He had to get a boat back to Miami as soon as possible.

They all looked at him with blank stares, then looked over at Maria. The priest smiled. "God has given you an angel to watch over you, my son. You are with the 'man' in charge. Maria."

MORRO BAY, CALIFORNIA
SEPTEMBER 21, 1962

CHAPTER 2

A re you crying, Dad?" Nancy slouched forward, leaning her head over the backseat.

"No, I'm fine." Johnny wiped his eyes with the back of his hand. "I just haven't been to this place since your mother died."

The town of Morro Bay lay in a pile of shanties and cobblestones curled around a small harbor and overshadowed by the massive rock that gave the place its name, Morro Rock. A calm, azure-blue sea lapped at the docks like a panting dog. Small boats with faded paint rocked, their masts swaying like upside-down pendulums. The same fish places he remembered as a teenager still hunched over the water with their neon beer signs buzzing in the dusk of twilight. The windows were caked with salty dirt. The cook at Elmo's had taken the trouble to rub out an eye-sized circle of clean glass.

Cabrilho and the early Spanish explorers had dropped anchor here. The rock was hard to miss. Of course the railroad and the main highway leading from Los Angeles to San Francisco had done just that. Now it was just a fishing village and a place to buy gas for the visitors heading up the twisting highway to Hearst Castle. It was one thing more, however. It was the summer home of Lorenzo Pera, the Mafia boss who controlled West Coast gambling.

Johnny Pera hadn't been here since he was a senior at Stanford, over twenty years ago. The years had been kind to him. He was six-foot-two with dark hair and shining brown eyes, and his mustache completed what other people called his "Clark Gable good looks." Even though he was forty-two, just being in Morro Bay made him feel sixteen again.

The briny air and circling gulls smelled and looked just like he remembered. He shouldn't have been surprised to get an invitation to his parent's fiftieth wedding anniversary, but he was. He hadn't spoken to either his mother or father in the last fifteen years. Not since he had gone to seminary and betrayed what his parents had called "the faith of his homeland." He had gotten a card and flowers when Karen had died two years before, but no phone call. Their silence implied to Johnny that his wife's death was no doubt part of God's ongoing judgment on him for becoming a Protestant.

It was almost comical in a sad sort of way. His father had made his fortune in the rackets doing God only knew what, and yet God's judgment was leveled at his son. Johnny's sin was in betraying the Italian homeland, the church, and the pope. Murder could be forgiven; betrayal could not.

He pulled his bright green Avanti into the service station. The Studebaker always attracted attention. It took no time at all before a young man in a grease-smeared yellow smock came bounding out of the concrete bunker with the star painted on its side. His teenage face was covered with bright red pimples the grease couldn't mask. He jerked the nozzle out of its place and grinned. "High-test, mister?"

Johnny nodded, and the man began to pump gas. Johnny's son, Mitch, opened the passenger door and stepped out, placing his hands on the small of his back and bending backward to work out the tightness left by hours of driving from San Francisco. "Not much of a place is it?"

Mitch was handsome for a twenty-year-old, with sandy-brown hair that was straight like his mother's. He was a good student and played football, something she had never approved of. "It has its points."

Johnny looked over his shoulder at where his daughter, Nancy, had sat back and curled into the corner of the backseat. She was seventeen. Her feet, clad only in white socks, were curled under her. Nancy could always look comfortable no matter where she was. Her straight, blond hair fell around her face like a torn curtain. It made her brown eyes look that much larger. There was a knowing innocence to them, like she knew everything there was to know but refused to participate. "You all right, sugar?"

"I'm fine, Daddy. Are we there yet?"

"Yes, almost. Your grandfather's place is just down the road."

"My grandfather." She slurred the words. "I don't even know why we bothered to come. They've never bothered with us."

"You've seen your uncles, Arturo and Dominico. They've come to visit us, and they'll both be there, along with their kids."

"Just wake me when it's time to go back to San Francisco." With that, she closed her eyes, as if to shut out the unpleasant interruption of the world.

Johnny climbed out of the car as the service station attendant was replacing the gas nozzle. It was obvious the teenager wanted to see under the hood. Johnny watched as the lanky mechanic made his way around the car and popped the hood. Leaving the young man to his ooh's and ah's, Johnny stepped over to where Mitch was standing, taking in the streets of Morro Bay.

"You actually spent time here?"

"Every summer from June till September. Those were the months not even the lizards could live in Las Vegas."

Mitch shook his head and grinned. The dimples in the cheeks deepened when he smiled, and his dark eyes danced. "Sometimes, Dad, I just can't imagine what it was like for you as a kid, being driven everywhere like little Lord Fauntleroy. How'd your old man ever let you go into the Marines?"

"He didn't have any choice. The war was on. I was twenty-one and a graduate of Stanford. Plus, I was married to your mother. I was a man the same as he was."

"Yeah, but from the way you tell it, he was some kind of king."

Johnny shook his head. "Not really. He just acted like it."

Minutes later they were driving back down the small winding highway. Haystacks dotted fields of mown hay, and bright gold poppies sprinkled the side of the road. Johnny recognized the massive oak tree on his left that would have been perfect for a tree house if it hadn't already been occupied. Nestled into the large limbs was a platform that faced the road. A low wall formed a sort of blind with a gun emplacement behind it where his father had positioned a guard to keep watch on the gate and the road below. A twelve-foot-high rock wall, broken glass embedded in concrete along the top, rimmed the perimeter of the house. At sunset the shards would pick up the last rays of the dying sun in the Pacific and sparkle like a gigantic diamond necklace.

Johnny pulled the Avanti into the patch of sand in front of the massive iron-and-brass gate and rolled down his window. He stared straight ahead for a moment, clenching and relaxing his fingers on the steering wheel. He took a deep breath. The years came flooding back into his mind. Still staring stonily at the gate, he pushed his head out the window and yelled loudly, "It's Johnny, Johnny Pera."

He heard a buzz and then the hum of a motor as the gate opened.

The bars, iron studded with polished brass lion heads, swung open to the world that Johnny had known such a long time ago, the world of his boyhood. He had been happiest then, having picnics and playing on the beach without a worry. He had learned to swim, to explore the deep blue water. He had nurtured his innocence and given it up. It was here that he had fallen in love for the first time, experienced his first kiss, felt his first rush of manly passion. But that was another life, not his, not now, not ever again.

Johnny aimed the car down the rocky road and shifted into low gear. The road dipped down a long slope that exposed a sandy beach strewn with bits of dark green kelp. Off shore the kelp beds swayed with the tips of the plants rippling on the surface of the foamy surf. A prominent spit of land curled out from the beach into the water, knifing through the surf and forming a small beach some two hundred yards into the Pacific. This was the spot where he had gone years ago to be alone with his thoughts. No one could approach it without being seen. It was called Cutlass Beach because it cut through the water and emptied into the open ocean. It had one other advantage. It was beyond the kelp beds, so one could lie comfortably in the warm sand without wallowing in the slimy fronds. Seals would play there, and abalone beds were on the rocky sides of the spit. Otters would often float on the surface, balancing clams and abalone while they pounded on their bellies with rocks.

Nancy sat up in the backseat as they rounded a bend in the road and the house came into view. The mansion sat on a bluff overlooking the beach below. Orange steel pilings crisscrossed their way into a concrete foundation. A wraparound deck gave the house an appearance of a huge white coconut sheet cake atop a brown plate. The style had been contemporary some forty years ago when it was built. The white tiles on the roof sparkled with a pink hue in the setting sun. Windows ran the entire length of the beach side of the house. Even from the road, they could see the lights inside pouring onto the ocean below, shafts of illumination playing on the foam as it broke on the rocks.

Johnny could remember standing on the deck at night and throwing bread crumbs to the fish below. It was like living in an aquarium.

"Wow," Nancy said in a breathy, soft voice. "I didn't know. You never told us."

"I'm not sure I could have described it."

Mitch looked at him. "No, Dad. I don't think so. This is the kind of thing you have to see for yourself."

Nancy scooted closer to the front. "And we're staying here tonight?" she asked.

"I can't promise that. We were just invited to the party. We might have to go back into town and find a motel."

"Guess you don't rate, being a preacher," Mitch said.

"It's complicated. You have to understand the family. When I told them I was going into the ministry and went to seminary, it was like I was resigning from the Italian race and giving up the name Pera. It was like I was telling them they didn't raise me right."

Nancy laughed. "From what little we know about your family, Daddy, I'd think there would be a little more they ought to worry about in terms of what they pass on to their children than the kind of church they go to."

Johnny glanced back at her. "You have to understand something about the family and its business, sweetheart. They live two lives—personal and business. They never mix the two. What they do with gambling and the rackets means nothing to them when it comes to sitting down around the table at night. You might very well think your grandfather runs a string of five-and-dimes to listen to him at home. What I did struck at the core of their personal world, who they see themselves to be, how good they think they are in God's eyes. If they love their family and keep the sacraments, then they can sleep well at night. Everything else they justify. They see themselves as supplying a service to people who are corrupt anyway, people who deserve everything that happens to them.

Nancy shook her head. "Amazing."

"It's like a different world," Mitch added.

"Very different."

Johnny drove the Avanti into the rock driveway and rounded the circle in front of the main entrance. Two men flanked the double doors, one with a shotgun slung over his arm. Another young man opened Johnny's door. He had dark, thoughtful eyes that looked like they did more than take in what was readily available for everyone else to see. They looked deep inside you. "Welcome to Seacove, sir."

Johnny climbed out. "Thank you." He reached out and shook the man's hand, giving him a smile. "I'm Johnny Pera."

"I know who you are."

The words made Johnny's smile disappear for a moment.

Johnny had never seen the young man before, so he must have been shown pictures. How his parents had gotten recent pictures of him, he could only guess.

Johnny, Mitch, and Nancy walked up the stairs to the deck, and the man with the shotgun pushed open one of the large doors. They stepped inside where a maid greeted them and showed them the way to the great room. It was a sight Johnny had seen many times before.

Suddenly, however, he froze in front of something he hadn't seen before in the house. There on the wall were pictures of each of Lorenzo and Pia Pera's children. Recent pictures. In Johnny's picture, he was holding Karen in his arms. His dark eyes and square, handsome jaw were distinctively Pera features, along with his curly black hair and mustache. He remembered when the picture had been taken. Karen looked beautiful—dark hair, pouty lips, and smiling eyes. A lump formed in his throat.

He caught up with Mitch and Nancy and stepped into the great room. The large circular fireplace in the center of the room held a blazing fire. Red tile peeked between Oriental carpets, bear rugs, and sheepskins. The furniture was distinctive red leather, soft as butter, and was set off with antique lamps.

Across the room a massive form jumped to his feet. The man had a face that looked like a shovel with a wide smile and a glittering array of white teeth. His gray-and-brown hair swooped down over his forehead and flopped into position in a violent swerve that was pasted to the side of his head. "Johnny, Johnny, my boy, is that you?"

All at once it came back to him. It was hard not to recognize Rocko "Fish Face" Benedeto.

The giant lumbered forward, extending a massive gnarled paw, rough, with fingernails chewed to the core. Rocko pumped Johnny's hand ferociously, squeezing it like a vise. "Boy, we didn't know if you and your kids were going to show up at all." The sound of his voice was like gravel being spilt over a tin roof. "Wouldn't blame you if you didn't."

"Where's the family?"

Rocko released Johnny's hand and waved his paw. "Aw, you know your mama. She and Isabella drug your papa and some of the boys out to see that new movie, *Lawrence of Arabia*. They went over to San Luis. Ought to be back later."

"What about the rest of them?"

"Arturo's on the deck out back with Dom. Baldy went with Isabella and your folks. Are these your kids?"

Johnny stepped back to give the man a better look. "Yes, Mitch and Nancy."

Rocko grinned. "Nice to see they favor your wife." He laughed. "Although you always were the pretty boy of the family."

Mitch stepped up and tentatively shook the man's hand. Johnny saw his son wince slightly as Rocko gave him the familiar grip.

"Pleased to meet you, son. I got lots I could tell you about your old man when he was a kid. Lots." He dropped Mitch's hand and stepped over to Nancy. He bowed. "And you must be the looker in the family. Welcome to Seacove, Missy."

Nancy smiled sweetly, then looked back up at the walls. They were covered with art, an unorthodox mixture of impressionist paintings along with a few works that appeared to be Renaissance in style. Johnny could tell that she was determined to have little to do with the people who made up his family's friends. It was almost as if she saw herself guilty by association.

"You folks must be hungry. I think Anna has some things in the kitchen you might find to suit you, some sausages and a few cannolis."

"Is Anna still working here?"

"Shoot yes, boy. They're going to have to drag that poor woman out of the kitchen when she goes, and even then she'll have her fingers clutching that oven."

Johnny looked over to where Mitch was looking out the window. "You go ahead on out there, Mitch, and introduce yourself to your uncles. Nancy and I will go to the kitchen." He glanced at Rocko. "No need to worry about me here. I know my way around. Why don't you stick with Mitch there and guard his precious ears."

Rocko laughed. "Yeah, I better do just that."

Taking Nancy's arm Johnny guided her down the hall and through the large dining room and the swinging doors that led to the kitchen. The place hadn't changed in all the years he'd been gone. White and blue tiles covered counters with polished wooden cutting boards embedded into them for work with the sharp knives. The appliances were new and shone like they'd been polished with a soft cloth. Anna stood in the corner talking to a woman seated on a stool with her back turned to them. Anna's face fell when she saw them.

He grinned. "Rocko said you might have something to eat back here, if it's no trouble."

Anna dropped her hands to her side and smoothed her apron stiffly. The woman was just as he remembered, puffy cheeks with long black hair that had now turned a shade of gray. It reminded him of cotton candy left out in the rain, stiff and frozen in place. Her eyes glistened tearfully, a look that surprised Johnny.

He stepped forward. "This is my daughter, Nancy."

Without saying a word, Anna moved to the large double refrigerator and opened the door, removing a tray of sausages and a bowl of antipasto. The other woman swiveled around to face them. She was an attractive woman with dark eyes. Her thick black hair rested on her shoulders, and she smiled with bright, wide lips. Her long legs were crossed at the knee. "I was sorry to hear about Karen," she said.

Johnny stood stunned for a moment, not knowing what to say. He swallowed. "Thank you." Looking back, he realized that Nancy had suddenly become aware of the tension in the room. "This is my daughter, Nancy."

The woman smiled. "Pleased to meet you, Nancy. You look so much like your mother."

"Thank you." Nancy didn't take her eyes off her father, and Johnny knew she was dying to know what was going on, but he knew he could never tell her.

"Nancy, this is Gina, Anna's daughter. We were old friends a long time ago."

Gina smiled. "Yes, a long time ago."

"But so much has changed," Johnny added.

Gina's smile widened. "But amazing, isn't it? The more things change, the more they stay the same."

The silence of the moment was broken by the sound of breaking dishes. Anna had dropped a group of plates, and shards of crockery slid across the polished tile.

CHAPTER 3

T he greenish-brown jeep showed unmistakable signs of what had once been Army ownership—bent fenders and formerly black stars, now turned gray. The tattered top flapped furiously in the wind, making a popping noise that sounded like rapid gunfire.

Occasionally the jeep backfired, belching a small cloud of smoke that carried with it the aroma of spoiled milk mixed with soot. Everything about the vehicle smelled old, and the seats were cracked. Bare springs poked through the cracked and brittle vinyl-covered fabric. It was the sea that made riding in the thing bearable. The smell of the sea was almost overwhelming, like green saltwater taffy bubbling in a steaming pot.

The driver gripped the wheel and turned the corner at high speed on the winding highway, lifting two of the wheels slightly off the road. It fell back to the highway, jarring the men inside. The driver let up on the gas pedal to settle the jeep down and to keep the man in the small seat in the rear from pounding on his shoulder again. The man was an anxious sort, perhaps more concerned with his own safety than the mission.

The nervous passenger would beat on the driver's shoulder and bellow like a stuck bull. No doubt what they were carrying in the back made the man's discomfort even worse. The ladder and carpet were bad enough, but the guns would make anyone nervous. The floor was filled with ammunition and small canteens filled with water. They had dried fruit and some cans of Spam. He knew they wouldn't be able to cook the Spam, but they could eat it from the can with a spoon. It tasted horrible that way with its fat, jellylike coating covering the top, but when the jelly was scraped off, the meat was edible.

The man beside him was calmer. He held on to a small bar that was just under the windshield and let the wind whistle through his jet-black hair. The shotgun between his legs bounced from side to side, occasionally passing just under his Adam's apple. There was more than a nervous flinch each time that happened. The irony of blowing one's own head off due to a sudden rut in the road was something that evidently rippled through the man's head each time the muzzle of the 12-gauge passed under his neck. He would gulp and try his best to secure the weapon in the crook of an elbow. But each time they hit a sharp curve, the large double-barreled gun would come bouncing back.

When they came to the stretch of the road with the rock wall and large oak tree, the driver pressed the accelerator to the floor once again. They buzzed past the tree and large iron gate. Perhaps it was a mistake to take this stretch of road at such high speed. If anything, it might attract attention, and that was the last thing he wanted. It was too late though. He had done it. It wouldn't be long now. Just a few more minutes.

The sun was setting behind Morro Rock, bathing it in bright orange as the gulls circled overhead. The fog in the area had disappeared, and he hoped the night would be warm, though that was doubtful. They had sleeping bags, but the idea of shivering all night long never appealed to him.

They were being paid well, $10,000 each, and this was for something he could believe in, something important. No doubt doing the deed would feel little different from squashing a bug. Any bug can be squashed. But getting to and finding the bug was the problem.

They were dressed in army fatigue jackets and faded green army dungarees. His high-top combat boots were laced up halfway with the excess lace wound around his ankles. Fully laced boots would have cut into his calves like dull knives while driving. Only their flat black sweaters gave them away as civilians, and the turtlenecks were more for warmth and comfort than authenticity.

He slowed down as he came to the broken sign, JERRY'S BAR-B-Q, HOT EATS CHEAP. The road he was looking for was just beyond the next bend.

Rounding the bend, he spotted it. He whipped the wheel to the left and slammed on the brakes. The jeep went into a controlled skid, sideways down the highway. The problem was, he was the only one who knew it was controlled. The man in the backseat took up his pounding and yelling once again and didn't stop until the tires of the jeep spun forward, launching them across the highway and down the steep sandy road.

The jeep bounced heavily on the dirt road, creaking and rattling painfully. The man next to the driver clung to the barrel of the shotgun in desperation, his face turning pale. He let go of the bar and maintained a death grip on the gun, bouncing up and down in his seat. There was little the driver could do to end the man's fear.

He downshifted, jamming the transmission into low gear. A normal car would have found its hubcaps planted deep in the sand, trapped belly up like a tuna fish on a fishmonger's cutting table.

The jeep's wheels spun, scattering a hailstorm of rocks and sand, then with a lurch caught hold and ground its way down the steep slope. Rounding a curve, the jeep's occupants got a panoramic view of the Pacific. The sun was setting, sending blazing red arms over the water and tickling the beating surf with pink fingers. The sand stretched out before them, wet with the retreating tide and studded with rocks and the remnants of fresh kelp.

The driver pointed the jeep straight down the road, swinging the wheel from side to side to avoid the rocks in the middle of what had once been a barely passable road. It was hard for him to take his eyes off the water. It shimmered in the twilight. Several fishing boats bobbed from side to side, making their way out for a night of fishing.

When they reached the beach, he swung the jeep to the left, out onto the wet sand. The ride was smoother now. Picking up speed, the vehicle sent a spray of foamy brine off its back tires and into the air. The wall was straight ahead, jutting out into the water. The setting sun painted the angry, sharp glass on the top of the wall. It wouldn't take them long to climb the wall. He knew that. They had everything they needed. They would be over the top and up the Pera beach in no time. From there they would wait. They would wait for the bug there. He would come to them.

The Pera mansion had miles of private beach, and this was the end of it. The place was also deserted; no other homes were nearby. But that didn't mean they were home free. He knew that. There would be miles to travel, and if the police were alerted, they might have more than a small fight on their hands. Everything had to be done quickly, and whatever he had done in terms of breakneck speed in getting them here would have to be repeated. They would have to retrace their steps and do it without thinking.

He edged the jeep up next to the wall and stopped. The engine idled as the passengers sprang out. He was going to sit behind the wheel and keep the engine running just in case they were discovered. It paid to be safe. The nervous one who had been riding in the rear walked around and glared at him, giving him a silent scolding with his dark eyes. He then stepped to the back of the jeep and picked up the carpet. It was a roll of sand-colored shag that blended comfortably into the color of the rocks and cement. Jumping to the hood of the jeep, he tossed it up to the top of the wall and over the outcropping of sharp glass.

The other man took out the ladder and slid it into position beside the wall and in front of the jeep. He shook the aluminum ladder, burying it deeper into the sand. He hoisted the extension into place, once again shaking the ladder to ensure that it was grounded firmly. Planting his foot on the first rung, he climbed it carefully, occasionally stopping to make certain it was not giving way in the sand.

It took no more than a few minutes before the two passengers had gone over the wall. The driver was the last to go. He balanced himself on the carpet at the top of the wall and pulled up the aluminum ladder, dropping it over the other side. Then he dropped to the soft sand.

The twelve-foot drop was jarring, but the sand made it bearable. No place was impregnable, and while the house itself might be difficult to get into and out of safely, their contact on the inside had assured them that they could wait on the beach for their target to arrive. It would be the next day, hopefully in the morning, but it would happen. In the meantime they could enjoy a nice evening on the beach.

The timing was perfect. They had needed to make the drive in daylight. The road to the beach was easy to miss; to find it in the dark was impossible. What they didn't need, however, was so much day-light that a casual passerby would spot them. They had followed their orders. Tomorrow it would be over.

They shoved the ladder into a mass of green plants and spent the next few minutes gathering kelp on the beach to cover it. The three of them then hurried down the beach and away from the wall. There was no guarantee the man they were after would come this far. The one thing they had to be sure to do was to stay close enough so that it wouldn't take long to get back to the wall. Where they waited might be critical.

The beach was empty except for a few rocky outcroppings. The tide was going out and the sand was wet. The slope that rose from the beach was covered with a mat of green ice plants. It was hilly, and the few small dips in the sand might conceal them.

The sun finally slipped beneath the waves. All that was left was a faint pink glow, followed by darkness and the light left by the stars on the top of the waves. The stillness of the open water became more pronounced with the onset of night. The Pacific stretched out before them as far as the eye could see. The only thing on the water was the winking of several sets of lights from boats. One, no doubt, was the patrol boat belonging to the Pera family. The others were fishing boats going back to Morro Bay.

They ran along the sand past the first rock jetty. The surf was breaking over the top of it, pounding on the slick rocks and sending streams of saltwater into the air. A flock of sandpipers picked their way over the beach, searching for buried clams and mussels exposed by the retreating tide. The birds strutted on their spindly legs, peck-ing at bubbles in the sand that might contain their dinners. The run-ning men were practically on top of them in the growing darkness before they took flight.

Suddenly, the man in the lead came to an abrupt halt. He held out his arms. Up ahead were two men walking. Cigarettes glowed in the darkness. More than likely they were guards sent to explore and secure the beach.

He signaled toward the hilly slope, and the three of them ran for the protection of the plants. Moments later they were crawling on their hands and knees, peering over the hills at the oncoming cigarettes.

The men were walking slowly, taking their time looking at the beach and the retreating surf. Their forms couldn't be seen yet, only the glow of their cigarettes.

The rumbling laughter of the guards mixed with the crashing waves. The only questions were, how far would they walk? Would they get to the end of the wall?

The driver looked back at the wall, suddenly sickened. The carpet they had placed on the top of the wall was still there. How could he be so stupid? Even in the darkness, the tan shag seemed almost neon to him. Or did it just seem that way because he knew it was there? If the two men walked that far they might very well see it. Then they would know. Everything would be lost.

CHAPTER 4

Minutes later Johnny stepped out onto the rear deck with Nancy in tow. He couldn't have made a speedier exit from the kitchen. His face had a slight flush to it.

"What was that all about?" Nancy asked out of the side of her mouth in a low voice.

"Nothing. Anna was just clumsy tonight." He had no intention of explaining anything to his daughter, but he knew that wouldn't stop Nancy. She was like a terrier latched to a mail carrier's trouser leg. Fortunately, Mitch was with Johnny's two brothers, Arturo and Dom, behind the large spotlight on the deck. They were using it to shine down on the surf below and illuminate the fish who came up for food.

Mitch saw them and waved them over. "Come over here, Dad. There's a couple of otters down there."

They walked over to where the three men were standing. Arturo was the more thoughtful type. His nose was large and his thinning hair was draped over the top of his head. He usually maintained a serious expression, even when he was just having fun. Arturo was the oldest. Life for him was work, seldom play. He smiled and stepped toward them. "I'm glad to see you, Johnny. We didn't know if you would come. We have rooms for you and your kids down at the beach house. It's a place we built ten years ago on the other side of Cutlass Point."

"I wasn't sure we'd be staying. I was thinking about taking the kids back into town to a motel."

"There's no need for that."

Johnny watched as Dom swung the light around and pointed at the fish below. Mitch leaned over the rail to get a better view. Johnny glanced back at Nancy. "OK, we'll stay then. If we're on the other side of the point we'll be out from underfoot."

"If you're worried about Papa, don't. I know he wants to see you. He and Mom have both felt bad for you since Karen's death, and I know they want to bury the hatchet. They ask about you all the time."

Johnny stepped back and pulled Nancy forward.

"Nice to see you again, Nancy," Arturo said.

"Great to be here, Uncle Art. This is a great place."

Dominico left the light in Mitch's hands and joined his brothers. He had a round jaw and a head of heavy, black wavy hair. His shirt was open to mid chest. "Great to see you, Johnny, and you too, Nancy." He looked back in Mitch's direction. "You got yourself a great kid there. Star quarterback, I'd guess."

"Actually, he's a wide receiver. Mitch has speed."

"Like his old man," Dom grinned.

"Maybe faster."

Dom slapped his arm. "But not a boxer though, right? I seem to remember you were a fleet champion in the Marines. You still work out on the bag?"

Johnny nodded. "Yes, I do. It's hard to quit."

"Turning forty ought to slow you down, I would think."

"Forty-two actually, but if anything it makes me go harder."

A short time later the three brothers were seated around the fire in the great room. Dom and Arturo sipped port and sucked on thick cigars. Johnny watched the smoke rise, blending with the wood smoke going up the chimney. Rocko had taken both Mitch and Nancy down to the beach house, and that gave the three brothers a chance to catch up on each other's lives. Family business was not discussed, however. Johnny was now an outsider, and his brothers knew it. No matter how clean-cut the business in the casinos seemed to be, there was always the tinge of illegitimacy to it. Johnny was squeaky-clean, and that was just how he wanted to stay.

"So you're out of the preaching business?" Dom asked.

"Yes, for a year now."

Arturo leaned back. "Why did you leave?"

"Karen's death changed all that. I needed her too much and didn't want to be the object of people's pity."

Dom laughed. "You must have had all sorts of women throwing themselves at you, good-looking guy like you are."

Johnny blushed. "That was a problem too."

Rocko came into the room and pulled up a chair next to them. He took a cigar out of the humidor and clipped off the end. He struck a wooden match and lit the tip. It blossomed into a torrent of gray smoke. Waving the cigar at them, he smiled. "Don't let me interrupt you boys. I'm just killing time. I got your kids bedded down for the night, although I doubt if they're in bed. The sound of the surf has them all stirred up."

"I bet it does."

"So what are you doing now?" Arturo asked.

Johnny raised an eyebrow. "You don't know?"

Arturo grinned and flicked the ash off his cigar into the fireplace. "We know you work for a security company. That's all."

"Yes, I'm selling investigations and security. I guess they needed someone with a spotless reputation."

"And being related to us didn't curse you?" Dom laughed.

"It didn't help. I'll admit that. But my record is pretty clean, and they knew what I'd been doing before that."

"Winning the Silver Star in the Pacific didn't hurt you either, I'm sure. We might just be needing your services ourselves," Dom said.

Arturo waved off the remark. "No need to bring that up."

"I did notice you have the tree guard in place, and I couldn't help but see the man with the shotgun at the front door."

"That's not all," Dom added. "We've got plenty more you haven't seen."

Rocko let out a string of curse words. "The Cubans." He held up his cigar. "This is the only thing they are good for."

"What would the family have to do with Cuba?"

"I think we've said enough," Arturo growled. "Johnny's not in the business end of things."

"And this is no longer our business," Dom snapped back. He stared at Johnny. "Papa has all the casino action west of the Mississippi. The boys in New York and Chicago want to get gambling back into Cuba. They figure if the place can get straightened out then they'll have the ticket to do anything they want."

"Yeah, but there's this Castro guy," Rocko added. "He's sort of become a roadblock."

"Right, " Dom went on. "So they figure if they could take care of him they could get Papa to help them get the action going again.

Some of Papa's old cronies sort of roped him in on the play. They made a real point of it too."

Arturo flipped what remained of his cigar into the fire. "Yes, and Papa told them he was out of it, day before yesterday. His plate is full. He doesn't need the pain."

"Yeah," Dom added. "And you know how Trafficante and Giancana can get when you tell them no. Plus, there's Enzo 'The Cat.' The man gets purely hostile when you stiff-arm him."

Johnny sat back. "I don't think Papa would be making friends with the Cubans either."

"Either side," Dom shot back. "You go ahead with plans, and you make the Cuban commies into enemies. You back out, and the exiles who are filling up Miami hate your guts. Either way you got people out to tear you to shreds."

Arturo sat forward. "Papa thought it best to keep a wide circle from the whole thing. His business it too good for that. He doesn't need the hassle. If and when somebody else solves the Castro problem, then Papa will help them do business, but not before."

Rocko flicked his ash into a large, crystal ashtray. "The problem is Giancana in Chicago. He's Capone's old gunman. The man thinks that anybody who ever says no to him is an enemy. He don't care what the reason. Your papa's between the rock and the hard place. He's got to say no to somebody. He can't go forward, and he can't go back."

Arturo held up both of his hands. "All right, we've said too much already. This isn't Johnny's problem. It's ours. He's here to pay his respects to Papa and Mama, not get into this." He shrugged his shoulders at Johnny. "Don't worry. We've got things covered here. This will all blow over in no time. Kennedy blew that first landing in Cuba, that Bay of Pigs thing, but he won't make that mistake again. You'll see."

Dom smirked. "Our big brother here has some faith left in the democratic process and this president of ours. He thinks the man is going to pull a rabbit out of his hat, but the rest of us think it's going to turn out to be a roaring tiger. No matter what happens, the old greaseballs from New York and Chicago won't be here to help the folks cut their cake."

It was some time later when the front door opened. Johnny could hear the sound of what he was sure was his sister Isabella's laugh from the hallway. He assumed it was Isabella since he rarely ever heard his mother laugh. He could also hear his younger brother, Baldassare. The man's voice was loud. There had always been a brashness to him.

Johnny got to his feet and walked to the hallway. His mother saw him first and shot him an icy smile. Then his father spotted him. Lorenzo Pera was still spry for seventy-six years of age. He was thin with gray hair pulled back over the top and sides of his head. Unlike Johnny, his prominent Roman nose had a crook on the end of it that gave it a beaklike appearance. Men in the business called him "The Crow," and his beady black eyes made the label appropriate. His smile spread over his face.

"Johnny, my boy, it's good to see you." He stepped forward with long, sure strides.

Johnny held out his hand. "Great to see you, Papa. You look good."

The old man laughed and glanced back at Johnny's mother. "I should. I got to keep up with your mama you know." He slapped at his flat stomach. "She's got me eating healthy." His eyes sparkled as he grinned. "Of course tomorrow all bets are off. I get steak and cake."

"I'm glad." Johnny gripped him by the shoulders. "Wouldn't want you missing out on the party."

"No," he laughed. "It's going to be a celebration of patience."

"My patience," Pia said as she stepped forward.

"Yes, Mama." Johnny released his father and walking over to his mother, embraced her.

"Are you still . . . what you are?"

Johnny knew what she was driving at. His mother was a dedicated Catholic. She would have preferred to see him dead and buried in Catholic holy ground than to see him become a Protestant believer. He nodded and continued to smile. "Yes, Mama, I'm still what I am. I haven't changed. I'm like you that way. Once I find something I believe in, I stick to it."

Baldassare stepped forward, grinning from ear to ear. "Pretty boy." He stuck out his hand. "It's great to see you, pretty boy."

Johnny stuck out his hand and shook his brother's. "Great to see you, Baldy. Glad to see you're not in jail or six feet under."

Baldy grinned, then playfully slouched into a boxing position with both hands balled into fists. He started to bob and weave. "No way, Johnny, my boy. You got to get up pretty early to put one over on Baldy." He threw a couple of mock punches. "I stick to business, family business."

Pia put out her hand and stopped Baldy's punches. "Johnny's not interested in the family, dear. He has a higher calling."

"Enough of this talk," his father said. He reached back and grabbed Johnny's arm, leading him into the great room. "Johnny's not here for that. He's here for the party. Where are the children?"

"Rocko took them to the beach house."

Johnny spent some time talking to his parents in the great room, but he couldn't take his eyes off of Isabella. She was unusually quiet, sitting in an overstuffed leather chair with a glass of port, staring into the fire. Her laughter as she had come through the door had turned into a cold, somber stare. He leaned closer to his mother and lowered his voice. "How is Isabella doing?"

Pia shook her head. "Not good." She bit her lower lip, her eyes taking on a ghostly stare. "Two divorces can take the life out of a woman. When your hope dies, you die with it." A spark shot into her eyes. "Maybe you should talk to her. She always respected you."

Isabella was the only daughter, his mother's favorite. Anything that touched Isabella in the slightest way had an impact on their mother.

"I'll do what I can. You two should get to bed. Tomorrow's going to be a big day for you."

He said good-night to his parents and watched them head off to bed, then he wandered over to Isabella, who was still staring into the fire. "Are you still painting?"

She looked up at him and nodded her head. "Yes, I am."

"I'd love to see your work."

She got to her feet and put down her glass. A faint smile drifted over her face. "I'm upstairs in the loft. I turned it into a studio where I sleep."

"Probably where you live too," Johnny smiled.

He followed her, limping slightly up the stairs. His old war wound always seemed to react to the cold night air. The sconces that lit the upstairs hallway were seashells that sent a faint glow over the rich, wine-colored carpet. Isabella's work hung along the adobe walls. Most were beach scenes, and occasionally one depicted a boat tossed about during a storm. *Isabella painted her own soul,* Johnny thought, *moments of tranquillity in an otherwise stormy sea.*

She pushed open the door and stepped inside, turning on the lights. The loft was like he remembered. Two sides were glass with spectacular views of the beach and the ocean. A sliding glass door opened out onto the upstairs deck. The ceiling was also a massive skylight where Isabella had hung gauzy white curtains between the redwood beams to cut down on the morning glare.

Johnny stepped over to one of Isabella's large easels. It was spattered with paint, and brushes teetered on the edge of the tray. The canvas on it had a light-blue wash with strokes of white arching upward like the bristles of a porcupine. "Another seascape?"

"Yes," she nodded. She was wearing jeans and a skin-tight blue turtleneck with billows of cotton rolling down her neck. She rubbed the insides of her arms. "I love the sea. It's dark and full of mystery."

"Like you." Johnny looked at her and smiled. His little sister was no longer a girl, but her art brought out her childlike innocence. With a brush in her hand, she could be the little girl at play, removed from the pain of being a woman.

She stepped over to the window and looked out on the ocean. "I'm not that mysterious. I just hate my life. That's all."

Johnny walked over to her and put his hands on her shoulders. "Sis, if you do, you're the only one who does. Everyone else loves you."

She glanced back at him over her shoulder. "I'm twenty-seven, and I have two ex-husbands who might disagree with you."

"They're fools. You're a wonder just waiting to happen."

She began to cry softly, wiping the tears with the back of her hand.

Johnny turned her around. He took a handkerchief out of his pocket and dabbed her eyes with it. "Isabella, God loves you just exactly the way you are. He made you, and God loves the things He makes."

Her lip continued to quiver. "God makes things beautiful." She shook her head. "But I am not beautiful."

He tightened his grip on her shoulders. He knew better. Isabella was like a slender Mona Lisa. "Isabella, you're a beautiful woman. For all the things you see clearly when you're painting, how can you possibly miss what you look at in the mirror?"

She took the tips of her fingers and tapped them to her chest. "In here. In here, Johnny. I'm not beautiful inside. God couldn't possibly love what He sees in here. And how can you speak of God's love? He took Karen from you and took the thing you loved most to do in life."

She pulled away from him and stepped to the side, hugging her arms the way a child would shiver in the cold wind. "You even have your wound to remind you of all the horrible things you've seen. How can you possibly think that God is love?"

He swallowed hard. Reaching down, he tapped his leg. "This is a constant reminder of how very much God does love me. He allowed me to live, for a purpose. He sent Karen into my life to show me His love for a time. Now that she's gone He is center stage in my life, which is where I want Him to be. And Karen is also where I want her to be, with Him."

She bit her lower lip. "You have a simple Christian explanation for everything, don't you, Johnny?"

"There's nothing simple about it." He shook his head. "I feel pain. I feel pain in my leg and in my heart. I live one day at a time, knowing that God loves me and believing just that. Other people suffer too, but they may turn inside and find nothing to comfort them because nothing is there. There is only the cross, God's ultimate proof of His love."

"I just can't believe that. It's just too simple."

"It's not that simple, Sis. I wish it were. I'm a lonely man. For over twenty years I've been like a tree with no roots, and these past two years I've been that same tree without the branches. Karen's death took the life out of me. I take walks and want to tell her what I've seen, but she's not there to talk to. I had a part of me snatched away, with nothing to replace it." He tapped on his chest. "Now there are times when I feel like I have nothing inside."

He paced across the room, then turned. "People think I left the ministry because I had women chasing me, trying to feel sorry for me." He shook his head. "That's not true. I let them go on believing that though, probably because it makes me feel good. It strokes my ego. The fact is, I left the ministry because I felt lonely and hollow, empty inside. No amount of platitudes or verses of Scripture seemed to be able to fill up the holes."

"Why are you telling me this, Johnny?"

He stepped closer to her, putting his hand on her shoulder. "Because you're in pain, Sis. I guess it takes one to know one."

After Johnny left, Isabella went into the bathroom. She turned the sparkling handles of the bathtub and tested the gush of hot water. Placing the rubber stopper into the drain, she shook her hands and dried them off with a blue terry cloth towel. She stepped into her studio and picked up a sharp X-Acto knife, then moved to the sliding door. Opening the door, she walked out onto the deck.

The cool breeze of the ocean blew across her face, and she pushed her hair back to allow it to hit her cheeks with full force. Stepping up to the railing, she pushed the arms of her shirt up past her elbows.

She stood there for a moment, staring at the red ribbon scars on the insides of her arms. *One more time*, she thought. *Just one more time*.

Taking the knife, she slowly raked it across her left arm, watching the red threads widen and trickle down her arm and through her fingers. *Just one more time*.

CHAPTER 5

The sun was bright the next morning as catering trucks backed up to the door and a band assembled on the beach. Long tables were being set with white silk and gold-plated cutlery. Florists went back and forth with bouquets of yellow roses, grouping them into large cut-glass vases. A group of carpenters constructed a dance floor on the beach, while sound men set up a PA system.

Johnny knew his father would spare no expense. The man had engaged a brass band and an array of Vegas entertainers that included magicians and crooners who knew the Italian language and could sing songs of the old country. The family was all important in the Peras' thinking, and this event would surpass any wedding party that had ever been thrown.

Johnny and Mitch, dressed in swimming trunks and T-shirts with the Stanford University Indian logo on them, wound their way past the tables and onto a long stretch of open sand away from the festivities. They wouldn't have long to toss the football, but it was something Johnny wanted to do with Mitch before they had to change. He waved at Mitch to go long as he heaved the pigskin in his son's direction. "Hey, not bad," he shouted as Mitch snagged the ball. "You're going to make a wide receiver yet."

Mitch threw the ball back, grinning. "Your arm's not bad either, Dad, for an old man."

Once again, Johnny threw the ball in Mitch's direction and looked up to see his father plodding his way through the sand. The elder Pera looked relaxed in khaki trousers, a white polo shirt, and sparkling white tennis shoes. The outfit matched the silver in his father's hair. But Johnny could see that the old man's face was somber, not at all what he would expect. He caught the ball as Mitch threw it back. "What's wrong, Papa?"

The man stuck his hands in his pockets. "It's your sister. She had an accident in the middle of the night, and she's asking for you. We would have gotten you last night, but your mother said no."

"What sort of an accident?"

"She cut herself."

"Cut herself?" Johnny turned and started toward the house, but Lorenzo grabbed his arm.

"It wasn't exactly an accident. She's cut herself before, many times. Your mother went to check on her last night, and she was up in her tub bleeding to death. We took her to the hospital and brought her back this morning. The doctor gave her something to calm her, but your mother is worried and so am I."

"I see."

"I'm not sure you do. We've spoiled her, given her everything but happiness, it would seem. Every time she's tried to do something on her own she seems to fall flat on her face. We thought her first husband would be the answer, but he couldn't put up with her. Then we sent her to art school in San Francisco, where she met her second husband." He shook his head. "In a sad sort of way we figured he'd be right for her since he was an outsider and we didn't approve of him, but he didn't work out either. She tries. We try. But nothing seems to work. "I've tried to be a good father to her, paid her lots of attention. Why is she this way?"

"I don't know, Papa."

"Why would she do a thing like this on our fiftieth wedding anniversary? Can you tell me that?"

Johnny shook his head. "No, Papa, I can't."

"I am glad you're here. Frankly, I wouldn't know what to do about this if you hadn't come."

"And she wants to see me?"

Lorenzo nodded. "Yes, your mother wants her to come down to the party later, but she won't budge. She just wants to see you. You know how close she always felt to you."

"OK, Papa. I'll do what I can."

"Yes, you do what you can, and then I want to talk to you when you're finished."

A short time later Johnny pushed open the door to Isabella's room and stepped inside. She was propped up on her bed watching the surf pound on the beach below the window. On the far wall a TV set flickered. Lucille Ball was making candy on a conveyor belt, and the canned laughter seemed somehow inappropriate to the circumstances.

He walked over and sat down on the edge of her bed. "Papa told me you wanted to see me."

She looked at him and nodded. "Yes. Mama wanted to send for a priest, but I wanted you."

Johnny smiled. "I guess I'm sort of a priest."

She reached out with her bandaged arm and took hold of his hand. "Can you help someone with no hope?"

"I can try."

"Can people be forgiven?"

"Yes, of course they can."

"Sometimes I feel like a person slipping into a dark hole. The only difference is I want to go down there. I want to slip away to where no one can ever find me. I actually like watching myself bleed. It's almost as if the bad things inside of me are draining away."

Johnny patted her hand. "Isabella, you can't go to where no one can find you. God will always be able to find you, and when you leave this life, you will be standing before Him. The only question will be, have you asked Him for forgiveness?"

"You make forgiveness sound so easy."

"It isn't difficult for a God of love, Isabella. He already wants to forgive you."

"What about you? Can you forgive Papa for what they've done to you over the years, shutting you out of their lives? I'm not asking for Mama. She still has hard feelings, but Papa loves you."

"I have nothing but forgiveness in my heart for them. But forgiveness doesn't take root in people's hearts unless they are willing to ask."

"Can't you just tell them that you forgive them? It would mean so much if you made the first move."

"I told them that when I came home. They both know that I hold no bitter feelings. But I'm not sure they will ever experience it unless they ask me. It's like you and God. He loves you and always has. He is always willing to forgive you, but you have to ask."

"All right, preacher man. You've delivered your commercial. I'll think about what you've said. All I ask is that you find a way to forgive them. Look for it."

Johnny smiled. "OK, Sis. I will. Are you going to be joining us today?"

"I suppose I'll have to. Mama will die from embarrassment if I don't show up for the festivities. People will be coming from all over the country, and you know how she is if she has to explain where her children are. You know that's the only reason she let Papa invite you, don't you? You'd be more embarrassing to her if you weren't here than if she had to laugh and force a chuckle when you launch into one of your sermons."

"No sermons today, Sis. I'm playing it straight, like a good boy."

People had already started to arrive when Johnny went downstairs. Waiters from the catering company in short white jackets were circulating around the great room with silver trays filled with small crackers piled high with meats and cheeses. Others carried trays with mounds of caviar, and some bent low to offer the guests an array of oysters on the half shell. He picked up a spicy meatball that had been skewered by a toothpick with a flag in it.

Rocko was mingling, his deep belly laugh echoing in the noisy crowd. Beginning as a giggle, delight seemed to erupt from deep inside his massive gut and resonate until it exploded into rapid-fire guffaws. Johnny smiled as he popped the meatball into his mouth.

"Johnny, my boy, come over here. There's somebody I want you to meet."

Johnny walked over to where Rocko was standing. The man next to him had gray hair pulled back straight and a wedgelike nose. His pointed chin accentuated a perpetual frown. He wore a dark double-breasted suit with a blazing red tie. Holding up a thick cigar, a square black onyx ring flashed in the sunlight.

Johnny felt totally out of place. He was still barefoot and wearing his swim trunks and T-shirt. He forced a smile.

Rocko put his hand on the man's shoulder and steered him in Johnny's direction. "This here is Enzo 'the Cat' Gatto. He came here all the way from New York City."

Johnny reached out and shook the man's hand. "Nice of you to come all the way from New York."

The man studied him up and down. "So this is the black sheep of the Pera family." He laughed. "Or should I say the white lamb? I haven't seen you since you were playing stickball."

"That's been a long time ago." He looked down at himself and grinned. "You'll have to forgive my dress. I haven't changed yet. My son and I were outside playing football."

Rocko reached out and put a hand on Johnny's shoulder. "Johnny here was a football star in college. He was a war hero in the Pacific too. Was wounded in action and got the Silver Star."

The man blew out a puff of smoke at the notion.

"The Cat is your papa's contact with the government. He knows them all."

"Which government?" Johnny asked, smiling.

"Ours," Rocko shot back, slapping Johnny on the back. "Ours."

"The Crow is letting us down, backing out of an important deal. You should talk to your papa and tell him not to be such a big disappointment, you being a war hero and all."

"My father's business is not mine. He knows what he's doing."

"I rather doubt that," Gatto murmured. He stuck the cigar in his mouth and pointed his finger at Johnny. "The family has been very good to your papa. We set him up on the West Coast and made him a very wealthy man. Now it's time to pay the fiddler."

Johnny smiled. "Mr. Gatto, the Pera family is the only family I know anything about. If you'll excuse me, my father is waiting for me. He wanted to talk."

"You remember what I said," Gatto added. "You talk to him and explain about serving his country."

Johnny could hardly wait to get out the door. He wandered through a barrage of early guests, forcing himself to smile, aware that he wasn't presentable in polite society the way he was dressed.

Just as he started to leave, Baldassare reached out and grabbed him. He had a cigar protruding from his mouth and was wearing a blue suit with wide gray pinstripes and a pink shirt. Baldy always liked making a statement wherever he went. "You going back to see Papa?"

"Yes, if I can find him."

"I saw you talking to him earlier. I hope you can talk some sense into him. Giancana can help us with the unions, maybe get us some of that pension fund money to help us build more hotels."

Johnny shook his head. "I didn't talk to him about any of the family's business, and I don't intend to. What you do with your lives is your business. It has nothing to do with me."

Baldy grinned. "It should. You're getting part of the profits."

The very idea his brother thought that way made his blood boil. "I'm not getting a thing. I haven't taken a dime from this family since I went off to college. I had a scholarship there, and after that the Marines paid me. You can keep your money."

He hurried out the door. Making his way through the crowd on the deck, he went down the stairs and onto the beach. His father was still there talking to Mitch. This was the one grandson the old man hadn't spent much time with, and, unless Johnny missed his guess, he knew his father had taken a strong liking to him. Mitch was hard not to like. He was strong, good-looking, and had a natural smile.

"Hey, you two," Johnny yelled. "Why aren't you throwing the ball to your grandfather?"

Lorenzo held up both hands. "I'm afraid I'm too old for that. I just watch now."

Mitch threw the ball to Johnny. "You'll have to come see Mitch in a game this year, Papa. He's pretty good."

Lorenzo shot Mitch a glance. "I bet he is, if he's anything like you were."

"He is, and more." Johnny tossed the ball back to Mitch. "You'd better go get changed for the party, Son. Your grandfather and I have a few things to talk about. I'll be along in a bit. In the meantime, watch yourself with those pretty girls inside."

"Sure, Pop. I will." He tossed the ball into the air and caught it, then made his way to the beach house while Lorenzo and Johnny watched.

"That is one fine young man," Lorenzo said.

Johnny nodded. "Yes, he is. He reminds me of you a little. He's hardheaded and won't quit."

Lorenzo chuckled slightly. "I'm so glad to see that I'm leaving him with a few of my good points. I have lots of regrets in my life, but I think not knowing and spending time with him"—he jabbed his finger in Mitch's direction—"is one of my biggest."

He looked at Johnny. "I've been a fool in so many ways. You are a part of this family. I don't care what you are, and I don't care what you do. And you're Italian no matter what church you belong to."

"What are you trying to say to me, Papa?"

The old man hung his head and folded his hands. "This is hard for me. I can't remember the last time I said something like this. It might have been when I took a dime from my mama's purse and she caught me. I was ashamed."

"Say what, Papa?" Johnny knew he wasn't making this any easier for him.

Lorenzo murmured a string of curse words under his breath. He then looked Johnny directly in the eye. "I want to say I'm sorry. I'm sorry for the way we treated you. When Karen died, I wanted to go to you, but your mother thought that you might come back to us. I felt like a crummy spider for not going to you when you needed me."

Johnny reached out and took him in his arms. "Papa, I forgive you. I've always forgiven you. I know you were doing what you thought was best. I know you loved me, and I know you loved Karen."

Lorenzo, tears rolling down his cheek, leaned back and looked at Johnny. "We did love Karen. We knew she was best for you even when you were in college. We knew she'd make you a good wife and bear you wonderful children. And she did."

"Yes, she did. She was a good mother."

Johnny put his arm around Lorenzo as the two of them started back toward the house.

"I don't think your mother is going to be able to say anything to you. She is a strong Catholic."

"I know, Papa. Just so you and I are square. That's enough for me."

"We are, aren't we?"

Johnny nodded. "Yes, we are. I'm glad the kids and I could come today."

They looked up just as Gina was coming down the stairs from the deck. She was wearing a bright blue full dress with her dark hair swept up. Lorenzo stopped him when he saw her. "I didn't know she was going to be here. She was your mother's idea, and that was before we thought you might be coming. Anna's been with us a long time."

"That's OK, Papa. That was a long time ago."

"You know she had your baby, don't you?"

Johnny froze. "No."

Lorenzo nodded. "Yes, she did. We found out she was with child that year you went back to college. Your mother thought we should send her away to have the baby, and I paid for it. There was no reason for you to know. After that your mama worked hard for you to marry Karen."

"I just came back that summer and Gina was gone. No one said anything to me about it, not even Anna."

"She wouldn't have. Anna is loyal to the family. But don't you worry. Gina went on and built her own life. She's been back from time to time, but of course you were never around. There was no need to worry about what you or Karen might think. She built her life and you built yours."

"Is that why Mama was anxious for Karen and me to get married?"

Lorenzo shrugged his shoulders. "It might have been. You know your mama. She doesn't ever want embarrassment to the family. Maybe she figured that if you were married to Karen she wouldn't have to worry about you and Gina. Karen came from a good family, and Gina . . ."

"A servant's daughter."

Lorenzo shook his head. "But I can't figure that one out. Our parents were servants and lived on the streets of New York. We're no better than she is. You're the son of servants and farmers, if you ask me."

Johnny watched as Gina mingled with the guests on the beach. She was a beautiful woman, and she had been his first love. What had happened in the kitchen the night before suddenly made sense. But what had happened to the child—his child?

CHAPTER 6

T he Pera library was large with glass-covered oak shelves filled with books that Lorenzo had never read. He had bought them more for their leather covers than for anything else. Pia kept a collection of the New York Times best sellers, most of which were totally ignored. Lorenzo leaned back in his overstuffed leather chair to get a good window view of the party on the beach below where Pia was circulating among the guests.

Arturo was busy going over the receipts from the casinos for the previous month, but it held little interest for Lorenzo. "Do we have to do this today?"

Arturo stood up straight. "No, Papa. You don't have to do this at all. You do have a few people to see, though."

Lorenzo nodded slowly. He knew these things were customary at weddings, funerals, and celebrations where members of the extended business family gathered. He hated mixing business with family gatherings, but everyone expected it. They didn't come this far just to raise a glass in celebration.

"I want to see Isabella first. Send Baldassare after her."

Arturo nodded at one of the men standing at the door. He then looked back at his father. "She's not going to be in the best shape today."

Lorenzo was staring out the window. "Your mama. She is beautiful, is she not?"

"Yes, Papa, she's very beautiful."

"I always thought so from the first time I ever saw her. She was twelve years old and playing the piano in the church. I thought she was an angel sent from God. She had long graceful fingers that glided over the keys like a skater over the ice."

He swung his hands in the air. "It is the way she moves even when she doesn't think she is being watched." He tapped his chest. "It's part of her, this gracefulness. She floats through the air like a butterfly and gently lands on the people she talks to. I was too young to know what love was when I first saw her, but I knew that graceful butterfly had landed on me."

Arturo moved closer to him, then looked out the window. He could see his mother and the way she was mingling with the guests. "Papa, this is a special day for you and Mama. It isn't often you can find two people who've loved each other for so long."

The door opened and Isabella stepped though it, followed by Baldassare. She was wearing a black dress with long sleeves that had lace at the wrists.

"You wanted to see me, Papa?"

"Yes, yes." He waved his hand at Arturo and the others. "You all go away. Give me some time with my daughter."

One by one, the men in the room filed out. Lorenzo got up from his chair and walked around the massive desk. He sat down on the corner. "You look too good to wear black today."

Isabella pulled at the ends of her sleeves. "It's one of the few dresses I have with long sleeves.

He shook his head. "I don't understand. Why would you do such a thing to your mama and me on our wedding anniversary? You want us to greet our guests by telling them our only daughter has killed herself?"

Isabella backed up and collapsed into a leather chair. "Papa, you don't understand."

"No, I don't."

"You have everything just because you want it. You tell a man to go and he goes. You want a business to fail and it fails. You want a singer out of Vegas and he can't find work." She glared at him, narrowing her eyes. "You want someone dead and he turns up dead. You can have anything you want. But the one thing I want, not to exist, I cannot have. Why is that, Papa?"

"Because it is wrong."

"What's so wrong about it? Is it because I'm your daughter? I'm no better than anyone else. Nothing I have is mine. It all belongs to you." She pointed to her chest, tapping her finger. "The only thing I have is me, and what I want to do with the only thing I have, you won't even let me do that. My life is mine. And if I want to throw it away, I ought to be able to do it."

"It is a sin."

"No worse than any of your sins, Papa. Do you think because you build churches that your sins are better than mine? You go along with those people in New York just because they are powerful, and yet you commit far worse things than what I want to do. They tell you what to do, and you do it. It doesn't matter who you hurt."

"I am not doing what they say." He clenched his fist and banged on his chest. "I make my own decisions and I say no." He stuck his finger at her to make his point. "You will see who I say no to."

He walked over to the door and opened it, glancing back in her direction. Sticking his head out the door, he shouted in Arturo's direction. "Is the Cat waiting to see me?"

"Yes, Papa." Arturo snapped to his full height, immediately recognizing by his father's tone that this was not the time for delay.

"Go get him. Tell him I will see him now."

Several minutes later Arturo opened the door and stood aside for Rocko and Enzo to step in. Baldassare followed them into the room. Rocko had been assigned as the New York boss's nursemaid. Rocko was just the type, a glad-hander who knew where the booze was kept. He walked over to the far side of the room and stood aside to watch.

Enzo smiled and walked up to Lorenzo's desk. Reaching into his coat pocket, he pulled out a long, white envelope. "Congratulations on your golden wedding anniversary, Don Pera. I have a little gift. Something for you to use to get something for your beautiful wife. My family and I wish you every happiness."

Lorenzo looked over the man's shoulder to where Isabella was watching. Normally he would never let her see him do business, but this was different. He had a point to prove, and she had to see it.

He reached out and took the envelope, then laid it on the desk. Nodding at the man, he tried to seem subdued. "Thank you, Don Gatto. You are being very kind to us."

Gatto lifted his chin, obviously proud of the gift. "We are always kind to our friends. It grieves me when I hear that our friendship may not be repaid or respected. We offer our hand of friendship, and you swat it away like a fly that has landed on your dining table. All we ask is for respect."

"I would never refuse your friendship, Don Gatto."

Gatto stepped forward. "You already have. We had an arrangement and you backed out. Now I am embarrassed. I have people I told you would help, and when you say no, it makes me look bad."

"I have no desire to shame you. I just refuse to deal with this Cuba business—for now." Lorenzo waved his finger. "The future is different. If and when we have control of Cuba, I will help you. You are a big man. You already have so many men. What can you possibly want with my poor help?"

"I have already told your son." He glanced at Arturo. "You have such a large gambling interest. When you step in and say you are with us, the whole industry gets ready to go along. We will need plenty of money to rebuild Cuba, and your help now can start to turn the spigot."

"This is politics. Let the politicians handle politics."

"They will, but they need our help."

"Listen, we're both businessmen and this is business. I have the gambling in Vegas, and people come to Vegas from all over the country. People from New York come to Vegas to gamble. People from Miami Beach come to Vegas to gamble. The more people come, the better my business. Why should I build another Las Vegas in Cuba? I do that, I'm gonna lose business."

Baldassare spoke up. "Did you say Giancana was going to make sure we had union pension funds to build another casino?"

Enzo smiled at him. "Yeah, and plenty of money too."

Lorenzo got up from his chair and walked around the desk. "Even so, Don Gatto, I said I would help and I will. It will hurt me to see the Cubans get their land back, but I'll help them put it together when they do. Because that's the kind of man that I am. I look out for others even if it cuts my own hand off. But I won't do this." He shook his head. "I would be foolish to do this. You have plenty of pull without me."

"And that is your final word?"

"Yes, that is my final word. You have my help when the island is retaken, but not before."

"People won't be happy about this."

"You mean Giancana and Trafficante?"

Gatto nodded.

"Giancana is a thug, and Trafficante is a pimp. It shouldn't take all that much to keep them happy. They don't know better."

Gatto blinked furiously behind his glasses. He glanced at Rocko, who merely shrugged.

Lorenzo waved a hand at Rocko. "OK, take our friend and show him our hospitality. Make sure he gets plenty of steak and lobster. Nothing is too good for him."

Lorenzo put his hand on Gatto's shoulder as he walked him to the door. "I'm sorry I couldn't be of more help to you, my friend, but I will help when the time comes."

Gatto looked at him. "I'm sorry too. I will go now. I don't feel much like celebrating today, but give my regards to Pia. I have bad news to pass on, and they always like to get it quickly and face to face."

When Rocko and Gatto left the room, Lorenzo looked over to where Arturo sat quietly. "You think we should have helped them?"

"I think we should have tried." He shrugged his shoulders. "I don't think anything will come of it, so it really couldn't hurt us."

"Look, we have a visible business in this country, the bright lights of Vegas. How do you think it's going to look if the press finds out we've been involved with some government plot to assassinate a foreign leader? And don't think they won't. It's only a matter of time. And when those guineas fail, we gonna look bad. You see how it is if we go along with them? If they win, we lose business. If they fail, we lose business. This way, my way, we only lose if they win."

"And you don't think they're going to win?"

Lorenzo shook his head. "Not a snowball's chance in the Las Vegas desert. That man over there, this Castro fella, is too strong. I don't care how many soldiers they have working the hit. If our CIA and an army we trained couldn't bring him down, then a few grease-balls from New York, Chicago, and Miami can't do the job. This ain't the twenties any more. Al Capone isn't pushing the buttons. He's dead."

"All right, Papa. Have it your way."

"You bet I will. I'm going to protect this family and our business from those people and their castles in the air."

He looked over at Isabella. "You see, young lady, I can say no to those people. I don't have to do what they say. I'm my own man. I grew up with them in New York. Walked the streets with them. But I don't live with them. I live with you."

She nodded her head. "Yes, Papa, I see."

"And what I do, I do for the family. I don't do it to please myself. I do it for you, your mother, and your brothers. I've always tried to put our family first, and that's never going to change as long as this old heart keeps beating. I'll fight for you and also say no to the fighting if I want to."

"OK, Papa, you can say no. Why can't I say no too? Do I have to be owned like one of your hotels?"

Lorenzo walked over to her chair and looked down at her. "You are very valuable, much more valuable than any hotel. You are a gift, a beautiful gift. To take such a thing and throw it away is an insult to the giver."

"Now you're starting to sound like Johnny. You're not going to give me a sermon, too, are you?"

"Maybe Johnny's right. He was always smart."

"And have you and Mama forgiven him?"

"I've already talked to him about that. It was me who needed to ask for his forgiveness, and I did." He shook his head. "I've never done that before in my whole life."

"I'm glad." She got to her feet and smiled. "That makes me feel better. I've missed Johnny. I remember when I was in the second grade. He played with me and never treated me like just a kid."

"Well, you'll be happy to know that he's back."

She put her hand on his arm. "Good, Papa. Thank you."

He watched her leave the room, then walked over and took a white shirt and tie from the closet. He put them on, followed by a blue blazer. Pia would be proud of him. He wasn't going to the dinner on the beach dressed like a thug. He would be a gentleman.

He then stepped over to where Baldassare was seated. Raising his hand, he slapped him hard across the face. He then held up his index finger, shaking it in Baldassare's face. "Don't you ever do that again, not ever."

Baldassare rubbed his cheek where the slap had landed. "Do what, Papa?"

"Talk when I'm talking with someone outside of the family. You just sit there like a marble statue and say nothing." He pointed to the door. "You think that man doesn't know you want Giancana's union money?"

Leaning down, he looked directly into Baldassare's eyes. "He knows, and now he knows I have at least one son who disagrees with me. I want to be strong in front of a man like that, but you made me weak, you and that foolish mouth of yours."

Baldassare hung his head. "I'm sorry, Papa. It won't happen again."

Lorenzo straightened up. "Make sure it doesn't."

He walked to the door and out to the hallway. When he got to the great room, he saw Johnny coming through the front door. Lorenzo broke out into a broad smile. Johnny was wearing a dark suit with a maroon striped tie. He looked nice. He held out his hand. "Hey, Son, Mama will be proud of us."

Johnny beamed at Lorenzo's outfit. "Yes, she will."

"I just got finished talking with Isabella." He shook his head. "She worries me. I really don't know what we'd do without you."

"She's a wounded woman, Papa."

"Yes, and I don't know what I did to make her that way."

"You didn't do anything, Papa. Life breaks everyone, and afterward some are stronger at the broken places."

CHAPTER 7

Johnny sat at the table with Nancy and Mitch, watching his parents as the band began to play one of Sinatra's tunes, "Old Black Magic." The waiters poured champagne and moved among the tables, keeping the lobsters piled high and removing the remains of what had gone before. Rivers of aged Chivas Regal flowed, and laughter echoed out over the ocean. It was going to be a beautiful afternoon.

Isabella sat at the corner of her father's table and pushed her food around her plate. Johnny had let so much of her life slip by him. She had gone from a little girl, innocent and full of smiles, to a bruised and broken woman. The years had not been kind to her soul.

His brothers were involved with their own families. Arturo's wife was solemn and matronly. Dominico's wife, however, was bouncy. She flitted around the tables like a bee drawn to open flowers, chatting and smiling as she went. That hadn't changed. Baldassare was a different story. He now had a fourth wife, a showgirl with cotton-candy blond hair and a high squeaky voice. He was still chasing women, only now he was marrying them.

Johnny watched the young man who had met them at their car bend over Gina to fill her glass. No doubt he was armed. Arturo and Dom would not leave things to chance. He was positive that soldiers of the Pera family were carefully observing the entire gathering.

Occasionally Gina glanced in his direction and smiled. He wondered if she knew that he'd been told about their baby. She seemed cool and calm, not at all like he expected. Just seeing her sent daggers of guilt through him. His father had said that she'd gotten her own life, but something like that was hard for any woman to recover from, and he was responsible. Johnny was never the type to let a debt go unpaid. His conscience was much too tender for that.

Baldassare stepped over to Johnny's table and signaled for him to join him at the bar. Johnny looked at his kids. Obviously his brother had something to say he didn't want them to hear. He got up and followed Baldassare to the large black-and-chrome bar that had been erected on the beach.

"Scotch and soda," Baldy told the bartender.

"Ginger ale for me," Johnny added.

"Always the Boy Scout, aren't you?"

Johnny grinned and picked up his soft drink. "And you're living up to your reputation too, Baldassare 'Bad Boy' Pera."

Baldy picked up his glass and banged it against Johnny's soda glass. He placed his elbows on the bar, sipped his drink, and stared at his wife, who was seated several tables away. "She's something, ain't she?"

Johnny nodded and smiled. "She's something, all right."

"I always go for what catches my eye."

"Ever found someone who catches your heart?"

Baldassare laughed. "Hey, Boy Scout, when it catches my eye, my heart goes along with it. But you shouldn't talk, Karen was a looker. But as I recall, you always did fall in love with beautiful women." He cast a glance in Gina's direction. "So you and I aren't all that different."

"So why did you want to talk to me, Baldy? You want to discuss women?"

"Nah, I just want you to use your influence on Papa. Make him see things my way for a change."

"I can't do that. First of all, I don't know anything about the family business and don't want to. Second, given what I know about Papa, chances are he's right and you're wrong."

He started to walk away, but Baldassare grabbed him by the coat sleeve. "He needs your help. He's in dangerous water, only he's too bullheaded to know it."

Johnny's father got to his feet, picked up a gold knife, and tapped on the edge of his champagne glass. The chatter and laughter died quickly, and the band stopped mid song.

Lorenzo cleared his throat. "I'd like to say a few words." He glanced down at Pia. "Mama and I are happy you could all come and enjoy this occasion with us. Nothing is better than a man's friends and family. The rest of the world can go to blazes as far as I'm concerned."

As if on cue the guests, some jumping to their feet, broke into cheers and applause. Johnny's father motioned them back down.

"We have so much to be thankful for. First of all, we are thankful for our children." He looked in Johnny's direction. "And I'm happy my son Johnny could be here with his kids."

Johnny knew that naming him took a lot for his father to do. Most of the people knew that he hadn't been a part of the Pera family for over twenty years, and they knew why. By saying his name in front of those gathered around the tables, his father was telling the people on the beach that he was sorry.

"He graduated college." Lorenzo grinned. "And he was a football star. He was in the Marines and won the Silver Star in the war." Lorenzo picked up his glass and held it up in Johnny's direction. "And he has two beautiful kids."

Johnny was beginning to feel uncomfortable. His father appeared to be singling him out and ignoring his other children. He could see Arturo's wife squirming in her seat. Even Dom's wife had stopped her self-appointed hostess role and was listening intently for the sound of her name along with that of her husband. This was becoming unwelcome praise as far as Johnny was concerned.

"Just him being here proves that we are a family once again." Lorenzo raised his glass. "I want to propose a toast"—he looked around at the gathering—"to the family."

This time all the guests got to their feet and held their glasses high. "To the family," they shouted in unison.

After the toasts, while everyone else sipped coffee, Rocko chased several of the younger grandchildren around the tables. The man loved children. He made growling noises, his hands extended and his sausage fingers wiggling in the air. He would be tickling any captives he might be able to track down.

Johnny rejoined the family, and Nancy watched Rocko as he ran after the children. "I think he's a scary man."

"Rocko? Get serious. He's a teddy bear."

"I am serious. He's in your father's business, isn't he?"

Johnny nodded. "Yes, he has been for years."

"Look at those hands of his. He might be trying to tickle children right now, but my bet is he's broken a few necks with those." She leaned forward with her chin on her folded hands, continuing to study the big man. "He's scary and he's big. Can you imagine how someone owing Grandfather money would feel with him coming through the door?"

Johnny stared at her. "You are an unusual young woman. I don't think I could find many women your age who spend the time studying people the way you do."

"Well, Dad, look around you. This may be our family and four hundred of 'our' closest friends," she snickered, "but it's also one of the greatest collection of murderers, pimps, loan sharks, and thieves ever assembled on one beach."

Johnny patted her hand. "You sure are cynical for one so young, but then you're an idealist like your mother. Only idealists turn into cynics. They see the glory in their minds spoiled by reality."

Nancy smiled. "You're an idealist too, Dad. Where do you think I got this desire to save everyone?"

"OK." Johnny laughed. "You got a double dose of it, from me and your mother."

"Probably. You wouldn't take a dime from these people in the worst times you and Mom had. You'd just as soon eat ketchup soup as to tell them you had any needs. Maybe that's idealism mixed with pride. Me, I'm just a people watcher. I like to figure people out. Take that woman over there." She pointed in Gina's direction. "She's been shooting you glances all day, and from the way you looked at her last night, I'd say she was BOM."

"BOM?"

"Before our mom."

"You don't know what you're talking about."

"I don't? I know about people, and I know what I saw."

"Gina and I were friends, but that was a long time ago. She was your age and I was your brother's age."

Nancy slumped over in his direction. "How good of friends?"

"Just friends."

"Did you love her?" She batted her eyes in a way she always did when she wanted something.

Johnny swallowed. "I thought I did. But that was a long time ago. Kids your age fall in and out of love as often as they change their clothes. I was too young to know what I wanted back then. Mostly I just wanted somebody I could talk to."

"Do you think you could still have feelings for her?" Nancy glanced back in Gina's direction. "Because unless I miss my guess, she still has feelings for you."

"So much has happened since then. I've changed. I married your mother. I went to war. I became a Christian. My whole world has turned over since I knew Gina Cumo."

Nancy reached out and tapped his chest lightly. "But the man on the inside is still there."

Johnny looked up to see his parents walking toward their table. Two young men were following them. He stood up as they approached.

"Johnny, why don't you take a drive with me down the beach?"

"Now, Papa? The party's still going on?"

Lorenzo looked at Pia. "Yes, now. Your mama and I have been talking. There's something I should discuss with you."

"OK, if you insist." He looked at the two men behind his father. They were obviously armed. "But I'd rather be alone with you."

Pia shook her head. "No, you have to take someone with you."

"I'll be all right. This is my place, my beach." Lorenzo looked at Johnny and smiled. "Besides, he's not in the business. If he's more comfortable talking to me with just the two of us, then that's fine by me." He looked at Johnny. "I'd take you inside, but Rocko says there's lots of people in there waiting to see me."

"I still don't think you two should go alone," Pia said.

"Johnny have you met Junior here?" He stepped back and pulled one of the young men forward. It was the man with the dark eyes who had greeted them when they drove up, the man who said he knew Johnny.

"I saw him, but we were never introduced."

"You two have the same name, but we call him Junior. Junior's been with the family since he was a little kid. He practically grew up here on the beach."

"Pleased to meet you." Johnny shook his hand.

"Why don't we take that pretty green car of yours you came in with?"

"My Avanti?"

"Yeah, that's it." He grinned. "I like that. Sounds Italian."

Johnny said his good-byes to the children, then walked off with his father in the direction of the garage. "This has to be pretty important, Papa, to take you away from your party."

"You know how I am. Once I get to thinking about something it just doesn't go away by itself."

Johnny laughed, then put his arm over Lorenzo's shoulder. "Yeah, Papa. I know how you are."

"Especially when it involves money."

"Money?"

"Yeah, your money."

"I don't have any money."

"Yes you do. You just don't know about it."

A few minutes later Johnny was backing the Avanti out of the garage where it had been stored. "You want to go into town or down the highway?" Johnny asked.

Lorenzo shook his head. "Nah, your mother would have fits. She's such a cautious woman." He signaled with his hand like someone shooing away a pesky fly. "Let's just go for a drive down the beach. I own a lot of it you know."

Johnny nodded and shifted the car into gear. He rounded the big driveway in front of the house and headed down the asphalt roadway that led to the beach. Within moments he had pulled out onto the sand.

"Go ahead," Lorenzo said. "Open her up and let's see what she'll do."

Johnny stomped on the gas pedal, sending the bright green car into a fishtail on the sand. He straightened the wheel and launched them over the beach on a roar. His father loved speed. So much of Lorenzo's life had been death defying in many ways, and he always welcomed the thrill, any thrill at all. "Mom is going to have your hide, you know."

"Go ahead. Let's see some speed."

Miles of beach owned by the Pera family stretched out before them. The afternoon sun bounced off the bright blue ocean, and sandy hills were flooded with a warm bath of intense light. Birds flew as Johnny carelessly sped down the middle of the beach. He suddenly stomped on the brake and twisted the wheel, sending the car into a series of skids and turns. The nose of the vehicle wound up pointing back in the direction of the house.

Lorenzo was laughing and clapping his hands. "That was good. That was very good." He took a moment to get his breath. "Why don't we get out and walk for a bit? I have something to say to you, and I'm not sure I can do it with my heart pounding."

They got out and started walking down the beach. The waves broke over the sandy beach, sending sheets of foam lapping in their direction. "You remember when we used to go digging for clams out here, Papa?"

Lorenzo nodded. "Yeah, and your mama would make clam sauce for the spaghetti. Fabulous stuff, rich and red with good wine." He motioned with his hands, raising them to make his point. "The smell would fill the whole house. I loved it. You know all this oyster, lobster, and steak is good, but I'd give the world for your mama's sauce on pasta."

Several seagulls circled the beach in slow loops. Johnny put his arm around him. "Yeah, Papa. Those were good days."

"Very good days. We've had other good times too, and you missed them. We kept you away, and you should have been here."

"Papa, I understand. You and Mama were only doing what you knew to do."

"And we were wrong. But we didn't forget you."

"I know you never forgot me, Papa."

"No, I mean we set something aside for you, something that belongs to you."

Johnny looked at him. He knew his father always measured love with money. It was why he had refused to accept it from them when he and Karen were struggling. As far as Johnny was concerned, it clouded the issue.

"Papa, I don't need your money."

Lorenzo held up a hand as if to stop him. "I know you don't need it. But we need to give it. By rights it's yours. I don't want you to have to wait until I die to get it, that's all. Your mama and I set some stocks and money aside for you. We did that when you were a little boy and added to it as the years went by."

Johnny knew he was making a point. He was trying in the only way he knew how to express the fact that their love for him had never been put on hold. It was the Pera way of saying I love you.

A flock of sandpipers scurried down the beach, then suddenly flew away.

Johnny watched as three men in military attire stepped out from behind the dunes. "I wonder what they want?"

"I don't know," Lorenzo said, "but they shouldn't be here. This is a private beach, not one for military exercises."

"You stay here, Papa. I'll go see what they want."

He walked forward, taking long strides to intercept the three strangers. The closer he got, the more uneasy he became. The men were not carrying military-issue arms. One carried a scoped rife, another a shotgun, and the third seemed to be sporting an automatic weapon that was not U.S. issue. "Are you men lost? This is private property."

The men smiled. Their look made him even more suspicious. Two of the men sported beards.

The man carrying the rifle stepped closer to him. "No, we're not lost." Johnny thought he detected an accent. "You are." With that he swung the rifle and cracked Johnny on the side of the head. Johnny went down in a heap. The man stepped on him and rammed the butt of the rifle into his temple. Then everything turned black.

CHAPTER 8

Johnny jerked awake and fluttered his eyes from the smelling salts. An ambulance was pulling away in the distance, and Rocko had him in his lap. His mother was standing by in tears.

"What happened?"

"Your father's dead," Rocko said in a gravelly voice.

Johnny got up on his elbows, his head still a blur. Dom was pushing back the crowd that had gathered. Arturo was talking to a group of the family soldiers.

"We got to get you into the house," Rocko said. "The police want to talk to you."

Rocko helped Johnny to his feet while a man in a light-blue seersucker suit started asking questions.

"I'm Lieutenant Williams of the San Luis Obispo County sheriff's office. We need to ask you a few questions."

"Can't you wait till we get him in the house?" Rocko snarled.

The man backed away and dutifully followed them as Rocko placed Johnny's arm over his shoulder and walked him toward the car. He loaded him in the passenger seat and climbed in behind the wheel. Rocko shifted into gear and rolled the vehicle through the scattering crowd.

He pulled up outside the front door in a matter of minutes. He squeezed his way out of the seat and went around to Johnny's door. Rocko lifted him from the seat and once again placed Johnny's arm over his shoulder.

Making their way through the great room, Rocko glided him down the hall and into the library. Gently, Rocko led him to a leather sofa to sit down.

"You all right, kid?" Rocko reached over to the table and poured him a glass of water.

Johnny placed the cool glass up to his forehead, rubbing it over his face and head.

Rocko looked back at the group gathered in the doorway. "Somebody get the kid here an ice pack. Make it quick."

Johnny placed the glass to his lips and began to drink. A minute later the man in the seersucker suit walked into the room, followed by Junior carrying an ice pack.

Johnny took the blue ice pack and placed it on his head. His head was still throbbing.

"OK, Lieutenant, he's all yours," Rocko said, "but just for a little while. We've sent for the doctor, and Johnny needs to lie down."

"I have just a few questions. How many men were there?"

"Three," Johnny croaked.

"You ever see them before?"

Johnny shook his head. "No, never."

"What did they look like?"

Johnny gave him a description of the men while the lieutenant scribbled notes. He also gave a careful description of the weapons they were carrying. He looked up. "They weren't military, though. I could tell that. And I think they spoke with an accent."

"What kind of an accent?"

"Spanish or maybe Italian. I'm not sure."

"Would you recognize these men if you saw them again?"

"You bet I would."

"Good. We'll send over an sketch artist, a lady who works with us out of the art department at the college. You can give her a picture of the men you saw."

"Sure," Johnny said. "Sure."

"You're not going to be going anywhere anytime soon are you? You're our only material witness."

"I'm not planning on it."

"Can you think of anyone who might want to kill your father?"

Johnny looked over at Rocko for a moment. "You've got to be kidding. I grew up in this house, and I can't remember a time when somebody somewhere didn't want to see my father dead."

"We'll be keeping in touch. You stay close to home."

Rocko walked the man to the door and then turned back to Johnny. "We ain't gonna count on those people. We'll find out for ourselves who done this. You did real good, though kid." He smiled. "Handled yourself fine."

Johnny placed his head in his hands. "No, I didn't. We should have listened to Mama and taken people with us."

Rocko stepped over to him and placed one of his big paws on his shoulder. "You can't beat yourself up about that, Johnny. Who would have thought those people would have gotten over the wall and into the compound? We have men who walk that stretch of beach too, walk it every day. I'm going to have to talk with them."

"Where's Mama?"

Rocko shook his head. "She's not doing good. The doctor's looking in on her now before he comes to find you. The woman is broken. To have this happen on their fiftieth anniversary makes it worse."

"I better go see her."

Rocko shook his head. "Might not be the best idea."

Johnny got to his feet and left Rocko in the library just as his brothers were coming in. He walked down the hall to his parents' room and opened the door. Seeing the familiar room again, he wondered anew how his father had managed to live with it. The room was pink, his mother's favorite color. The canopied bed, Old English style bureau, and chest of drawers were polished oak. Along the top of the walls were shelves holding his mother's collection of at least a hundred porcelain dolls dressed in frills, hats, and lace. Curiously, most of the dolls were blond.

Johnny focused on his mother, who hadn't seen him yet. Sitting on the love seat that had been turned around to face the window, she was staring out to sea. Gina sat next to her. Pia had already changed into a black, high-neck dress that made her ivory skin even paler. *How like Mama. Always proper.*

Gina spotted Johnny and walked over to him.

"I wanted to say something to Mama."

Gina shook her head. She spoke in a low whisper. "I don't think that would be helpful right now."

Johnny ignored her and walked over to where his mother was seated. He put his hand on her shoulder. "Mama, I'm so sorry, so very sorry."

She ignored him, but he could see her face tighten. A coldness came over her. She hunched forward, pulling her shoulder away from his hand, and continued to stare at the ocean.

Self-consciously, Johnny stuck his hands in his pocket. "We should have listened to you, Mama, and had people go with us."

"You should have listened to me." The words were cold and emotionless. "Your father would have done as I said. If it hadn't been for you, he would still be here."

Gina took him by the shoulder and pulled him away. She signaled him with the movement of her head to follow her into the hallway.

When they stepped into the hall, Gina closed the door. "Please don't take this too harshly. Your mother is in deep grief. It's only natural for her to be angry and to lash out at someone."

"Maybe she's right. I should have listened."

Gina touched his cheek and ducked her head so she could make eye contact with his downcast eyes. "Maybe, like her, you need to listen. I won't argue." Gina smiled. "You are your mother's son, much as you'd like to deny it. But this time it's not your fault. Those men weren't there by accident. They would have . . ." Gina stopped, suddenly running out of energy.

Johnny looked back at the closed door. "Then why doesn't she know that?"

"She needs some time to understand things better, that's all. Give her time. This has been a shock to her."

Johnny bowed his head. "I won't even be able to go to my own father's funeral or the viewing with Mama looking at me like it's my fault."

Gina put her hand on his arm. "I'll explain things to her when it's time. I'll tell her that you love her. That's all she needs to hear. Sometimes things happen to us that we have no control over. People feel wronged and violated, but they get over it. They recover."

"That's what I told Papa this morning. I told him that life breaks everyone and afterward some of us get stronger at the broken places. I know this has broken Mama, but it's broken me too. We need each other now more than ever."

Gina softly wrapped her arms around him and held him. "You'll get stronger Johnny. This is not your fault."

Johnny spent the rest of the afternoon walking on the beach. Earlier, both Mitch and Nancy had come to see him and they had been sympathetic. Their grandfather was someone they had never known, except by reputation, so there hadn't been much to say. Mitch had tried to talk, but Nancy had simply sat there and listened to him.

Johnny's self-accusatory thought roared through his brain. He had wanted to be alone with his father, not shadowed by goons who could overhear them talking. His father always seemed to have men, family soldiers, who hung around him and looked for every opportunity to look good. They were fixtures in his father's life like cuff links and bedroom slippers, always there and usually ignored. Yet when his father had needed them, Johnny had sent them away.

It was easy to see the reactions of his family. After all, he was the outsider. How did he know what to do? He hadn't been around for over twenty years, and now he had shown up and gotten his father killed, all because of his desire to forget that his father was a Mafia boss if only for a brief time. He had trusted his instincts when he shouldn't have. Now his family blamed him for what had happened.

Rocko had been comforting, but he wasn't family. Gina had been tender and kind, but in some ways that bothered him. He should have asked for her forgiveness.

What had she thought for all these years? he wondered. *Had she thought that I just didn't care that she was pregnant, that I had gone off to Stanford to be a big star and didn't give a second thought about her?* On reflection now, what had happened seemed odd. But he didn't know about her and the baby. He never knew. *Did Gina know that?*

CHAPTER 9

Nancy spent the better part of an hour in the house watching people rush around in a frantic search for someone to tell them what to say and do. Her grandfather had been the main-spring of the entire operation, and without him no one knew what to do next. She shrugged her shoulders and joined a group of guests walking out the main door. She would go to her room and read.

As she walked along the pathway to her room, she spotted a large, red barnlike building on the hill above the beach house. It was painted red with white trim, a red metal rooster stood on the top of one of the turrets, and she could see hay in the loft. The stretch of white fencing told her what the place was, and she couldn't wait to see it firsthand. One of the things her father had told her when she agreed to come was that the Pera family had a stable full of horses.

She took a turn on the path and climbed a set of flagstone steps that led to the open area the barn was sitting on. A large oak tree stretched its limbs over the path and shaded the fenced-in area. She had loved horses for a long time, but given the fact that they lived in the hills of San Francisco, she rarely got a chance to ride.

She walked up to the barn, slid the big door open, and stepped inside. The stables were pristine, whitewashed with polished stalls. Saddles were arranged on racks, and halters, bits, and bridles hung on wooden pegs. Everything was in order. Horses poked their heads over their stalls, eyeing her as she walked past. They were magnificent.

She put a foot up on a bale of hay and watched a black quarter horse stallion race around the stall. He was like something wild, tossing his head, snorting, and then running to the other side of his large pen. He stopped, stared at her, then shook his head.

"I see you've taken a liking to Jesse," a voice said behind her.

She turned around and saw the young man who had greeted them at their car the night before. "Yes," she nodded. "He's beautiful."

She swallowed. If the truth be told, she thought the young man was beautiful too. His dark eyes had a penetrating look to them, and his high cheekbones sloped down a perfectly chiseled face to a well-rounded chin.

He picked up a halter from one of the pegs, walked over to Jesse's stall, then opened it up. Looping the halter over the stallion's head, he led him out into the barn. "We might as well give you a better view then."

Nancy walked around the horse, patting him and rubbing him. She smoothed his mane and rubbed his head right between his eyes.

"I think he likes you."

"I like him."

"Would you like to ride him?"

Nancy nodded. "Yes, I would. When?"

The man smiled. "How about right now?"

"You're allowed to do that?"

He laughed. "Of course I am. Jesse needs a little exercise. You might as well give him some."

"I'm not sure I got your name," Nancy said.

"It's John, but people call me Junior."

"What would you like me to call you?"

"Whatever you like." He smiled.

"I'll call you John. That's my father's name."

John handed her the halter and, reaching for a rack, grabbed a saddle blanket and placed it on the stallion's smooth back. When he found just the right saddle, he placed it on the stallion and cinched it into place. "You probably know how to do this. You look like a horse-woman."

"Yes, I've done it a few times before."

"I'm sure you have. I just know his equipment." He then took a bit and bridle and put it into the horse's mouth.

Leaning over the saddle, he smiled at her. "Jesse is quite the horse. Just because he likes you doesn't mean he won't try to throw you. Give me just a minute and I'll saddle my horse. I'll need to go with you just to make sure."

"Make sure of what?"

He grinned. "Make sure you come back with him of course."

She laughed. "Oh, I'll come back with him. I wouldn't steal my own grandparent's horse no matter how much I like him."

He returned her laugh. "I'm not worried about that. If Jesse does throw you, I don't want you swimming in the surf while he trots on back to the barn. He'd like nothing better than that and, while I might find it funny, I'm sure you wouldn't."

"No, I wouldn't."

He took a second horse out of a stall, a long-legged, square-jawed gelding. He went to work saddling it. Nancy placed her foot in the stirrup and climbed on top of Jesse. The big horse began to stamp his feet and kick his back legs.

John climbed on his own horse and chuckled. "I told you he wasn't easy."

"That's OK. I don't want him to be too easy. I've had my fill of merry-go-rounds."

He walked his horse past her, leaned over to open the barn door wider, then rode out. Nancy followed.

"Follow me," he said. "The path to the beach is down here."

He rounded the barn and picked his way down a path to the beach below. Nancy followed him closely. The sun was beginning to set, and the warm glow on the breaking surf was breathtaking. The sea was a deeper blue at this time of day, and the tide was coming in.

He stopped at the beach and waited for her as she rode up to him. "You strike me as a horsewoman, like your grandmother."

"Why is that?"

He laughed. "It's a theory of mine, a theory about strong-willed women. But it probably wouldn't interest you."

"Please go on. I'd like to hear it."

He began to walk his horse down the beach. Nancy pulled up close beside him and kept pace. "My theory is that strong-willed women like the feel of control they have over something strong, large, and masculine. That's why they gravitate to horses, especially stallions. They can command them. They can control them." He looked over at her, flashing a smile. "They think."

"Interesting. And you think I'm strong willed?"

"I know you are."

"You don't know anything about me."

"Yes, I do. I saw it when I first laid eyes on you. You don't want to be here, do you?"

Nancy shook her head. "Not really."

"I see that from the way you carry yourself. You're here more as a critic than anything. The way you walk around and look at things. It's like you're staring into a fishbowl and complaining to the owner about the variety of fish he keeps in his tank. You don't think they're either beautiful or edible."

"I think that's a nasty thing to say."

"But it's true isn't it?"

"What if it is?"

"It offends me because I'm one of the fish." With that he kicked the sides of his horse and broke out into a canter.

Nancy followed suit, sending a sharp kick into Jesse's sides. He bolted, sending her flying past John.

"Hold on, little missy, not quite so fast." He galloped, catching up to her. "Pull up on those reins. Let's not get too carried away."

She tossed her head and laughed. "Why? Are you afraid to go fast?"

"I'm afraid you don't know what fast really is. You don't know Jesse, and, like most of the men or boys you've had in your life, you only think you're in control."

Just the thought that this man claimed to know her sent a ripple of anger up her spine. She had always made it her business to know people, never to be known by them. She gave Jesse a swift kick in the sides, which sent the horse bolting forward at a swift gallop. Huge clods of sandy beach came tearing up behind her and onto John.

The stallion tore through the beach and over the sheets of oncoming water like a runaway locomotive. Nancy leaned down and gave him his head. She was determined to show this man who thought he knew so much about her just how in control she really was. He would never be able to catch her, and he would never be able to know her, not now, not ever.

The spray from the surf caught her full in the face as the big horse stretched out into a full gallop. Jesse's hooves beat through the sand and the rolling tide, sending small pieces of kelp flying behind.

The wind whipped Nancy's hair as she rode the speeding roller coaster of horseflesh. She looked back and saw John trying his best to catch up to her, but she knew he couldn't unless she slowed Jesse. She had no intention of doing that. She would run this John whatever his name was right into the ground and leave him begging for mercy.

Suddenly Jesse hit a stretch of water and veered violently to his left, back toward the open beach. He seemed to stop and spin, his front legs in the air.

Nancy came off the back of the big horse and hit the water hard. the oncoming waves pounded her space and spun her over and over in the sandy surf. The force pulled her under and dragged her out. She flailed her arms wildly, grabbing for the sand, anything that could control her and show her up from down.

Within moments she felt two strong hands lift her up from the water. John. He grabbed the back of her blouse and dragged her from the waves. She felt helpless, like a lifeless doll being taken out of a washing machine and tossed onto a pile of wet clothes.

"Are you all right?"

She nodded, spitting water.

He smiled. "Good. I didn't want to have to give you what they call the kiss of life. That would be messy, and you just might slap me."

He pushed the hair away from her face and then ran his hand over her cheek. "Too much speed for you, girl. Occasionally these fish you stare at bite."

"I'll be fine," she sputtered.

He looked up the beach. "Jesse's already on his way to the barn. I guess you'll have to ride behind me, or walk."

She didn't like the way he smiled when he said the word walk. Kicking at the sand under her feet, she got to her feet. Her skirt was caked with wet sand and pasted to her legs. She pulled it down and tried to knock some of the sand off. "I guess I didn't impress you very much."

He grinned. "I wouldn't say that. You impressed me a great deal—with your bullheadedness."

She glared at him, then looked over at his horse. It stood passively, waiting for him.

John walked over to the horse, picked up the reins, and, planting his foot in the stirrup, swung aboard. He held out his hand to her. "Want a ride back?"

She shook her head. "No thanks. I'll walk."

He laughed. "Bullheadedness is the word for you all right. You are like your grandmother."

CHAPTER 10

Johnny made his way over the rocks and across the spit of land known as Cutlass Point. He had changed out of his party clothes into deck shoes and jeans. His gray pullover sweatshirt gave him some warmth. This had been his thinking spot so many years ago, a place where he escaped from his family to be alone. As a child he had come here when the house was filled with out-of-town guests. Johnny knew who these guests were. Their loud talk and laughter, the smell of their cigars, and the aroma of alcohol sickened him.

In those days his father had thought him to be a mama's boy, but that wasn't the case. He was just a boy who had fallen in love with books and poetry. They lifted his spirits and taught him what it was like to be a hero. His books taught him about virtue and justice. Sir Walter Scott and his writings about Camelot had done much to introduce him to what it meant to have honor. As a Marine he had felt the stirrings those books produced. But even as a child he had been ashamed of his father's work. Something inside him died every time the business acquaintances of his father came to the house. He had felt that way today during the party. The sight of those same people brought back all those memories.

But Johnny knew he couldn't condemn them. They were no worse than he was. His years of Bible study had shown him that much. After what his father had told him about Gina having his baby, his tender conscience was making it difficult for him to fault anyone else for committing sin.

Johnny hiked over the rocks, at times slipping and having to go down on all fours for balance. The stones were slippery in places because the tide was coming in. If the tide was exceptionally high, Cutlass Point could be cut off from the beach and then become Cutlass Island. Even then, however, its beach would still be accessible.

The moon hung low, just visible behind Morro Rock. Its light shimmered in the water as the waves broke on either side of him. Fishing boats in the distance had their red-and-green running lights on. Fishermen had an optimism that Johnny found compelling. Every day brought fresh hopes for them no matter how many illusions had been shattered in the past. He imagined, however, that after a period of time a man's habits took the place of his hopes. The boats would go out and do what they had always done because that's simply what they did. Johnny never wanted to share that fate. He wanted the idealism of his longings to motivate his life.

The climb to Cutlass Point was a journey into the past for Johnny. There had been no war when he had been here, and no Karen. He had not yet become a man. His life had been high-school football, his books, and the glittering lights and bright shapes of his desires.

A dense fog was rolling in from the evening mist. The whole place might be shrouded by the fog for days on end, one of the things the Central Coast of California was noted for.

He scrambled over the last of the rocks and stopped short of the beach. Squatting low on the rocks, he wrapped his arms around his knees. A woman sat on a blanket facing the sea. Her hair was covered with a scarf, and her dress was pulled up with her legs. He knew at once that it was Gina. What had once been his spot had become their spot so long ago.

He got to his feet and took a deep breath. Skipping down the rocks, he balanced himself and jumped from one rocky landing to another. He knew this was something that could no longer be put off. Try as he might, he knew he couldn't leave here without making things right with her.

"Gina," he called out.

She rolled over on her knees and got to her feet. "Johnny, come on down."

He stepped off the last of the rocks and onto the small beach, then walked toward her. "I thought I'd pay a visit to the old place."

"I thought you might come here." She smiled. "The house is not a very pleasant place to be right now."

"No, it isn't."

She reached down and picked up a large red-checkered thermos. "I brought some coffee, just the way you like it, black."

"Thanks. That was thoughtful of you."

"Somehow I knew you'd come here."

He laughed and glanced back at the main house with its lights blazing. "I always liked this place when things weren't right at home."

She unscrewed the top of the thermos and poured a cup of the hot coffee into the red plastic top, then handed it to him. "It's going to get a bit chilly. You might need a little of this in you."

"Thank you." He took the cup and sipped it.

She put a hand on his shoulder. "I'm sorry about your father. I liked him very much."

"Thank you." He sipped the coffee and glanced out at the oncoming fog. "You know, Papa and I used to come out here and talk."

"I didn't know that. But there always was a lot of talk around your family table."

"Yes, but sometimes there are some things a man can't say in front of other people. He has to hear his own voice and not be afraid of anyone correcting him or butting into his own thinking. I guess Papa always thought I was safe, that I'd just listen to him. He would bring me out here and talk to me."

"About what?"

"About his past. About Italy and his parents. About death sometimes, his fear of dying and his questions about God. He would let down his guard. Of course back then I didn't know anything, and I suppose it's a good thing I didn't. Papa just needed to be listened to. It does make for a bittersweet return home. Now it would seem it just might be my last. I should have done more years ago to bring us back together."

"Why would you say this might be your last visit?"

"I have so little in common with this family, and now with Mama blaming me for what happened today, I rather doubt they'll have me back."

"You had nothing to do with your father's death."

"Mama gets her mind made up about things and there's no turning back. She's been that way for years."

"Time has a way of changing things."

"What about you? Has time changed things for you?"

"Of course it has." She chuckled. "I hardly recognize myself anymore."

"You're still as beautiful as ever, maybe more."

"Thank you. But so many other things have changed. I went to college and then law school at Santa Clara."

"Really? Are you a lawyer?"

"Yes. In fact, I'm a partner now. My firm represents your family and its holdings. I know my connections with your father had a lot to do with us landing the account, but it's been very profitable for the firm and for the Pera family as well."

"Good. I'm glad to hear that."

"That's really why I was here this weekend."

Johnny held the cup to his lips and looked at her.

She smiled. "I suppose that comes as somewhat of a blow to you. Perhaps you thought that since I had heard about Karen's death that I was here as some sort of a historical vulture."

"No, I didn't think that. I was just surprised to see you."

"My mother was a bit upset seeing the two of us together in the same room last night," she laughed. "Dropping and breaking dishes was a dead giveaway I suppose."

"She seemed a bit cold. I can't remember her that way."

"She knew you were coming and she knew I was coming. But when she saw you in the kitchen with me, that just sent her over the edge."

"I can understand that."

"Here, let me pour you some more coffee." She reached over and placed her hand on his as he held the cup. She filled the cup with steaming black coffee. "I remember you liked this stuff even before you should have. Your mother would screech at you to drink more milk, but you would sneak off to the kitchen to drain the coffeepot."

"One of my many vices, I suppose."

She smiled. "I don't think you had too many, as I recall."

"I did have a few, but none you didn't know about."

"Yes." she nodded. "We both knew a lot about each other. The thought never crossed our minds that we would have a life without each other."

Johnny sipped his coffee. "When I got back from school that year I was surprised to see you gone. I had written to you, but my letters were always returned. They told me you had gone away. No one told me where. I suppose I figured you had simply decided that you'd had enough of Johnny Pera," he laughed. "And I could understand that."

She set the thermos down in the sand and walked over to where the waves were lapping up onto the beach. She took a step into the water and watched as the waves lashed at her ankles. "I had forgotten how cold this water is."

Johnny stepped closer to her and sipped his coffee. "It was never too cold for us when we were young."

She looked back at him. "It never is." Turning back, she looked off at the sea and Morro Rock beyond.

"Gina, my father told me today what happened to you that year. I'm sorry. I never knew. No one ever told me. No one ever told me anything."

"You were the fair-haired boy, Johnny, the football star who was destined to take this family out of the shadows and into the light of day. How could they spoil that? They knew you and I knew you. You're too responsible. If you had known what had happened, you would have dropped out of school and pumped gas at a filling station. You wouldn't have taken money from them. They couldn't have that, and neither could I. I would have felt guilty for the rest of my life."

"I would have found a way."

"Your father found a way for you, and so did your mother. Your father supported me until I had the baby and then paid my way through seven years of college and law school. After that, he gave me his business. Your mother found a way by making certain that you married Karen. She burned my bridges and yours too. I've lived a life and so have you. I was married and divorced. My husband didn't exactly take kindly to my career. He wanted a woman by the fireplace to cook and sew. I've never been that. You had a life with Karen, and from what I hear, it was a wonderful life. You certainly have two beautiful children. God knew what He was doing with us."

"I have to ask you about the baby. What was it and what happened to it?"

Just then the chugging sound of an engine reached them, and a searchlight cut through the gathering fog and swung its piercing beam across them. A shot rang out and a slug ricocheted off a nearby rock.

Johnny dropped his cup and grabbed Gina, pulling her to the sand. He wiggled on top of her to pin her underneath him.

He looked up and saw the patrol boat edging its way out of the fog. Its engine was idling, and two men were on deck. One had a rifle in his hand, and the other held the searchlight. The man with the light put a bullhorn to his mouth, and his voice boomed over the water. "Who are you? This is a private beach."

Johnny held up his head and yelled. "I'm Johnny Pera. You idiots are shooting at the family."

"We're sorry, sir. We have our orders."

"Well, they don't include shooting us. Next time ask questions before you fire on somebody you don't know. You could have killed one of us, and we've had enough death here for one day."

"We're sorry, Mr. Pera," the voice boomed. "It won't happen again."

The boat burst into a low growl and swiveled in the water, heading back out to sea. Within seconds it disappeared into the fog.

Johnny looked down at Gina beneath him. She was a beautiful woman, and their eyes became riveted to each other.

"I seem to remember this spot," she smiled.

He laughed. "Yes, I guess it was, now that I think about it."

She chuckled slightly. "Well, make up your mind. Either kiss me or let me up."

He could feel the flush coming to his face. Then he laughed. "I'm sorry." He got up and, taking her hand, pulled her to her feet.

She brushed off her dress. "I'm the one who should be sorry. I've taken advantage of you." She looked at him. "I know you're a lonely man right now, Johnny Pera. Anyone can see it in your eyes. I shouldn't have come out here."

Johnny looked out into the fog. "I guess it shows. I see Karen everywhere. I feel her, but I just can't touch her. I have so much to say to her, words that I never got the chance to say. She's just not here to listen. And then, Papa today . . ."

Another voice sounded from the rocks behind them. "Mr. Pera, Johnny Pera. Are you there?"

"It's John," Gina whispered.

"We're down here, Junior," Johnny shouted. "What's the problem?"

"Your daughter, Nancy," he shouted. "She fell off a horse. She's fine now, but a bit shaken."

"All right," Johnny yelled. "We'll be right there." He looked at Gina. "Duty calls, I guess."

"Yes, duty."

They started to walk toward the rocks. Johnny stooped to pick up the thermos and the lid that served as a cup. He then took her hand.

"For a moment there, I wasn't sure what you were going to do," she said.

"I wasn't either."

CHAPTER 11

The next morning Johnny was awakened by a knock on his door. He stumbled out of bed dressed in his boxers and T-shirt, cracked open the door, and peeked out. Arturo was standing there, dressed in a suit and tie. "Come on in," Johnny said.

Arturo walked in and took a seat in a rattan chair. He threw a leg over one of the arms and watched as Johnny took out a pair of khaki pants. Arturo surveyed the room. It was paneled in redwood and had a large picture window that looked out to a deck and the beach beyond. "I forgot how nice this beach house is," he said.

Johnny nodded. Opening a drawer, he pulled out a navy blue polo shirt. "Yeah, it's quiet too." He turned on the faucet and took out his razor. In a matter of moments he had lime-scented shave cream on his face and was stroking what there was of his beard.

"I came to get you for a family meeting."

"What sort of a meeting? Funeral arrangements?"

Arturo shook his head. "No, Papa worked that out some time ago. We need to meet to decide what to do."

Johnny patted his clean face with a dab of bay rum. "That doesn't involve me. I have nothing to do with the family business."

"You do now. You were there when they took out Papa. You're involved, all right."

Johnny tucked the shirt into his pants and snapped on his watch. "I can't see where that makes me any more a part of this meeting. I've already told the police everything I know."

Arturo smirked. "You can't think that we're letting the police handle this. Just because you've been a preacher doesn't make you stupid."

"Is Mama going to be at this meeting of yours?"

"Of course she is. She's part of the family."

"Then I'd better not go for sure. She holds what happened against me."

Arturo got to his feet. "It was Mama who sent me to get you."

"Arturo, you don't seem to understand. Just because my last name is Pera doesn't make me a part of this family. I haven't belonged in over twenty years."

Arturo reached out and grabbed his arm. "Look, Johnny, we weren't there for you when you needed us. I feel bad about that. But you're here now, and we need you. Now let's go. We have breakfast laid out in the great room."

Johnny followed Arturo out the door and along the pathway that led to the main house. As they went through the front door, Johnny could see that the whole clan had gathered there, everyone including Rocko, Junior, and Gina. Even Isabella was there, cowering in the corner with her feet pulled up under her. Her face was white, paler than ever against her black sweater. Johnny walked over and stooped in front of her. He placed his hand on her leg. "You OK, Sis?"

She nodded and bit her lip.

"You shouldn't be here. You should go back to your room."

Several men were scouring the room with electronic wands. He saw one of them take off a lampshade and unscrew the bulb. He looked inside and pulled out a small, black disk. He held it up for Arturo to see before slipping it into his pocket. One of the other men pulled an extension cord out of the wall, rolled it up, and stuck it in his pocket. They worked for several minutes more as the family sat in silence. Then the man in charge, a man with a leather utility belt, straightened up and spoke to Arturo. "It's clean now."

Arturo nodded and poured himself a cup of coffee from a silver coffeepot. He held it to his lips and waited for the men to leave. "We have everyone here now. We have to decide where to go from here and who's going to be responsible."

Dom forced a smile. "It looks like you're the responsible one, big brother."

"That's not the issue," Arturo said. "We need to know where to go from here."

Baldassare spoke up, waving his hands. "We find the killers and the ones who paid them and we hit them back. We hit them back hard."

Johnny shot to his feet. "Hold on a minute. I don't intend to be here while you people plan murder. I don't want any part of it." He looked at his mother, who was seated on the couch next to Gina. "Plus, we have ladies present."

"Look," Dom said, "We don't have nobody here who shouldn't be here. Gina is our lawyer and Mama, well, she's Mama."

"Johnny is right," Gina said. "I can't be a party to any illegal plans you might have. That sort of activity isn't protected by any attorney-client privilege."

"All right," Arturo said. "We don't have to discuss that. But we are not going to wait on the police to investigate this thing. We all know it's much bigger than they are capable of dealing with. It might even involve the government."

Baldassare let out a series of curse words. "Government? It's bigger than the government. It's the families of New York, Chicago, and Miami. Let's not kid ourselves here."

Rocko put his fist to his mouth and cleared his throat. At times he could seem almost shy when addressing a family gathering. "Look, you all know that I was loyal to your father. There ain't nothing I wouldn't do for that man. But we ain't about to get into no shooting war with New York, Chicago, and Miami. That would be stupid. And what if it's just one of them or none of them?"

"Rocko's right," Arturo said. "There's no sense in going off half-cocked and stepping into something. That would be bad for business, very bad."

"Then what would you suggest?" Dom asked.

"I'd suggest that we find out. Do our own investigation," Arturo shot back.

"We better start with Giancana in Chicago," Baldassare said. "We got something he wants."

"And something he ain't gonna get without Papa," Dom shot back.

"Then we go to Enzo in New York and on to Trafficante in Miami," Baldassare said. "We listen to what's on the streets, what other people know about what's gone down. We talk to friends, our friends, and call in markers. The word's got to be out. Nobody can never hide nothing on the streets."

"You better be prepared to make a deal," Rocko said. "A man's got to give something to get something."

"Look, Trafficante and Giancana wanted that action in Havana real bad," Dom said. He stuck his hands in his pockets and kicked at the tile with one of his feet. "They needed Papa, and Papa wanted their help with the union pension funds. Papa wanted the funds to build more hotels, and we could have had them too, with him alive. Frankly, I think what we're dealing with is politics, not business."

Arturo sipped his coffee. He had a coolness and a thoughtfulness that were in total contrast to his brothers. "I hear Bobby Kennedy's already got plans for how to respond to this Castro should he take one of our ambassadors out. The people in Washington figure that could happen with the hit teams sent into Cuba after Castro. You know how it works. Castro takes out our man in Panama, and we take out his brother Raúl."

Baldassare clapped his hands. "That sounds like our kind of action."

"In a way it is," Arturo went on. "Of course, if Castro decided to take Papa out instead just to show that no one was unreachable, then he would have made his point without triggering the Kennedys. If he can remove a Mafia don, he can take out an ambassador, or the president, for that matter."

"Don't forget the Cuban exiles," Dom said. "This Javier Lage is a big man in Miami, and our CIA is in bed with him. Those people weren't too happy when their Brigade 2056 went down at the Bay of Pigs. The CIA has this Task Force W operating, and I hear they have over three thousand operatives, more than enough to send a few to California for Papa. Killing Papa would make sure the rest of the family went along with their plans."

Arturo sipped his coffee and looked at Johnny. "It sounds like we're going to need someone with government connections, someone who can find out the truth."

Johnny held up his hands. "Don't think about involving me in this little scheme of yours. I don't want anything to do with it."

"You've never wanted anything to do with the family," his mother suddenly said.

The sound of her voice from the couch brought every head in her direction.

"You're not being fair to Johnny," Isabella said. "He has nothing to do with family business, but that doesn't mean he's never wanted to be involved with the family."

Johnny reached over and patted her shoulder.

"Hey"—Dominico snapped his fingers—"don't you have a war buddy with the FBI? Some guy you saved during the war?"

"Frank Bass, but he wouldn't have anything to do with this."

Baldassare smiled. "He might if you asked him real nice like."

Johnny could see the lights go on in his brother's eyes. He knew Frank Bass might be the perfect government informant, and so did Baldassare.

Johnny stuffed his hands in his pockets and walked toward the large picture window. He looked out at the beach and the fog that was drifting in. The misty haze duplicated exactly what he was feeling. He wanted nothing to do with his family's revenge. He was removed from them in so many ways, not the least of which was the blood lust that seemed to move them.

As the group continued to talk, Arturo walked over to him. "Johnny, I think I know what you're feeling."

Johnny shot him a glance. "How could you? I feel bad enough about Papa without all this. I don't want anything to do with what the rest of you are thinking about."

Arturo looked back at the family. "I'm not sure you know what we're thinking. They're over there feeling helpless. Do you really think the authorities care what happened to Papa? As far as they're concerned, it's just one more greaseball they don't have to worry about. There's no justice to be had. If you could come up with some evidence, anything at all, people would have to listen. That's all we're asking for, proof."

"And you expect me to believe that?"

Arturo shrugged. "It's the truth, believe it or not. And think of this. If it is Castro who's involved, what's to stop him from going after someone else, someone higher up? You might be saving the whole country some heartache."

"And you think the family hero is going to put on his armor and chase people down for you? You've got to see me as that same gullible kid who left to go to college. Well, I'm not. I've been through war and I've been through life. Nothing good can come of this."

Arturo grabbed his arm and turned him around. "You want Baldy to charge off into the streets of Chicago and New York? Maybe you think Dom can weasel his way into the good graces of the CIA and make them admit wrongdoing. They'll both try, and where will that leave you when they wind up dead? How do you think Mama's going to feel then? Unless we find out who's actually responsible for this, people will be killed, innocent people, maybe people in this room."

"You're the obvious choice. You're smooth. You know what to say and who to say it to. You know all the people involved. They would talk to you. My vote is for you, big brother."

Arturo smiled and sipped his coffee. "You're forgetting one thing."

"What's that?"

"Frank Bass. He's your friend, not mine. You saved his life in the Pacific, as I recall."

"So what?"

Arturo put his hand on Johnny's arm. "Look, we do our homework in this family. We know everything that's important to know. I know you've been away from us, and that's probably the biggest reason that we've done our homework on you."

"Are you saying you didn't trust me?"

"Johnny, when you left this family, no one trusted you. I'm not sure anyone believed you could separate yourself from us for all those religious reasons of yours. I knew you. You're an idealist. That's why you went into the Marine Corps. But let's just say other people had their doubts. They wanted to know what you were doing and what you thought. They also wanted to know about your friends."

"So you checked on Frank Bass?"

Arturo nodded. "Yes. He's the field director of the FBI office in Miami Beach. I didn't say anything about that little fact in there. He might be critical to us."

Johnny pulled his arm away and turned back to the window. "Don't talk to me. I don't want anything to do with it."

"Johnny." He could hear his mother's voice. "Johnny, come back here and talk to us."

He turned around and walked back into the room.

Dom spoke up. "I was just telling Mama that just because you didn't want to help us didn't mean that you don't care."

"Is that true, Johnny?" His mother asked. "You won't help?"

"I don't want anything to do with this blood lust, Mama. I won't have that on my conscience."

"Why?" she asked. "Don't you have your papa's blood on your conscience already?"

Johnny bit his upper lip. "Mama, I didn't have anything to do with that. You know that."

"I know if it weren't for you, he'd still be here today."

"That's not fair, Mama," Isabella said.

His mother took out a handkerchief and held it to her eyes. "I know it is true. Your papa had protection, but Johnny didn't want them around. Now he doesn't want us to find his killers."

The eyes in the room turned in Johnny's direction.

"You did love Papa, didn't you, Johnny?" his mother asked.

"Of course I did. With all my heart."

"Then why won't you help us?"

"I don't want any part of your revenge."

"Look," Dom said, "Suppose we tell you that we'll take any evidence you produce and give it to the police, let them take action. Will that satisfy you?"

"But you won't do that. I point the finger at someone, and you'll have Rocko and his soldiers hit him. Then you'll shrug your shoulders and smile. You'll blame the streets or someone else, but it'll be you all along, and I'll be responsible. I might as well pull the trigger myself. I think Arturo ought to go and do this."

Baldassare laughed. "No way. Everybody knows he's clean. You just take some woman as your wife and you'll be able to wander the streets as a tourist. Put a camera around your neck and gawk at the buildings. Nobody will care. You could have the run of the place."

"He's got a point," Dom said.

"The kid's right," Rocko growled. "You're a civilian. Some folks will know your name, but only those people you need to talk to. One of these boys gets loose on the streets, and there's no telling who's carrying a grudge. People could let loose without any questions. Then where would we be?" He grinned. "I think you're the man. I'd follow you, and I'd be there to give you cover. Might take a little of the heat off you too."

Dom's smile widened. "There ya go. You two could be a team, one clean and one dirty."

Arturo stepped forward. "Johnny, what if we made you a promise? We will have nothing to do with extracting revenge for Papa's death. The people responsible may be beyond our reach anyway. We're not going to take out Castro. And if you get us evidence that it's some other family, then we'll take it to the police. We won't start a war. That would be bad for business. It's not like it used to be. We don't work that way anymore. We run casinos in Nevada. It's legal there, and we don't want to mess things up."

"Besides," Dom said, "don't you sell investigations now? Sell us then."

His mother folded her hands and stared up at him. "Do this, Johnny. You owe it to us."

"All right, I'll do it." He looked at Arturo and pointed his finger. "But I'm holding you to your promise. No one will die because of me. You will let justice take its course."

"Absolutely." Arturo smiled. He motioned toward Gina sitting on the couch. "You take Gina along as your wife. You traveling with her won't arouse suspicion, and if there's a deal that has to be made, she's our attorney."

"Do we have to do that?" Johnny asked.

"I think it's a fine idea," his mother said. She reached over and patted Gina's hand.

"It'll be good cover," Rocko added. "Plus I'll go along and take Junior here. He's all I'll need. We'll be there to back you up and get you wired with any connections you might need."

Arturo slapped Johnny's back. "Then it's settled. You'll leave after Papa's funeral."

CHAPTER 12

Javier stuck his head out the door of the chopper as it banked. The swaying of the helicopter, along with the sight of the water below him and the small patch of ground off the coast of Honduras called Swan Island, made him more than a little queasy. Several peaks on the island were dotted with radio towers. For twenty hours a day, the towers broadcast Spanish language messages aimed at overthrowing the Castro regime. Radio Swan was completely operational, and the place seemed to be safe, at least for the moment.

The pilot adjusted the pedals and pulled back on the stick, lifting the rear of the chopper and settling it onto the helicopter pad. The rotors whirred overhead, and Javier jumped out, hunching his shoulders and running with his head down. The notion of a headless commander held little appeal for him.

Javier Lage was now the Cuban exile commander. When he wasn't running underneath the spinning blades of a helicopter, he looked the part. He was over six feet tall with dark hair, albeit a bit receding, and dark eyes. His mustache and Vandyke beard had flecks of gray around the edges. He thought it gave him a dashing appearance and made him look wiser than his thirty-five years. He had a broad forehead and high cheekbones and almost always wore a leather bomber jacket, even in sultry climates. He fancied himself a man's man with great appeal to women. Clark Gable had been his American movie idol.

The trees near the edge of the pad were so thick that he could barely see the tin-roofed houses scattered among them. The concrete-block houses were ugly, but they could withstand the storms of the Caribbean in late summer and fall. Of course, one might have to sit quietly inside with no roof overhead.

Several men came to the edge of the clearing, saluted, and then clutched desperately at their caps as the chopper picked itself up off the pad. As the chopper flew away, the men wobbled in its dust-filled wake.

"Commander Lage, it's nice to have you with us." The man's missing teeth gave him the appearance of a jack-o'-lantern.

Javier returned his salute. "Is Hunt inside?"

"Yes," the man nodded. "He's with two more gringos."

Javier smiled. "Good. I hope they brought food and money."

The man lifted a broad banana leaf, and Javier ducked underneath and spotted the trail that led to the command bunker. A torn cardboard sign, VICTORY TRAIL, marked the path. The air was smoky from fire burning some of the underbrush; there was little else that could be done to keep the lush greenness in its place. Cutting it back with a machete was too difficult and took too long.

He lifted the hasp on the metal door, pushed it open, and ducked through the low doorway. E. Howard Hunt sat at the radio console with an open mike in his hand. Two other men were beside him, people Javier didn't know.

Hunt squeezed the red button on the microphone and held it up to his mouth. "Hammer One, this is Swan One; he's here and the chopper's away." There was a pause. Hunt glanced in Javier's direction and held the headset closer to his ear. He pushed the button down again. "He's alone. Say again. OK, Hammer One, we're out."

Hunt put the mike and the headset down on the paper-strewn metal table and got to his feet. E. Howard Hunt was career CIA. Eisenhower had placed him in charge of the Cuban exile groups before Kennedy was elected. Now it was easier to keep him in place than to find someone who could pass muster with the Democratic National Committee. He was lanky with blond hair that was showing more than its share of scalp. He smiled and stuck out his hand. "Great to see you, Javier."

Javier gave Hunt a vigorous handshake. This was the man who was responsible for recruiting him.

"I've got a couple of people for you to meet," Hunt said. "This is the director of Operation Mongoose, Bill Harvey."

Javier shook the man's hand.

"And this is Cliff Cox. He's handling our Italian friends."

"The Mafia?" Javier asked.

Cox nodded and shook his hand.

Javier grinned. He looked around the windowless concrete bunker. The air came down metal chutes, which had grated filters set high on the outside walls and spouts letting out on the floor of the bunker. The grates and the position of the air chutes were designed to keep grenades and smoke bombs out of the bunker. Wire cage lights hung from open-beamed ceilings. Several bunk beds lined the walls, and two tables and red plastic-covered chrome chairs flanked an electric stove. "So what do you think of our operation?"

"Not too bad." Cox grinned. "Though I wouldn't call it a tourist resort."

"I doubt if it's in any of the brochures," Harvey added.

Javier nodded. "Just so it's not on Castro's maps." He looked at Harvey. "I hear your people have been blowing up sugar plants and short-circuiting electric plants."

Harvey smiled. "Yeah, we been making some havoc on that island."

Javier looked at Hunt. "Do you really think that's a good idea? We're training a new invasion force, and this can only hurt us. When Brigade 2056 landed at the Bay of Pigs, the General Intelligence Directorate—the DGI—had thrown a hundred and fifty thousand potential rebels in jail. We had no one left on the island to join us. That was partly why we failed. This small stuff can only make them mad enough to do the same thing. It can expose our contacts and place us at risk, and for what? A few lights blinking on and off? It's stupid."

"We're trying to build up a presence on the island and let them know we haven't forgotten about them," Hunt said. "We have six hundred case operatives and three thousand agents."

Javier grunted. "If you ask me, Operation Mongoose is just Operation Goose. You're doing all the wrong things just to show the American Congress that you're doing something."

"We're doing the best we can with what we have," Hunt replied.

"Not if your best is the wrong thing, you're not. I'd rather have you doing nothing than the wrong thing."

"Cox is moving ahead with his contacts," Hunt said.

"The Mafia? I hear they're backing out."

"That problem has been taken care of," Cox said.

"By whom?"

Hunt smiled. "Let's just say we have the situation well in hand. If things go according to plan, you will land with Castro, his brother, and this Che Guevara already eliminated. That ought to make your march into Havana a cakewalk."

"Cakewalk?" Javier clasped his hands behind his back and began to pace. "Seems to me I heard this term before. People were going to join us at the Bay of Pigs, and Kennedy was going to supply air cover." He glared at Hunt. "Instead, we got nothing." He spat out the words.

"That will change," Hunt said. "Kennedy's not going to let that happen again. He's even got his brother Bobby coordinating the effort."

"Oh, fine. Now let me see." Javier lifted his gaze to the tin ceiling. "If I'm on the beach and need something, something like tanks or airplanes, I go to Harvey here. He picks up the phone and calls you. You search through your files for Bobby Kennedy's number and call him. If we're lucky and his brother isn't too busy, then Bobby will dash over and see if he can talk to him. Kennedy will discuss the pros and cons and how it will look in the next election with his advisors. Then they will all decide that it will be much better for them politically to have us fight it out and be the heroes without their help. Meanwhile, me and my comrades will be fighting and dying."

Javier arched his eyebrows and looked at the three men. "How do you expect me to fashion the speech when I send my men off in their boats to fight the waves getting to the beach, assuming you can give us good maps and get us there?"

"You paint a pretty bleak picture," Cox said.

"Humph," Javier grunted. "I should. I've lived it."

"You're forgetting one thing," Cox said.

"What's that?"

"Castro was alive then," Cox went on. "He'll be dead when this landing takes place. Without Fidel, the Russians will be powerless, and his commie friends on that island will be shucking their uniforms and looking for a place to dump their rifles."

"You're putting a great deal of faith in that bunch of hoods."

Hunt spoke up. "We have a right to. Through the years we've seen them at work when they had something on the line. It was a while back, but the Saint Valentine's Day Massacre ought to stir your memory a little."

"And they have something at stake here," Harvey added. "They had a good deal going for them under Batista. The casinos were full and overflowing with cash. This could be the biggest score they've ever pulled off."

"And they're solid behind this, all the families," Cox said. "Their people in New York, Chicago, Miami, all around the country are backing this play 100 percent. We couldn't ask for a better deal."

His head went down momentarily, then back up with a smile. "Of course, we had a few problems with one of them, a hardhead in California. But that's been taken care of. Everything is a go now, green lights all over. You just have your people ready to go. With what we've got planned, you won't need much to pull it off."

"You're all forgetting one thing," Javier said.

"What's that?" Hunt asked.

"That Saint Valentine's Day Massacre. The one man Capone was trying to get, Bugs Moran, wasn't there when it happened. They missed him." He pointed his finger at them. "You better hope they don't miss Fidel."

CHAPTER 13

To Johnny, Chicago seemed like a mean-spirited town. Its history was one of fires, slaughterhouses, and hooch-runner murders; yet it was more than that. The fire of 1871 had caused it to become a city of steel girders, elevators, and high-rise structures. Wave after wave of immigrants had turned it into a city of the world dropped into the middle of America's heart. It stretched out for miles—gray buildings, signs, and plumes of smoke. The clamor of the streets was a mix of Polish, Russian, Norwegian, and Yiddish all at the same time, along with the special lingo of any number of gangs.

San Francisco was different. There was a charm to the city that was hard to duplicate. Even though he and the children had lived there for less than two years, they had come to love it. San Francisco was a romantic city. Chicago was a city at work.

To Johnny, Chicago was a place he went when he had to go, and he had to now. As Arturo had explained it to him before he got on the plane, to do nothing would be dangerous for them. It would be like hanging out a sign and saying they were out of business. The brothers were restless for resolution, even if they had to let the police finish the job.

O'Hare airport had been named after Butch O'Hare. Butch was a Navy flier who had been killed in the Pacific while protecting his ship from the Japanese. He had won the Congressional Medal of Honor. Most people who stopped to read the airport sign knew that, but there was more to the story. Butch O'Hare's dad had been a mobster connected to Al Capone, and he had turned state's evidence to put Capone in jail. But his cooperation with the government had allowed his son Butch to go to the Naval Academy, and Butch's dad had been consequently gunned down. But when the story was told and the heroism of Butch O'Hare recounted, Johnny knew that heroism was first found in Butch's dad. It was part of the legacy of the mob that none of them liked to talk about. Butch's dad had been a rat. That was—and always would be—the unpardonable sin. Johnny related to that. In his family's mind, he had committed the only other unpardonable sin: He had left the Catholic Church.

Thoughts of the family business flooded Johnny's mind. The business had been made in this city, and its tentacles had reached into the Midwest and finally into the West where his father had been The Man. There had always been a swagger about being a Pera, a pride that was inborn and produced a heart of iron. Johnny had been soaked in that family pride, and it had made him want to be a star on the football field, perhaps had driven him into the Marine Corps. Now that pride was making it impossible to say no to his mother, even though he wanted to. He was someplace he didn't want to be, with people he didn't want to be with, to accomplish a job he didn't want to do.

The drive into downtown Chicago was cramped. Rocko was in the front seat with the driver. He chatted and laughed with the man like they were long-lost friends.

He looked back over the seat at Johnny, Gina, and Junior and thumbed in the direction of the el train that was passing them by. "We shoulda taken the el. It's cheaper."

Gina smiled and shook her head. "Yes, but carrying your bags to the hotel makes up for it."

The taxi turned onto Michigan Avenue and pulled over to the curb in front of the Blackstone Hotel. The edifice of the old hotel was aging but elegant with columns that stood by large glass doors. They piled out of the cab where two bellhops rushed up to them with chrome baggage carriers.

Moments later Johnny, Junior, and Gina were standing in the lobby waiting for Rocko to get their rooms. He came back from the desk bouncing the keys. "I got us three rooms on the fourteenth floor." He grinned. "It's really the thirteenth floor but you know how superstitious people are. They just name it fourteen and then everybody's happy."

The group made themselves at home in Johnny's suite, which overlooked Grant Park and Lake Michigan beyond. A chocolate-brown sofa and love seat flanked the large window. The glass-topped coffee table had a large bouquet of birds-of-paradise.

Junior prowled the room, looking under the shades of the blue and tan lamps and taking a chair to stand on and explore the bulbs that hung from the crystal chandelier.

Rocko seated himself on the couch and pulled out a sharp penknife to clean his nails. He shook it at Junior. "I wouldn't bother with that. I booked us under Smith and Jones." Glancing at Gina, he grinned. "You're Mrs. Smith. You have a room of your own, though. This here's a two-bedroom suite I got for you and Johnny."

She forced a grin. "That's considerate. I'm sure no one can find us under that name."

Rocko shrugged his shoulders and smiled. "Sorry. It was the best I could do. Sam Giancana's got this town wired. We use the Pera name and they're gonna know where we are and how to find us. The cops are on Giancana's payroll. Shoot," he let the words drool out of his mouth like spilt molasses.

"Why don't you explain to us again just what we're supposed to do here in Chicago?" Johnny asked.

"Simple. We need to find out if the man killed your father."

"And how do you propose to do that?"

Rocko grinned. "Ask him."

"Just that simple?"

Rocko laughed. "Sure. Why not?" He put his index finger to the corner of his eye. "I'll know just by looking at him when we bring it up. I can smell out a liar quicker than a hound can find a coon."

"We're going to need more evidence than that."

"And we'll find it by asking around." He closed his knife and dropped it back into his pocket. "We're also going to see if we can do some business with old Sam." He glanced over in Gina's direction. "That's where the pretty lady comes in. If we swing a deal, she can write up the papers."

"A deal for what?"

Rocko grimaced and wagged his head back and forth like a pendulum. He waved at Junior, who was climbing down from the chair. "Explain to the man, Junior."

Junior pulled up a chair and turned it around, sitting and leaning forward on the back of it. "Giancana has the unions in his pocket, and they have pension money. We'd like to get his help in arranging loans to finance new hotels in Vegas. It's part of why the family's so nervous about us doing nothing. If we seem to be weak, then they are less inclined to help us."

Rocko reached over and slapped him on the back. "I like this boy. You see why I like him, Johnny? He's smart. He knows where the bodies are buried."

"And why would Sam Giancana want to help us get loans?" Johnny asked.

Rocko stroked his chin. "For a while it was because your papa was willing to help him with this Cuba thing. Then it became Giancana's greed. He wants a piece of one of the casinos we already own. He can't get a gaming license himself, and we already have one. Those things are better than pure gold. They're a permit to print cash."

He leaned forward in Johnny's direction. "Greed, my boy. Sam's got it and we understand it. As long as he stays greedy, we got him by the tail."

"And how is this greed of his going to help us find Papa's murderers?"

"If Sam did it, we're going to find out. If he didn't do it, then he's going to help us find who did." He leaned back into the couch. "That is, if he wants a piece of the Vegas action. You see, he's got the unions, but we've got the Nevada politicians and the Hollywood acts. He needs both of those to operate a casino."

A short time later Johnny heard a knock. He opened the door and found Rocko and Junior standing there. Rocko shook a piece of paper in his face. "I got us a meeting with Giancana," he grinned, "and a little dinner too. Small place around the corner called the Russian Tearoom. Now you get your wife and we'll go."

"That's not funny. She's not my wife."

"OK. But get her anyway."

It was a short walk to the Russian Tearoom. The place had dark curtains and carpet that looked to be Persian. A cloth painted with dancing Cossacks covered a red lantern that was hanging in the main dining room. Shadows cast on the wall gave the appearance of larger dancing figures. They followed the man who greeted them to their table.

Rocko picked up a menu and flashed a smile. "What do you think of this place?"

"Interesting," Gina said.

"Yeah, Giancana hates this type of eating place. It's not Italian. So I figure he don't know anybody here. It's safe for us." He glanced down at the menu. "So just pick something out as long as it's meat. Those Russians can't get meat too wrong."

Junior picked up his menu and opened it. "Wanna bet?"

When they finished their soup, a red oily mixture that tasted like vinegar with squeezed beets, Sam Giancana walked in flanked by two men. He wore a crumpled white suit and a straw fedora, and soldiers wearing double-breasted, pinstriped blue suits flanked him.

Rocko shot to his feet and flashed a grin. "Sam, my man." He waved his hand. "Come on over and pull up a chair." He watched as Giancana stepped closer to the table. "Sorry we don't have room for your boys, but we got a chair for you."

Giancana snapped his fingers like he was summoning a lapdog. One of his men pulled out the chair for him while the second man busied himself with clearing diners from a nearby table.

Giancana wove his fingers together and slouched forward with his hands clasped under his chin, his dark eyes twinkling in Rocko's direction. "To what do I owe this visit of yours?"

Rocko leaned back, and a smile crept across his face. "We just came from the Crow's funeral. The family wants to thank you for the beautiful flowers you sent."

"My pleasure. I always admired and respected the man. Terrible thing what happened to him, and on his fiftieth wedding anniversary too." He shook his head. "Terrible thing."

"You know these people?" Rocko asked. "This here is Johnny, the Crow's son."

Giancana nodded at Johnny.

"Johnny ain't in the business, but he's along to pay his respects."

"I appreciate that," Giancana said.

"And this here is Gina Cumo, the family's lawyer."

Giancana raised his eyebrows at the sight of Gina. "Not what I would expect."

Rocko laughed. "Few people do. She can be quite a distraction in a courtroom, but she's good, real good."

"I'm sure."

"And this is my man John, but we call him Junior. He's young yet, but a good man."

Giancana pointed in Rocko's direction but spoke to John. "You pay attention to what this man teaches you. He's the best in the business and was loyal to Lorenzo."

John nodded silently.

Rocko leaned back in his seat. "We'd like to find out what you know about that contract, what you've heard on the street. You always seem to have an ear about things like that, and we figured you'd know. The family doesn't want to start a general war, too much good business for that sort of thing."

Giancana unfolded his hands and waved with his right one. "I hear things, but I don't know too much, nothing for sure. Give me a couple of days."

"Fine, fine," Rocko batted his hand in Giancana's direction. "We'll be here and be in touch with you."

"Where are you staying? I could contact you there?"

Rocko circled his finger in the air. "We're around. Staying from place to place and seeing the sights. Johnny here ain't seen much of Chicago. I want to take him to some of the old haunts. Best that we contact you."

Giancana nodded. "You know where to reach me."

Rocko looked in Gina's direction. "We brought Gina so that maybe we could conduct some business."

"What kind of business?"

Rocko smiled. "We're still interested in any financing you could arrange with the Teamsters' pension funds. The family would look on that as a great favor. Arturo would be pleased."

A smile crossed Giancana's lips. He put his hands together. "One hand washes the other, my friend. The Crow had a deal with us on this Cuba thing, but he backed out. Now how am I gonna break my back if there ain't nothing in it for us?"

"The Cuba thing is out for us. The Crow made that clear." Rocko slouched forward. "But I think other arrangements could be made. We might be able to get you in on the Vegas loop, under our name and protection, of course."

"My union money and you get a piece."

Rocko shook his head. "No, our good name and gaming license, the union's money, and you get a piece. Matter of how you look at it."

"I see." Giancana narrowed his eyes. He turned and looked at one of his men, who got up and left the table.

Rocko leaned his head back. "And of course if you turn over on Lorenzo's hit, we'd look on that Vegas arrangement with even more generosity."

"And I'm the rat."

"The filthy rich rat," Rocko shot back.

Giancana slowly got to his feet, pulling his suit coat together and fastening a button. "Let me think about it and see what I can find out. You give me a couple of days and then call me." He smiled at Gina, took her hand, and kissed it. "Meanwhile, enjoy your stay in our fair city." He released her hand, still smiling at her. "If there's anything else I can do to be of service, you have only to give me a call from wherever you are."

Rocko stood up. "We will, Sam. We're looking forward to doing business with you."

Johnny watched the two of them walk to the door, along with Giancana's remaining soldier.

A short time later they finished their meals and headed out the door. "What did you make of that time?" Johnny asked.

"He knows." Rocko nodded. "Knows everything."

"Does he know because he planned it?"

"That I'm not sure of, but I'll find out. While we're here I'm going to ask around. We'll give him some time and then call him."

"And what about this deal you're trying to pull off?"

"I can tell you one thing. It won't make a hill of beans worth of difference if he fingered your papa or not as far as that deal goes. Sam Giancana would just as soon stab your mother in the heart and then turn around and climb into bed with you if he thought there was a buck in it for him. The man's a shark, and if there's blood in the water, he don't care whose blood it is."

Johnny grabbed Rocko's arm. "There were a few things in there that I didn't like."

"What?"

"The man seemed too much at ease, like he was sitting in a rocking chair, reading from a script. I gotta say it made me more than a little nervous too when one of his men left early."

"You think he's setting us up?"

"Could be. I don't know what to think. You know the man."

They rounded the corner and started up Michigan Avenue. They hadn't gone a half-block before Rocko grabbed Junior's arm and nodded in the direction of a long, pea-green Ford that was keeping pace with them. The driver looked at first like he was hunting for a parking place, but the car passed two spaces and continued to roll slowly along the avenue. Besides the driver, Johnny could make out three or four shadowy passengers. Suddenly when the street was clear of other pedestrians, the Ford stopped. One of the passengers rolled down the windows.

Rocko pulled out a revolver and dug his fingers into Junior. He shot a glance at Johnny. "Hit the deck," he yelled.

Junior leaped from his spot and pulled Gina down. Johnny looked up to see Junior tumbling on top of Gina, burying her beneath him as shots rang out.

PART 2
THE DARKNESS

CHAPTER 14

Johnny stepped out onto the balcony overlooking Lake Michigan. The stiff breeze ruffled his hair. It was hard for him to imagine how he had wound up where he was, doing what he was doing. In many ways he had always been the favored child. He had been the star athlete and the one picked for success. His parents had money, and even though his family's name and reputation had kept him out of polite society, it hadn't prevented him from hobnobbing with the entertainment industry. He had won the Silver Star on the island of Saipan and had left the Marine Corps a bona fide hero.

And then came the happiest day of his life. He had become a Christian, and he was determined to do it with his whole heart.

He heard a knock. Stepping back into the room, he walked over to the door.

"Hey kid," Rocko walked into the room, slapping Johnny on the back. "Kinda brought back the war for you last night, didn't it, kid? Duck and cover, stuff like that."

"I can't say that I enjoyed it."

"I'm going to see Giancana today. I called him up and arranged a meeting."

Johnny narrowed his eyes. "You really think that's wise, after what happened to us last night?"

"I don't think he had anything to do with that." Rocko shrugged his shoulders. "Why should he? What's the percentage in making trouble with the only people who can get you the prize you've always wanted? It don't make any sense."

"The timing is just too coincidental."

Rocko shook his head nonchalantly. "Maybe. Maybe somebody who knew Giancana was meeting with us set that up. Either way, Sam's got to know what happened, and he can do something about it."

"And what am I supposed to do about arranging your funeral?"

Rocko laughed, a deep, guttural belly laugh. He slapped Johnny on the back. "Kid, you're the one who's killing me. Don't you worry none about me. You got to baby-sit Gina today. I'm the one who should worry about you."

"What am I going to do with her?"

"Buy her a hot dog. Take her to the Art Institute. Women like that kind of stuff. I'll know where to find you if you're there."

It was a short time later when Johnny knocked on Gina's door. She was wearing a pleated plaid skirt and a white blouse with ruffles. Her hair was swept back and tied with a blue silk handkerchief.

"Rocko and Junior left for a meeting with Giancana, and I have instructions to take you to the Art Institute today."

She stepped back, chuckling as he walked in. "Instructions? You make it sound like an assignment."

Johnny smiled. "Sorry. I didn't quite mean it that way."

She picked up her purse. "Not quite, but almost, I gather. This must be very difficult for you, not only having to go someplace for your family, but having to be with me."

Johnny nodded slightly. "I'm sorry. I must confess it does make me feel more than a little uncomfortable."

She slung the bag over her shoulder. "Have you ever noticed how much you say, 'I'm sorry'? You even confess. I'm not your priest. What happened between us those many years ago was just as much my fault as it was yours."

She walked to the door with a smug look on her face. "Sometimes you men look on women as helpless victims. It's like we don't have brains of our own and wouldn't know what to do with them if we did. I wanted you just as much as you wanted me back then. I loved you and you loved me. It's as simple as that. I had a baby and it was yours and mine, but I wanted it. That was my choice. So quit carrying around all this guilt Johnny Pera. It doesn't become you. Now, I want to go to the art museum and I will go, with you or without you. It's your choice."

Johnny held his hands up in surrender. "I would love to go with you."

The arched doorways of the Art Institute were impressive, as were the second-floor red banners advertising its Impressionist art.

Massive stone lions stood on either side of the stairs. Large stone urns between the lions held an impressive array of bright flowers.

The halls were active with mothers and children. Johnny spotted one man in a black turtleneck sweater who was stroking a wisp of a gray goatee as he studied a multicolored work of modern art.

"What are you smiling at?" Gina asked.

"That man over there." Johnny chuckled. "He strikes me as an art lover." The marble hall made each step ring out with a crisp, deliberate sound. Had it not been for the echo of the children's laughter, a man might easily pick up a whisper. The place was designed for looking, not talking.

"And aren't you an art lover?" Gina lowered her voice slightly. "You seem to like your sister's work."

Johnny took a few steps, pausing in front of a dark Rembrandt. The painting had eyes that seemed to stare right through him. "Isabella is special to me. She paints from her heart." He looked back at her. "But I'm afraid she has a troubled soul."

"We all have troubled souls." She stepped closer to him. "No matter how much oil we pour on top of the water, there is always a storm underneath."

She turned her gaze to him. "Your soul is troubled even though you think you have all the answers. Like I said back at the hotel, regret is your master. You came to your parents' anniversary party because you felt ashamed about being apart from them. When I saw you in the kitchen that night, guilt was written all over your face. Your mother pricked your conscience, and that's why you're here on this fool's errand." She laughed. "I get paid to be here, but you, Johnny Pera, you pay with your pain."

"Somebody murdered my father just as I was finding him again." He stuck his hands deep into his pockets, then glanced at her. A slight smirking smile crossed his lips. "I bet you're a sight to behold in a courtroom. No doubt you play a jury like a violin."

She laughed. "I do quite well, thank you."

"Perhaps I feel responsibility more than most. When I played quarterback, I felt responsible for every loss."

Gina's eyes sparkled. "And no doubt you credited your team members for every win."

He bowed his head, a chuckle rumbling in his throat. "Another point for you, Counselor." He looked up at her. "I can't win when it comes to a duel of wits with you."

"You forget, I grew up with you. You always made your bed and picked up your clothes. You rinsed your dish when you finished eating. You were the perfect son in an imperfect household. Blame is something you cling to like a badge of honor. No matter what your family is responsible for, you can't take the blame for them."

"And what about you, Gina? You seem bright. Maybe you're too bright to be the mouthpiece for a Mafia don. What made you take on our family as a client, a family you knew all too well?"

She grinned. "The money. Your father paid quite well. Besides, I already owed him a lot. He's taken care of me."

Johnny shook his head. "You went into the law to pursue justice, only to wind up defending injustice."

"Is that what you think of your family?"

He nodded. "Pretty much."

She pushed her arm around his elbow and started to drag him reluctantly in the direction of the modern art exhibit. "Then here we are together. Both of us defending the wrong. How does it feel?"

"It feels lousy." He stopped and glanced around, then lowered his voice. "When we do get to the bottom of this thing, we're going to do it my way. We'll take what evidence we have and go to the police. There will be no slow moving cars with tommy guns, no blades shoved into some guy in a dark alley. We're playing this straight down the line."

"Then you'd better make sure you get something you can make stick. I can help you with that."

He looked her in the eye. "One thing you never told me."

"What's that?"

"The baby."

She looked down at the floor.

"Tell me about the baby."

Her eyes met his. "It was a boy. He looked a lot like you."

"What happened to him?"

She put her hand on his arm. "Look, Johnny, he's never had a father, certainly not you. He's fine where he is and with what he's doing. He knows nothing about you, and he's a grown man. I would never tell you anything without first talking to him, and I'm not about to do that. You'll just have to live with that and come to peace with God over that one."

"OK. I can do that."

"Are you sure?"

Johnny shook his head. "No, I'm not sure, but I'll try. I'll just have to trust that you know what's best."

"Johnny, you aren't to blame for that alone. You had no idea. If I had written you and told you, or if your parents had communicated to you, you would have dropped everything and run home to marry me. I know that."

"I certainly would have."

"And like everything else you've ever done, you would have been motivated by your sense of responsibility." She shook her head. "I wouldn't have wanted that. You would have missed Karen and never had those two wonderful children of yours." She smiled. "And I wouldn't be a lawyer. Look, this is your field not mine. You're the one who's supposed to get into the head of God. But isn't He supposed to be in control of these things? Why do you have to have the control and all the blame?"

Johnny nodded. "You're right." He shook his head. "I do blame myself for so much. I've always taken the responsibility for everyone's happiness but my own. And I can't be wrong, not now, not ever. I suppose you could say I've divided the world into two parts, right and wrong. And I've always had to come down on the right side with both feet, no matter whose toes I tromped on to do it. It's a lesson I'm learning."

The two of them spent the rest of the afternoon in the museum before going down to the cafeteria to order two Chicago-style hot dogs. Gina had hers smothered in chili and onions, and Johnny had his with spicy mustard and layers of sauerkraut.

They were finishing up when Rocko stepped through the door and spotted them. He hurried over to their table and sat down across from them.

He pushed his fedora back and grinned. "You two having a nice time catching up?"

Gina smiled and patted Johnny's hand. "Yes. I think we've talked our heads off today."

"Good. I'm glad."

"What did you find out from Giancana?" Johnny asked.

"He's tracking down who took those shots at us last night, but in the matter of your father, he thinks he has a lead." Rocko scooted closer to them and glanced around the room. "Sam thinks it was the Cubans."

"Which ones?"

Rocko's lip drooped slightly. "Well, he ain't so sure about that, but he thinks the Cat would be able to tell us in New York. Gatto's got them people wired as far as Castro's men are concerned. They got an embassy there, ya know. They're United Nations members."

"So we go to New York and see this Gatto?" Johnny asked.

Rocko nodded. "Probably. We got a few loose ends to tidy up here first. I think I got us a deal. We'll use the union pension funds to finance the new casinos. Giancana wants a piece of the El Morocco. We can still run it, and he'll get us good financing from the unions to open up new clubs. Ain't that great?"

"I don't care a thing about that," Johnny shot back. "I just want this matter of Papa's killing resolved. We're going to need hard evidence too."

Rocko waved both hands at him. "All right, all right. I know. We'll get that." He leaned forward. "We just gotta get this too. If this is in the works, those brothers of yours won't go off half-cocked."

He looked at Gina. "Am I right or am I right?"

Gina nodded slightly. "Yes, you're right. This deal has been very important to them. They want to own Las Vegas, and if they have to give a small piece of it away to do it, I'm sure that will be just fine with them."

"One thing, though." Rocko held up one finger for emphasis. "We got to make sure Giancana's on the level. I know some other fella here in town who might be able to tell us that. Sam Giancana ain't exactly on his top-ten list, if you get my drift. We got to see him."

He reached into his pocket and pulled out a small piece of paper, then shoved it across the table in Johnny's direction. "Here's the man's name and address. You and Junior go see him tonight and ask his boys about your papa. Find out what they know. If he ain't gonna pin Giancana with it, then our backside is clear. I got somebody else I got to see."

"What about me?" Gina asked.

Rocko shrugged and smiled. "Look, dis ain't no job for a lady. These guys are pretty unpleasant sorts."

"So I'll just sit in my room, watch TV, and wait for a call to bail you out of jail."

"That's about it."

CHAPTER 15

The chophouse at the Blackstone was called The Grill. The places were set with fine linen and shiny silver with gleaming steak knives that could pass for meat cleavers. Rocko hadn't shown for dinner, and Gina dropped her napkin beside her plate. Like always she had gone her own direction and ordered butterfly shrimp. "You boys make sure you don't stay out too late tonight."

"We'll be fine." Junior pushed a large chunk of steak into his mouth. It had been well coated with A.1. sauce, which dripped down his lip as he chewed.

"How do you know you're even eating meat?" Johnny asked.

Junior smiled and continued to chew. "I know. It's good too."

Johnny cut a thin slice of his pork chop.

"And where are you meeting this man?" Gina asked.

"One of the River North clubs, a place called Blue Chicago," Johnny said. He stuck the pork in his mouth.

Gina got to her feet. "You both be careful. That isn't exactly your part of town."

Junior smiled and patted the bulge under his arm. "We'll be careful."

Johnny could tell the kid was packing a revolver. In his dark suit and steel blue tie, Junior would look like a cop. The only problem was that most of the bar owners in a town like Chicago knew who the cops were, which would make Junior's appearance strange. Johnny was sure Junior would stick out.

"Let me know when you two get back. I'll be watching TV in my room, trying to stay out of the way."

Johnny got to his feet and laid down his napkin. He reached over and nudged Junior's elbow, getting him up. "I hope you'll be all right. Maybe we can do something fun tomorrow unless Rocko has more information for us to follow up on. Sounds like you'll be doing some paperwork on the El Morocco."

"I'm starting that tonight."

A short time later their cab rolled past the Moody Bible Institute. The large structure was imposing, and the lights were on in many of the dorm rooms. It reminded Johnny of his own world, a world where people loved each other and didn't try to kill one another.

The cab pulled over to the curb in front of Blue Chicago. The club's windows looked like a ship's small portholes. Worn red curtains were bunched in the windows, and blue neon notes glowed in the darkness. A buzzing and hissing neon sign read BLUE CHICAGO.

Sad trombone music mixed with the soulful mood of a saxophone flowed out the open door along with a cloud of smoke.

Johnny paid the cabby as they got out and took their place in a short line. The people were filing in, past a black man almost as large as the door he was guarding. Johnny paid the cover charge, and both of them stepped inside.

The bar was an elongated horseshoe that took up the space closest to the door. Bottles gleamed in racks around a center wooden island, and the red, amber, white, and brown liquid filtered what little light there was, creating a display of color. People were crowded around the bar, some shouting at the bartenders and others backed up with their elbows on the bar, listening to the band on stage.

The three men working the bar were dressed in black pants, white shirts, blue vests with sparkling sequins, all set off by crisp black bow ties.

Numbing, choking smoke filled the place, making it not only difficult to breathe but also to see.

They made their way around the bar to the table area. The small tables were surrounded by ice-cream parlor chairs. The stage at the far end of the room was occupied by a band. A bass fiddle, piano, saxophone, clarinet, and slide trombone were playing what could pass for "Saint Louis Blues."

Taking a table in the back of the room, Junior signaled for a cocktail waitress. The woman in a tight, peekaboo black dress sashayed her way over to them and smiled. Her teeth sparkled.

"I'll take a beer," Junior said. "Draft."

"And you, sir?"

"Just a club soda for me."

The woman hurried off.

"Not much of a drinker, are you?" Junior asked.

"Not really. The stuff always made me feel queasy. I don't see much sense in drinking something that makes me feel sick." He inched over closer. "You mind if I ask you a question?"

"No, sure. Go ahead."

"What's your real name? Calling you Junior makes you seem sort of young."

Junior laughed. "I was thinking the same thing about you." He covered his smile and tried to make a sober face. "Johnny seems like a kid's name. I don't meet many men who go by kid's names."

Johnny smiled. "I suppose you're right. My real name is John, of course. I can't remember ever being called by anything but Johnny, unless it was by a priest or someone who didn't know me."

"That's my name too. John."

"Then why do they call you Junior?"

"I don't really know." He shook his head. "No one's ever told me. They just planted the label of Junior on me when I was small, and it kind of stuck."

"We both seem to be stuck in our childhood."

"I guess so."

"I suppose a man never gets too far from his childhood, no matter how hard he tries. It seems like I've been trying all my life, and yet here I am."

Junior nodded. "Yes, here you are, doing something you don't want to do."

"I'll be fine. I'll make the best of it. I've been in rougher spots."

The waitress came back with their drinks. A woman in a slinky red satin gown walked to the middle of the stage and picked up a large microphone. Her crisp clear voice sounded out and filled the room as she broke into the lyrics of "Saint Louis Blues."

The entire room began to sway back and forth with the music. Johnny leaned forward to get Junior's attention. "You feeling a bit out of place here?"

Junior nodded. He looked around the room. The place was filled with black patrons. "I feel like we're two white marbles in a bowl full of buckshot."

Johnny chuckled. "You might say that. It's going to make it easy to see our contact though. He said we couldn't miss him in here. His name is Aldo. He's a large Italian man with a bald head."

Junior laughed. "He must have wanted a spot where no one he knows ever goes to."

"This would no doubt be the place."

After each song the woman performed, the room erupted into applause. Johnny continued to check his watch, growing more and more impatient. "I'm not sure this guy's coming. Rocko's note said he'd meet us here at nine P.M. and it's almost ten. I think we've been stood up. That worries me."

"Worries you? Why?"

"Gina's back at the hotel, alone. I don't like that."

Junior jumped to his feet and peeled several bills from a roll he was carrying in his pocket. "Let's go."

Johnny and he began the task of winding their way through the standing-room-only crowd. The audience had grown since the woman started singing, and people were pressed up next to one another. They squeezed their way between the people and finally stumbled out the door.

The street was clear of people, except for four Latin looking types standing near the dim street lamp. The four men looked Johnny and Junior over and began talking among themselves.

"We better see if we can get a cab," Johnny said.

As Junior stepped out into Clark Street, the four men drifted in Johnny's direction. "Where ya going, bub?" one of the men asked.

Johnny looked in the direction of the four men. Two of them were wearing blue sweatshirts with stripes down their sleeves. The man who spoke to him was wiry and dressed in torn jeans. It was the fourth man, however, who concerned him. He hung back from the group, but Johnny could see that he was quite large, a barrel chest with a girth to match. He was wearing motorcycle boots with metal buckles.

Johnny forced a smile. "We're going back to our hotel."

"What's the hurry?" the man in the torn jeans said. "The night's young." He laughed. "Even if you ain't."

Johnny held up his hands. "I think we've had plenty for one night."

Junior spotted what was happening from the street. He walked back to the curb. "Just go on about your business," he said, "and we'll take care of ours."

The man kept staring at Johnny. He pushed his lower lip out and spoke in a whiney drawl. "What's the matter? You brought your kid out here to score and can't find a lady who wants you?"

"We're not looking for trouble," Johnny said.

The man squinted his dark eyes and reached into his back pocket. He pulled out a switchblade and sprang it open. "Maybe you was looking for something else and maybe you found trouble."

Junior tried to reach into his jacket, but before he could produce his revolver the two men in sweatshirts were on him. One sent a punch into Junior's midsection while the other reached around to grab his arms.

The man with the knife stepped closer to Johnny, followed by his large friend. "Now let's see what you got."

Johnny braced himself as the man came at him. He stepped aside at the last instant and sent a punch into the man's head, dropping him to the sidewalk. The knife slid along the pavement. Johnny signaled the larger man like he was calling for a small puppy. "Come ahead if you want."

The man held up both fists and moved toward him. From where Johnny stood, it looked like the man's hands were the size of baked hams. He heard the man behind him scuffle to his feet and saw Junior struggling and kicking the two other men.

Johnny stepped forward and sent two swift punches into the big man's face. The blows snapped the man's head back, but the man stayed on his feet. Johnny circled his target, repeatedly darting in close and delivering one punch after another.

The big man seemed confused. He shook his head, then grimaced. He looked back over Johnny's shoulder to the man in the torn jeans. Holding up his hands, he waved furiously. "Stay out of this," he yelled. "The old man here is mine, all mine."

Johnny circled over in Junior's direction where he was still struggling with his two attackers. One of the men was trying to hold Junior's arms while the second was delivering punches to his midsection. Johnny kept his eyes fixed on the big man, then suddenly shot a foot out, sweeping the legs out from under Junior's assailant.

The thug hit the pavement hard, and Johnny danced back onto the sidewalk, circling the big man to the left.

The big man suddenly rushed him with his arms extended. Like a bull goring a bullfighter, he caught Johnny in his arms and rammed him into the side of the brick building. Johnny felt his knees buckle. The man was powerful and strong, like a gorilla.

A pair of swift blows into Johnny's gut knocked the air out of his lungs. The gorilla spun Johnny around and clamped arms around Johnny's chest. "I'm going to squeeze the air right out of you," the man said in a breathy whisper. "I'm going to teach you a lesson, but it'll be the last one you ever learn, 'cause you're gonna be dead, plumb dead."

Johnny's ears were ringing. There had to be a way to get his man to release him, even if for a second, and it had to happen fast. Johnny lifted his right foot and sent his heel down hard into the man's instep.

The man yelped in surprise and extreme pain, and Johnny felt the viselike grip release slightly. A swift kick to the man's shin broke the grip completely. Johnny spun around and delivered a swift punch to the man's groin area, which produced another agonizing scream of pain.

The gorilla was doubled over in pain. Johnny grabbed the man's thick shoulders and launched a knee in the direction of the big man's forehead. It was like kicking a football that had been overinflated. The man stumbled backward and dropped onto the sidewalk, twisting and turning in pain.

Johnny could see that Junior had kicked the man whose feet he had knocked out from under him, and he was now delivering punches to the man who had attempted to hold him.

Johnny looked over at the man in torn jeans, who had now retrieved his knife. "Come ahead," Johnny said. "It's your turn now."

The man turned and ran, and was soon followed by the two men who had been attacking Junior. That left only the big man writhing in pain on the sidewalk. It would be some time before he would be going anywhere.

Seconds later a long, black Cadillac pulled up to the curb. A large man with a bald head appeared at the rear window. "You Johnny Pera?"

Johnny nodded. "Yes."

The rear door opened. "Get in."

Johnny helped Junior into the car and climbed in behind him.

"Where's your hotel?" the man asked. "I'll take you."

"Just take us to the music shell in Grant Park."

"You two don't look like you're in any shape to walk far."

"We'll be fine," Johnny said. Rocko had warned him properly. He had no intention of giving away the location of their hotel, even if it meant they had to crawl back to their front door. "We just ran into a few of your local boys out for a good time with the tourists."

The man laughed. "Yeah, we could see that. We watched those three run off and from the looks of the fella on the sidewalk out there, he ain't gonna be running no place anytime soon." He stuck his hand over Junior in Johnny's direction and grinned. "I'm Aldo, Aldo Casale. I knew your papa back in the old days, before he became a big fish."

Aldo was a giant of a man. He wore ice-cream white from neck to toe, suit, vest, and shoes. He virtually glowed in the dim light. Even his pasty, oatmeal-like skin on his bald head seemed to shine. Only his black beady eyes and thin gash of a mouth gave away his face. Johnny shook his hand. "Nice to meet you. You a friend of Sam Giancana?"

Aldo twisted his face and spat. "No way." He shook a pudgy finger in Johnny's direction. "Don't you trust that man. He'd as soon kill you, gut you, and leave you to the birds as look at you. Rocko put the word out that you wanted to see me, and here I am. I'm sorry I was late."

"We are too," Junior nodded.

"Rocko's looking for people who might know who had a hand in killing my father."

Aldo sank back in his leather seat and took a deep breath. "It's dangerous to even speak of it." He shook his head. Turning in Johnny's direction, he widened his eyes. "I can tell you this. If those brothers of yours are planning on getting even, they better take a deep breath. The people behind your papa's death are invincible. They can't be found, and even if you did find them, they can't be prosecuted."

"Prosecuted?" Johnny asked.

"Yeah, I know you boy, or know of you. You're straight, on the up-and-up. You're probably out to prove something, and you need to forget it."

"Why is that?"

"Like I said, they're invincible, can't be touched."

Johnny shook his head. "I'm afraid I don't understand."

The man leaned forward so he could look Johnny in the eye. "Figure it this way. The people who had the most to gain by your father's cooperation wasn't anybody in the families—the families could take or leave his help."

He shook his finger, "But these people. They couldn't afford for your papa to back out. They were afraid if he did, the rest would follow."

"Who are you talking about?"

Aldo smiled. "You know them, not well, but you know them. You write a check to them every year. In a way you might say that you paid them to do your old man in."

Johnny shook his head. "I'm afraid I'm not following you."

"You worked for them one time. The government." He spat out the words. "Our own U.S. government. They're the ones with the high stakes in this game. They already got egg on their face, and they ain't about to get it thrown at them again. When your papa said no, he said no to them. Now I don't know who they used. I don't know who pulled the trigger. But I know it was them all the same."

Johnny sank back in his seat.

Aldo held up his finger once again. "One more thing. You better think about who had the most to gain in your own family. The people who did this thing had to have somebody on the inside. The Crow was untouchable, except for the people he trusted."

A short time later Johnny and Junior limped back in the direction of the hotel. Johnny's head was spinning, and not just because of the fight. If this Aldo character was right, then there was only one man who could help him, a man he had sworn he would never call on. Johnny had saved his life during the war, and he had shared Christ with Johnny in return. Johnny didn't want to presume on that relationship, but he might have to if he couldn't find another way.

Johnny put his hand on Junior's shoulder and grinned. "You carried yourself pretty well tonight for a boy."

Junior chuckled, his eyes dancing. "And you ain't so bad yourself, for an old man."

CHAPTER 16

The tiny, sputtering fishing boat had originally been painted white, but now the wear and lack of maintenance had turned it into streaks of gray and burnt orange. It had never been designed to make regular crossings between Miami and Cuba, but it did. The captain was a patriot who ran human cargo for a profit. He pushed the throttle shut and, after a few more dying gags, the *Santa Aida* became silent, gliding into the small bay north of Trinidad, Cuba. Javier had smiled at the boat's name as he boarded. *Aida* meant "help," and if ever a boat needed it, this one did.

He scanned the trees along the shore for a signal. A flashing light blinked on and off seven times. Javier pointed it out. "There she is. We can go."

The captain pulled back on the throttle, choking the little boat back to life. It chugged toward the shoreline. Javier knew he wouldn't have much time to make this rendezvous. Even though the beach might be clear now, Castro's men could happen upon them at any time. It never paid to delay.

He had brought guns and explosives with him in the hopes that Maria Gonzales and her followers would welcome him in their camp. He also needed her to do something. She seemed to be one of the few people on the island that he could trust, and she had to be cultivated. There were so many double agents in Cuba that one never knew whether anyone was a patriot or a member of Castro's DGI. But Maria had loyal followers and was connected to a priest as well. There was something about her passion that made Javier think he could trust her.

As they got closer, the captain once again cut the engines. Javier stepped over to the small rubber boat sitting on deck and heaved it over the side. With the line attached to the rubber boat, he drew it closer and began to toss his supplies into the bottom of the raft. It took him several minutes to completely load the bundles. He turned to the captain and saluted, then lowered himself over the side and into the bobbing raft.

The rubber raft squashed beneath his feet as he grabbed the line that started the tiny engine and jerked it. It sputtered and then droned on in a soft buzz as Javier adjusted the choke. Moments later he was making headway to the shore. He would land the supplies, and then those who were waiting to leave Cuba would take the little rubber boat back to the *Aida*. The little fishing boat couldn't carry more than fifteen to twenty people. That would mean at least two trips from the beach, but it would be worth it to the captain. Javier knew that each person who escaped Cuba had to pay dearly for it. It would make the trip very profitable for the man.

Almost twenty minutes later the small rubber boat nudged its way to shore. Several figures ran toward Javier from the darkness. He hoped they were Maria's people.

Two of the men grabbed bundles in the bottom of the raft while a third took the line along with Javier. Together they towed the small raft through the wet sand to the dry beach. It took only a matter of minutes before the raft was emptied and the first group of exiles was on its way back to the *Aida*.

Javier moved through the trees to a clearing where he saw Maria standing with two men. Even in the dim light of the tress she looked beautiful. The green fatigues she wore couldn't hide her figure. Her dark eyes, mocha complexion, and thick black hair were only made grander by the mannish uniform. But the woman was all business. When she saw him she barked, "Let's go. We have a long walk." With that she stomped off into the trees with Javier tagging along behind her in the line of men.

Shortly after dawn they came to a small house in a clearing. It was a simple place with a bleached-out tin roof. The dark wood was made up of remnants from several other houses. Rubber tires positioned around the flat front porch gave the appearance of a railing.

Two men dressed in straw hats and torn trousers stood outside the house. Spotting Maria, they waved.

"These men are farmers?" Javier asked.

Maria smiled and nodded. "Yes, they grow tobacco."

Javier stepped up to them and shook their hands. Most farmers only thought about their crops, and it took a lot for one to leave his fields. "How is the crop this year, señors?" he asked.

The men smiled widely. The older man with a gray beard spoke up. "We have already begun the picking, señor, and it has to be done by hand, carefully. We start with the *libre de pie*, the leaves on the bottom." He grinned. "They are the ripest. When we have them all picked, they will go to the curing barns on poles and sit there for fifty days."

"Sounds like quite a process," Javier said.

The old man nodded and laughed. "You don't know. We will have these same leaves for over two years, curing and fermenting them before we can ship them out to be made into the cigars you smoke." He took out a dark brown cigar and handed it to Javier. "Take this one, señor. Smoke it and enjoy."

Maria slapped Javier on the back. "Don't get them talking about leaves. They never quit." With that she laughed and walked into the house.

Javier followed Maria. A small fire licked the sides of an iron stove, while eggs and sausage sizzled in a large flat skillet on top. Hunched over the fire was a woman, stirring the eggs with a polished wooden spoon. She looked back at Javier with burning dark eyes. Turning back to the stove, she continued to stir.

Maria dropped the pack she'd been carrying and set down her rifle. She motioned in the direction of the woman at the stove. "This is Caterina. You be careful with her. If she doesn't like you, she'll put a hex on you." She held up her hands and wiggled her fingers in Javier's face. "A bad, bad hex." She laughed.

Javier found a stool and began to unlace his boots. He had to dry out his socks. "You have both ends of the spirit world covered, I see." He smiled. "You have your priest and a witch."

Maria tapped the side of her head with her index finger and grinned. "You betcha. It doesn't pay to cross either one. A girl can't be too careful. But Caterina can cook too. You'll like that."

"And your man from Havana ought to be here today?"

"Hector, yes. You'll like him. He brings us much information."

"Is he safe?"

Maria nodded. "Yes, Hector's brother Juan is a baseball pitcher, a good one, maybe Cuba's best. Hector wants him to play baseball in the United States someday, be a millionaire."

"He's dreaming."

"We're all dreaming. He keeps working on Juan's head to persuade him to go." She shrugged. "Sometimes he says yes. Sometimes he says no. But he always thinks about it. I think he's waiting for his mother to die, but she won't. The woman's too stubborn to die. Women are like that, you know. They don't do what you want them to do. They always do what they want to do."

"I'll have to remember that."

Javier took his seat at a rickety table. The fourth leg of the table had been bound with wire, and it tipped slightly in his direction when he sat down. Caterina spooned out the eggs and sausage on a chipped plate in front of him, then ladled a portion of food on Maria's plate. Stepping outside the door, she banged sharply on the sides of the skillet. Men came running, but there wouldn't be that much to go around.

He pushed his eggs around his plate and then sipped his black coffee. "How did you get into this?"

"I was born into it."

"How does one get born into a revolution?"

"My brother was killed fighting for Castro. I watched him sweat, bleed, and die for the man and his dream. You should have seen the light in his eyes when he talked to us around the table at night. He believed Castro was going to take us all into Utopia, make Cuba into a paradise on earth. He was a true believer."

She stirred her eggs, taking a small bite. "But when the revolution came, it just became worse for my people. Neighbors watched them; relatives reported on them. Friends became spies for the government. There was no more love here, only speeches and empty promises. My father was dragged out into the street by Castro's men and beaten to death. He died in my arms."

"I'm sorry to hear that."

"My brother's death, trying to get Castro into power, was in vain. It was a waste. At least my father died for the truth, and I am going to die for the truth."

"What about your own life? Surely you had one before all this. You're an attractive woman. You must have had a husband."

Maria nodded and pushed her plate away. "Yes, I was a teacher. My husband now serves in Castro's secret police, the DGI." She leaned forward and gritted her teeth, speaking with a hiss. "He was the one who reported that my father was a capitalist sympathizer. I divorced him. A sin, I know." She shook her head. "But I would never share the same cup of coffee with the man, much less the same bed. The only reason he is not dead to me now is that I want the chance to kill him myself."

She got up from the table and scraped what remained of her breakfast onto a tin plate. She walked to the door. Holding it out, she shouted at the men on the porch. "I have more here if you are hungry."

Javier sat back and watched her. Maria Gonzales was exactly what he had been looking for, someone he could trust. She would never pass on any information, not if her life depended on it. And she would not hesitate to kill, even her own husband.

Javier followed her to the door. "I have a favor to ask you, a big favor."

She swung around, looking him in the eye. "A favor?"

Javier nodded; his eyes were down. He glanced up at her but found it hard to look into her burning eyes. "Yes, a favor for the Americans."

Maria flung the now-empty tin plate in the direction of the far wall. It glanced off the boards and rattled to the floor, spinning like a top thrown by a child. "The Americans!" She spit on the floor.

"Yes, the Americans." He looked up at her. "I know you don't trust them, but they are our only hope. They gave me the weapons and the C-4 to give to you in the hope that you could do something for them. It might mean the difference."

"The difference in what?"

"It could provide the excuse for an American landing. You don't know what it's like to be pinned down on a beach by tanks and artillery when all you have are small arms. Like it or not we need the Americans."

Maria marched over and picked up the plate, then handed it over to Caterina. Then she swung around and planted her hands on her hips. "Our people die trusting those Yankees and all their speeches. They're all talk. Their words are mixed with our blood."

He shrugged his shoulders. "All they need are a few pictures. I've got a cameraman coming in a couple of days. He can take them. All you have to do is take him there."

"Where?"

"A place where the Americans believe there are Russian missiles. They can send over U-2 planes to take aerial pictures later, but they need to know the missiles are there first. I can show you the place on a map. It's a couple of days walk for you and a few men. It's very important. That's why we can't trust anyone but you with this."

The old woman Caterina stepped away from the stove and waved her hands in the air. "Nooooo . . ." She looked right at Maria. Her lips quivered. "You can't do this thing. Something bad will happen to you. You mark my words."

Later in the morning Javier watched as a string of men made their way into the clearing. They were not farmers. They wore battle fatigues like Maria, their hats pulled down over their faces and their boots caked with mud. Automatic weapons were slung over their shoulders. The man in charge held up his hand to the formation, stepped forward and hugged Maria.

Maria took the man's hand and led him over to Javier. "This is Hector Ortiz. He is our man with the regime."

Javier stuck out his hand. "Javier Lage. It is good to meet you."

Ortiz was a slightly built man with a broad forehead, wide nose, pockmarked face, and thick glasses. In any other place Javier would have pegged him as a college professor.

"You brought us guns and explosives?"

Javier nodded. "M-16s and C-4 plastic explosives. Do your men know how to use them?"

Ortiz nodded and grinned. "Oh yes, señor. These men will do very well with them. I cannot stay long, however. I need to get back to Havana before I am missed." He reached into his shirt pocket and pulled out a set of papers. "Here are the plans to the factories Miami requested. You will blow them up?"

"I have people who will. What of the team of men sent by the Italians in the states to kill Fidel?"

Ortiz shook his head. "All dead. They were discovered."

Javier put his hand to his face and raked it down his nose and mouth. He cursed and took a deep breath. "There will be more. This is a job that must be done and those people have pledged to do it."

"They must be careful who they seek help from. The streets have ears."

CHAPTER 17

New York was hot and sultry, a sauna with an overcast sky. Johnny and the group drove through Queens and made their way over the East River by way of the Brooklyn Bridge.

When the cab pulled up, bellhops came racing out to take their bags. Rocko grinned at the crystal chandeliers when they walked through the glass doors.

Johnny, Rocko, Junior, and Gina checked into the prestigious Waldorf-Astoria. Rocko had picked it out. "We'll need to tell people where we're staying. Nothing says 'power' like the Waldorf."

Johnny knew the two-hundred-dollar-a-night price tag also brought safety since the staff was known for its discretion and security. The elegant hotel with its gleaming crystal chandeliers, gold fixtures, and plush upholstered furniture was a genteel fortress.

After dropping off their bags and looking over their suites, the group caught another cab and made their way to the Hamptons. It was a long drive, bridge after bridge and multiple causeways, but it finally spilled out into a stretch of road that was open to the sea.

Gina leaned forward and tapped Rocko on the shoulder. "This Enzo Gatto fellow must do pretty well for himself."

Rocko laughed. "He ought to. He runs all the action up here in New York, the unions, the docks, the markets. Nothing passes through this city that he don't get a piece of."

Gina sat back and nodded. "He does have it wired."

"I'll say he does," Rocko shot back. "The man's been around forever. Long enough so he don't have to live on the East Side no more. He can afford the Hamptons with their tennis courts and pretty blondes on every street corner. This place may be New York, but it ain't New York, if you get my drift."

The cab turned into a driveway with an iron gate and bright lamps. Even though it was twilight, huge spotlights instantly popped on, bathing the yellow vehicle with beams of intense light. The driver lowered his window and shouted into the speaker that was hanging on the brick wall. "It's the Pera party."

Instantly, a motor hummed and the massive gate cranked open. They made their way down the drive to the modern house that sat overlooking the water. Trees lined the driveway, and tennis courts and a swimming pool flanked the house, which was set in a dazzling array of manicured lawns. A stone lion and a bear stood at the end of the driveway, their paws extended and their mouths frozen open with silent roars.

As the cab pulled up to the front door, two men in white dinner jackets hurried to open their car doors. When they were inside the impressive foyer, a thin man with balding gray hair and a black tuxedo stepped in front of them. His smile was artificial and practiced. "You are the Pera party?"

Johnny stepped forward. "Yes, here to see Mr. Gatto."

"Please follow me. Mr. Gatto is in the library."

They followed him through the hallway and down another hall with murals of Roman structures, the Coliseum, and hillsides filled with olive trees.

The butler ushered them through two dark cherry doors. Book-filled oak-and-glass cases covered the walls, and a massive mahogany desk sat in the middle of a bay window, with a blue leather high back chair behind it. Their host was seated in front of a blazing fire, watching a television set that had been placed in the wall over the fireplace. He sat forward and clapped his hands, glued to a football game.

"Hey," Rocko shouted, pacing forward. "What ya watching?"

The man shot them a glance over his shoulder. "Notre Dame." He grinned. "They're winning." He waved them forward. "Pull up a chair. We ain't going nowhere, and there won't be no dinner till this game's over. The wife's outta town. Bermuda."

Enzo Gatto held up a thick cigar, his square black onyx ring gleaming in the dull light.

Rocko sat down on an overstuffed flowered chair, squashing a belch of air as he sank into the cushions. He swung his legs around and planted his heels firmly on a matching ottoman. "Yeah, that's great."

Gatto waved his finger at the TV. "They're Catholic ya know."

Rocko chuckled. "Yeah, I know."

Gatto beamed. "Almost like going to church to watch Notre Dame football." He glanced at Johnny. "Don't you agree?"

Johnny smiled and sat down on the couch. "Some people would say that."

Junior and Gina took places on the long couch beside Johnny. They looked almost as out of place as Johnny felt.

Enzo Gatto looked and sounded very different from what Johnny remembered. Maybe it was because he wasn't on a business trip, or perhaps it was because he was in his own home. It could even be the fact that he was locked into a football game. In any event, Johnny decided that he liked the man better this way. He'd have to remember to pass along to his brothers that they should always conduct their business with the Cat while there was a Notre Dame football game on.

Johnny scooted forward so that he could talk to the back of the man's head. "What do you hear about the men sent to Cuba on that job?"

Gatto waved his hand while he continued to watch the game. "'Nuttin'. We ain't heard a word. Figure they're all dead."

Johnny sort of liked the idea that he could ask the man questions and that he was so preoccupied by the game that he might even answer them without thinking. He decided to go on. "So you're sending some others to take their place?"

"Sure, sure." Gatto waved his hand with his answers, a don't-bother-me gesture.

"When?"

"Soon, soon, very soon."

"Don't you think Castro might get mad at being targeted and decide to hit back, maybe hit one of our own guys?"

"Nah." Gatto pushed the thought away, then got to his feet and marched up to the set, turning the volume up. He backed up to his chair without turning around and sat down.

"Why wouldn't he?" Johnny shouted.

"Why wouldn't he what?" Gatto had forgotten the question.

Johnny leaned forward. "Why wouldn't Castro want to hit one of ours?"

"The man's too stupid. He don't know nothing about our operation or who does what. He wouldn't know where to start."

Johnny looked at Rocko and shook his head. He didn't believe what Enzo Gatto was saying. From what he heard, Castro had an excellent national intelligence force.

"If Castro didn't whack my papa, then who did?"

Gatto got out of his seat and took a few steps forward so he could get a better look at the play unfolding. "I figured the exiles did it. They don't want us backing out, none of us."

"Not the CIA then?"

It was the first thing that got Gatto's attention and pulled him away from the ball game. "The CIA? Where did you hear such nonsense?" He shook his head. "Boy, don't let people get the idea you're thinking that way. It's dangerous. You'll wind up on some government list and be hounded till you die. What's worse, we'll all be put on their list. We won't get no cooperation from them, not now, not ever."

"Are they cooperating with you now?"

Gatto clamped a bite into his lower lip as if there was something he wanted to say but couldn't or wouldn't. He put his hands to his face and rubbed it, running his fingers through the gray hair on the sides of his head. Johnny's question had brought the man to the point of exasperation.

"That's my business. I don't want you gumming up the works. I got plenty of contacts with the Cubans here in New York. I'll set up a meeting with you and one of their people in the embassy. You can ask him your questions." He grinned. "He might even give you a nice cigar."

It took almost an hour for Notre Dame to crush a lowly Navy team, and Gatto squealed with delight at every play, almost as if he had a son playing for the Fighting Irish.

"Great game, don't you think?"

Johnny shook his head. "Sort of like a grizzly bear taking on a panda, if you ask me."

"Hey, them other boys had some pluck to them. They scored three points, didn't they?" A smile spread across his face. "'Sides, I only root for winners. I ain't got no time for losers."

He walked to the doors with the TV still blaring. "Let's go get some dinner. They been waiting it for us."

One by one everyone filed out, with Enzo Gatto bringing up the rear and slapping Rocko on the back. The man was still feeling his oats after Notre Dame's runaway victory. "You got that deal cinched with Giancana?"

"Almost," Rocko said. "We got some details to work through."

"But he's going to put you in charge of the casino, ain't he?"

Rocko glanced ahead at Johnny. "That ain't decided yet."

"He better. You're putting the grease to the thing."

They walked into a large dining room with dark Queen Anne furniture. Renaissance style art hung on the walls. Enzo Gatto was a traditionalist with a distinct Italian taste, which also showed in the meal—antipasto, a spicy minestrone soup, and pasta with veal.

Gatto glanced at Johnny. "Drink your wine, boy. It's good for you."

Johnny swirled the wine around in his glass and took a sip.

"You played football didn't you, boy?"

Johnny nodded.

"But not for Notre Dame."

"No, Stanford. I played quarterback."

"Too bad Notre Dame didn't want you."

Johnny smiled. It always gave him great delight in bursting someone's bubble. He smiled. "They recruited me, but I chose Stanford instead."

"You didn't want a Catholic school?"

"I wanted Stanford."

Gatto shook his head, then pushed another forkful of veal into his mouth. "From what I heard, you joined another team anyway, after the war."

"If you're referring to my becoming a Protestant, yes, you could say that. I went into the ministry."

Gatto rolled his fork in Johnny's direction. "I guess if a man wants to be a priest but likes women too much to stay away from them, that would be the way to go."

"That has nothing to do with it. I became a Christian."

Gatto dropped his fork. "You were born a Christian. I was there when you was baptized as a baby." He pointed to his eyes. "I saw it with my own two eyes. Come on now, admit it. It was the women, right?"

Gina cleared her throat. "Take it from me, Johnny has remarkable self-control when it comes to women."

Johnny shot her a quick glance. Given his history with her, the very idea she would say such a thing was ironic and almost mocking. But he knew she didn't mean it to be taken that way.

She could see the look in his eyes and the irony of what she had just said seemed to embarrass her. "Of course he is normal, like any other man. But he is also virtuous. I admire him."

Gatto lifted his glass and held it in Gina's direction. "Words like that from such a beautiful woman go a long way." He glanced at Johnny. "You should be proud."

Johnny smiled at Gina. "I am."

CHAPTER 18

Colonel Scott Gordon was a man of many talents. He performed magical acts at the children's hospital and always made the best Santa Claus for his own children during the Christmas season. It had less to do with his size, which was six feet, four inches of spring steel and rawhide, but more to do with his deep voice. His melodious laugh could easily blossom into rolling ho-ho-ho's at a moment's notice.

He swaggered as he rounded the gate and returned the guard's salute. These late night meetings with the president had little appeal to him. Most of the day would be spent preparing for it in his

Pentagon office and then, without going home, he would be forced to sit and wait until someone called with a final word where and when the meeting was to take place. Meanwhile, Jackie would either try to keep his dinner warm or give up and put it into the fridge. Tonight would be hopeless. His meatloaf would be in the refrigerator.

The guard standing by the French doors spotted him and turned the ornate gilded handles to let him in. "Evening, sir."

Scott stopped and looked at the man. "Evening. George, isn't it?"

The man smiled. "Yes sir."

"And your wife is Roberta?"

The man nodded and smiled. "Yes sir. You got that right."

Scott walked down the long West Wing hall and stepped into what was called the sitting hall. If it had been left up to Scott to name the place, he would have called it the stewing hall, because most of the visitors paced back and forth stewing over some meeting that was about to take place. What had been designed as a place of relaxation was anything but.

The main feature of the West Wing sitting hall was a large, fan-shaped window with a carved ornate arch that rose from the floor and curved halfway up the dazzling array of window panes. The large couch in front of the window was a bright honey color with red, blue, and yellow throw pillows. Scott set his beaten leather briefcase on the sideboard table and paced over to the couch in front of the window. As cars passed the White House, the glare of their headlights smeared the trees on the front lawn before going on into the night. The people in the cars were no doubt going home, which was exactly what he wished he were doing.

He picked up one of the pictures on an end table, that of the president sailing on Cape Cod. Kennedy had a broad grin on his face and his hands on the tiller. Scott Gordon knew the feeling all too well, the feeling of being in control with the wind at your back. There was nothing like it. The group of pictures arranged on the table were all the Kennedy clan, some frolicking on the beach and some playing games of touch football.

Scott smiled at the thought. No doubt a lot of that had ended with the Kennedys' move to Washington. Here a man had to fight for his family, hang on to it like a determined growling dog. Even then people pulled you away. Washington was a place where a man could be condemned by his competence. The more a person knew, the more late-night meetings he was forced to attend and the more business trips he had to take. He had a deep longing to settle down into a command where he could actually do what he came into the Marine Corps to do.

Scott stood up straight when he heard the door open and, as he turned around, he was glad he did. General Maxwell Taylor, the chairman of the Joint Chiefs of Staff, entered the room. The lanky man wore his dress uniform. His steel-blue eyes looked down his straight nose. He would have looked like a general even if he'd been wearing only his skivvies.

"Gordon?"

Scott snapped his heels together. "Yes sir."

Taylor smiled. "I thought it was you." He motioned him forward. "Follow me, Colonel. We need to pick your brain tonight."

Scott filed behind the man and followed him to the Oval Office. Taylor opened the door and stepped aside for him.

The president was seated behind his desk with the presidental flag to his left and the American flag to his right. The large blue oval rug had the seal of the United States in the center, the legs of the eagle outstretched with arrows in one set of talons and an olive branch in the other. No doubt the eagle would be using the arrows tonight. If that were not true, there would be no need for him.

Scott knew more than a little of the history of the Oval Office. Anybody who worked in the White House did. The president's desk had once belonged to President Rutherford B. Hayes, a gift from

Queen Victoria in 1880. It had been fashioned from the oak timbers of the HMS *Resolute,* a ship recovered by whalers in the Arctic. Matching Chinese vases adorned the marble mantelpiece with a portrait of George Washington prominently displayed over the fireplace. Matching red-and-white striped sofas flanked the fireplace, extending to the foot of the great seal on the floor. But the chairs on either side of the president's desk were what caught Scott's attention. They were hard, straight backed, and solid oak, set directly at the president's elbows, which made them even more uncomfortable.

Scott hung back, but it was hard to miss the discussion going on at the president's desk. His brother Robert was seated in one of the hot seats, the one to the left of the president. A man Scott had only seen a few times, a spook with the CIA, occupied the one to the president's right.

The president stared directly at his brother. "This was supposed to be taken care of, and now you come in here to tell me the job's been botched." He rapped his knuckles on the desk with each word.

"We don't know that for sure yet, Mr. President." Robert's voice was shrill. Even though he was the president's brother, Scott knew Robert Kennedy always took care to address the president properly. There were enough people working at the White House who saw John Kennedy as a lightweight, without his brother adding to the image by being too familiar.

"This isn't some random shooting on the streets of Chicago," the president went on. "We're talking people operating in a foreign country who can't even speak the language. They have no family in Cuba. Why should anyone go out of his way to help the Cubans?"

"Because they want Castro out of the way as much as we do."

"I rather doubt that."

The president turned his attention to the man seated to his right, glancing back at Bobby. "I think we should go the other way. Cubans need to free Cuba, not some goombahs from the south side of Brooklyn."

Bobby leaned forward. "Mr. President, we've already discussed this. The force we have is nowhere near ready. We've already taken a bloody nose with this group, and I have my doubts whether we can find any Cubans in Florida that will ever trust us again, for perhaps a long while."

"Do you agree, Cliff?"

The man to the president's right glanced at Bobby Kennedy and then leaned forward in the direction of the president. "I think that is changing, Mr. President. We're finding some good men who, I think, can do the job, and we're using them now."

The president lifted his gaze to where Scott was standing with General Taylor. "General, I'd like to get the military's assessment of our situation there." He shot glances at both men seated in the hot seats in front of him. "Something that doesn't have politics mixed up in it, or people trying to cover their keisters."

Taylor stepped forward. "Mr. President, that is why I asked Colonel Gordon to join us tonight. He's prepared the readiness report on Operation Mongoose and Task Force W. He's an expert on Cuba. He's been stationed in Guantánamo and Miami and knows a lot of our people both on and off the island."

The president placed his hands behind his head and leaned back. "Scott Gordon. It's plain to see where your ancestors come from, Gordon. Do they make good Scotch whisky?"

Scott let a faint smile cross his lips. "Don't know much about that myself, Mr. President. We'll leave that for the Irish to decide."

The president chuckled. "And I'm sure we will too."

Kennedy picked up a piece of paper in front of him and held it up. He smiled. "I've been reading a little about you, Gordon. You served in the Pacific, fighting the Japanese."

"Yes sir." Scott nodded.

"Got a Silver Star too, I see."

Scott stared straight ahead.

Kennedy shook the paper and grinned. "Wish I could say the same. All I got in that war was a nice long swim and a perpetual back-ache." He laughed. "Makes me a rocking-chair hero, I guess."

He looked at the paper then up at Scott. "I'll read your report, Colonel, but I'm going to need more from you, much more."

"That's why I'm here, Mr. President."

"It may involve you spending some time away from home."

Scott nodded somberly. "One of the things I took on when I joined the Corps, sir."

Kennedy got to his feet and leaned down with his hands on his desk. "Fine. I'm glad to hear that. I'd like you to go to Florida and see for yourself how ready Operation Mongoose really is. Go where you need to go and see who you need to see. Bring me back a report I can trust. I need to know how many men we can count on and how ready they are to launch a serious attack against Castro. I want to know their morale and what their leadership is like. Do you know Cliff Cox?" He looked down at the man to his right.

"I've seen him, sir."

"Well, Mr. Cox will give you all the assistance the CIA can give. He'll leave no stone unturned for you. I need your honest assessment, Colonel. I don't care whose toes you step on to get it."

Scott saluted and turned to leave.

"One more thing, Colonel."

Scott stopped in place, then turned around.

"Your wife and mine share the same name, Jackie."

"Yes sir."

"I also suspect they share the same desire to see more of their hus-bands. Please give your Jackie my apologies." He smiled. "I might just have to call on you to apologize to my Jackie some day."

CHAPTER 19

The Jax Hotel was a seedy dive on the lower East Side on Delancy Street. It was a short walk from Little Italy, and most of the people surrounding the building spoke Spanish. Johnny took them to be Puerto Rican. The building was painted a bright shocking pink with a series of pea-green metal fire escapes that snaked up the front. The landings on each floor were fenced in with sharp spikes, and the awnings, which fanned out over the oval windows of the first two floors, were painted the same color as the fire escapes.

The four of them presented a stark contrast to the other people on the street. Both Rocko and Junior were wearing gray suits with red-and-white ties. Johnny was in his blue blazer and khaki slacks. But it was Gina who caught everyone's eye on the street. She was wearing a short, bright red dress that swung around her shapely legs as she walked.

As they started to walk up the stairs, Johnny spotted a man sitting on the top step. The man held out his hand. "Got a quarter for a meal, friend?" he asked.

The man was unshaven and was wearing a torn Harvard sweatshirt. His brown dungarees were ragged at the knees, and the shoes on his feet didn't match. He wore a dirty sneaker on his left foot and a broken-down combat boot on his right.

"Looks like you need some shoes," Junior smirked.

"Nah, these suit me just fine." He held up his left foot. "This one helps me to run from the cops." Putting it down, he picked up his other foot. A broad grin crept across his face. "And this one is for kicking."

Rocko laughed. "Kicking what?"

"Folks and dogs what need kicking."

Rocko bent over in laughter. "I like that in a man, somebody who knows what he's doing." Reaching into his pocket, Rocko produced a dollar bill. "Take this, but don't bother to lie to me about it. If cheap wine is what you want, this ought to do you."

The man reached out and took the greenback, grinning from ear to ear. He doffed a slight salute in Rocko's direction. "Thank you kindly."

"Where did you get the sweatshirt?" Johnny asked.

Reaching down, the man pulled his shirt out. "This shirt? I got it when I was going there."

"Harvard?" Johnny asked.

The man nodded. "Yep. I graduated in 1958, poli sci."

Johnny's eyes widened as Rocko laughed. "Political science?" Johnny asked. "Why didn't you do something with it?"

The man smiled and waved his hand at the street. "I am doing something with it. I sit here and think. I think lots."

Rocko reached down and patted his shoulder. "Well, pal, you just keep thinking. You keep your belly warm with that wine too."

They headed up the stairs and walked through the glass doors with copper-colored bars on them. "When you give a hungry drunk a dollar," Johnny said, "an hour later you're still going to find a hungry drunk."

Rocko snickered. "Yeah, but he won't be thinking about no food."

"He won't be thinking," Johnny added.

Rocko stopped at the first flight of stairs and looked back at Johnny. "You know, kid, I don't think you ever did figure out what our business was all about." He stroked his chin. "We supply people with what they want. We meet people's needs."

"Needs?"

"Well, desires. I know you preacher people live a life where you're all the time telling people they shouldn't have desires, but that don't change the fact that they do. People have wants and likes, and we match them up with a supply. It's as simple as that. Pure business. Supply and demand. They have the demand, and we have the supply. They ask, and we say yes. That man out there asked, and I said yes. I don't question who he is or what he does. Figure that's his business."

As they climbed the stairs they could hear noise erupting on the floor above them, incomprehensible shouts and bellows, seemingly coming from several men all trying to be heard at once. Johnny grabbed Rocko's sleeve. "Are you sure this is the place?"

Rocko nodded. "The Cat said this was where the Cubans hung out. They got offices on the second floor. We're supposed to talk to a Felix Gonzales." He arched his eyebrows and snickered. "Hey, that makes sense. The Cat is sending us to Felix, Felix the cat, get it?"

"Yeah, I get it."

Rocko turned and plodded up the stairs, shaking his head and obviously tickled with himself. "Figures, Enzo sending us to another cat."

When they got to the top of the stairs and rounded the corner, they saw men wearing green fatigue uniforms crowding the hallway. A large man with a full black beard was waving his hands and shouting at two men who were backing away. Others joined in the shouting contest, shaking their fingers.

The two men who were receiving the tongue-lashing backed away, holding up their hands in surrender and mumbling excuses. They shuffled backward in unison, easing blindly toward their open office door.

Johnny pulled on Rocko's sleeve, bringing the big man to a halt. He leaned forward and nodded at the two retreating men. "Let's hope one of them isn't our man Felix."

They watched as the big man in charge stomped into his office, followed by his two lackeys. The man slammed his office door shut. One of the men who had been the subject of the tirade poked his head out of his door. He stepped out into the hall and straightened his shirt.

Rocko turned his head and spoke in a low whisper. "Yeah, with our luck we get the whipped one to deal with. What we want is the top dog."

The hallway had become silent. People still shuttled in and out of the offices, but they clutched their papers close and scurried to where they were going. There was an air of fear to the place. Everyone knew who was in charge, and no one wanted to cross him.

Rocko straightened his suit and stepped into the hall. Johnny and the others followed along. They had taken only a few paces before the man who had slunk out of his office moments before spotted them. He lifted his chin and stepped into the middle of the hall in front of them. "Do you have business here?" he asked.

Rocko nodded and glanced back at the other members of the group. "Yes. We're here to see a Felix Gonzales. Is he here?"

The man lifted his baby-smooth chin. "What is the nature of your business with Mr. Gonzales?"

Rocko scratched the back of his head. "That's private, sort of between us and Felix Gonzales."

The man stepped forward. He was over a head shorter than Rocko, but that didn't stop him from showing his newfound confidence. He put his hands on his hips and looked up into Rocko's eyes. "This is the new Cuba. We have nothing that is private. You state your business with me and I tell him. If he has an answer for you, then I will let you know. If he wants to take his time to speak to Yankees from America, he will tell me and I will tell you."

Rocko shrugged his shoulders. "We seem to have struck a roadblock here, Johnny. I don't know what to say to this mouse. You tell me."

Gina smiled and spoke up. "Let me have a minute with him. You men watch and learn."

Rocko stepped aside as Gina moved forward. She put her arm through the man's arm and together they walked down the long hall. Johnny could tell that Gina had gotten his complete attention. She slipped her hand down his arm and held his, patting it as she talked.

A few minutes later the man left the hall and went toward another office. Gina waited for him and gave him one last smile as he turned back to look at her. Then he went inside.

Gina turned sweetly around and walked back toward them. "This shouldn't take long."

"What did you say?" Johnny asked.

Gina smiled. "I told him we had information that could help to preserve his president's life. I told him we knew about the American Mafia and its plans."

"We could have told him that," Johnny said.

Rocko smiled. "Not the way she told it, we couldn't." His grin widened. "Boy, you have got a lot to learn. You just can't bring yourself to go around the back way, can you? You can't tame a tiger with only a whip and a gun. Sometimes it takes a saucer of cream." He looked at Gina and smiled. "And I'd say we have a nice saucer of cream with us, boys."

Gina frowned and planted her hands on her hips, glaring at Rocko. "Men. You people can be so simple. Look, I'm a forty-year-old mother, not some pin-up girl on a garage wall. I deserve a little more respect than that. I'm not a saucer of cream for anyone. Now you apologize."

Rocko bowed his head. "I'm sorry Gina. I was only trying to tell the boy you get more flies with honey than you do with vinegar."

She stepped closer to him. "I'm not honey either. I'm a grown woman with a brain. You can be nice to someone without coming on to them. Someone needs to teach you to show a little respect."

"Yes ma'am." Rocko nodded.

It was only a short time before the smooth-faced guard reappeared. He pushed his head out the door and looked down the hall, away from where they were standing and toward the door occupied by the big dog that had yelled at him. Then looking at them, he signaled them to come.

The guard closed the door behind them. The room was typical of a hotel tenement house with its orbed light hanging in the middle of the ceiling. Peeling wallpaper scenes of little boys at play—flying kites, batting baseballs, fishing, and running with dogs—were dog-eared at the corners of the room and torn away in patches.

The man behind the desk looked up at them. He had a close-cropped beard and military haircut. "Manuel tells me you have information which concerns the safety of our president."

"If your name is Felix Gonzales, we do," Rocko said.

Pushing himself slightly away from his desk, the man crossed his legs, reached into a box, and brought out a long, chocolate-colored cigar. "I'm Leonardo Padura." He bit off the end of the cigar and spit it onto the floor. Next he picked up what appeared to be a shiny silver derringer pistol, held it to the end of the cigar, and pulled the trigger, sending a steady flame from the end of the barrel. Padura smiled at them as he put away his lighter and puffed his cigar to life. "I have to hear what you have to say before I can take up the time of Gonzales."

He pulled the cigar out of his mouth and motioned to them. "Tell me what you have."

Rocko stepped forward. "First we need to know something."

"And what is that?"

"A short time ago one of the leaders of the Mafia, a man in California, was assassinated. His name was Lorenzo Pera. We need to know who was responsible, who the triggermen were." Rocko held his hands out plaintively. "You help us, and we make you and Gonzales heroes."

"That's easy," Padura sneered, waving his hand. "Give me something hard."

Johnny was growing more and more impatient with the arrogance of people pretending to be something they were not. "If it's so easy, then tell us the truth."

Padura took the cigar from his mouth and flicked ash onto the floor. "The CIA, of course." He grinned. "You have to take this up with a Cliff Cox from your American Central Intelligence Agency. He's the man in charge of killing Americans."

"You're lying," Johnny said.

Padura pulled the cigar from his mouth and pointed it at Johnny. "No, you are the liar." His eyes flashed. "Don't you think we know who you are? You're Pera's kid. You got nothing I want except grief and vengeance. You parade in here with your suits and ties and think you can pull the wool over these stupid Cubans' eyes. What do we know? We're farmers come to power, living in palaces built by someone else, dictators using American money."

He got to his feet and leaned on his desk with both hands. "Now I told you the truth. You silly Americans can go ahead and believe your government, but over the years we in Cuba have come to know them for what they are—murderers and thieves."

He stood up straight, clamping his teeth once again around his cigar. "Believe what you want. I don't care. Your CIA committed the murder of your father, just as it did mine. The only difference between you and me is I know the truth when I see it. You don't. Your stupid patriotism stops you from thinking."

He waved his hand. "Get out of my office. You're wasting my time. There's nothing you can tell me that I don't already know. You have nothing but blood lust in your minds. But I tell you this. When you're through with this pathetic little journey of yours, you're only going to discover what I've already told you. Then you will have to curl up in your beds and sleep with it. Adios. Get out of my sight."

The four of them filed silently out of the man's office. Johnny felt more than a little embarrassed. He knew that he didn't have vengeance in his heart, and yet he also knew that was exactly what this trip seemed to indicate. He also knew the Cubans had good information.

They started walking down the hallway with the baby-faced guard keeping pace at their heels. When they got to the stairs, the man caught Gina's eye, motioning with his head back into the hall.

Gina stepped back and talked to him. She nodded and smiled.

"What was that all about?" Johnny asked. "Making a date?"

She lowered her voice. "Don't be silly. Just because that man back there made you feel like a fool doesn't mean you have to act like one."

She looked at Rocko. "He wants to meet us in Central Park tonight at eleven. He says he knows a few things we weren't told back there." She smiled. "I think he wants a bribe."

"That we can do," Rocko said.

Junior had been silent, taking in the sights and looking tough. "One thing I'd like to know," he said. "Who told him about us if it wasn't Enzo the Cat?"

"Good question," Rocko said.

"He had us pegged right down to who we were and why we're here. And he didn't seem all that sympathetic."

Johnny looked at Rocko. "Why should he be? Supply and demand, right? Somebody wants a murder and somebody delivers it. Right, Rocko? Simply business."

CHAPTER 20

Baldassare's plane landed at Miami International shortly before three P.M., the wheels skidding and biting the runway as the pilot reversed engines. He could no longer wait to get a report from his preacher brother. Pacing the floor of the beach house and staring out at the water had long since lost its appeal. It was time to take action. If Santos Trafficante hadn't ordered the murder of his father, Baldassare knew the man would know who did. And he wasn't about to take sweet smiles and promises from the man either. If dons like Trafficante thought the Pera family could sit by while they were systematically murdered, then no one's life in the Pera household would be worth a plugged nickel.

Arturo was opposed to this trip, but then Arturo was the family businessman. He had no stomach for war. But Baldassare had gotten on the phone. He'd lined up a place to stay on South Beach, a rental house, along with guns, cars, and a few Trafficante enemies he knew who would like nothing better than to have the old man put away for good. He'd also brought three of the family's best soldiers. They might not have the respect Rocko had, but they all knew how to pull a trigger.

Bruno was a giant of a man who could intimidate anyone just by standing next to them. His neck was thick and his jaw looked like something chiseled out of marble.

Renzo was a smooth operator. He liked to shoot from a distance and was a marksman. His dark hair, oiled into place, gave him a slick appearance.

Marco was most like Baldassare. The man was brash and over-confident. He had Italian good looks and was a ladies' man. His weapon of choice was the sawed-off shotgun. At close range it left nothing to chance.

They picked up their bags at the carousel. Baldassare barked out orders. "Renzo, you go pick out our car. Make sure it's a Caddy and black."

Renzo smiled and hurried off to the rental counter.

"Marco, you check on the guns we're buying from the Oatmeal Man. Tell him I want them delivered to this address." Baldassare handed Marco a piece of paper with the address on it. "They got to be first-rate and untraceable. Do I make myself clear?"

Marco nodded. "We going to some clubs tonight, Baldy? I'm sure feeling like it after that long plane ride." He rubbed his backside. "I thought I'd never be able to stand up again, and now I want to dance."

In less than an hour they were piled into a gleaming white Cadillac. They drove across the Julia Tuttle Causeway. The blue water of Miami Beach spread out on either side of the road. Boats, large and small, idled their way back and forth. Some had sails raised and were cutting through the water. Others were powerboats that were sending out trails of white water mixed with diesel fuel.

Baldassare shouted at Marco from the backseat. "I thought I told you a black Caddy."

Marco was at the wheel. He cast a beaming grin back in Baldassare's direction. "The only convertibles they had were white, Baldy."

"That's another thing. Who said anything about a convertible?"

"Aw, boss." Marco droned out the words with a pitiful tone. "It's Miami Beach." He held his hand up to the sky. "The sun is shining. There's no fog like in California. We got to live a little, ain't we?"

The house they had rented came equipped with a cook, and Baldassare had been assured that the pantry was fully stocked. But perhaps the best thing from his perspective was the fact that there was a security guard. There would be no sudden uninvited guests, and that would allow the four of them to sleep in relative peace.

They pulled up to the white gate and gave the guard their phoney names and false identification. The man checked their picture IDs, and then he backed away with a smile and waved them through.

Their beachside street was quiet. The house was white stucco with red tiles on the roof and green metal balconies that sported planters with blossoming red and yellow poppies. A tennis court was on one side of the house and a swimming pool on the other.

"Whew." Renzo gave out a whistle. "This must have set you back a pretty penny, boss."

Baldassare smiled and nodded. "Yeah, it's expensive all right. Hopefully we won't have to be here too long."

Renzo grinned slyly, his bare teeth gleaming. "Just find 'em, hit 'em, and go, right?"

"We hope," Bruno added.

When they went inside, they could see that the place had been decorated in the typical Miami style, art deco. The marble fireplace rose from floor to ceiling. Potted plants, flowers, and palms stood all around the main room. The furniture was a riot of color, bright oranges, yellows, blues, and reds, on white.

The four of them set down their bags and stepped on the Oriental carpet that covered the parquet floor. Marco was the first to speak up. He looked over at Baldassare. "Your mama would have a hissy living in this place."

Baldassare smiled and shrugged. "Yeah, kinda nice, isn't it?"

Renzo stepped over to one of the large mirrors hanging on the wall. He smoothed his hair, grinning at his own reflection. "I like it myself." He swung around and looked back at Bruno. "What do you think, champ?"

Bruno stepped forward and collapsed into a huge club chair. "I don't care one way or the other. Just so long as it has a good bed." He put his fingers together and placed them behind his head. "A roof is a roof and a bed is a bed."

"That's my man," Baldassare said. "Always thinking of the most important things."

"When do we start?" Marco asked.

"Tonight," Baldassare said. "We've got to get the man's attention first. Hit him where it hurts the most."

Marco clapped his hands and rubbed them. "Good. I like the sound of that."

It was close to eleven P.M. before the four of them got back in the white Caddy and headed toward the bright lights of Miami Beach. The gun delivery had gone as planned, but Marco thought the automatic weapons were seriously out-of-date. One was an M-3 grease gun with a 30-shot clip and the other was a Thompson. Both were vintage Korean War. They had been well maintained, but he still didn't like them. The shotguns were first-rate though, two pump-action 12-guage Brownings, sawed off to make them easy to conceal. The pistols were two Colt .45 automatics and two Ruger .357 Magnums.

Renzo sat in the front seat, gripping the .45 and pointing it at oncoming traffic.

"Put that thing down," Baldassare barked. "You don't know who belongs to any of those oncoming headlights. We could be passing by a Miami police car, and you wouldn't know it till he turned around and switched on his flashers."

"Just getting the feel of the thing. That's all."

"Well, put it down."

Bruno looked over at him. "This is a boat we're going to hit?"

Baldassare nodded. "Yeah, a floating gambling casino. It looks like something out of Mark Twain though, a Mississippi River steamboat. I hear it's Trafficante's pride and joy. If things go right, they won't even know we're there."

"They'll know all right," Marco shouted. He laughed. "They'll know when they get to counting the money."

A little over an hour later they shoved off from the docks. The small cruiser they had rented had twin outboard engines, which gave the boat plenty of kick. They had put tape over the name of the boat and the numbers on the side. When Marco pushed the throttle forward, it rose out of the water like a sea monster that had been harpooned. They sped out of the harbor, bound for the open sea. The sea was a dark blackish blue, a well of deep ink.

It took them almost an hour to find the casino. The sternwheeler was cruising beyond the three-mile limit, its lights ablaze and its bright red paddles slowly turning.

Marco swung the wheel and gunned the engine, pulling them alongside. They bounced off a series of tires before coming to rest at a floating dock. Dixieland jazz poured from the ship. Baldassare climbed out and adjusted the shotgun slung across his back. The three who would be going aboard all wore blue raincoats to conceal their weapons. Bruno carried a duffel bag around his waist. He lumbered out of the boat, followed by Renzo.

"All right," Baldassare shouted, "take the boat for a spin around this thing, but don't get far. We ain't about to swim back to Miami."

Marco gave a slouchy salute, kicked over the wheel, and gunned the engine. The water erupted into white foam as he headed out to sea.

"Let's go," Baldassare said. "We got to pay the man a call. We'll go up and take a little spin around."

They walked up the ramp that led to the main deck. The windows were large, exposing gamblers and dense smoke. Men and women shrieked and screamed at the craps table while others passively watched the wheel turn on the roulette table. Still others pulled at the one-armed bandits, watching the wheels spin and waiting in vain for the coins to drop out.

"Money in our pockets," Renzo hissed.

"Ought to be a lot of it too." Baldassare's eyes sparkled at the sight of an obviously full house. "This ought to get Trafficante's attention."

"Ya think so, boss?" Bruno asked.

"Yeah. That brother of mine will be going around, asking silly questions no one will answer and apologizing for taking up too much of their time. Me, I'd just as soon kick in the door and hold a gun to the man's head. Maybe then we'll get some straight answers."

They circled around to the stern. A few of the more romantic types had ventured back there and were standing at the rail, taking in the glow of Miami's distant lights. The smoke from the two overhead stacks drifted lazily overhead, mixing with a few sparks that twinkled in the gray, sooty mixture.

They continued to circle until they spotted a man wearing a pistol at his side. The man was standing outside, smoking a cigarette. Baldassare reached into his pocket and produced a Lucky Strike. He planted it in his lips. "You go on ahead, Bruno. When I get the man's attention, you make sure he goes out."

Bruno nodded.

"Make sure you smile at the man though."

Bruno walked on ahead. He passed the man, nodded and smiled, then stopped at the railing just beyond.

Baldassare and Renzo walked on until they caught the man's eyes. Baldassare stopped, the unlit cigarette bobbing in his mouth. "Hey, buddy, got a light?"

The man reached into his pocket and produced a Zippo lighter. Bending over to light his cigarette, Baldassare saw Bruno spring from the rail. Bruno came down on the back of the man's neck with both hands. The man's knees buckled, and he collapsed into Bruno's arms.

Baldassare motioned in the direction of the door. There was a small peephole. "Hold him up."

Both Baldassare and Renzo pulled black stocking masks out of their pockets and scooted them over their faces. Then they reached under their raincoats, Baldassare producing the Thompson and Renzo the grease gun he didn't exactly care for. Renzo knocked on the door as Bruno held the semiconscious man up to the peephole.

The small hole slid open. Then it closed followed by grunts and the sound of chains being unfastened.

Bruno stepped over to the rail and tossed the man he was holding overboard before slipping on his mask and pulling out the shotgun strapped to his back.

When the door opened, Renzo gave it a kick, sending the man at the door sprawling onto the floor. The three of them stepped in, closing the door behind them. Baldassare leveled the machine gun at the tellers who were counting stacks of bills. "Don't bother counting it, boys, the money is all ours."

He motioned to Renzo and Bruno. "Get the money into the bag. I want everything over a ten-dollar bill. Trafficante can keep the rest."

The two men moved to the counting tables, large long tables that had no doubt once served as a place for cleaning and gutting fish. Bruno took the duffel bag from around his waist, and the two of them began throwing in stacks of bills. The stacks were high with purple wrappers holding the bills and denoting their denominations. They worked feverishly, their hands flying over the tables as they moved down the line of cash.

Baldassare kept the tommy gun trained on the clerks. He watched as one of the men eyed a red buzzer. "I wouldn't even think about it," he said. "You work for a crook, and its crooks who are taking his money. You touch that and you'll be longtime dead."

The man slid back from the buzzer. He began to breathe hard.

A few minutes later Bruno snapped the bulging bag shut and swung it over his shoulder. "That's it, boss. We got it. We got it all."

Baldassare motioned to Renzo. "Tie them up."

Renzo reached into his raincoat pocket and produced two large rolls of duct tape. He began to move among the clerks, strapping their feet together and then their hands. Finally, he tore off several strips of the sticky silver tape and glued their mouths shut.

Baldassare backed away. "OK, boys, we got a boat to catch."

The three of them slipped out the door and took their masks off. They slipped their weapons back into place under their raincoats, then made their way around to the front of the boat, passing a number of couples whose attention was diverted by their companion. Baldassare knew they made quite a sight, two out-of-place men in raincoats when the sky was clear, and one giant. Still, people were people. Everybody had a life to live, and that didn't include doing anything about a sight they didn't understand in the first place.

They ran down the gangway to the floating dock. The sea was calm and the sky was clear, but there was no Marco.

"Where is he?" Renzo asked.

"He'll be here," Baldassare said.

"I didn't see him on the other side. Wasn't he just supposed to go around in circles?"

Baldassare nodded. "Yeah, but what a man is supposed to do and what he does can be two different things."

They waited for what seemed like an hour but was probably no longer that fifteen minutes before they saw the lights of the boat. Marco had the thing going full blast, lifting it out of the water on a dead run for the side of the big steamer. As he approached the floating casino, he killed the engine and floated up to the side, banging the tires once again.

He had a big grin on his face. "Hey, you finished fast."

Bruno loaded the bag into the boat and Renzo jumped in. "We've been done for a while and standing here like sitting ducks waiting on you."

Baldassare stepped into the boat. His eyes were hard as he looked at Marco. "Where have you been?"

Marco held up both hands. "I had to take her out and let her rip didn't I? Couldn't very well do that while turning tight little circles around this steamer." He looked up at the steamer. The music was blaring as loud as ever. "Besides, you three had all the fun. I couldn't just stand aside like some kind of cab driver."

Baldassare looked back up the ramp, in the direction of the music. "No, I suppose you couldn't. How would you like to have some real fun?"

"Sure." Marco's eyes brightened.

Baldassare handed him the Thompson, then took out his mask. "Put this on. I want you to go back up there and break up that party.

I want a real fireworks display with this tommy gun. Do you think you can do that?"

"That would be great."

"No people though. I don't want anyone to die unless it's you. I just want you to shoot up the lights and spray the windows with bullets. And I want you screaming at the top of your lungs too. Tell all those people in there that this is a mob boat and that the same thing will happen to them, only worse, the next time they come back." Baldassare leaned closer to him and looked him dead on. "I want your words quoted in all the newspapers. Don't mumble. Get it right."

Marco nodded. "You bet, boss. I'll do it."

He jumped out of the boat and ran quickly up the ramp.

"You think that was a good idea?" Renzo asked. "There might be security guards in the casino with guns."

"Would you stick your head up if someone was waving a Thompson submachine gun around?"

"No, I wouldn't. But then I'm no hero."

Suddenly, they heard a fury of gunfire, the sound of the Thompson in low static thuds, followed by screams. The music stopped, replaced by the sound of Marco's shouts. Then the Thompson started up once again, along with the rattle of broken glass.

It was only moments later when they heard the sound of Marco's footsteps flying down the ramp. Screams were coming from the Casino, loud wails and sharp cries of fright.

Marco jumped into the boat and dropped the Thompson to the deck. He threw the throttle into full position, and the boat launched itself out of the water and into the open space. It landed with a thud, sending Baldassare and the other two sprawling over the slick seat cushions and onto the deck.

"What are you doing?" Bruno bellowed.

Marco looked back. "I had to kill a guard. He pulled his gun." He grinned. "I can tell you one thing, though, ain't none of those people ever coming back to that place, neither them nor any of their friends."

WASHINGTON, D.C.

TUESDAY, OCTOBER 2

CHAPTER 21

Ray Jeffers had put in more than a full day at the Capitol, but it didn't seem to be enough. He stood on the steps in the light rain, waiting for the spooks who were going to take him to God only knew where. He had his black overnight bag with a change of clothes. Those were the only instructions he'd gotten. The rain pelted his dark gray fedora. The drops were big and heavy, and he was thankful it wasn't coming down harder.

Ray knew his trench coat wouldn't last too much longer, but not because of wear. He'd grown by two suit sizes since he had taken the job of congressional security chief.

He watched as the dark blue station wagon rounded the corner and pulled up next to the curb. Two dark figures were inside. One of them rolled down a window. "Ray? Ray Jeffers?"

"That's me." He stepped off the curb and climbed in.

The car rolled away, and Ray unbuttoned his coat and slipped it off. He shook it slightly and laid it across the seat next to him. "Where are we going?"

A young man in the passenger seat looked back at him. The man had a mustache, no doubt to make him appear older. He stuck out his hand. "I'm Agent Leads, and this is Agent Bodine. I'm afraid we have a long drive ahead of us. We're going to West Virginia."

Ray smiled and shook the man's hand. "Leads and Bodine. Those your real names?"

Leads chucked. "Sure. Our parents would be very surprised if they weren't." He looked at Ray's bag. "You bring clothes and shave gear?"

Ray nodded. "Yes, but my wife wants me home tomorrow night."

"We'll have to see if we can do that." He laughed. "We have you in a four-star hotel tonight, a resort."

Bodine turned the corner and joined in Leads' laughter. "Yeah, a resort. Some people would call it the last resort."

"You mind explaining that to me?"

"In time," Leads responded. "In due time you'll know everything. You have to know. We'll be working through you with the members of Congress."

Ray sat back in his seat, trying to get comfortable. "Normally the only way the CIA works with Congress is to tell them as little as possible. Direct questions bring only stutters followed by a clearing of the throat."

"We deal with a need to know, and right now you have a need to know," Leads said.

"Then I consider myself privileged."

The drive was long for Ray, punctuated only by a pit stop for coffee and two jelly doughnuts. They drove through the deep woods of West Virginia for hours before they pulled into a driveway that led to the hotel. The hotel was massive, a white structure that seemed to cover acres of ground. Large columns rose from the front, giving it a Roman-forumlike appearance.

Ray scooted forward in his seat, his eyes widening at the look of the place. "You were right about the four-star hotel. What's it called?"

"This is Greenbriar," Leads said. "You'll find your room comfortable and roomy, but you can't call home and talk to mama about it."

"And why not, pray tell?"

Leads looked back at him, staring him straight in the eye. "This whole trip is top secret, like it never happened. You can't tell anyone where you've been or what you've seen. Tomorrow when we drop you off at home, it will be like a fairy godmother whisked you away for the night. We've brought you here so you can have this place in your mind in case you have to brief the members of Congress, and that won't happen unless and until we tell you. You're here because Congress trusts you. They will listen to you when they have to."

"And they won't listen to you?"

Leads smiled. "You said it yourself. They get coughs and the clearing of the throat whenever they ask Alan Dulles and John McCone questions. I guess we're not sure if they'll believe us when they have to."

Alan Dulles was the retiring director of the Central Intelligence Agency, and McCone was his successor. Ray knew Leads was probably right. Every time either one of those men said good morning to a congressional member, they felt like they had to stick their heads out the window to confirm it. To make matters worse, the botched job the CIA had done with the Bay of Pigs landing caused them to doubt the agency's competence along with its truthfulness.

The next morning started early, five-thirty. Ray sat by a window in the dining room stirring the remains of his mushroom omelet by six-fifteen. The early light had bathed the expansive lawns with a deep green luster. The lawns stretched out almost as far as a man could walk. He was on his fifth cup of coffee by the time his spook baby-sitters walked into the dining room.

He motioned to the empty seats in front of him. "I wasn't sure when you'd be down, but you can order if you like. I'm all packed up."

Leads waved his hand. "That's OK. We had cereal in our room. We better get going. We have a full day ahead of us."

Ray scooted his chair forward and picked up his cup of coffee. "Do you mind telling me just what it is we're going to see?"

Bodine slouched forward. "We are going to show you the last resort of Congress. Underneath this hotel is a series of bunkers. Congress will be brought here in case there is a danger of nuclear attack. The members may not have much warning, and they certainly won't have a lot of time to make up their minds."

The coffee cup shook in Ray's hand. He set it down slowly, shaking his head. "Now I know why they call you people spooks. You scare people to death. Make up their minds about what? What's to decide?"

Bodine glanced around the room, then looked Ray in the eye. "The space we have available is just for the members of Congress. No one else will be allowed inside, except for security and maintenance."

"No one else? Did I hear you right?"

"That's right, Mr. Jeffers. This facility is just for the members of Congress, not their staff." He dropped his voice lower. "And not their wives and children."

"You mean you expect a man to abandon his wife and kids to a nuclear blast while he scurries away to some hole like a rat leaving a sinking ship?"

"These people have larger responsibilities."

"Larger than a man's own family?"

Bodine nodded. "Yes sir. It's called the Constitution. They knew that when they took the job."

"And you expect me to talk them into that?"

Leads sat forward. "We'd like you to try. They need to be briefed by someone they trust."

"All right," Ray said. "Give it to me straight. Is there any reason why we're going through this doomsday scenario now? Am I just some item on your to-do list that you're finally getting around to, or is there some special danger these people are facing right now?"

"Cuba," Bodine blurted out.

"Cuba? Get serious."

"Our intelligence reports indicate the Soviets may be constructing medium-range missile sights on the island. If that is true, there's a chance that we'll invade."

"A good chance," Bodine added.

"Then the problem is solved," Ray shot back.

"Maybe," Bodine said. "Maybe not. There are forty thousand Russian troops on that island, and they have tactical nuclear weapons. If they attack our landing forces and use those things, then all hell will break lose. We'll have a disaster with our landing troops, and the president may launch a nuclear strike against the Soviet Union."

Ray sat back in his seat and took a deep breath. "And that's when I can expect a call from you or someone in your office?"

Bodine nodded. "Yes, that's when."

It was only a short drive to the green steel gates behind the hotel. A guard ran out from the small shack nearby and threw a switch, which sent an electric motor into operation. The gates separated, and Bodine drove the car through the gates and down a hillside to a concrete bunker. They got out of the car and walked down the slope.

Bodine stepped inside and threw a switch, illuminating a series of banked lights. They stepped inside and walked down a long corridor with shower nozzles on top and in the sides of the wall. Bodine pointed them out. "These are for the people who don't quite make it in time. It's for decontamination."

"Whew." Ray let out a sigh. "For a minute I thought they were showers from the German concentration camps. You know, the gas showers."

"No." Bodine shook his head. "But we do have a crematorium in here, just in case."

"Yeah, just in case." Ray forced a chuckle. "A comforting thought."

They passed a series of cases where shotguns and automatic weapons were arranged in neat rows. Ray pointed to them. "These are for the locals who also want to survive, I take it?"

Bodine nodded his head. "You could say that. We want to have plenty of firepower. You can assure the members that they won't need to worry about their security."

Rounding a corner they stepped into an auditorium. An American flag was hanging on a red backdrop, and three wooden podiums were on a small stage. A bank of cameras pointed to a large, photographic mural of the Capitol with a blue sky in the background.

"This is the Capitol room," Leads said. "It will be where the House of Representatives convenes."

"What are the cameras for?"

"For members of Congress to make broadcasts back to their home district. They may need to reassure people."

"Oh, yeah. I'd sure be reassured if my congressman was safely tucked away in some bomb shelter telling me everything was OK. Make me sleep tight, for sure."

"The room for the Senate is next door. It's a little smaller, but we try to keep things functional."

Ray followed the two men while Leads continued to give a running account of the construction. "There is enough air for seventy-two hours in here, and after that it will have to be decontaminated." He looked back at Ray. "But you'll be happy to know that the shelter is built over a series of wells. The members will have pure water every day and plenty of power too. So they shouldn't suffer too badly."

"Unless they think about their families," Ray added.

Leads went on, not missing a beat. "The dining facilities can handle three thousand meals a day with enough food to last for three months. This ought to interest you." He opened a door and stepped into a room, turning on a light. The bank of caged lights overhead showed off an array of orange metal bunk beds, all lined up neatly in a row. The beds were made with gray blankets and thin white pillows and had very little space between them.

"Who's this for?" Ray asked.

"The members of Congress," Bodine said. "It ain't exactly like the hotel upstairs, but it will be a lot safer."

"And you expect them to live down here for who knows how long?"

Bodine nodded. "Yes, if they want to stay alive."

"We have motion pictures, books, magazines, and lots of board games for them to pass the time."

Ray began to laugh.

"What's wrong?" Leads asked.

Ray shook his head. "I was just trying to imagine Strom Thurmond sleeping on a top bunk and playing checkers all day."

Bodine walked off and turned a switch and illuminated another room. Ray got the idea the man was all business. Or maybe it was just the nature of this particular business. "We have lounge facilities, showers, small closets, and lots of communication equipment." Bodine pointed to the ceiling. "Several times a day we can extend an antenna into the air and pick up as well as send radio signals to the president, who will be in a separate secure location."

"That ought to comfort them."

Bodine frowned. "I get the idea that we're not exactly selling you on this place."

Ray shook his head. "I'm trying to imagine the members of Congress actually living here, and somehow it ain't coming to me."

Leads stepped closer to him. "Well, Mr. Jeffers, you'd better let it come to you. What you say when it's time may mean the difference between people living and dying, not to mention a Congress continuing to function."

"Will there be any point to having a government if the country is baking under a nuclear cloud? I don't mean to be difficult. I'll do my best. That's all I can promise."

"If this should happen," Bodine spoke up, "we will need to make careful arrangements. There can be no flights from the airport. We don't want to see a mass migration; the Russians have spies everywhere. If they were to see large groups leaving together, there is no doubt they would order a nuclear attack."

"Then how do you propose to evacuate them?"

"They will have to leave by car, a few at a time. That is why we brought you here by car, so you could see what it's like. Nothing must seem unusual, just members of Congress leaving in small groups. They must not pack bags. We have clothes here for them and lots of toiletry items."

"So they're going to be wearing orange prison garb in here?"

"Flight suits," Leads spoke up.

It took several hours more to show Ray the complete layout and to explain communication, taking him to the command and control center. They also showed him the kitchen and pantry area, including a list of menus. The three of them were standing by the outer door when Bodine turned to ask, "Do you have any questions?"

"Just one."

"What's that?"

Ray looked Bodine in the eye. "Am I on your list? Do you have a jumpsuit for me?"

Bodine shook his head. "I'm afraid not. We have security here." He glanced at Leads. "We're not on the list either."

CHAPTER 22

Central Park was designed to be an oasis away from the hustle of Manhattan. Of course, on many weekends the skaters and joggers could knock a man down who was simply walking there and enjoying the view. The park's reputation as a place to be avoided at night went as far back as the Great Depression, when out-of-work men would camp out in the confines of its brambles. Johnny was well aware that it wasn't a place to take a woman at eleven P.M., but that was exactly what he was doing. Gina had insisted on coming with him to meet the man they had met in the Cuban hallway that morning, and Rocko had thought it was a good idea.

Gleaming lamps highlighted the dark shadows of the park. The lamps twinkled in the darkness, doing little to illuminate the shadows. Walking along the pathway, Johnny and Gina could see a carriage being drawn by two horses.

Gina clutched at his arm. "That's very romantic, don't you think?"

Johnny scratched his brow. *This is the last place I ever wanted to be with Gina*, he thought, *someplace romantic*. "Yes, it is."

"You don't mind that we skipped the mob scene tonight, do you?"

"It would have been safer to have the four of us."

She laughed, clutching his arm tighter. "You're a big strong man. I'm not worried. I didn't want to overwhelm our informant with four of us trying to convince him to open up."

"You could be right."

"Of course I'm right. Does that bother you?"

"'Course not. Why should it bother me?"

"Sometimes I get the impression that women in your world are made to be seen, not heard. They adorn what you do, never do things themselves. The more passive they are, the more applause they get. Of course, applause is the wrong word. It would be more like tacit silent approval."

"Ever notice how easy it is to look on somebody else and their life and pass judgment? You see me and my world as somewhat foreign to you. You think you know me just because you've heard some radio preacher blaring into a microphone. If that were true, then I'd know you because I read Perry Mason mysteries. I'd go off on how crooked lawyers are and how they are always chasing ambulances. Why don't we just call a truce to this and accept each other as we are, accept the fact that when God made us He broke the molds. I won't carry around any warped ideas of you and your world, and you can be free from any notions you may have about preachers. Fair enough?"

Gina nodded. "Fair enough."

As the carriage passed them, the driver tipped his stovepipe silk hat, then whisked his hand under his gray handlebar mustache. The couple in back were huddled under a blanket, totally oblivious to anyone else.

The carriage had no sooner passed them when they picked up the sounds of another horse up ahead and saw a lone rider in the faint darkness. "Mounted policeman," Gina said.

It took a couple of minutes before they were close to the policeman. The horse was jerking his head and stamping at the path with his hooves. The officer drew rein on the big, chestnut-colored horse and waited for them, holding the reins in his left hand. The man made a dashing figure with his badge shining on his blue cap. He had a dark complexion, dark eyes, and black hair that lapped around the back of his collar. The pistol butt on his left hip gave off a soft glow, and his high boots had a gleaming luster to them. "Evening, folks," he said, tipping the bill of his cap with his hand that held the reins. "You going for a walk?"

They stopped and Gina put her hand out to the horse, patting his muzzle. "Yes, officer," Johnny said. "It seemed like a good night for a walk."

The horse pulled away and swung around in a circle as the policeman kicked him in the sides and jerked on the reins to settle him down. He pulled hard on the reins with both hands, jerking them down and from side to side. Finally coming to a stop, the officer smiled. "You're from out of town, aren't you?"

Johnny nodded. "California." He smiled at the officer. "Are you using somebody else's horse tonight?"

The officer leaned down and patted the side of the horse's neck. "Nope, old Trigger here is my horse. He sat back up straight. "Well, you be careful on this walk of yours. Don't venture too far off the transverse or away from the lights. Central Park isn't the safest place to be after dark. You never know who you're going to find out here, and I wouldn't want anything to happen to tourists in our fair city."

Gina spoke up. "Officer, can you tell us where to find the Belvedere Castle?"

"It's straight on up ahead, past the Ramble, but I definitely wouldn't go there at night. Too many things can happen where no one can see. Why don't you come back tomorrow morning if you want to see that?"

"We may do that," Johnny said. "Maybe we'll just look from a distance tonight."

"Good idea." The policeman pulled up the reins on his horse and pointed down the path. "Just continue on and you'll come to it."

"Thank you, Officer," Johnny said.

They both walked away, Johnny holding Gina's hand.

"I think they try to scare tourists," Gina said.

"I doubt that." He turned and looked back at the officer who was walking his horse slowly in the opposite direction. "Odd though."

"What's odd?"

"That policeman. Some things don't add up."

"What things?"

Johnny continued to stare at the retreating backside of the horse. "That horse wasn't his horse. I know horses, and for one that animal's age, he acted kind of skittish, like he was in the wrong place or had the wrong rider on him. Horses are creatures of habit, and his habits were being disturbed."

"You were quite a rider when I knew you."

"Yes, and that man knows very little about controlling a horse. He certainly doesn't strike me as someone who does it for a living. He didn't even look the part of a policeman."

"Why would you say that?"

Johnny shook his head. The policeman had disappeared into the darkness, and Johnny turned while they continued to walk. "Part of it is silly, I suppose. The cops in this city are Irish mostly, especially mounted police. He looked Italian."

"That is silly. Remember what we said about judging people?"

"You're right, but a couple of other things bother me too. His hair was too long for a uniformed policeman. Most of those guys are conservative, especially horse-patrol police. Plus, he held the reins with his left hand."

"What's wrong with that?"

"He was left-handed, and his gun was on his left hip. No self-respecting policeman would be in a position where he couldn't readily draw his weapon. I know cops. I work with a security company. It's my business to know cops."

They hurried down the path, picking up their pace. Johnny's instincts told him something was wrong about that night, something he hadn't counted on.

They passed the Bethesda Fountain, which had become a hangout for hippies of all sorts. A number of the brightly dressed and hobo-like creatures were huddled in small groups to keep warm. Johnny could smell the sweet aroma of marijuana. They smiled, bobbing their heads. Some waved passively.

They crossed the Bow Bridge. The moon shone brightly on the water, and their feet sent out a soft patter over the wooden structure. The Ramble was on their left, a mixture of hedge work and brambles that formed a maze in the darkness. This was a place for drug deals in Central Park, especially in the darkness. It was easy to conceal one's self in the high brush and tangled growth.

Hurrying past it, they came to Belvedere Castle. The structure loomed in the darkness, its turrets looking out on the expansive lawn below it. It had been designed as a fantasy playground for children, someplace where knights could joust for the hand of the fair lady. Only now its tunnels, halls, and slides were often used as a retreat for drug dealers, thieves, and perverts. The officer was right. This was definitely not the place to be after dark.

In the darkness, beside the castle, Johnny spotted the orange glow of a cigarette. The man stepped out from beside the wall and crushed it out. "Is that you?" he asked. "I've been waiting."

"Yes," Johnny said. "It's us."

Looking around in all directions, they stepped over to where the man was standing. He was wearing a blue windbreaker over his green military garb. It seemed to Johnny that the Cubans were all obsessed with appearing military, or at least dressing like Castro dressed. But unlike Castro, this man's face was clean shaven. "This is good of you to see us," Gina said.

The man shook his head. "I couldn't let you think you had gotten the truth today. I did speak to Felix when I saw him this afternoon, and he agreed to meet you. But he just couldn't come tonight. He has more information, and I think you ought to hear it."

"When can we meet him?" Johnny asked.

"Tomorrow night, ten o'clock, in the cemetery of the old Trinity Church. You know the place?"

Johnny nodded. "Yes, I know it." He pointed down the hill toward the large lawn. "Why don't we walk down there." He looked back up at the dark castle. "This place has ears."

The man nodded, and the three of them walked down the hill in the direction of the castle.

"Why are you doing this?" Gina asked.

The man lowered his head and studied the shine on his boots. "I do not like the man in charge at the Jax. He is overbearing and arrogant. He looks down on us and treats us as people without a brain."

"We saw a little of that this morning," Johnny said.

"If I can get some information from you that might offer some protection for my president, then I could go to our ambassador. I would tell him my information has been rejected. And if what you tell me is accurate, then I could be the hero, as you Americans say."

Suddenly, a horse and rider bolted out from the trees across the lawn. The rider was some distance away, but they could see it was the dim figure of a policeman, his gun drawn. The horse was coming on at a full gallop.

The look of the determined rider brought the three of them to a frozen halt. They didn't have much time; the man would be on them in a matter of a minutes. "Run," Johnny yelled. He pointed down the hill. "We'll split up. You go down to the Ramble, and we'll run back to the castle."

Gina kicked off her shoes, and the two of them began to run for the dark castle. It was all uphill, but Johnny knew it was a place the man on his horse would find difficult to explore. They might even get lucky and actually find some drug dealers. Right now, anyone with a gun would offer welcome protection.

As they neared the top of the hill, they heard shots. Johnny looked back. The man on the horse had gunned down the Cuban they had been talking to. Now he jerked on the reins and began to gallop the horse in their direction.

Johnny pulled on Gina's hand, and the two of them ran for the darkness.

As they got closer to the castle, another shot rang out. The slug ricocheted off the stone wall in front of them. Johnny spotted an opening in the castle, a dark, waist-high tunnel. They ran for it, Johnny pushing Gina ahead of him.

Bending over, they scurried through the darkness into the belly of the stone castle. They came to a chute that ran up one of the turrets. A steel ladder was riveted to the wall. Johnny pushed Gina onto it. "Climb," he whispered loudly.

The two of them climbed the ladder, arriving at a landing where they could crawl over and see the lawn below. Johnny slithered over to one of the small openings and looked outside.

"You see anything?" Gina asked.

"No, but we can't stay here. He knows the opening we went through, and it's a straight shot to where we are now. We'd better keep moving."

They spent the next few minutes crawling over and around the tunnels and obstacles inside the castle. Most of the time they were in total darkness, feeling their way through cans and broken glass. Johnny took the lead, brushing aside some of the debris so Gina could slide forward on her knees. They soon hit a long tunnel made out of corrugated metal. Each movement they made echoed down the darkness. When they came to an opening, Johnny stuck his head up. There were stars overhead. He pushed his way up the opening and slid out on top. Bending over, he helped Gina.

"This would be a good place to stop," he said. "If he tries to come through that tunnel, we'll be able to hear him long before he gets here."

They sat next to the small opening. Gina looked at him. "Why would he want to kill the Cuban?"

Johnny looked at her. "He wanted to kill us. The Cuban was just a witness."

"Us?"

"Yes, it was a hit."

"That policeman we saw?"

Johnny nodded. "Yes, when he met us, there were witnesses close by, that carriage. And there was too much light."

"So he knew where we were going?"

"You told him, but he probably knew anyway."

Gina shook her head. "I don't understand how he could have known. I didn't even tell you until late this afternoon. Either the

Cuban said something to this Felix Gonzales fellow, or there's a leak someplace with the four of us."

"That's not possible."

"Well, one thing's for sure. We'll know tomorrow night when we show up and meet this Felix. If he fingered us, he'll be there with friends."

"Just tell me one thing."

"What's that?"

"Tell me you'll be armed tomorrow night. I don't care if you're a preacher or not, and I sure don't care about these New York City gun laws."

Johnny looked at her, searching her face. Panic was written all over it. He nodded. "I'll be armed." He looked at her. "But now we ought to get you taken care of. You've got blood on your legs."

She looked down at her dress. It was dirty, and her stockings were torn at the knee. She sighed.

HOMESTEAD AFB, FLORIDA
TUESDAY, OCTOBER 2

CHAPTER 23

I t was late afternoon when Scott Gordon's plane touched down on the runway of the naval base just outside of Homestead, Florida. The plane was a C-130 transport, hardly built for comfort. The ride had been ear-shattering with vibrations pouring through the body of the transport and the passengers. It had been the first military flight he could get from Washington. He dressed in his fatigues and carried a buttoned-down .45 automatic. This was a business trip, all business. The only thing he wanted was to do his job for the president and get home to Jackie and the kids.

When the hatch on the plane opened, Scott jumped to his feet. He picked up his travel bag and scurried down the aluminum stairway.

The tall man waiting for him at the bottom of the ladder extended his hand. "Welcome to Florida, Colonel. I'm Cliff Cox, CIA."

"I thought as much," Scott said. He didn't like government spooks, but he was going to have to fight to keep that feeling to himself. There was no need to antagonize anyone, especially when he might need them.

"I thought I could take you into Miami tonight, see the sights, and have a few beers. I could bring you up to speed."

Scott headed for the terminal, walking at a fast pace. "No, we'll go to see your Cubans tonight. I want to get a look at their setup."

"They'll be plenty of time for that." In spite of his height, Cox was having a difficult time keeping up with Scott's pace. "You've had a long flight. You'll be needing to find a spot to drop your things."

"I'll drop my things in your men's camp tonight."

"You're not staying at their camp, are you?"

"Of course."

"It's pretty Spartan there. Besides, there will be nothing to do tonight. They do most of their training in the day. There won't be anything to see."

Scott stopped and looked at him. "Aren't they planning on a night landing?"

"Yes, of course."

"Then why are they only training in daylight?"

"So they can see the targets better."

Scott forced a smile. "I see. Then when they land they'll have to wait till dawn until they can return fire? Is that what you're telling me?"

"No, of course not. It's just that we have the target range all laid out. Plus, the mosquitoes are horrible at night. You're going to be uncomfortable."

"Listen Cox, I'm a Marine. I've been uncomfortable for twenty-three years. It's what I get paid to do. Maybe I should explain something to you. I've been asked to judge these men's readiness for battle. That includes their morale. I can't think of a better place to judge an army's morale than by sitting around the campfire with them at night and eating their chow. Can you?"

"I guess not."

"Then why don't you show me to your car. You can brief me while we drive out there."

Cox took Scott to the parking lot and pointed out a baby blue, bug-eyed Sprite. It was cramped, but Scott dropped his bag in the back of the seat and climbed in, squeezing his feet forward into the small compartment. Cox had the top down, and he hopped in without opening his door. He started up the little car and roared off with the sound of the throaty little engine rattling in the parking lot.

"Homestead is quite the place itself," Cox said. "They have a park in the city that has over five hundred varieties of fruits, nuts, and vegetables."

"I like that," Scott responded. "Something practical."

"They can grow anything down here."

"Let's hope they can grow an army."

"Colonel, you have to understand. These men are still a little green by American standards. Many of them were pulled off the streets of Miami just a short time ago. Some speak no English."

"I don't care who they are or what they are, just so they follow orders and shoot straight."

The drive to the camp took them straight into the Everglades. Marshes of saw grass stood out in all directions, and turtles and alligators filled murky water.

The little car roared down the dirt road, scattering rocks and sending out a blanket of dust that rose into the air and then gently descended on the pond. It created a choking, insufferable, dusty mist that caused birds to take flight. The saw grass soon gave way to groups of standing Cypress tress.

"I hope you don't expect to find some well-oiled spit-and-polish machine, Colonel."

"I don't expect anything. My job is not to train troops; it's to report what I see and think to the president. I'm his eyes and ears out here. That's all. Don't look to me for anything. I'm not going to give you any advice. My job is to advise the president."

It took another forty minutes before Cox rounded a bend on the dirt road. The throaty roar of the Sprite caused several heads to pop up. The men were sentries, but by the time they checked out the noise, he and Cox had already gone by. They needed to place men out in the open, standing in the road behind a barricade, Scott thought. Then they could be certain that some tourist, or, worse, some news reporter wouldn't blunder into their camp.

When they turned the next corner, the camp came into view. Stretched out in front of them was a large parking lot, almost empty except for a couple of pickup trucks, several beat-up cars, and a jeep. A shack and a large pond, complete with dock and speedboat, were beyond the lot. There was also a wind boat that was used for the shallow water of the swamp.

Cox pulled into a space near the shack and climbed out. The screen door to the shack slapped open, and a man in a T-shirt, fatigue pants, and combat boots stepped out, a broad smile on his face. He quickly made his way over to where they were standing.

"Cox, good to see you," the man roared. "You almost missed me." He stepped over to them, his hand extended.

Cox shook the man's hand. "Well, I'm glad I didn't. I brought you a special guest. This is Colonel Scott Gordon."

The man put his hands on his hips and stared at Scott, his smile never wavering. "To what do we owe the honor of a visit from the American Army?"

"Marine Corps," Scott corrected.

The man's grin widened. "Of course. The Marines."

"Colonel Gordon, this is Bolivar Leon. He is second in command of the brigade."

Scott shook his hand. "I'm glad we didn't miss you."

The man leaned back and waved his hand up in the air. "Friday night, you know. I was going into Miami for a few laughs. You know, see the women."

Scott looked over the camp. "I was told you had three thousand men. I only see a few hundred at most."

Bolivar grinned. "Like I said, Friday night. Many of my men have their own cars. Some of them never stay here at night. They drive back home when we're done in the afternoon. Too many mosquitoes here, and they like mother's cooking better."

"A commuter army," Scott said.

"You might say that. But this is their home. We took them off the streets and can't expect them to lock them away with family so close by."

"And where is your commander?" Scott asked.

"Javier? He's still in Cuba. Castro's agents are everywhere. Javier has to find people we can trust. Our lives depend on that."

Scott walked to the edge of the parking lot and looked out over the camp. "No doubt you have some of Castro's agents among you." He turned and looked back at Cox and Bolivar. "Of course, they're probably back in Miami now filing their reports. I mean, it is Friday night."

A short time later, Scott and Cox strolled through what was left of the exile army still in camp. "I suppose I should have gone with you to Miami tonight," Scott said. "I would have seen more of the brigade there."

"I'm sorry about that. I didn't want to waste your time."

"You haven't, not by a long shot. I'm going to learn a lot just this weekend. If you're going to find out about an army's morale, you need to find out what their dreams are. What we have left here are men who couldn't find rides back into town, men with no families. They will be a little down and somewhat disgruntled. They'll tell me everything I want to know about what they think of their commanders and this operation in general. I couldn't have asked for a better slice of their time."

"I hope you don't judge the whole operation by this?"

"Listen, Congress is shelling out a lot of money for this operation, and the president is actually counting on these people to fight. The security here is abysmal. Anybody could come waltzing into this camp and never be seen. Of course, why would they need to? They can learn anything they need to know on the streets of Miami and much more from talking to some woman whose son brags to her. Frankly, I think I could take a troop of Boy Scouts and whip these people to a stand-still."

They both looked up to see Leon running toward them. He handed a piece of paper to Cox.

"Colonel, this is from Javier Lage, the commander of this army. He's coming back from Cuba, but he has a job there that may prove of interest to you." He smiled. "That is, if you're really interested in discovering what we're up against."

"Of course I am."

"Then you may have to find a secure line and call the president. This will require presidential approval." He chuckled slightly. "You might want to call your wife too, and get her OK. She may not want you in Cuba."

CHAPTER 24

The old Trinity Church on Broadway and Wall Street was built in the 1840s. The brownstone church with its buttresses and spires had at one time been the tallest structure in New York City, and its location made it the ideal place to be married or buried. The bells from the 280-foot tower still sounded out over the financial district, and Johnny lifted his eyes as the clock gave off a melodious chime before beginning the deep bongs that totaled the number eleven.

Rocko and Junior had stationed themselves at opposite ends of the block, Junior reading a newspaper, which was hard to do by lamplight, and Rocko was sipping a cup of scalding coffee. Johnny made sure the two of them were in place before he and Gina started up the walkway. The snub-nosed .38 he was carrying in a holster on his belt gave him a degree of security; at the same time it sent a sense of dread through his body. He had no intention of ever joining his family as some sort of enforcer, and yet here he was, packing a gun and looking for information that could well lead to revenge. He kept telling himself that he was searching for information that could bring about justice, but he knew he also had to keep other members of the family, especially Baldassare, in line.

The walkway to the church was gray cobblestone. The cemetery, dotted with moss-covered monuments and stone crosses, was just beyond the walkway. Lamps cast a soft yellow glow on the walk, bathing it in a warm light. The towers of the church stood silent when the last of the eleven bongs ended.

"Papa would have loved this place. Since it's an Anglican church, it's not too Protestant." He smiled.

Johnny stopped to look at one of the markers. Two angels somberly pondered a marble slab. "Look at this one. 'We cannot save our skins without saving our souls.' How true."

"Do you really think so?"

Johnny nodded. "Yes, I do. People go to great lengths to save their own skins and totally overlook the deeper issues of life. A life without meaning isn't life. It's just breathing."

"Maybe that's what you're doing on this trip, saving your soul. I think a man's soul is in jeopardy if he can't forgive or find forgiveness. I think you find it very hard to forgive yourself. No matter how much you see this long separation from your family as a result of your calling and you becoming a Protestant, I think you believe you could have done more to patch things up with them. You miss your dad, and you miss those twenty years you could have had with him."

Johnny knew that what she was saying was true. He had been out of the family, an outsider. And he blamed himself. No matter what his parents' problems had been with his conversion, he should have tried harder at reconciliation. Instead, he had been content to remain beyond their reach.

Suddenly, a crow took flight from the burial ground, flapping its wings as it flew low and then swooped skyward. *Perfect*, Johnny thought, *I'm here tonight with Edgar Allan Poe.*

"Spooky, isn't it?" Gina chuckled.

Johnny nodded. "Of all the places to meet in New York City, why would the man pick here?"

"Maybe he was trying to make sure he could recognize us. He's never seen us, and who else would be crazy enough to come here at this hour?"

"Yeah, let's hope you're right. Let's hope he's not trying to send us some sort of hint about what's to come. In a way, I like these old graveyards right in the middle of town. Back then people saw death as a part of life. They surrounded the dead with the living."

"I hear these Cubans are into voodoo and witchcraft. Maybe this Felix is a follower. Maybe he thinks that what he's got to say concerns death and ought to be encircled by it."

Johnny smiled. "Now there's a comforting thought."

"Well, we know this isn't exactly going to be on the up and up, don't we? You said so yourself. No one else could have gotten information out about where we were going to be last night. If it wasn't one of us, it had to be the Cubans, some man our informer told. And if that's the case, then maybe he could have been the target after all. Maybe we were the witnesses."

"My gut instinct tells me no, and for tonight's sake, I hope my gut instinct is right."

"Why would you say that?"

"Because if I'm wrong, and information from the Cubans is what gave us away last night, we're walking into a trap. If the Cubans wanted to kill their own man, then we're still the witnesses who need to be disposed of. If tonight's meeting is on the level, maybe just this Gonzales fella knows about it. Of course, learning about his buddy's death isn't exactly going to make him want to talk his head off to us. Would you?"

Gina shook her head. "I wouldn't be found within ten miles of this place."

"We'll soon find out."

They turned the corner on the walkway at a junction beside the cemetery. This would allow them to walk the entire oval around the graveyard while looking for a man they hoped wouldn't show up. Then they would know that the near miss wasn't because of something they had unsuspectingly said to somebody. In a way it would be a relief, but they would have to start from scratch.

Suddenly a tall, shadowy figure in a trench coat materialized by a bench next to the graveyard. Gina grabbed for Johnny's arm, digging her nails into his wrist. Johnny patted her hand.

They walked closer to the man, who remained standing. Johnny was more than a little nervous about the voluminous trench coat the man wore. He could be concealing any form of weapon under it. Johnny reached down to his belt and put his hand snugly around the butt of his .38. If there were any sudden moves, any moves at all, Johnny was going to push Gina to the ground and draw his weapon. He wouldn't wait to fire.

The shadow stepped closer to them, then looked around nervously. He held out his hand. "I am Felix Gonzales. Are you the people I am supposed to meet?"

Just the sight of the man's right hand gave Johnny a sudden shot of comfort. "Yes, but could we see both of your hands?" Johnny wasn't about to let go of his .38 while the man had even one of his hands concealed under his coat.

Gonzales smiled and produced his left hand. "Of course. I don't blame you for being cautious."

Johnny reached out and shook his hand. "Not after what happened to us last night." He glanced at Gina. "This is Gina Cumo."

Gonzales dropped Johnny's hand and then, bowing slightly, he picked up Gina's hand and kissed it. "Charmed, señora. I only wish we could meet under better conditions."

"She is the one your friend talked to when we set up our meeting with him."

Gonzales' eyes danced. "I can see why he was so agreeable to meet with you."

Gina bit her lip slightly. Johnny knew she wasn't comfortable with or influenced by flattery. "We're sorry about your friend. I can't help but think it was because he took such a chance in meeting with us."

Gonzales shook his head. "Everyone is talking about it now. Most think it was some robber in the park."

"Did he still have his wallet?" Johnny asked.

Gonzales shrugged. "You know people. No matter what you tell them, they still blame America and New York City. It is the reputation of your city. Reason doesn't count for very much."

"Then why would you come to see us, knowing what happened last night?"

Gonzales smiled. "They were trying to kill you, weren't they? I figure they'll need another night to make more plans. By then I'll be gone. Besides, with what I have to tell you, you will become an ever richer target, and my usefulness as someone who knows their secret will have passed."

"So you'll be in the clear?"

Gonzales nodded. "Exactly. And if you tell me what I hope you can, then I may even get promoted. The people of my country will be grateful."

The man clutched at Johnny's sleeve and, with Gina following, pulled him over to the bench where he had been seated. "Let me tell you, señor, the repeated attempts by your government to assassinate our president will only produce a similar response from us. Your own president will fall, and you will have only yourselves to blame."

Gina stepped forward. "Are you saying there is a threat to the life of President Kennedy?"

Gonzales smirked. "We are better prepared than you could ever know, better prepared for whatever you may try to do to us. I think your country sees us as some sort of what you might call a jerkwater Banana Republic, the kind you have been dictating to for years. I can tell you, that has all changed under Fidel. We have allies now, allies with powerful missiles. We have a good army and an excellent security force. We have men walking the streets of Miami Beach who hear everything. We have men who have infiltrated this so-called exile army of yours. We have those who know how to kill your president and can do it without our names ever being mentioned. We will know, of course, but the world will not. Cuba is no longer a satellite puppet of the United States. We are our own country, not some place for your Mafia to set up its gambling profits on the backs of my people."

Gonzales was obviously an ideologue. His convictions had been hammered out in the revolution, and he was not about to change. Johnny figured he could no doubt be persuaded to accept a bribe or to offer some sort of assistance, but only if the net result would be favorable to Castro and his regime. Johnny was almost reluctant to help. If finding out the truth out about his father's murder could only result in prolonging Castro's military dictatorship, then maybe the present lie would be better.

"Your country and its troubles with ours are of little concern to us at the moment," Gina spoke up. Johnny was glad she did. He bit his tongue at the words his time in the Marine Corps might have produced. "Ours is a private matter," Gina went on. "We have a murder to investigate, and we think you might know something about it."

"You are referring to this Mafia leader's murder in California?"

"My father," Johnny added.

That response brought a bone-chilling look from the man. "Your father?"

"Yes, but I am not in the family business. We are just trying to find out who might be responsible. Enzo Gatto gave us your name. I understand he knows you."

Gonzales laughed. "Yes, he wants to be a business partner. Wants Cuba involved in his drug trade." He reached up and scratched his eyebrow, then lowered his voice. "We have discussed nothing about your 'group's' involvement with politics. Do you think my country might have sent a squad of assassins to kill your father? Why would we do such a thing? If the information I have is correct, your father was refusing to go along with plans to infiltrate Cuba and kill my president. He would be a hero to us, not someone we would want to see dead. It was not us, señor. If anyone, it was the exiles, the traitors. You need to take up your case with Javier Lage down in the swamps near Miami."

He waved his hands. "This Trafficante fellow is in bed with him about his plans, and your CIA too. These are the people you should be talking to. They are the ones responsible for your father's death."

"I wouldn't exactly expect you to tell us that you are responsible," Johnny said.

Gonzales puffed out his chest. He lifted his chin and glared at Johnny. "I can tell you, if I was responsible I would say so. I am not afraid of you and your Mafia soldiers. We simply have no reason to do what you might suggest."

He straightened his coat, as if he had been offended. "But I must ask you in return. Do you have information about the Mafia's plans to kill my president?"

"I know they sent a three-man team into Cuba with poison for him."

Gonzales laughed. "Yes, we know that. We found them. They are all dead. We can only hope the rest are as stupid as they were."

Johnny held up the palms of his hands. "Then neither of us is going to be of great value to the other."

Gonzales held up a finger. "One moment, señor. I have a name I can almost guarantee knows the identity of your father's murderers. The man's name is Cliff Cox. He works for your CIA. He is in charge of this whole CIA-Mafia connection. He will know everything. He may even have shot your father personally."

"OK," Gina spoke up, "Fair enough. If we run across anything that may involve a plot to murder your president, anything more than what we have already told you, we will contact you personally."

Gina's words brought a smile to the man's lips. "Fine. I will accept the word of the beautiful lady." He opened his coat and reached into his suit coat pocket, producing a business card and handing it to Gina. "This is the card of a small bookstore on the Lower East Side. If you call and leave a message there for me, then I will return your phone call from a safe phone."

Gina nodded and opened her pocketbook, dropping the card into it.

"Is our business concluded?" Gonzales asked.

Johnny nodded. "Yes, thank you."

Gonzales glanced at his watch. "Good, then I go." He started to leave, then turned back and looked at Gina. "I will be expecting a call from you, pretty lady." With that, he turned and walked away.

Gina turned to Johnny. "What did you make of that?"

"He told us nothing new."

"What about this man's name, this Cliff Cox?"

"No doubt the Cubans blame everything on the CIA, including the murder of Cock Robin. But I can tell you one thing. He told us everything Enzo Gatto wanted us to hear."

"Why would you say that?"

"He let it slip. In my years of working with people, when they touch their face while talking, it shows a reluctance to say what they are thinking. Also, he knew too much about Mafia business, things that only Gatto could have told him. You should know that by now, everything this family does is kept under close wraps. Nobody says anything to anybody unless it's a lie they can profit from. We weren't listening to Felix Gonzales tonight. We were listening to Enzo Gatto."

"You could be right."

"Of course I'm right. Gatto's trying to protect somebody, somebody we can get to by giving up a name of somebody we can't get to. It's also why Gonzales was here tonight. Think about it. He knew we had very little to give him that he didn't already know, yet he spilled the beans. Why? Because he had information to pass on that Gatto wanted us to know. This man is in Gatto's back pocket."

"You think he wants Cuba in the drug trade?"

Johnny grinned. "Why not? Drugs are like a time bomb ticking away at our whole society. It's one more weapon to these people, a weapon they can use against us and make a lot of money doing it. And why in heaven's name did you promise to call that man if we found out anything about a plot to kill Castro? The man's a snake. Why would you tell a snake that a semi is coming down the highway?"

"I wanted to keep communications open with him, in case he came across anything."

"Anything he comes across will just be another lie from Gatto."

A gunshot suddenly echoed in the street, followed by two more.

Johnny and Gina ran through the cemetery and down the walkway away from the church.

When they got to the street, they saw Rocko in a full run. He grabbed them and hurried them along. "Let's go," he yelled. "We gotta get outta here before the cops get here."

They ran behind the big man until they came to where Junior was standing. "What happened?" Junior asked.

He fell in running behind the three of them. "I saw a couple of guys back there," Rocko panted. He was waving the .38 in midair. "One of them pulled a gun and took a shot at me. I returned fire." He shook the gun. "One thing I know, and you better learn it too. Never bring a knife to a gunfight."

Johnny reached out and grabbed Rocko's gun. "Give me this thing. I don't want you shooting anybody."

In the distance they heard a wailing siren.

CHAPTER 25

Baldassare read through the newspaper accounts of the big robbery and watched the television reports the next day. The death of the guard bothered him. It made the police that much more voracious in their investigation. They were determined to catch the seagoing bandits, the "pirates," as they described them. That this was a Mafia war was not lost on the media either. Marco had seen to that. Two things were absolutely certain: Trafficante's gambling business had suffered a serious setback, and they had the old man's undivided attention.

Marco came through the swinging doors of the kitchen, eating a ham sandwich. "You know what our final count is from last night?"

Baldassare turned from the large picture window—he'd been expecting police cruisers to pull up any minute. "No, what?" he growled.

"Nine hundred and seventy-two thousand dollars. That's quite a haul. It ought to pay for this trip and then some." He mashed his teeth into the sandwich. "And it's going to cost Trafficante a whole lot more than that. That was just the better part of one night's haul. It'll take them most of a week to put that boat back into shape, and weeks after that before they can scare up some new customers, if they ever do."

He chuckled and fell into one of the overstuffed chairs, putting his feet up on an ottoman. "Scare, that's the right word for it." He waved what was left of his sandwich in Baldassare's direction. "People are going to be plenty scared to go back into one of his clubs. The way I got it figured, we cost that old man ten to fifteen million. That ought to get his attention. He'll know better than to fool around with the Pera family again."

Baldassare shook his head. "I just wish you hadn't shot that guard."

"He went for his gun. What was I supposed to do?"

"It's going to make this thing hot for us. Most of the time the cops only pretend to look for Mafia robberies. Deep inside, they're happy to have us going at each other's throats." He shook his head. "Now with this killing, things will change. They will be looking at the airport to find out who has come in over the past few days. Then they will go over the records of rental car companies, hotels, motels, and rental houses. At the most we'll have three or four days to do what we need to do and get out of here."

"We can do that. No problem."

"Yeah, sure, but we'll have to keep looking over our shoulders. And we can't fly out of Miami. I figure we're gonna have to drive to Atlanta in order to go home."

Baldassare looked out the window and saw Renzo and Bruno pull up in the Caddy. When they came through the door, Renzo had a smile on his face. "We got it done boss. Just like you asked."

"Where'd you dump the guns?"

"About three or four miles out of the harbor. We watched for a while to make sure no one was around."

Bruno nodded. "Yeah, boss, we watched real good. There weren't nobody no place close by."

"Did you dump the masks?"

Renzo nodded. "And the raincoats too. Everything got wiped down and then went over the side."

"OK, fine." Baldassare stepped over to a white-and-gold antique-looking phone. Picking up the receiver, he pulled a slip of paper out of his pocket and dialed a number.

"Hello. I'm calling for Santos Trafficante. Tell him Baldassare Pera is calling." A man's voice came on the phone. "Santos, this is Baldassare Pera. How are you?"

He paused, listening. "I'm fine here. Just got into Miami with a few friends. I was hoping to get together with you. You know, tie up a few of Papa's loose ends. When can we meet?"

Renzo stepped into the room and joined the audience of listeners. He smiled, then rubbed his hands together vigorously.

"No, I want to meet at your club. You know the place. All right," Baldassare said. "We'll meet you tonight."

He set down the receiver and walked over to the large window overlooking the pool and the beach beyond. He stood there for a few minutes, rocking on the balls of his feet, his hands clasped behind him.

"What did he say?" Marco asked. He walked across the room and stood close to him.

"You know, looking out at the beach and seeing the children playing makes me think, remember. I can remember Papa flying a kite with me. He knew just what to do, explained to me what made the darn thing fly. Back then I thought the old man knew everything. He always knew everything."

He turned to Marco. "But it was his power that I admired the most. He could tell somebody something and it stayed told. There were no questions, no arguments." He held out his index finger in Marco's direction and wiggled it. "Everything he touched did what he wanted it to do. He had power. I wanted to be just like him, have power, make people respect me."

He nodded in the direction of the phone. "That old man on the other end of that phone only thinks of me as the Crow's kid, but he will learn to respect me too. He will fear me and what I can do to him." He balled his fist. "He will respect me and fear me, or I will crush him like an insect."

"What did he say?" Marco asked again.

"We're going to meet him at his Top Hat Club tonight. Then we'll talk. Of course, we'll do the talking and he'll do the listening. Tonight he's going to believe that I have all the cards."

It was close to seven P.M. when they rolled out of the guarded gates. The Top Hat Club was in the Coconut Grove area of Miami Beach, directly across from City Hall. That brought some snickers. Trafficante's men only had to cross the street to spread the money around.

"You sure this place is safe?" Renzo asked.

Baldassare nodded. "Safe as the Rock of Gibraltar. The old man didn't want it here, but I insisted. Papa told me about this spot." He glanced across the street at the City Hall. "Who's going to engineer a hit across from the police station?"

They walked through the glass doors and stepped onto the plush wine-colored carpet. A man in a gold pillbox hat and a red cutaway jacket greeted them. The man snapped his heels and plastered on a broad smile. "Can I get you gentleman a table?"

"We're here to meet with Mr. Trafficante," Baldassare said.

"Is he expecting you?"

"You bet he is," Marco shot back.

"This way please." They followed him down the hall and into the main dining room.

Turning the corner after passing through the dining room, the man in the pillbox led them to a sitting room. He motioned to the large couch on the far wall. "If you gentlemen will wait here, I'll see if Mr. Trafficante can see you now. Whom shall I say is calling?"

"Tell him Baldassare Pera is here to see him."

The man opened a door and closed it behind him.

Marco stepped over to the wall and eyed a collection of seascape paintings. He shook his head. "Ever notice how it is that the ugliest people surround themselves with the prettiest things?"

Baldassare crossed his arms. "Papa used to say that a man only opens his heart to two things, beauty and pain."

"Well, maybe that pain we dished out the other night will open up Trafficante's heart." Renzo smirked.

The door opened. "Mr. Trafficante will see you now."

Baldassare turned to the men. "Let me do all the talking."

They made their way through the door and walked into an inner office. Paintings of Rubenesque nude women hung on the walls. A massive black desk sat in the center of the room, but Trafficante was seated behind a wooden dining table. The man was a lump of flesh with a balding head peeking out from a few strands of jet black hair carefully combed over the top. His tuxedo coat and starched shirt were on a hanger behind him, and he was down to his thin sleeveless T-shirt. Gray hair protruded out of the deep V under his neck.

He speared a sausage with his fork and tore off a piece in his mouth. "Come in." He waved them forward. "Hav'a yourselves a seat. You boys hungry? I can order whatever it is you want."

Baldassare shook his head. "No thanks, Don Santos."

Trafficante picked up a decanter of red wine. "Have some vino with me. A man can't never get too much wine." He laughed. "Your papa used to say that." He tapped the side of his head with his index finger and smiled. "Your papa was always a smart man. I always said dat. Of course a smart man don't always have the smartest kids." He grinned. "A man can pass on lots of things, but sometimes his brains don't go after him."

"It's too bad you couldn't take my father's 'no' for an answer when it came to this Cuba business."

Trafficante leaned back in his chair and pushed the remainder of the sausage into his mouth. He chewed it, smacking his lips while he shoveled ziti onto his plate. "Cuba, dat's another thing. Your papa, he no hafta worry about no Castro. He could sit out dere on the West Coast and rake in the suckers in Vegas. He was fat and pretty. Me now," he pointed to his ample chest, "dat man is in my backyard. I hafta worry about him. Your father though, I always know he'sa my friend. He certainly wouldn't come into my town and knock over one of my best places, shoot one of my guards, and run off to play at the beach."

He paused and then aimed his fork in Baldassare's direction. "Dat was a very stupid thing to do."

Baldassare smiled and nodded, then shrugged his shoulders. "Yeah, I read about that. Whoever did it sure was stupid, killing a guard."

Trafficante picked up a forkful of pasta. "Come on now. We botha know it was you and these boys of yours dat did dat. Don't insult me by trying to tell me any different. Why would you go and do something like dat? Your daddy didn't leave you enough of the business? Don't you go and try and tell me any different, capisce?"

Baldassare took a sip of his wine, then leaned forward. "If it was us, we'd only do something like that to get your attention, just to let you know it would cost you more not to cooperate and tell us what you know about Papa's death. You know these Cubans. If any of them had a hand in Papa's murder, you'd know about it."

"What, me?" He dropped his fork. "You think I had anything to do with my friend Lorenzo's murder? You insult me. You do better to look to your own house for that. I know people who want to get into that Nevada action of yours. Maybe they figure that with your old man out of the way they can swing a deal."

"You mean Giancana?"

"Yeah, sure." His voice rose. "Sam Giancana. He wants a place there and can't get one. Your papa's kept him out for years."

Baldassare glanced at the other men, then looked Trafficante in the eye. "That may be, but our money's on the Cubans, and they're in your back pocket. You're the boss when it comes to Miami, and nothing happens without your say-so."

Trafficante chuckled, a subtle rolling laugh. "You got dat right, boy, and don't you forget it." The laugh died abruptly. "And you don't come into my town and shoot up one of my places. You do dat and you become food for the 'gators in the swamp. Am I making myself clear?"

"Then tell us what we want to know. Maybe we'll see that whoever did this gives you your money back." Baldassare shrugged his shoulders. "Otherwise they just might keep up this nasty business, and then nobody wins. We want the people responsible, then we go away."

Trafficante slugged down several gulps of wine. "OK, OK, know what I'm agonna do?" He slid over a pad of yellow paper and picked up a pen. "I'm agonna write down a man's name and give you a place to meet him, one of my places, the Thatched Hut. You boys will like dat place." He began to write. "This man is a government man who works with all the Cubans, CIA. He knows everything there is to know about what they do and what they don't do. If anybody can help you, he can."

He ripped the page off the pad and handed it over to Baldassare. "I'll set up the meeting. You be there, all of you, and you'll find out just what it is dat you need to know."

Baldassare got to his feet, and the rest of the men stood up. He folded the paper and stuck it in his pocket. "OK, Don Santos, we'll do as you say. But hear us on this. If we don't find what we're looking for, we'll come back to see you. I just hope you don't have any more bad luck with the gambling joints you run."

He looked around the room. "You got it nice and easy here, a nice place, real nice. It would be a shame if somebody cut into your action."

Trafficante waved his hand at him, as if he were shooing away a pesky fly. "Buonasera, boy, Buonasera."

"Arrivederci."

CHAPTER 26

Maria sat on the front steps of the tiny dilapidated farmhouse. The boards of the gray porch were water-soaked, which made the splinters soft and pliable. She couldn't bring herself to go in the house. Her dark eyes were riveted to the small trail that came down the mountain and into their valley.

"This makes two days you wait," Father Yago said. The priest was more impatient than she was. His hands were clasped behind him, and he paced behind her on the porch.

She picked up a small stick and used it to write on the ground. "Yes, I know. Right now I don't care about this photographer Javier promised. I only want my men safe. They've been on that beach waiting, and it's not a secure spot for them. Castro's men could easily find them. Then where would we be?"

Yago shook his head. "I know. Men are not so easy to replace."

"Especially these men. I know their wives, their sisters, their mothers."

"And is this not a dangerous mission for them?"

Maria shook her head. "No. It's easy." She held the stick she had been writing with and broke it in two. "The hardest part is getting this man from the beach and sending him back to Miami."

"Then God will protect them. He walks with them. What about this Javier? Where is he?"

Maria smirked. "He's gone back to Miami. He says he's going to get me more equipment, antitank weapons."

It was dusk when Maria saw the small column of men coming down the trail. One man marched out in front while the rest of them walked with their rifles at the ready. It made her proud to see them doing everything she had trained them to do. The point man was watching for any potential ambush. That way the whole patrol wouldn't be jeopardized.

She walked toward them, greeting the first man as he walked into the farmyard. "Pablo, I'm so glad to see you. I was worried."

The man grinned, flashing a toothy smile. "What's to worry? We got him." He nodded back in the direction of the small column.

Maria stood by Pablo as the rest of the men sauntered down the hill and onto the beaten ground surrounding the house. She counted them. *Twelve. No, thirteen. My twelve and the photographer.*

The stranger was a man she would never have expected to see in a place like this, doing a job like Javier had told her this man would do. He was tall, handsome, and looked to be over forty. He had a square jaw and the look of military about him, including his short haircut, which was graying at the temples. His seawater blue eyes were arresting. There was a thoughtfulness about them, a depth that spoke of intelligence.

Ciro led the group, a broad smile plastered across his face. He stopped in front of Maria and stepped aside for her to see the stranger. "Maria, I'd like to introduce you to Colonel Scott Gordon." His grin widened. "He's a Marine."

Gordon smiled and stuck out his hand. "Ma'am, happy to meet you. I've heard a lot about you."

Maria shook his hand. The man had a viselike grip, and his broad chest and muscled arms stretched the seams of his shirt. She noticed his wedding ring. "Colonel Gordon? We weren't expecting . . ."

"Yeah, I know." Gordon laughed. "I wasn't exactly expecting to be here either. At the last minute I switched with the CIA photo guy who was coming, and we were delayed for a couple of days. I hope I didn't put you out."

Maria shook her head. "No. Of course not," she lied. In spite of the long wait and danger to her men, the thought of actually having a Marine Corps Colonel standing on Cuban soil and not behind the fence of Guantánamo Naval Base gave her a sense of hope. Maybe there would be an American landing after all. Maybe it wasn't just empty words.

Gordon shrugged his shoulders and lifted the two cameras by the straps. "Taking pictures isn't that big of a problem. I'm here mostly to meet you, see what you've got going, and take you back with me."

"Take me where? Miami? This is my home. My work is here."

"Yes, and you're doing a darn good job of it, from what I hear. I'm supposed to see to the readiness of an exile landing force and, frankly, from what I can see, they aren't near ready. One of the things that has to take place is to have a good cadre of people like yours ready for them. In order to do that, you have to know them and they have to know you."

Maria started to walk away, then she turned and looked back at him. Her eyes hardened. "I don't trust those people. They should have stayed in Cuba in the first place. As far as I can see, they turned tail and ran once, and they'll do it all over again."

Gordon stepped closer to her. "And they don't trust groups like yours. They landed once at the Bay of Pigs, expecting help, and got nothing."

Maria threw up her hands. "The DGI threw hundreds of thousands of patriots in jail to rot." She pointed her finger at him. "All because those people on the streets of Miami leaked what was going to happen. Castro knew about the landing. Now you want me to go there and show them my face?" She dropped her hands. "Then I come home and they arrest me."

"I won't let that happen. Your identity will be protected."

She pointed at her face with both hands. "And who will protect my face? People know me."

"You will only be introduced to people we know are secure."

Maria shook her head vigorously. "This is my home. These are my people. I live and I die here with them." She gave him a swift gesture with the back of her hand. "We won't talk about this anymore. I'll do what I promised to do, take you to this Russian base, no more. Take your pictures, but keep your promises for people who will believe them."

Gordon stepped closer to her; his eyes seemed to soften. "I understand, and I don't blame you one bit." His voice was soothing, like warm cream. "You have suffered enough. The president knows that. We want to do this thing right this time, but we need your help to do it. We need to know the strength of the Russian element here, on this island and what our men are going to face when they land. The Cuban exiles will land first, but they will have full air support. Then we will land."

"Then why do you need these pictures?"

"We are going to send reconnaissance U-2 aircraft to take a full set of pictures, but we must know first just what they are going to see, and, perhaps more important, what they aren't going to see until it's too late. Those U-2 pictures will be proof positive, but a flyover involves a great risk internationally. Francis Gary Powers was shot down over Russia. We need to see if they have ground-to-air missiles capable of doing that."

Maria paused. Her mind churned. Her gut instinct had stood her well in the past. But this man, this Scott Gordon, confused her. She wanted to trust him. "All right." Maria held up her hands. "We go at first light tomorrow morning. Then you can have your pictures. Tonight you can put your things in the house."

Gordon picked up his pack and slung it over his shoulder. "I'll stay with your men tonight, if you don't mind. I learn things better that way."

"Do what you please." With that Maria stomped off into the house.

The next morning while it was still dark, Maria stepped out onto the porch and stretched. It startled her to see Gordon sitting on the steps. He had peeled the wrapper from a dehydrated meat pemmican bar and was using a sharp knife to cut slices. He pushed the thin shavings into his mouth with the blade. "What are you doing out here?" Maria asked.

He turned his head, flashing her a grin. "You said first light. I'm waiting for first light."

She went back into the house and then emerged a few minutes later with two scalding cups of black coffee. Stooping over, she handed one to the colonel. "Warm yourself up."

He took the cup. "Thank you."

She held her cup to her lips, muttering. "I don't know why, but I want to trust you. It goes against everything I've ever been taught. Never trust a Yankee."

She held up a hand. "Don't ask me what it means. I don't know. It means what I said. I trust you, nothing more."

She watched her men emerge from the barn. They rubbed the sleep out of their eyes and yawned. Leaving Gordon where he sat, she stepped off the porch and walked in the direction of the men. "I'm only taking Father Yago, Ciro, and Damien. We will travel light and fast. The rest of you stay here and wait."

Taking the three men she had called, she led them to the house and up the steps. "You three get something to eat. The rest can wait. We leave in fifteen minutes."

Gordon sipped his coffee and nibbled on a fruit bar, which was nothing more than a dried up sliver of fruitcake.

His silence and unspoken amusement annoyed Maria.

"You have a problem?" She growled the question as she took another sip of the hot bitter liquid.

"No problem. You seem to run a tight ship. I would have suggested only two men myself. But why the priest?"

"I have my reasons. Ciro and Damien are young, and they kill without blinking an eye. Plus they are unmarried. Father Yago goes because he can pray. We need prayer. He also swings a machete well, and we are going through the bush. There are no roads. Satisfied?"

"And he's unmarried too." Scott smiled.

True to her word, within fifteen minutes the five of them headed up the trail. Ciro went ahead of them carrying an automatic weapon. Damien was next with his sniper rifle, complete with silencer and scope. Maria and the priest followed, with Gordon bringing up the rear.

They walked the trail out of the valley and down into the valley to the west of them before they came to a clear, running stream. Ciro glanced back at Maria, who motioned upstream, toward the mountains to the south of them. He headed up the stream, bouncing from rock to rock before he moved into the heavy growth.

"I would suggest we stay away from the stream," Gordon said. "Too many people come to the streams."

Maria shot him an angry glance. "My men know that, Colonel, and so do I. Just because we're illiterate peasants doesn't make us stupid."

"My apologies, ma'am. You're right. You're still alive. That must make you smart."

The group spent the next six hours breaking through brush and hacking their way by machete through the undergrowth. Father Yago was a terror with his machete, swinging it tirelessly in long swaths. He obviously kept his blade sharp.

When they came to a small clearing, Maria snapped her fingers and the men fanned out around the patch of grass. They sank to the ground and kicked their feet out, exhausted and hungry. "We take a little while to eat," she said. "Drink lots of water. You'll need it."

Father Yago inched closer to Gordon and wiped his face. Sweat was pouring off his forehead. He smiled. "This what you expected, Colonel?"

"Pretty much."

Yago smiled, then looked in Maria's direction. "No, I mean her. Is she what you expected?"

Gordon took a couple of long gulps from his canteen, then shook his head. "No, I can't say that she is."

The priest drank from his canteen and laughed. "Yes, I know. Maria is very special. She is blessed."

"What do you mean by that, Father?"

The priest continued to look in Maria's direction, then caught her eye and smiled. "It is very simple, señor. God respects her and she respects Him. God gives to her and she gives to Him. God laid down His life for her and she lays down her life for Him and His people. There is just one thing more, and I'm afraid it is something that is very hard for human beings to do."

"What is that, Father?"

"People have such long memories, but God forgets quite easily. When we confess our sins, He puts them behind His back forever." Yago shook his head slowly. "He will never look at them or remember them ever again. But we are not like that. We want all our justice here and now where we can see and taste it. We want revenge. We want the scales to be in balance to accommodate our puny sense of right and wrong."

He pointed his finger at the bright blue patch of sky overhead. "But God is the one who has suffered the greatest offense, and God is the one who forgives."

The priest gazed at Maria. "I think when Maria truly feels God's forgiveness, she will learn to forgive as well. Only then will the sting be taken out of her heart."

Just as they were finishing their lunch—some broiled pork wrapped in leaves—they heard the whir of rotors overhead. Grabbing for their weapons and packs, they tumbled backward into the dense brush.

The sound of the overhead helicopter grew louder, the rotors kicking at the dirt around them and flattening the grass. Maria crawled forward, straining to see. The thing hovered overhead, men peering out the door behind a heavy machine gun. Russian. She could see the red hammer and sickle insignia painted on the side. It hung in the air like a hungry bird of prey. She only hoped the men in the door wouldn't decide to lay down a stream of fire at the brush where their small group lay hidden. They had obviously seen something.

Moments later, it lifted higher and thundered off toward the mountain peaks in the distance, the echo of its blades still rattling in their ears.

Gordon jumped to his feet and pointed to the men. "Let's get moving, and fast. If they did see something, they'll radio a patrol and it'll be here in minutes."

Maria dusted off her pants. She was caked in dust and dirt. She glared at him. "These are my men, Colonel. I give the orders here." With that, she looked at the group. "You heard the man. Let's get moving."

In unison they headed down the hillside and into the denser undergrowth. The vegetation would be thicker there, making them harder to find. They could also make better time going downhill.

Ciro squeezed himself through the thick trees, while the priest swung his machete furiously at the greenery. They labored for what seemed to be hours, pulling at branches, yanking at limbs, and pushing their bodies through thick, tall grass. Some time later they heard the sound of falling water below them.

Maria snapped her fingers, getting the men's attention. "Let's fan out over the stream. I want to make sure we're alone here before we go down."

They moved away from each other across the slope and began a slow decent toward the falling water. The ground was soft, giving way under their boots. They slid downhill, grabbing for branches to prevent a fall. Soon they were standing on the lip of a small, dark, tree-filled valley. They could see bits and pieces of the stream through the trees.

Maria squatted down, looking below. She signaled to Ciro, who jumped over the edge and skidded out of view. They could see the dust his boots were making in the soft ground.

Exploding to the surface, she shivered, a smile widening over her face. Whatever it meant to die, she knew this was what it meant to live. For now, she felt free inside.

She moved to shallower water and started to scrub every part of her body. There was always something about what she did that made her feel dirty, but it was a dirt that no amount of water could ever wash away. She carried it in her heart—the hate, the anger, the bitterness. But she could leave all that now, in this place. She could be a little girl again.

It was then that she heard the laughter from across the stream. Her head jerked up, and she could see them. Five Russian soldiers were staring at her, laughing and whistling. They spoke in a language she couldn't understand, but she could read their eyes. They were motioning for her to come out.

Maria crossed her arms in front of her and stepped back. She glanced over to where she had covered her automatic rifle. If she could get to her weapon and make the men come to her, she could surprise them.

Several of the men jumped to their feet and pointed their rifles at her. They pulled back the hammers on their automatic weapons. One man, obviously the man in charge, drew his revolver and stepped out into the water. He motioned for her to come toward them, then pointed the pistol directly at her.

Maria stopped midstream. Her heart was pounding. Surely her men had heard the Russians.

The man with the pistol cocked it and took aim.

Maria began to cry. Then she slowly waded toward the men in their camouflage uniforms. The water dripped off her back, curling down her spine. *This will be over soon, one way or the other.*

CHAPTER 27

T he Thatched Hut was like every other seedy bar Baldassare
had seen in the Nevada desert—with one big exception.
This one was on the ocean with the surf washing up outside
the large set of sliding windows. A moonfaced bartender poured multicolored concoctions, and girls in bikinis hung on the arms of sailors
and fighter jocks. The jukebox throbbed with the sound of Roy
Orbison, lamenting a "devil woman," no doubt with this place in
mind.

A pilot at the bar was demonstrating his maneuvers for a bikini-
clad blonde sitting next to him. I HATE THE 82ND AIRBORNE was

scrawled in red lipstick. This was a Navy bar. The Army was not welcome.

There was a feel of death to the place. The pilots risked their lives every day when they climbed into their cockpits and pulled the hatch down. From the looks on the flyboys' faces, however, it was plain to see that death was a powerful aphrodisiac.

The sadness of the place was almost overpowering, a suffocating atmosphere of male privilege and female abasement. The waitress was a hatchet-faced woman with inch-thick makeup. She bent low over their table and cracked a smile as she set down their drinks.

Renzo pushed two of the twenties they had taken from the boat heist at the woman. "Keep the change," he said.

She grinned, stuffing one of the bills into her sagging top. "Sure thing, mister. Anything else you boys want, just ask for Hilve."

Baldassare was anxious to meet the man Trafficante had given up, if for no other reason than to see the fingerman for his father's murder face-to-face. The Cubans may have pulled the trigger, but the government loaded their guns. In all the years when the business had been the subject of federal investigations, he had never thought they could stoop so low as to actually murder a member of the family. Now he knew better. Trafficante thought the man was invulnerable, and couldn't be touched, but Baldassare was determined to prove him wrong. If the Kennedy administration could hit his family, then he could and would hit back. And hard.

The four of them sat at a table along the far wall. Baldassare was determined not to let anyone get close to his back. Baldassare preferred to pick his own meeting places, but this was Trafficante's turf. They sipped their drinks and occasionally Marco glanced at his watch.

"Where is this guy?" Marco asked. "He was supposed to have been here twenty minutes ago."

Baldassare unzipped a pack of Lucky Strikes and slammed it against his finger to push one of the cigarettes out. Dropping the pack in his pocket, he pulled out his Zippo, flicked a flame, and touched it to the tobacco.

Bruno leaned across the table. "I don't get it boss. Why is this guy coming to meet us in the first place? If Trafficante tells him who we are, don't he know we want to kill him?"

"Trafficante didn't tell him we know he's the finger man," Renzo said. "He just told him who we are. This guy's like the IRS. They figure they can rob you and then get you to apologize for making them do it. He's probably just going to show us around, then try to explain to us how it was some Cuban group what got carried away. He'll say they're gone now and there's nothing he can do about it. Of course he'll smile and apologize, say it wasn't his fault. Then he'll slap us on the back and tell us he'll come and pay us a visit in Vegas."

Bruno blinked. "But we ain't gonna let him do that, is we boss?"

Renzo twisted in his seat. "No, dummy." He held up his hands in a simulated squeeze. "We're going to wring that federal jerk's neck."

"After we find out who the triggermen were," Marco added.

"Right." Bruno let the word out long and slow, a smile crossing his face.

Baldassare stared out the window. The sun was lower in the sky, turning the ocean a deeper azure blue.

Renzo nudged his arm. "Whatcha thinking about, boss?"

Baldassare pointed with his burning cigarette to the ocean. "I was just thinking how much Papa loved the ocean. He lived most of his life in Chicago, and his business was all in Las Vegas, but he couldn't get enough of the ocean. You reckon that's how people are? They all want what they can't have?"

Renzo grinned. "That's our business, boss. We promise people something they can never have, but they keep coming back for more."

"Gambling is a business of hope," Marco added. "Everybody's got to have hope."

"And what about you guys?" Baldassare asked. He took a puff from his cigarette. "What do you hope for?"

"I want a Corvette and a beach house with fine women." Marco smirked.

Renzo looked at him and smiled. "You can buy that. Me, I'd rather have the way to earn the money. I want a casino myself someday. That's where the money is."

"You been listening to Rocko?" Marco asked.

"Sure," Renzo nodded. "The man's been around. He talks about that all the time, dreams about it. He'll get one some day too. You can count on it."

"What about you, Bruno?" Baldassare asked. The burning cigarette bobbed in his mouth. "What are your hopes?"

Bruno laced his thick fingers together and sat back, circling his thumbs. "I been thinking about that. I just want me a good woman, somebody real nice who makes me think good thoughts, somebody who says really nice things about me, how I'm all loving and stuff. I want her to make good pasta and clam sauce and have lots of kids that have my name behind theirs." He sat forward. "And one day I want one of them to be somebody, somebody I never was, somebody like a lawyer, a doctor, or a plumber."

"A plumber?" Renzo laughed.

Bruno nodded. "Sure, why not? Them people are union. They ain't Republicans."

Baldassare saw a tall man in a multicolored floral shirt came through the door. He had sandy brown hair and wore khaki slacks and deck shoes with no socks. His shirt was pulled out, and he had a lump on his hip, no doubt a revolver. He spotted them and walked over to their table, a big grin on his face.

"You the people I'm suppose to meet, the ones Santos told me about?"

Baldassare got to his feet, pushing his suit coat aside and exposing the square butt of the .45 he was carrying in his belt. He nodded. "We're the Pera group. Who are you?"

"The name's Cliff Cox." The man held out his hand, which no one made any attempt to shake. He dropped it, never wavering in his smile. "I take it you're here to find out just what I might know about your father's death."

Baldassare nodded. "You got that right."

"We can't talk about that here. It's something I'm going to have to show you. You have a car?"

Marco nodded. "Yeah. It's the white Caddy parked out front."

"Good. Then why don't you follow me?" He jerked his thumb in the direction of the door. "I've got a blue Austin Sprite."

Marco leaned closer to Baldassare. "What kind of man drives one of those toy cars?"

"The kind of man who's too big for his britches. He might as well be too big for his car too."

They drove south then west along the Tamiami Trail. Bruno sat in the backseat with Baldassare. The sun hung low as they turned south once again. Ghostly Spanish moss draped the trees. Grassy fields seemed to be covered with scarlet hurricane lilies, their wiry spider-like heads swaying in the evening breeze. The small towns were punctuated with gas stations and soda fountains, and Kewpie dolls dancing in the windows.

Marco followed the tiny blue car as it turned onto a back road. The Everglades stretched out on either side of the road, vast marshes filled with water lilies and croaking frogs. A flock of pink flamingos took flight, spreading their wings and filling the sky with the sound of beating feathers.

"Wowzers!" Renzo shouted from the front seat. "Makes me think of Vegas."

"Why Vegas?" Bruno asked.

Renzo looked back, grinning. "The Flamingo, Bugsy Segal's old place."

"Everything makes you think of gambling," Bruno grunted. "Me, I just think of them 'gators out there. I'd like to get me one of them things and skin it."

"What in blazes for?" Renzo asked.

Bruno grabbed his right foot and held it up. "Cowboy boots. Them things would make fine cowboy boots, mighty fine."

The sun was dipping low over the treetops when the two cars rounded the bend that led to the pond. Baldassare sat up so he could see the camp spread out around one side of the pond. Smoke rose from a number of fires with small groups of men gathered around them. Cox steered his small car into one of the dirt parking places in front of a small weather-beaten shack, and Marco maneuvered the white convertible next to his.

Cox bounced out of his little car and leaned into theirs. "Hang on for a minute. I've got to check on something. I'll be right back and take you to the men with all the answers."

The four of them watched as the man practically ran into the shack. Marco looked back at Baldassare. "I thought he was the man with the answers."

Baldassare pulled out his .45. "I don't know, but I don't like it. You better check your rounds. I don't like the sound of having to face men. These people have an army here."

"And we don't have anything left of any heavy weapons," Renzo said.

In a matter of minutes, Cox came striding out of the shack. A man with a sloping mustache and deep dark eyes trailed him. Cox stepped up to the car, smiling. "This is Bolivar. He's in command here today, and he's given us permission to talk to the men you're looking for. I have to take you there, though. They're not in this camp."

Baldassare opened his door and got out. "That's fine, but you're riding with us."

Cox held up his hands and smiled. "That's OK. I'll drive slow. You can follow me."

"No way!" Baldassare shook his head. "You got an army here, and we aren't going to be driving into any ambush, not today, not ever."

Cox glanced at Bolivar, and the dark-skinned Cuban nodded. "OK," Cox said. "Have it your way. I'll go with you and keep you safe, if you like."

"We like," Baldassare said. He stood back and held the door open for Cox.

When Cox was settled in the middle of the backseat, Baldassare climbed in beside him. Marco started the car and spun the wheels into reverse. "Where to?" he shouted.

Cox pointed. "That road to your left."

Marco threw the car into gear, and they lurched toward the road. Baldassare pulled out his .45 and pointed it at Cox's temple. "All right, Mr. Government man, now listen up. Anything goes wrong, you die. My fault, your fault, the Cubans' fault, it don't make no difference. You're going to be just as dead. Am I understood?"

Cox nodded stiffly. "Yes, I understand. You won't have anything to worry about from me. We're just going to take a little drive and meet a man. Do you speak Spanish?"

Baldassare shook his head. "No."

"Then I'll have to get out and talk to the man, explain what you want. I'll translate for you so you can understand. The man we need to see doesn't speak a word of English." A slight but genuine smile crossed his lips. "He doesn't speak any Italian, either."

Bruno took out his Ruger .357 Magnum. The inside of the barrel looked like a long dark tunnel. He cocked it and held it to the other side of Cox's head. "Don't you make no mistakes. I pull this trigger, and there ain't gonna be no bullet holes cause you ain't gonna have no more head."

He reached down and tugged at Cox's belt, pulling out the .38 that was in a small holster. Holding it up, he laughed. "You ain't gonna stop nothing with this thing."

Cox eyed Bruno's huge frame. "I sure couldn't have stopped you."

They wound their way around the pond, the tires stirring up a dust cloud that floated out over the water lilies and into the marshy grass. A blue heron took off, folding its long wings into a perfect V as it climbed for altitude. Several large alligators floated just under the surface of the green slime on the pond's surface, their black eyes peering out.

Cox pointed to a smaller road coming up on their left. "Turn here," he said. Marco swung the wheel, and the Caddy hit several bumps and then a series of washboard ruts. It was like driving over the ties in a railroad bed, jarring, even teeth clenching.

When they emerged from the trees, the swamp stretched out in front of them, an endless sea of waving grass and lily pads. The causeway led to the trees beyond. Cox pointed. "There's a shack the other side of those trees. The man you're looking for is there." His eyes met Baldassare's. "I am sorry to hear about your dad. But if anybody can help you, this man can. I think you may be surprised by what you find out."

"I hope you're right." Baldassare's eyes bored right though Cox. "'Cause frankly, I don't much like what I know right now."

"Just pull over and stop," Cox said. He looked at Baldassare. "I have to go see this man myself. He won't even come close to you unless I talk to him first."

Bruno blinked in Baldassare's direction. "You ain't gonna let this man get away from us are you?"

Cox looked back at Bruno and then at Baldassare. "If I don't talk to him alone first, you might as well turn around and go back. He knows who killed your father and, more important, he knows who ordered it."

Baldassare looked at the distant shack. "All right." Baldassare waved the .45 at him. "You walk on over there and talk to the man. But stay in sight. I want to see you at all times."

"You won't be sorry."

Baldassare opened his door and got out. He watched as Cox climbed out of the car and started his walk toward the shack.

"I don't like this," Marco said.

Cox stood in the doorway of the shack, talking to someone inside, then stepped through the door.

Renzo stood up in his seat. "That ain't good, boss. He's gone."

Suddenly, a line of men jumped from the trees and landed in a prone position beside the road. They all carried automatic weapons. Two tripod-mounted machine guns glided into position.

A ripple of fear ran though all four of them, but it was too late. The men beside the road opened fire. The first spray of bullets pierced the sides of the Caddy and cut down Marco and Renzo where they were seated. Baldassare dropped down behind the car, and Bruno began to crawl behind the backseat and out the open back door. He slithered to the ground beside Baldassare.

Both men sat with their backs to the car, their hearts pounding. The machine gun rounds penetrated the side of the big convertible. Baldassare poked his head into the open door and could see Marco. The man lay on the seat, his open eyes staring into eternity. Baldassare reached back and grabbed Bruno's hand. He looked up into the evening sky and repeated the words, "Hail Mary, full of grace, the Lord is with thee. Blessed are thou among women, and blessed is the fruit of thy womb, Jesus. Holy Mary, Mother of God, pray for us sinners, now and at the hour of our death."

CHAPTER 28

Maria climbed over the embankment and fell belly first onto the small clearing on the top of the ridge. She struggled, her hands shaking. Gordon grabbed her hand, pulled her up. "You all right?"

She nodded, wiping her eyes. "Yes."

"I thought maybe we could go back into the brush and make camp for the night. That way we could get into position to take pictures tomorrow."

Maria shook her head. "No. We are too close. We'll go to the Russian base tonight. I want pictures at first light so we can get out of here."

Gordon glanced around at the men. "It's been a hard day. I think the men are all done in. If we have to do too much walking . . ."

"No." Maria cut him off. Her voice was strident and raspy. "I'm done in too. I want to get home. I don't want to be here any longer than necessary. We move on tonight."

Gordon turned to face the men who were lying on the ground. Both Ciro and Damien had their hats pulled down over their faces. "You heard the lady. Let's get to our feet and pack up. We've got some walking to do."

Gordon noticed Father's Yago's eyes. They were drawn to Maria. He got up and walked over to where she was sitting. Her knees were drawn up, and she had her arms wrapped around them, drawn tightly into a ball. The priest put his arm around her shoulders.

"Are you all right, my child?"

She looked up at him. Tears were glistening in her eyes. She mumbled a reply, her lips quivering. "Yes, Father. I'll be OK. Just memories of when I was a child."

The priest rubbed her shoulder. "That's all right, my child. All of us are still children down deep inside. We never lose that. I pray we never do. There is always hope inside the heart of a child, and you should have hope too. Soon all of this will be over."

She wiped her eyes, and, rocking forward, got to her feet. She slung her pack over her shoulder, picked up her rifle and looked at the men. "Let's go." She tried to make the command sound like her usual bark, but there was a crack in her voice. "We have to get in position."

Ciro took his usual place at point and headed off into the bush, followed by Damien. Maria stayed by Father Yago's side, and Gordon brought up the rear. The group pushed their way through the foliage, made even darker by the lateness of the day.

Gordon fell in behind Father Yago, who slung his machete in wide swaths. Gordon only hoped Maria was right about being close to the Russian base. The thickness of the growth made it difficult to traverse in the bright daylight, and darkness would make it impossible.

He watched as Maria attacked the vines and branches with her machete. The woman seemed driven, unaffected by fatigue or the low sun, she flung the blade back and forth. Her arm cocked back, and without so much as taking aim, she came down hard with the blue-steel blade, sending thick vegetation to the ground.

It was almost pitch black when they tumbled out of the dense undergrowth. Before them was a chain-link fence with three strands of barbed wire strung along the top. Gordon could see the guard tower to their left and a platform with a bank of spotlights. The lights bathed the fence in a harsh yellow ray. Beyond the fence was a series of concrete-block houses and an array of missiles.

Gordon reached out and grabbed Maria by the shirt. When she turned to him, he motioned with his head back in the direction of the forest. "Let's back up and look the place over."

Maria snapped her fingers and waved the men to retreat into the thick growth.

Maria placed her hands on her hips and stared at Gordon. "Well, here we are. Now what?"

"I'll make a series of cuts in the fence," Gordon said. "No doubt they have perimeter patrols who check the fence at night, so my cuts have to be low and hard to see. Just before dawn, Ciro and I will take out the guards in the tower." He glanced at Ciro. "You'll use your sniper rifle and silencer, and I'll use the crossbow I brought. We have to do it at the same time so they won't be alerted when just one falls."

Ciro nodded and grinned.

"Then we'll push through the fence and go over the hill. I'll take my pictures while you provide security. If we do this thing right, we'll be in and out of there in ten minutes tops. Is that understood?"

The men nodded. Gordon stared at Maria. He wanted to make sure she was in total agreement.

"I understand," she said.

"This mission is my baby," he said. "I'm in charge until we're out of here and back in the bush. I know just what I'm doing. It's a mission I've been trained for."

He looked at Maria. Having someone else in command might be difficult for her to stomach.

She nodded. "OK, Colonel. You're in command until we get out of here."

"Fine," he smiled. "Then we'll go back in the bush about twenty or thirty yards and bed down for the night. One of us will be awake at all times, and we'll be up an hour before dawn."

Gordon set down his pack and pulled out a small pair of wire cutters. He watched the lights play along the wire for a while, trying to judge the timing. As the lights swept along the chain-link fence, he counted the seconds, numbering them off—20, 21, 22, 23, 24, 25, 26, 27, 28, 29, 30. Then the light came back again.

He ran for the fence and lay facedown next to it, all the while keeping the time in his head. He made several small cuts. It was important not to create any noticeable holes. He had to make his cuts so the wire could be pushed open and then pulled back into place to give the appearance that it was still whole. Nothing must seem out of place to the casual guard who might walk by. He must also be certain that he created no telltale scent. The guards might have dogs.

He looked up. The intense beam was beginning its return trip. Scrambling to his feet, he dove headfirst into the brush as the light passed overhead.

Maria put her hand on him. "You get it done?"

He shook his head. "No. One more pass."

He waited for the arc of light to return and then ran back to his spot on the wire. Finishing his cuts and leaving only a few of the strands of wire to hold the entrance in place, he got to his feet and ran back to the group.

"OK, it's done for now. Let's get back into the trees and wait."

The group blended into the forest. It had been a long hard day, and Gordon was certain none of them would have any trouble falling asleep on the bare ground. The only problem might be sleeping too hard and too long. He motioned to the group. "Sleep on an arm and get yourself uncomfortable. That way you'll get just enough."

Damien took the first watch, and the group soon fell asleep.

Gordon had the last watch. He crept up close to the fence where he could observe any Russian patrols. He spotted two men, one with a large German shepherd on a leash. He had to make sure the group was ready to go when the patrol passed by again. The dog patrol was moving away from the guard tower, which was a break. If they continued that pattern, things would be OK.

He ran back to shake them awake. "OK," he said, "Here's how this thing lays out. Ciro and I will go to the tower. They have a dog patrol, and when it passes the tower, we'll kill the two guards."

He looked intently into each eye. "When the dog patrol gets past you, move through the wire cuts fast, but make sure you don't break the cuts. I have to put it back into place. Ciro and I will come through the wire, and I'll put down some red pepper about twenty yards before the dog gets close to the place where we went through. That way we'll be out of there before he gets close enough to sniff out our tracks."

"Dogs are bad," Damien said.

"Yes. The patrol passes by every thirty to forty-five minutes. If things go the way I hope they go, we'll be long gone before they pass by again."

"Isn't the pepper going to harm the dog?" Father Yago asked.

"It's temporary, Father, so don't worry."

Gordon reached into his pack and took out a black crossbow and two small arrows. He slung the bow over his shoulder and pushed the arrows behind his belt. Both he and Ciro moved to the edge of the perimeter and started down the long line of trees until they were directly across from the guard tower. The tall, metal structure had a catwalk surrounding a small roof with handrails. Gordon knew that most Russian men were addicted to smoking and that these men were no different. The warm glow of the lit cigars allowed a perfect view of the men's chins.

Gordon pulled the bow into position and laid an arrow in place. He nudged Ciro and pointed to the man on the left side of the tower. Then he whispered. "We take aim together. When you hear the spring on the bow, you fire."

"OK, I do that."

Gordon had never taken a good look at Ciro. He was a young man. That was plain to see. Perhaps he was very young. The beard on his face could hardly be called a beard. It was mostly fuzz. But Gordon was sure Ciro's nerves were steady. Maria was a thorough woman. She would never give a man a sniper rifle if he didn't know how to use it. He touched the young man's arm. "You OK?" he whispered.

Ciro nodded.

It was only a matter of minutes before they saw the small dog patrol. The big shepherd was straining at the leash. Gordon felt a slight breeze on the back of his neck. That was a problem. It sent a shiver of fear up and down his spine. If the dog picked up their scent right at that point, he might begin to bark and move toward the fence. They would then have to kill the two men and the dog along with the guards on the tower. Plus they had a chain-link fence between them and the patrol. It could be a bloody mess and noisy. He hoped it didn't come to that.

The guard holding the dog tugged on his leash, and they moved past the tower and down the fence. Gordon would give them some time to get out of immediate earshot.

He held the crossbow up to his cheek and sighted the guard on the right. Out of the corner of his eye, he could see Ciro doing the same with the guard on the left.

The man on the right side of the tower turned around. He was now looking in Gordon's direction. Easing his finger, Gordon took a breath and let it out slowly. He squeezed the trigger. The spring on the bow launched the arrow up into the air and straight into the throat of the guard on the right side of the platform. Ciro squeezed off his round almost simultaneously. Both guards dropped at once and without a sound. More important, they dropped onto the platform and not to the ground.

Gordon and Ciro ran along the fence line. Suddenly, the spotlight flashed in front of them. They froze. The light had Ciro pinned for an instant. Gordon could only hope that in the distance they might look like trees. The guards who could have gotten the best view were both dead.

The cut in the wire was right in front of them. They would have thirty seconds before the light returned. Gordon pointed to the spot and Ciro got on his belly and pushed his rifle through. Gordon followed, slithering under the wire.

He reached back and pushed the wire back into place. There was a slight break where somebody had gone through without being careful enough, but perhaps it wouldn't be seen.

Gordon stumbled to his feet and pulled out a small tin can filled with canine pepper. He ran toward the tower. Then he saw the spotlight making another pass. He dropped to the ground as the light ran over him.

Getting back on his feet, he ran another fifteen yards or so. He sprinkled the pepper for a couple of yards before dropping the small tin back in his pocket and running to the fence break.

Ciro pointed to the group. Three others were lying on the crest of the slope that led down to the missile emplacement. Both he and Gordon ran to join them and hit the ground.

"It ought to be dawn shortly," Gordon said.

He watched as a guard stepped out of one of the concrete-block houses. The man lit a cigarette and stood with his back to them, looking out over the missiles below and puffing on his cigarette.

Gordon looked up and saw Maria running. She was skirting the ground but running in the direction of the guard.

"What is she doing?" Gordon hissed.

The men looked back at him and shrugged their shoulders.

They watched as Maria approached the man from the rear. She drew out her knife and pounced on the lone guard. He had to be a head and shoulders higher than Maria and weigh a good two hundred and fifty pounds. She grabbed him from behind and rammed the knife into the man's chest. He sank to his knees, his lit cigarette dropping to the ground.

Maria bent down, slipped her arms under the dead guard's shoulders, and dragged him off into the darkness. She laid him down on the ground near a stack of boxes and arranged the boxes around and on top of the body. Then she turned and ran back to the still startled group.

She dropped to the ground beside Father Yago, panting.

Gordon crawled over toward her. He reached out and grabbed hold of her shirt. "What in heaven's name do you think you're doing with a grandstand play like that?" He growled the words with a soft guttural rumble.

She tried to push his hand away, but he held tightly to her. "He's the enemy, and I'm here to kill the enemy," she hissed.

Gordon pushed his face into hers and lowered his voice so that only she could hear. "Listen, I don't care what your personal feelings are. We have a job to do, and when your feelings get in the way of us doing our job, then you're the biggest enemy we face. You can easily make yourself unfit for command with plays like that. You have to think of the mission and your men, nothing else. Is that understood?"

He watched as tears rolled slowly down Maria's cheeks.

MIAMI, FLORIDA
MONDAY, OCTOBER 8

CHAPTER 29

The flight from New York to Miami had been filled with early snowbirds, older travelers bent on escaping winter. Gina rented a new dark blue Buick at the airport, and Rocko directed them to a hotel on the beach that he was very familiar with, the Marlin. The place was garish with glitzy art deco in all directions. The exterior was a multicolored Easter egg, painted in soft yellow pastels mixed with gold, aqua, and bright purple, and a blue neon light curled around the arches and gables of the old hotel.

Johnny had his own suite, without the pretense of having Gina in an adjoining room. When they got to the third floor, he didn't take the time to unpack. There was one comfortable club chair, a large green one with matching ottoman. He sat down in it and picked up the phone.

"Who ya calling?"

He hadn't noticed Rocko, who had walked into his room.

"Frank Bass." He dialed the number.

"Good, maybe he can help us."

"Frank Bass," Johnny spoke into the phone. "Can I speak to Frank Bass. This is Johnny Pera. We're old friends."

It took a short time before Johnny got an answer, but he beamed when he heard the sound of Frank's voice. "Hey, Jarhead, remember me? Well, I'm in town, the Marlin Hotel." He listened as Frank spoke. "You're kidding? He's here? Well, bring him on over. We'll all catch up. I'll buy you dinner and show you pictures of the kids. He's got a woman, a Cuban woman?" He listened as Frank explained. "Sure, he can bring her too. OK, see both of you at six-thirty then."

When he hung up the phone, he bounced to his feet, a smile on his face. "I've got another Marine buddy who just got into town today too. The guy's a colonel. Frank's bringing him over. I guess he has a Cuban woman with him."

"Just so we find time to talk to him about what we need. Your friend Frank is one of the reasons we wanted you in on this."

"Yeah, and Scott works at the Pentagon now. What Frank doesn't know, he probably does."

When six-thirty rolled around, Johnny had secured an extra large table at the Swordfish Grill on the bottom floor of the Marlin. Johnny had reserved two open seats beside him for his Marine buddies, and he stood and waved as they entered the room. "Hey you guys, we're over here."

Frank Bass was a stout man with a burley chest. He filled out his blue suit, and his crimson tie was pinned in place with a USMC medallion. He was clean-shaven with a square jaw and bright blue eyes. He looked like a Marine, even though his suit and tie said otherwise. He reached out to shake Johnny's hand. "Great to see you, hombre."

Johnny reached out and hugged the man, patting him on the back. "I'm glad to see you, Frank." He pushed him back and eyed Scott Gordon. The man was ramrod straight and was carrying an attaché case. Johnny reached over to grip his hand. "And you, I would never have expected to find you here."

They took their seats, and Scott seated the young Cuban woman. "And who is your friend?" Johnny asked.

Scott stood behind his chair and smiled. "Gentlemen, allow me to present Maria Gonzales. She's a VIP and in my charge." He took his seat.

"Nice assignment, Gordon," Johnny said. "You always had a way of getting the soft duty, as I remember." He then introduced the rest of his party. "So this is my crew. We're doing some traveling together. In fact, we've got a job to do that both of you might well be able to help us with."

They worked their way through the meal, starting with a large bowl of peeled shrimp on ice and hot crab chowder. Johnny noticed that Junior had circled the table in order to sit next to the Cuban woman. He didn't much blame him. "I see you're never far away from your work, Gordon. You brought your briefcase with you. Important papers for the president, no doubt."

"Pictures of Russian missiles for the CIA," Maria piped in.

Gordon shot the woman a hard look.

"I was sorry to hear about your father," Frank said. That seemed to distract Gordon, who looked in Johnny's direction.

Johnny nodded. "Yes, I was there when it happened. It was on my parents' fiftieth wedding anniversary."

"That must have been horrible," Frank said. "Have they found out who was responsible?"

"No, and I was hoping you could help me with that." He looked over at Gordon. "And if you can't, maybe Scott can."

"I'd be happy to help you in any way that I can."

Johnny leaned forward. "We think whoever is responsible for this has ties to the Cubans. Papa had refused to help with an operation that I'm sure both of you are at least familiar with. We have every reason to believe that whoever ordered Papa's murder did it in order to make people go along with the plan. But I can explain our thinking and get your ideas when we go back up to my room. I don't want to disturb your dinner."

Frank put his hand on Johnny's. "Have you called home lately, Johnny?"

"No, I haven't. Why?"

Frank cut a piece of his swordfish steak. "Because we'd like to know the whereabouts of your brother Baldassare. We've heard he's here in Miami."

Johnny looked over at Rocko, who had been listening. "Do you know anything about this, Rocko?"

Rocko shook his head. "Nothing. But you know Baldy. The man's a hothead. He probably came to pay a call on Santos Trafficante."

"That's exactly what the Bureau thinks," Frank said. "One of Trafficante's casinos was hit the other night. They took over a million in cash and killed a guard." He put the piece of fish into his mouth. "Nobody around here would be foolish enough to do something like that. Our boys at the office figured it to be outsiders. Trafficante's been involved with what you're looking into. Maybe Baldassare is trying to get his attention."

Rocko spoke up. "We got us a meeting with Trafficante after dinner tonight. I forgot to tell you, Johnny."

Frank looked Johnny in the eye. "You be careful with that man. He's dangerous. Make your meeting with him as public as possible.

But do me a favor and call home. I'd feel a lot better knowing your brother was still in California."

After dinner they went up to Johnny's suite for Key lime pie and coffee. They had twenty years of catching up to do. The three of them stood on the balcony, looking out on Collins Avenue.

"I see you've been getting a lot of that Key lime pie, Frank." Johnny said.

"Yeah." Frank laughed. "Comes with a desk job, I suppose."

"Speaking of jobs," Scott said, "Why did you leave the ministry?"

"I did that last year. It was a year after Karen's death." He put his cup down on the table. "Some people would find it hard to understand, but I think I can trust you two. I just found a deep longing inside, something I had to listen to."

"A longing for what?" Frank asked.

"For the something that was missing in me, that thing I once had with you two men on the beach there on Saipan."

"When you accepted Christ?" Frank asked.

"Yes."

"I'm not sure I understand," Scott said.

"A. W. Tozer once said, 'Thirsty hearts are those whose longings have been wakened by the touch of God within them.' There had been many times in the years before Karen's death when I felt out of touch with God. I had drifted, not with the things I was doing, but with the sense of romance I felt with God."

He shook his head. "Those times only made me redouble my efforts to be a success in the ministry. I thought I needed to work harder, be more disciplined, be more committed. But the faster I went, the more behind I felt. I wasn't listening to my heart, only checking off events in my daily calendar. I did my Bible study, prepared my sermons, worked with couples, attended meetings, visited the sick. My daily quiet times became a hollow ritual. It took Karen's death to tell me how empty all that activity really was. For the first time my loneliness woke me up to the fact that I'd been living the Christian life without the intimacy of God. Papa used to say that only beauty and pain open a man's heart. I guess it took great pain to open mine."

"But why this?" Frank motioned to the window where the others were mingling and talking in Johnny's room. "Why get involved now with your family's business?"

"Guilt, maybe. I felt somehow responsible, like I should have done more to make myself a part of my family and their lives, should have been trying harder. I sort of wrote them off as a hopeless cause."

"Johnny, your folks have been that way since they were in the old country," Frank said. "It has nothing to do with you. They were playing both ends against the middle trying to find a way to climb to power since before you and I were ever thought of."

"Yes, but God put me there, dropped me right in the middle of them and I did nothing, nothing but walk away. I embraced my new family and turned my back on my old one."

Gordon swung around and put his elbows on the iron balcony railings. "And you felt a sense of duty," he said.

"Yes. They said they needed me and I said yes. It took me twenty years to say it, but I finally did."

Johnny looked Gordon in the eye. "You seem thoughtful, Scott."

Gordon nodded. "I've got a lot on my mind too. I'm anxious to get back to Jackie and the kids. What you're talking about just makes me want to get on that plane even quicker. Just as soon as I can get that package of mine dropped off, I'll be out of here."

"That briefcase of yours?"

"Yeah, and a round of final inspection. I'm learning a lot I'd rather not know. I might be able to help you, though. I can set up a meeting for you with the CIA man who's been handling the Cuban thing. The guy's a snake. Frankly, I wouldn't trust him as far as I would trust the countries he and his people spy on. And you shouldn't believe a word he tells you. He'll look you in the eye, sweet and innocent, and lie through his teeth. All for our national interest, of course."

"Of course," Johnny laughed. "OK, you set it up, and I'll meet with him. I'll try to believe the opposite of whatever he says."

Frank had been looking through the window at the people mingling in the room. He watched as Gina talked and laughed with Maria. He cocked his head in Johnny's direction. "I was just wondering," he said. "That woman Gina in there, that's not the same Gina you told us about in the Pacific, is it?"

Johnny nodded. "The very same."

Frank rubbed his chin. "Wow. She's a looker." He grinned at Johnny. "That must make it tough for you. Is she married?"

"Divorced."

Frank shook his head. "You be careful, pal." He tapped Johnny's chest. "You know how you are with this guilt thing of yours, and you're a lonely camper right now. I'd keep my distance."

"I'm trying, but it's tough. The woman's a thinker too, a lawyer, the family lawyer. I think she's come to peace with our past, probably more than I have."

"Keep your distance all the same. A lonely man is on a slippery slope.

Scott had been restless during the evening. He had tried to enter the conversation, but he knew that his mind was elsewhere. He wanted to be home with Jackie, and he needed to deliver his final assessment of the situation with the Cubans to the president. He knew that the exile army wasn't nearly ready for an invasion, and, to make matters worse, the security there was abysmal. He had brought Maria with him to learn more of what he could about the Cuban resistance and perhaps even some names of people in Castro's government that might be able to help them. This wasn't exactly his job to do—that was more for the CIA—but he trusted the CIA even less than he trusted the Cubans. He knew that what he told the president had to be what he had heard with his own ears and seen with his own eyes.

The three walked back inside and Scott immediately looked at the leather briefcase. It was sitting beside the couch just where he had left it, but he knew instantly that had been a mistake. He should never have let the thing get out of his sight. He picked it up and tried to laugh and make small talk while they all made their way to the door, but he couldn't take his mind off his stupidity. The room was full of thieves, and, in spite of Johnny's involvement with these people, it was what they did for a living.

Rocko slapped Frank Bass on the back as they all walked to the elevator. "Hey, you know, for an FBI guy, you ain't so bad."

Frank smiled. "You won't think so if I have to put the cuffs on you."

Rocko laughed and held up his hands. "Not so fast, copper." He glanced at Gina. "I got my lawyer here with me, and I been a good boy, a real good boy."

"Just keep it that way."

When they said their good-byes on the street, Frank and Scott watched Johnny and his group walk away. Scott opened the car door for Maria. She got in. Both men then slid into the front seat. Scott looked back at Maria. "You have a nice time with Gina?"

She nodded. "Yes. She's a smart woman. I like her."

Scott chuckled. "You seemed to get a lot of attention from the young man in there."

She waved her hand at him. "Young men. You know them."

"Yes, I do." He turned around and slipped on his seat belt.

"Are you worried, Scott?" Frank asked.

Scott had a rather distant look as he watched the traffic speed by. He shook his head. "I'm thinking about Johnny. The man's over his head. He's been herding sheep for years, and there's a big difference between being a shepherd and a lion tamer. One mistake and he won't lose a sheep; he'll lose his head."

Frank nodded. "True."

Scott unsnapped the brass clasps on his briefcase and opened it. He rifled through the papers inside.

"Anything wrong?"

Scott looked up the street. Johnny and the group had disappeared. "Yeah, something is very wrong."

"What's that?"

Scott glanced back at Maria, then looked Frank in the eye. "The pictures that I was bringing back from Cuba—they're gone."

CHAPTER 30

When they pulled out of the hotel parking lot, Johnny felt a deep sense of sadness sweep over him. He missed friendship with men he knew and who knew him. There was something refreshing about being able to talk to someone he didn't have to impress. As a pastor he had very few friends. Being friends with anyone in his congregation meant he was playing favorites. Jealousy was the inevitable result. For a brief time tonight, he had been able to put all that behind him and it felt good.

Junior was behind the wheel, with Johnny and Gina in the backseat. Rocko sat up front with Junior, giving directions.

"Where are we going?" Johnny asked.

Rocko smiled. "Someplace safe. I made sure of that. I picked out a good spot. You'll like it. It's quiet like a church." He laughed. "In fact it is a church."

They wound their way through Miami and turned onto the old Dixie Highway. It wasn't long before the lights of the city were behind them. Trees covered with Spanish moss dotted the road, opening up into moonlit ponds. It was almost a picture postcard, a dark one.

Rocko pointed to a dark, overgrown structure beside the road. "There it is, just up ahead. Pull over."

Junior pulled over to an unlit curb and turned off the engine. They could see the building, but barely. A flagstone walkway wound its way from the curb to the main entrance. Most of the windows were dark.

"What is this place?" Johnny asked.

Rocko looked back at him. "It's called the cloisters of Saint Bernard de Clairvaux. I guess the church it was taken from is still in Spain."

Gina sat up. Suddenly, she was interested. "Taken from? This place is stolen?"

Rocko laughed. "You could say that. It comes from an eight-hundred-year-old church north of Madrid, Spain. William Randolph Hearst bought it. He was going to use the place to surround his swimming pool in San Simeon, California. The stones were taken down, packed in hay, and shipped across the Atlantic. But when they got here the boxes were quarantined. They stayed here until Hearst died. Then the problem was, how to put the forty thousand stones back together. I guess they solved it, cause here it is." He laughed louder. "The chapel is still in Spain, but the cloister is right here. Folks get married here and they have services."

The four got out of the car. "I don't see any other cars," Gina said.

Rocko smiled. "That's right. We're early. I kinda like it that way. Myself, I'd rather be the cat waiting on the bird than the other way around."

The doorway that led into the cloister had a distinctive, carved-stone coat of arms, a roaring lion with crossed swords. They walked up the steps and opened the door. All was silent.

"Man, it's quiet in here," Junior said.

"Sort of like a church," Johnny said.

"That'll all change when Trafficante gets here," Rocko added. "The man's got his self a set of lungs, and he ain't gonna be too happy with driving to this place. He'd rather talk to us over a plate of pasta and a glass of wine."

The inside of the cloister contained a sweeping set of hallways that circled an inner garden of palm and banana trees. Stone arches looked out on the garden, each with carved pillars. The roof overhead was all stone, each piece fitted into place with curvatures that vaulted into peaks in the ceiling. The floor was oak, dark and light squares of finely polished wood that echoed with each step they took.

They took the hallway to their right. Rocko laughed. "One thing about this place, we're gonna hear anybody who comes in long before we see them. It's why I picked it." He smiled. "Plus it really spooks old Santos."

They came to a small chapel. Even though it wasn't an original part of the building, it still maintained a Gothic look. The dark pews were padded with wine-colored cushions. The far wall had a series of confessional booths with doors and opaque screening to protect the confidence of sinners. A battery of candles glowed along the other wall, red and white candles, some low and some freshly lit. Their flickering flames cast shadows over the stones. The front of the church contained the altar and a pulpit. Behind that was a carving of the bleeding and dying Jesus on a cross.

Rocko stopped the group and pointed to the image of Jesus. "Now how can a man stand before that and lie to us? I ask you."

Johnny smiled. "I'm sure if anyone can, it would be Santos Trafficante. The man has practice."

Rocko pointed at Junior. "Stand over there in the shadows, and stay there until I call you. Kinda like to have Santos a little surprised from time to time."

Then he looked at Gina.

She shook her head. "I'm not going anywhere. I want to see and hear it all."

Rocko raked his jaw with his big paw. "Well, OK. It don't make us look too tough, bringing a woman along. But I reckon we can chance it."

"You're not expecting trouble, are you?" Johnny asked.

Rocko shook his head. "Nah, not here, not now. Santos will try and surprise us. I know the man. He don't like people to call him out of his ordinary routine, and we don't have much to offer him. He might tell us something, though, if he thinks he can get rid of us that way. Come here, kid. I gotta get you ready."

Rocko put his arm on Johnny's shoulder and led him toward the altar. He spoke in low tones so that only Johnny could hear. "You hear how I'm talking to you now?"

Johnny nodded.

"Well, if Trafficante takes you and talks to you this way, then you listen close, ya hear? A guy like Santos, he's a member of the mob. He's untouchable unless he tells somebody something they ain't suppose to know. He'll have soldiers with him, but he ain't gonna say nothing important unless you're the only one who can hear. A guy like Santos Trafficante don't talk to more than five or six people a day, and never on the phone. He don't want nobody hearing anything he has to say. And if he tells you something important, something he knows he ain't supposed to say, and one of them boys of his rats on him, then he's gonna get whacked. So he ain't gonna say nothing to nobody unless he's feeling generous and nobody's listening."

Rocko stepped back and pushed Johnny away slightly. He lifted his chin up and let his eyelids droop for effect. "But if he wants to say anything that might even be close to the truth, he'll pick you to tell it to."

"Why me?"

"Cause you ain't in the business. The cops ain't gonna bust you and force you to rat him out, and even if they did, it would be his word against yours. He knows you was always your papa's favorite kid. Maybe he'd do it as a tribute to your old man, ease his own conscience."

Rocko smiled at him and straightened his collar. Then he ran his hands down the lapels of Johnny's jacket. "OK, kid, you ready for this?"

Johnny shrugged his shoulders. "I guess."

"Good, kid." Rocko patted his cheeks with both hands.

Less than a half-hour passed before they heard the sound of footsteps in the hall. Junior drifted back into the shadows just as Trafficante, flanked by two of his thugs, stepped through the door. A blond woman trailed the group. She looked to be in her early forties, with hair piled on top of her head and a low-cut dress that clung to her ample figure.

Trafficante was wearing a pea-green double-breasted suit with a white rose stuck in his lapel. A swooping white hat cut a dashing line down his forehead, cutting across his left eye. He was carrying a pair of soft yellow leather gloves and a gold-tipped cane.

He stepped toward Rocko and cracked a broad smile. "Buonasera." Reaching over, he grabbed Rocko by the shoulders and planted kisses on each of the big man's cheeks. The grin never left his face. He patted Rocko on his stomach. "Hey, you gonna be a big old man some day. Maka your mama proud."

Rocko pulled Gina forward. "This is Gina Cumo, old family friend and our lawyer."

Trafficante cocked his head and glared at Rocko. "You figure you gonna need a lawyer?" He bowed to Gina and kissed her hand. "La bello donna. I love a beautiful woman no matter what she is."

Rocko nodded in Johnny's direction. "And this is Johnny Pera. You remember him."

"Sure." Trafficante reached out to Johnny and pulled him closer. He kissed his cheeks. "You play football. And a Marine, a hero, if I recall." He held Johnny by both hands and looked into his eyes. "And you went into the church business too. Am I right?"

Johnny nodded silently.

"And not a priest."

"Right," Johnny said.

"That's OK by me." He slapped Johnny's arms. "You still a fine man, the apple of your papa's eye."

He looked back at Rocko. "So to what do I owe the honor of this visit of yours? Why you come to see me, and in a place like this?"

"I figure we could talk without other ears around. I don't like people snooping around in family business."

"But why here? Why not my club?"

"You're busy there," Rocko said. "People come and go. Here we can have you without other people coming in to jabber."

"OK, OK. So what you want to talk about?"

He looked back. "Hey, this here's Gloria."

The woman smiled, showing a bright set of teeth.

Rocko dropped his voice to a low, rolling subliminal growl. "Why did you bring her here?"

Trafficante grinned. "Hey, ain't she gonna be welcomed in your family no more? The Crow never went anywhere without her when he came to Miami. You know that. I just figured you'd want to see her again. You know, see how I was treating her right."

Johnny could see that Rocko's face was turning red. "Now I've seen," Rocko said. "You're embarrassing her and the kid here too."

"What do you mean?" Trafficante reached out and took Johnny's arm. "The kid was a Marine, wasn't he? He's a man of the world. He can handle all that. He must have known his dad liked women."

"Send her back to the car," Rocko said. "I don't want her around."

Trafficante walked back to where his men were standing with the woman. He started talking to them.

Rocko took Johnny's arm and led him a few steps in the opposite direction. "I'm sorry about this, kid." He glanced back to where Trafficante was explaining himself to the woman. "I think Santos is just trying to get your guard down, make us forget why we came. The man's like that. If he can find a way to get under your skin, he'll do it."

Johnny watched as one of Trafficante's men led the woman out of the chapel. Trafficante turned around and grinned at him, then walked over to where he was standing with Rocko.

"OK, big guy," Trafficante said, "let's cut to the chase. You want to know if I had anything to do with the Crow's being whacked. Well, I didn't. I wasn't too happy about what he done, pulling out of this hit on Castro. I figured he owed us something, but he didn't see it that way. So he goes his way on this and we went ours. End of story."

"We figure it was the Cubans, and you got them people wired. They're almost like a private army of yours, and don't go to telling me no different. You scratch their backs and whack Castro and they scratch yours."

Rocko shot a glance to where Junior was standing in the shadows and nodded slightly. Junior stepped out into the light.

Trafficante noticed Junior right away. "Hey, you brought muscle. What you gonna do, try to take me out in a church?"

"I don't need muscle." Rocko clenched his right fist and flexed his muscles. "I got enough on my own. You know that. You got guys. We got guys. You reach over to the West Coast where we are, and we can reach over here too."

"Yeah, I already saw Baldassare and his little army. He came to see me and I sent him home."

"You saw Baldy?"

"Yeah." Trafficante smirked. "He tried to get tough with me, but I wasn't having any of that. He had guns. I had guns. You gonna try and pull a bad-boy Pera on me too? I had enough of that. You can't come into a man's home and make him feel like he owes you something."

Rocko shook his head. "Nah, we don't have to do that."

"Then why don't your boy over there walk your woman to the car too? That'll make it even. It'll just be us in here to talk."

Rocko walked over to where Junior was standing and called Gina to come and talk with them. Trafficante stepped up to Johnny and took his arm. He led him away. "Look, Johnny, I'm sorry. I didn't mean to embarrass you like this."

"You really think you can tear down a man in front of his son? You think I'm going to hear something about some girlfriend my father once had and that's going to make me forget about what happened to him?" Johnny looked him in the eye. "That's not going to happen. My father wasn't perfect. I know that. He was into crime up to his ears, and he had to wallow with people who did it. I don't forgive him for that. I don't have to. That's God's place, not mine."

"I know you're just trying to find out the truth, but it won't happen this way."

"I don't know much about how to make it happen, but I can promise you this, unless I find out the truth, all the truth, I'm going to be a sore on your backside for a long time. You're going to see me whenever you get up in the morning, and my face will be the last one you see at night. And I won't be alone. I have friends, friends who can make your life miserable."

"You talking about Frank Bass?"

Johnny nodded. "You bet I am. How'd you know I was with Frank?"

Trafficante smiled. "I got men everywhere in this town. We know everything. Look, I don't want no trouble with you, and I sure don't want no FBI on my tail all day. I got no beef with your family. They got their action, and I got mine."

He continued to walk with Johnny in the direction of the altar. Johnny could tell that the conversation was making Trafficante suddenly nervous. Sweat was beginning to bead on his forehead. It glistened in the candlelight. "I know you ain't no part of your family's business, and I trust you. We didn't really need your papa, just his blessing. Even now I got three men in Cuba to do what we want done there. We got it all planned out. We're gonna whack that lousy dictator during a big parade in Havana. We'll have shooters from three directions. That slime ain't gonna know what hit him. We even got us a Cuban patsy to take the fall. It'll be clean and tidy. They'll get their killer and it'll be one of them."

"Why are you telling me this?"

"I just want you to know that we didn't need the Crow to do this thing. We had no reason to kill the man, no reason at all. If I were you, I'd start looking closer to home."

"What do you mean?"

"Your papa wasn't letting some of his people advance, you know, get their own place."

"Their place?"

"You know, get casinos, get a business, make money." Trafficante balled his fist up in front of Johnny's face. "He was keeping things tight, not letting Chicago money in and not letting his own people spread out. The Crow was always like that, rest his soul. He was afraid if he let people branch out that they'd be on their own totally. He didn't want nothing happening in Vegas that didn't go into his pocket."

Johnny shook his head. "I don't know anything about family business, and I'd like to keep it that way."

"You better find out about your family's business and quick if you want to get to the bottom of this thing."

Later in the car, Johnny leaned over and spoke to Gina in the backseat. He lowered his voice. "You still got the number to that bookstore, that one the Cuban gave you?"

"Yes." Gina opened her purse and reached in to retrieve the card.

Johnny put his hand on hers. "Hang on to it. We may have something to tell him, something I don't think Trafficante in there wanted to come out. He just got nervous."

CHAPTER 31

Early the next morning Johnny heard a knock at his door. He was only half dressed in his khaki slacks and had been picking over what was left of an order of eggs Benedict. The paper on his bed was open to the funnies, and his hair was still uncombed. In most places he no doubt would still have been asleep since the night before had been a long one. But with the airy, next-to-nothing curtains, he couldn't help but get up with the sun.

When he opened the door, he saw Frank and Scott standing in the hall. Johnny could tell they had something unpleasant on their minds. "Come in. I was just eating breakfast."

Scott was wearing a set of starched fatigues, and Frank had on a rumpled, cream-colored suit. Only his shirt was pressed. "We have a problem," Frank said.

Johnny motioned to the couch. "Have a seat. I'll pour you some coffee and you can tell me about it."

"None for me," Scott said.

Frank picked up a cup and held it out. Johnny poured.

"Something was stolen from my attaché case last night while I was on the balcony with you," Scott said.

"Stolen? You've got to be kidding?"

"I'm afraid he isn't. What was taken is a matter of government security—some very important photographs of a Russian missile site in Cuba. Scott risked his life to get those photos. One of your friends must have taken them."

Scott looked at Johnny. "Those pictures belong in the president's hands. I could kick myself for not taking them to the rightful people when I first got back to Florida. I blame myself. Now I've got to get them back, and fast."

"Are you sure it wasn't the bellhop who delivered the coffee or the Key lime pie?"

Scott shook his head. "Couldn't have been. It had to be one of your three friends."

"Could it have been the woman you brought, this Maria woman?"

"No way. She put her life on the line to get those pictures the same as I did."

"Maybe she's got second thoughts about those pictures."

"I don't think so."

Johnny took a slug of coffee and sat down on the bed. He picked up his socks and put them on. "We'll think of something."

"We'd better," Scott said. "What about that big Mafia thug, the one called Rocko?"

Johnny shook his head. "I don't know what any of my people would want with the pictures. They have no interest in Cuba, apart from finding out what happened to my dad."

"They could be worth a lot of money to the wrong people," Scott shot back.

"Not to change the subject," Frank said, "but did you call home last night?"

"Yes I did, but I really didn't have to. We met with Santos Trafficante after our time with you last night, and he told us Baldassare had paid him a visit."

"I was afraid of that. Did Trafficante tell you where your brother is or where he went after this little visit of his?"

Johnny shook his head. "No, just that he'd been there. I got the idea that there were threats involved. You know Baldy, headstrong and stubborn. He was supposed to stay in California and leave this up to me, but the man has a tough time with just sitting."

"He's a hothead," Frank added.

"Yes, he's that all right."

"I'm going to check around town and see what I can come up with," Frank said. "I've been thinking about your brother ever since Trafficante's casino boat was knocked over." He held his hands up to Johnny. "Don't try to defend him. It just sounded like something Baldassare would do. The fact that I know he's been trying to bust Trafficante's chops didn't make me think about anyone else either." He shook his head. "Stupid thing to do."

"What about my problem?" Scott asked.

Johnny stuffed his feet into his shoes. He got up and walked to the window. "Maybe we can help each other."

"I'm all ears," Scott said.

Johnny walked back and opened a drawer. He took out a white polo shirt and shook it out. "Why don't we go out to those Cubans of yours today. You can talk to my people, and I can get to know this

Maria person. I might be able to tell if in fact she's had a change of mind. She probably wouldn't tell you. Frank can find some way to get into my people's rooms while we're gone. If those photos of yours are there, then he can get them."

"Get your shirt on and I'll show you an army that's determined to lose," Scott said.

Johnny pulled out a small holster and strapped it to his ankle. He then took out a small Walther PPK and stuck it in the holster, pulling his pant leg over it. He grinned sheepishly. "I'm learning to stay pre-pared."

Over an hour later they rounded the curve that led to the Cuban camp and got out. Johnny, Gina, Rocko, and Junior were in the Buick, and Scott and Maria were in a white jeep Scott had borrowed from the Navy.

Scott motioned to Johnny. "I'll take you and the rest of your people into the command shack, but Maria's staying out here. I don't want her face seen by these people, not just now. Maybe you two can use my jeep and take a drive later. I'll keep your people busy and ask questions."

"Fine by me." Johnny glanced at Maria. The woman was wearing fatigue pants and a shirt. She was beautiful.

The group followed Scott over the walkway and into the command shack. The place looked surprisingly comfortable on the inside, with a stove and cabinets. Two single beds were flanked by nightstands. A large desk sat in the middle of the room, and behind it was a radio set and a safe marked AMERICAN BANANA COMPANY. The safe was out-of-date but served its function.

Scott talked to the two men who sat at their desks. He glanced back at Johnny and the group, no doubt explaining who they were and why they were here.

The wall closest to the pond was only a half-wall with screens. It looked out on the water. Junior walked over to it and looked outside. He was soon followed by Rocko and Gina.

"What do you think?" Johnny asked. "Could you live here?"

"Not for long."

Scott brought the two men who had been at their desks over to meet them. "Allow me to introduce you folks to the commander. This is Javier Lage and Bolivar, his second in command. They run the camp."

Scott handed Johnny the keys to the jeep. "Why don't you take our friend out there for a spin? I'll take care of these folks and see that they get lunch."

Johnny took the keys and gave Scott a slight salute. "Sounds good to me." He glanced at Gina. "Just make sure you don't feed them to the 'gators."

Gina frowned at him. "And you make sure you don't get into anything dangerous."

Johnny laughed. "Don't worry about me."

He climbed inside the jeep. "Ready to go for a ride?"

Maria nodded. "Sure."

Johnny started the jeep. "I'm supposed to keep you out of harm's way, make sure your face isn't seen around here."

They started on the road around the large pond. Johnny wanted to make certain they didn't stay close to the Cuban camp. Prying eyes wouldn't do. He didn't much want to head back into town either. There might be incoming traffic that way, and he didn't want Maria to be seen. Scott had made that point quite clear.

They soon came to a smaller road on their left, which veered off from a large black oak tree. Johnny swung the wheel, and the jeep hit several bumps and a series of ruts.

When they emerged from the trees, the swamp stretched out in front of them, an endless sea of grass. On the far side there was a line of trees. The causeway they were on led to the trees beyond. "Nothing but miles of nothing," Johnny said.

"I wouldn't say that. I think it's pretty." A flock of blue herons took to the air. "And the birds are beautiful," she added.

They drove straight for the trees on the other side of the grassy sea. "Cuba's not like this, is it?"

"Some parts are, but not quite as pretty. We have nice land, though. The farmers are pleased, but they can't make a living there, not anymore."

"Communism?"

"Yes, the communists. The people who used to have anything have had it taken away and given to people who earn nothing because they are lazy. So now everyone is poor, even the people who used to feed the country. There is no reason to work anymore. Castro's legacy will be a nation of slothful serfs, sluggish and unable to take care of themselves. My brother died to bring him to power, and my father died because he gained power. I hate them, hate all of them."

"Hatred is a bitter pill to swallow. It only poisons you."

"Aren't you here because you hate the men who killed your father? The colonel told me a little of your story."

"I don't know them. How can I hate them?"

"You will hate them. You're the same as me."

Johnny smiled at her. "Well, I'm a sinner the same as you are, if that's what you mean. But I don't want to hate anybody. I just want justice."

"That's where it begins. You want justice the same as me. But there are men who will try to stop you. They will kill the people you love the most, and the rest they will force to their knees. You'll watch and the anger inside of you will grow. Finally, it will become hatred. Then you will be like me."

They came over the causeway, and the road banked into a stand of tall oaks. Ribbons of Spanish moss hung from the trees, and shade covered the road. "There must be people living here. There's a shack up there," Johnny said. "Would you like to stop and take a look around?"

Maria shrugged. "Why not?"

They drove behind the trees, and Johnny stopped the jeep. A small shack sat on a bluff overlooking the swamp.

They got out of the jeep and started up the hill. When they got to the shack, Johnny creaked open the door and they stepped inside. Inside were tables surrounded by a carpet of spent brass cartridges. "The Cubans must use this place," Johnny said.

Maria nodded. "Yes, probably to shoot alligators and birds. No doubt that's all they're good for, target practice against things that can't shoot back."

"You don't sound very hopeful about that group. I would think you would be. Aren't they trying to free your country?"

Maria laughed. "I think they're trying to free American dollars. Maybe they gave up after the Bay of Pigs. Power is all they want now, power and money."

"And so these pictures you took with Colonel Gordon, are they worthless too?"

Maria crossed her arms and shook her head. "I don't know, maybe. If they help the Americans invade, then they are not worthless. But if they just give the Americans an excuse to stay away, if the missiles scare them off, then they're less than worthless. They could harm us. We might never get the help we need."

Johnny opened the door. "Why don't we follow this path outside and see where it leads us?"

The two of them started down the path, skirting the marshy swamp. The ground was packed but damp, the product of a hard rain. Overhead, the trees spread out. It took them almost an hour of walking before they came to a clearing. A small pond was in front of them with a house on the other side. It wasn't much of a house, but there was a dock that had a rowboat tied to it. Smoke rose from the chimney.

"You suppose they're friendly?" Johnny asked.

Suddenly, a shot rang out and hit the tree next to where they were standing. Both of them flattened out on the ground.

"You varmints." The voice sounded out over the pond. "Didn't Jimmy tell you he never wanted to see your lousy hides ever again?"

Maria looked at him. "Does that answer your question? Nobody lives out here that's friendly."

Johnny inched his head up. "Don't shoot. We're unarmed."

He looked at Maria. She was wearing a shoulder holster with the butt of a .45 sticking out from it.

"Then stand up and come ahead, but real slowlike."

Johnny looked at Maria. "You'd better lose that horse pistol."

"No way," she said. "I'd be naked, and I don't know that man."

"Don't worry. I have an ankle gun, and I won't let anything happen to you."

He got to his feet slowly and held his hands over his head. "Besides, we just might learn something from an outsider here."

Reluctantly, Maria unstrapped her pistol and laid it on the ground. She got to her feet.

They slowly approached the house. The place was rundown and sat on a mixture of concrete and cinder blocks with a screened-in front porch. They made their way around the pond and could see several alligators submerged among the lily pads.

"Come on up and through the front door," the voice shouted. "I want to get a better look at you."

They walked up the rickety steps, and Johnny opened the screen door. Maria stepped in and Johnny behind her.

The man suddenly emerged from the open front door. He was barefoot and wearing frayed, cutoff jeans and a Miami Dolphins T-shirt smeared with red stains. He stared down the barrel of a bolt-action .30-06. "Who the blazes are you people, and what do you want?"

Johnny tried to force a smile. "I'm Johnny Pera, and this is Maria."

The man lowered his rifle and looked at Maria. "Humph. I thought you might be them Cubans. They always come snooping 'round where they don't belong. Nobody asked them to come here, but they done took over this place, 'cept for what belongs to Jimmy here."

The man waved his rifle. "Come on in. I'm cookin' in here."

The man backed up, the rifle still pointed at them. The front room had a worn brown sofa and chair with newspapers all over the floor. Stacks of newspapers filled the room, some over a man's head. One wall was covered by an enormous Confederate flag.

"I see you're still fighting the Civil War," Johnny said.

The man spat on the newspaper-covered floor. "Weren't no civil war. It was the war of Yankee aggression, folks trying to make other folks knuckle under."

"Can we put our hands down?" Johnny asked.

The man frowned and lowered his rifle. "I guess you can. You look harmless, Yankee tourists who get themselves lost. It happens." He waved the rifle, pointing them into the kitchen.

Johnny and Maria stepped into the kitchen. Their eyes widened. The place had two ovens and a six-burner stove. Ducks were hanging, coated in a glistening sauce. Pot-and-pan shaped mirrors hung on a rack over the burners. Two large cutting boards were scrubbed clean. One had an array of mushrooms and spices along with grated cheese, and the other a large roast that was sliced open.

"I take it you're a cook?" Johnny asked.

"Nah." He stood his rifle by the door. "Jimmy here is a chef. I studied in Paris for three years. I can make every sauce known to mortal man and a number mortal man ain't never heard of yet. Although mine are too good to be wasted on mortal man. Set yerselves down." He pointed to a red table with ladder-back chairs around it.

Reaching over the burner, he took down a large pan. He picked up a small clove of garlic and sliced it in two. Placing the pan on the burner, he picked up a bottle and sprinkled oil in the pan. He then shook salt on the bottom of it. "Got to have the salt. It makes the garlic dig itself into the pan." He picked up the garlic and swished it into the pan, rubbing it carefully.

Sitting the pan over the open flame, he reached into a pot and picked out a handful of crayfish. He dropped them into the bubbling oil and added a collection of spices. Picking up a wooden spatula, he stirred the mixture. He reached for a bottle of red wine and added it to the mix. "I hope you like this. It's my own recipe."

They finished the meal close to an hour later. Jimmy pushed himself back from the table and stared at Maria. "Ain't had me a meal across from a pretty woman in a coon's age. Figured if I was gonna shoot you, I ought to at least feed ya first."

Johnny smiled and rubbed his stomach. "I'd say we could die happy."

The man reached into a tin can that had the Quaker Oats man on it and pulled out a twisted black cigar. He bit off the end and spat it on the floor. He held it out to Johnny. "Care for a cheroot?"

"No, thanks," Johnny said. "I don't smoke."

"I'll take one." Maria smiled and reached for one. She bit off the end and spit it onto the floor, then grinned at the man. "What's the matter? You never seen a woman smoke a cigar before?"

Jimmy sat with his cigar hanging out of his mouth. "No, can't say that I have, least not a pretty woman."

Maria reached for a match that was standing in a cracked cup on the table and held it in her hand. She pushed her thumbnail over it, igniting a flame. Holding it up to her cigar, she puffed the thing to life. "I'm from Cuba," she said, continuing to puff a cloud of gray smoke. "You know, where they have those Cubans."

"Well, I'll be."

"We aren't all alike. I'm not with those people you see around here."

"I'll say you're not." He raked his match across the table and lit his cigar. "You know, we see many a queer thing out here in the Everglades, most of them from Mother Nature, but a few stupid things left by people."

"Like what?" Johnny asked.

The man got to his feet. "Come on with me. I'll show you something mighty strange. I come across it yesterday, and you ain't gonna believe me telling you about it."

They walked out by the path where they had come in. Maria stooped over and picked up her .45. She grinned at the man and looked at Johnny. "He said we were unarmed, so I left my pistol here."

Jimmy scratched his head. "That's some kind of pistol. Didn't think I'd ever see a woman carrying one of those."

"Maria is a different type of woman," Johnny said.

"You can say that again, mister."

They hiked through the woods and took a different path, one that led down the slope to the bogs below. Large dragonflies flitted across the path, their translucent wings shining in the light. Jimmy still carried his rifle, and Johnny kept it in sight. "You don't plan on using that on us, do you?" he asked.

"Nah, but we still have us panther out here. Mostly they kill a man's goats and chickens, but sometimes they take out after people. It don't do to get caught out here after dark. Bad business."

They cleared the trees and saw the road below them. Jimmy pointed to the swamp. "Right down there."

When they crossed the road, Jimmy stopped and squatted down. Johnny and Maria got low next to him "This here is the Everglades. Natural springs and rivers feed this sea of grass, along with city sewage, cow pastures, and citrus groves. All Florida is connected to this here place in some way or another, and we got almost every critter on earth that's fit to call a critter. The United States tried to best the Injuns who lived here, but they couldn't. The Yankees tried to whip my great-granddaddy's people here, but they couldn't." He looked Johnny in the eye. "We never did surrender, mind you. We is still unreconstructed."

He pointed to the dark water just offshore. "Old boss 'bino lives there. He's the ghost that swims, an albino alligator, pure white as the driven snow with big blue eyes. He ain't like nothing you ever seen before. Injuns say he's a spook, but I steer clear of him. That's what I thought I was seeing at first."

Jimmy got to his feet and looked at them. "But 'tweren't the old boss, not at all."

"What was it?" Johnny asked.

Jimmy shook his head. "Come with me, but you ain't gonna believe it. Pure foolishness it is, no doubt drunken foolishness."

He led them down a path to a spot next to the water, then pointed. They could see the rear of a white Cadillac with its Florida plates, UXV-1143. "Now why you reckon folks would want to drive their new Cadillac down into that swamp? It don't make no sense. Musta been plumb drunk when it happened."

IN A DACHA ON THE BLACK SEA
WEDNESDAY, OCTOBER 10

CHAPTER 32

The blustery old man of the Kremlin was always at his best on the beach. Biryuzov knew that much about him. The breeze and the warm weather always agreed with him and made him more thoughtful and less confrontational. He could take bad news easier when he was on holiday.

Sergei Biryuzov was now a marshal in the Soviet army and was considered somewhat of a missile expert, which was rare in the high command. Most high-ranking Soviet officers were refugees from the great war, ex-cavalry officers, people who were used to waving their swords in the air and making noises that sounded like Joseph Stalin.

They had to give good imitations of the man in order to have survived the great purges. Biryuzov was different. He looked the part with his high hat and cardboard-stiff collar, but he knew he was different. His swords were ICBMs and MRBMs. To him, the front lines were everywhere. He stood tall, over six feet, and had ice blue eyes.

The dacha was more than just a beach house. It was isolated and had a commanding view. Khrushchev could sit for hours and read the papers from the patio. It was his favorite thing to do. He devoured the Western press, absorbing every nuance of what the minds on the other side of the world were thinking.

Biryuzov's driver let him out at the front door, and he walked with long strides up the stairs, saluting the guards who opened the door for him. He made his way through the front sitting room and out the large French doors that led to the patio. Then he saw Khrushchev. The man was in baggy swim trunks and a red shirt. He was staring out to sea through the eyepiece of a telescope.

Biryuzov snapped his heels to attention and saluted. "Comrade Premier. Marshal Biryuzov, reporting as ordered."

Khrushchev waved him forward. "Come here, Biryuzov. I want you to look through this."

Biryuzov stepped forward and looked through the opening of the telescope.

"Do you know what you're looking at?" Khrushchev barked.

"Turkey, sir."

"That's right. And what else?"

Biryuzov stepped back. "Just Turkey, sir, the beaches of Turkey."

Khrushchev pointed a stubby finger in the direction they had been looking. "More than that, Comrade Marshal. You are looking at American Jupiter missiles aimed at my dacha." He hammered his right fist down on his open left hand. "They are staring right at us, daring us to do anything."

"The Jupiter missile is a liquid-fuel missile, Comrade Premier. It is not very accurate."

"They don't have to be accurate!" Khrushchev bellowed. "They have nuclear warheads on them. Who could survive even a miss?"

"Yes sir. You are right."

"Of course I'm right." He shook his finger in the direction of the water. "What do you intend to do about them?"

"I have just returned from Cuba, Comrade Premier. I have good news for you."

"Tell me. I need good news."

"We have successfully completed the most ambitious landing ever attempted by Soviet forces, and right under the noses of the Americans. It has been a remarkable logistical feat, Comrade Premier. We have placed MRBMs, medium-range ballistic missiles, as well as IRBMs, intermediate-range ballistic missiles, right under the belly of the Americans. In Cuba all those missiles are strategic weapons, capable of reaching the largest of the American cities, including Washington. We also have IL-28 medium-range bombers, MiG-21 fighters, antiaircraft missile batteries, short-range nuclear battlefield rockets, and forty-two thousand Soviet troops. Even though all this has taken place just off their own coastline, the Americans have hardly noticed.

Khrushchev leaned against the iron railing. "I don't like it."

"Don't like what, Comrade Premier?"

"I don't like those Jupiter missiles staring down at me while I swim."

"The supreme leader in Cuba is very happy with our missiles in his country." Biryuzov smiled. "He actually thinks he's doing us a favor."

"Us a favor? Where does he get such an idea?"

Biryuzov inched closer. "He believes that with our setbacks in China and the rise of Japan as a democracy, along with Western Europe, we need a show of strength to keep our allies in the Soviet orbit. He has confidence in what we can do. When you said our missiles could pick a fly out of the sky, Comrade Castro believed you. He has no questions about our ability and no idea of the gap we face. You said we were turning out rockets like sausages."

"I know. I know what I said. But American missiles outnumber ours by—what was your estimate?"

"Seventeen to one, Comrade Premier."

"He doesn't know that, does he?"

"No, Comrade Premier."

Khrushchev turned around and once more stared out to sea. "I love that man and love what he is doing." He glanced back at Biryuzov. "He's a believer you know. He wants to free the common man all over Central America, free him from the greed of the capitalists. But we are doing Comrade Castro a favor by having our missiles there. The Yankees have already tried to invade him once. They will do it again and again and again. They cannot have, will not tolerate, a socialist state in their own hemisphere. You know that as well as I do."

"But Comrade Premier, Minister Gromyko has already concluded that the conditions in which he can imagine an American intervention in Cuba simply do not exist."

"And you believe him?"

"He is our expert on the Americans. Why shouldn't I believe him?"

"Believe what you want, but prepare for the worst. Me, I choose to believe the worst. I always believe the worst. The Americans will not allow a socialist state ninety miles away from their home."

Once again, he turned and pointed out to sea. "And I cannot allow American Jupiter missiles to hover over my breakfast table." He gripped the iron railing. "The people have suffered enough." He shook his head. "The Red Army had to fire on strikers in Novocherkassk who were protesting rising food prices. The people don't have enough to eat, and what they have is in such short supply that the common worker cannot afford it. We fought the revolution because of this, and here it is again, once more at our doorstep."

"But Cuba, Comrade Premier, Cuba is finally safe."

"You did communicate my orders about the missiles, didn't you, Comrade Marshall?"

"To raise them only at night?"

"Yes. I want them down during the daylight hours and only raised in the vertical position and ready at night. Maybe the banana trees can hide them."

"Yes, Comrade Premier. I gave the order."

"Good. And the written military orders?"

Biryuzov nodded. "Just as you requested. For months now they have only been written in longhand, no typing whatsoever."

Khrushchev smiled. "Fine. I don't want any chances taken. This is all to be done undercover."

"I'm afraid I don't understand your reasoning for this, Comrade Premier. Why not let the Americans and the world know that we are there in force? Surely that would be better than having them discover it in secret. If they believe that we are trying to sneak up on them, wouldn't it be easier to conclude that we are planning a first strike? Surely that could prove dangerous."

"It is," Khrushchev snapped his fingers, "How do the Americans say? My rabbit in the air."

"Out of the hat, sir. The rabbit comes out of the hat."

Khrushchev pointed his finger. "Well, this rabbit is staying in the hat. The Americans are flexing their muscles, and they won't see mine until they need to."

"Sir, the American Strategic Air Command already has half of their bomber force ready to take off within fifteen minutes. They have raised their alert status to DEFCON 3. Some of their crews are away from their own homes for as much as eighty to ninety hours a week.

They are also getting their Minuteman missiles ready. Some are what the Americans would say are 'hot-wired' to short-circuit the necessary precautions. Our sources tell us that Strategic Air Command field officers have been given great discretion in when they are allowed to launch their weapons. Any nervousness at all could be fatal."

"Those missiles?" Khrushchev turned and looked once again in the direction of Turkey. "Those inaccurate missiles? Are you telling me some American colonel could send them flying into my house here on the beach and without orders?"

"Yes sir. That is what I am telling you."

"That is why I am telling you they must go."

Biryuzov shook his head. "The Americans will not do that. Turkey is a NATO country. America cannot make a decision like that apart from the NATO command. To do so would mean betraying their allies. They would give up their position of leadership, and the entire NATO structure might very well collapse."

"Good. That is just what we want."

"Not even Kennedy is that stupid, Comrade Premier. He will invade Cuba before he allows that to happen."

"More likely they will assassinate Castro."

"Yes, Comrade Premier. They will kill him and then invade during all the confusion. That is what our sources tell us, that the Americans have hired assassins sent to murder Castro. When that happens, they will show a pretense of a Cuban exile invasion along with a few populist groups followed by a Marine landing."

"In spite of our forces on the island?"

"The Americans do not know our strength. Their estimates are far too low. That is why I suggested that we make our presence known to them. When they know how strong we are, then perhaps we can have peace in the Caribbean."

"I will think about what you have said, Comrade Marshal."

CHAPTER 33

Junior saw himself more as an opportunist than as anything else. He didn't have the physical size of a Rocko, and he couldn't back people down just by walking up to them. Most of the intimidation he'd used over the past few years had been because of his connection to the Pera family. That and his brains. He had other talents too. He'd spent some time as a second-story man and a safecracker. He was a natural for that. He was athletic and had nerves of steel. It was as easy for him to hear the tumblers turn in a lock as it was for others to hear a lunch whistle. He had talent. He just needed to prove it. Up to this point, he'd pretty much felt like dead weight on this trip. That was going to change.

He stood on the gunnery range with a Cuban who was explaining the use of a fully automatic assault weapon. The weapon felt good under his cheek. The Cuban was an officer, but Johnny didn't think he looked all that smart. The man's name was Nasser.

Junior aimed the rifle and squeezed off a burst of fire.

"Hey, that's good," Nasser shouted. "You did good."

Junior lowered the rifle and grinned. "I bet you guys get real good with these things."

Nasser nodded. "Yeah, we do fine."

"You guys are such experts I'm guessing people want to use you for other work too." Junior had long ago learned that the way to a man's heart was through his ego. A man was most likely to say anything in the nature of bragging.

Nasser puffed up his chest and grinned. "Yeah, they do."

"Why, sure." Junior reached out and tapped the man on his chest. "They would want the best, and you're the best, right?"

"Yeah, we had a man in California hire some of us to take care of a problem. Got a plane ride. It was a nice trip."

Later over lunch Junior began to watch the exiles more intently. This bunch was more than an army. They had a vested interest in keeping their American hosts happy and could no doubt be satisfied with just a small retainer. And being caught might simply mean a slap on the wrists. They were perfect killers for hire. Most likely that's why Johnny had wanted them to come out here to the camp in the first place, to find out who might be involved and, more important, who had given the orders. He only hoped that Rocko and Gina had found out as much as he had.

He watched Rocko at the other end of the table. The man was a natural with people. He was sitting next to Bolivar, the man that Gordon had said was the second in command. Rocko was no doubt telling stories, trying to gain the man's confidence. Junior watched as Nasser, the officer who had been with him on the gunnery range, came over and talked to both Rocko and Bolivar.

Junior dropped his fork in the middle of his beans and looked at Gina. "How can you eat this stuff?"

Gina scooped up a forkful of the black beans. "It's not Italian."

"You can say that again."

"But it is edible, and I'm hungry."

They sat at the end of a long table. There was little talking among the men there, just the sound of metal forks and spoons hitting the tin plates and scraping up what remained of spicy pork and black beans. The tables were full of men, and few looked the part of any army Junior had ever seen. They were sweaty and bearded. Many seemed out of shape, and a few seemed to be much too old to serve in any army, much less this one. Junior thought they looked more like refugees from the unemployment line than men who were preparing to fight and die.

He watched Rocko get up from the far end of the table and walk his way. He could tell the man had something on his mind. Whatever Rocko was thinking, he tried to cover it up with a smile. Rocko stopped behind Junior and bent down close to his ear. "Hey kid, you really want to help? There is something you can do here that I don't think any of us could pull off."

"What's that?"

"You know how we been saying that whoever whacked the boss had to be involved with these Cubans?"

"Yeah."

"We ain't gonna find out anything hobnobbing with this here commander. We got to find a way to get close to the men. Somebody's got to know something. They ain't gonna talk to me, and they sure ain't gonna talk to Gina."

"Yeah, you're probably right about that."

"But you're young like they are. They'll drink with you, slap your back, and brag about what they know."

"What are you saying?"

"I figure if one of us was to stay around and sleep with these guys, you know, hang around the campfire at night, there might be something we could use."

"And you got me singled out for that?"

Rocko nodded. "Yeah. We can't leave Gina here, and I got myself a bad back. I need a firm bed. Plus, we got to figure on Johnny hanging out with his buddies. That leaves just you."

"OK, I'll do it."

It was late in the afternoon when Junior saw Johnny and Maria drive up in the jeep. Gordon had been pumping Junior with questions all during the tour, asking him what he thought of the Cuba problem and if he saw these people as ready to handle it. He'd pretty much shrugged off the questions, but knew he had acquitted himself well at the gunnery range. He had scored a number of bull's-eyes with the standard issue Colt .45 automatic, but it was the fully automatic weapon that really got him going.

Gordon took the assault rifle from his hand and laid it on a bench. "Not bad for someone who's not used to handling one of these."

"Thanks," Junior said. "Guess I'm a natural."

"I'd say you were." Gordon looked over in the direction of the jeep. "We'd better get over there. I don't want Maria's face seen around here, not just yet. I need to run her back to the hotel."

"Fine by me," Junior said.

They made their way over to the jeep. Rocko and Gina had already walked over to talk to Johnny, and Junior could tell that Rocko was discussing the plan of leaving Junior behind for the night. He stepped up to the jeep with Gordon by his side.

"You enjoy the swamp?" Gordon asked.

"It was interesting," Johnny said.

"Very," Maria added. She smiled at Johnny.

Junior could tell that Maria's sudden melting was not lost on Gina. "I'll just bet it was interesting," Gina said.

"Rocko tells me you're planning on spending the night here."

Junior shrugged his shoulders. "I guess so. But if I do, I'm keeping Gordon's jeep. You can all go back in the Buick. I'm not going to be stuck here with no way to get back on my own."

"Technically, it's a Navy vehicle," Gordon said.

"And you're a Marine," Junior said, "but I ain't gonna tell. We'll just say I'm you for the night."

"Sure, kid." Rocko reached out and slapped Junior on the back. "I'm sure the Colonel here can look the other way, just this once. 'Sides, you'll probably still be here with it when we get back in the morning."

Rocko looked over at Gordon. "What about it, Colonel? Can we leave Junior the keys?"

"I guess so."

Junior felt funny being left alone in the exile camp, but he made the most of it. The men sat around the campfire, swatting mosquitoes and drinking beer. He looked for Nasser to try to continue their earlier conversation, but the man always kept a good distance from him. He would smile and drift off into the darkness.

Junior made his way over to the tent he'd been assigned to and unzipped the mosquito netting. He climbed in and took off his boots. He was carrying two bags, one with a few clothes and the other with his equipment. He always liked to be ready. He took out his small Ruger .22 and the silencer he carried for it. The hollow-point bullets made it more of an assassin's weapon. It would do minimal damage unless fired at point-blank range into a man's brain. Wounds to the limbs or body would be painful but not incapacitating. The Ruger's best feature was the muffled report that sounded more like a wet pop.

Reaching into his equipment bag, he took out the sap. The sap was a flexible length of leather with one end weighted down with solid lead. He bounced it in his hand. He slipped it under his pillow and screwed the silencer into place on the Ruger.

He then tied a set of eating utensils to the top of the zipper. Stepping back, he smiled. The idea of sleeping in a strange place with men who may have murdered Lorenzo Pera didn't sit well with him, but at least now he could relax.

He lay down and turned over on his belly. Sleeping this way was uncomfortable, but tonight he wanted to be uncomfortable, very uncomfortable.

It must have been hours later when he heard the slight rattling of the eating utensils he'd tied to the net zipper. His eyes popped open. The camp was quiet except for the faint pop of what must have been the last of the campfire. He dug his right hand under the pillow and clutched at the sap. Rolling over softly, he dropped his left hand to where he had left the Ruger. It was there. His fingers wrapped themselves around the cold trigger and pistol butt.

He could see the dim figure of a man in his doorway. The man was slowly lowering the zipper on the tent's netting, pushing in to deaden the noise the eating utensils might make. He saw a flash, a dull glare from the dying fire. The man had a knife in his hand.

The man pushed his way into the tent and stepped toward Junior's cot. He raised the knife to strike, and Junior rolled off the cot and swung up with the sap. It connected with the man's head, snapping it backward.

Junior jumped to his feet and met the man. The man grabbed for the gun in Junior's hand, and Junior swung the sap again, this time hitting the man in the throat. The man's whole body shook, but he held Junior's gun hand tight. He came at Junior with the knife, slicing the side of Junior's cheek and sending out a trickle of warm blood.

Junior reached back and slung the sap once again, connecting with the side of the man's head. It seemed to stun him. Junior swung again, and once more he connected. This time the blow was to the man's face. The man released his grip on Junior and sank to his knees. Junior came down hard now, on the top of the man's head. It dropped the man to the floor. He was still.

Junior stood for a moment over the man, then turned him over. It was Nasser, the man who had shot off his mouth on the gunnery range. Maybe he had realized that he'd said too much. Another thought, even worse, entered Junior's head: Maybe he was here to kill him under orders.

Junior sat down and stuffed his feet into his boots. He stood up and tucked the Ruger into his belt. Picking up his bags, he stepped over the man and left the tent.

He moved through the camp cautiously. *Surely, there must be a guard,* he thought. He was met by the muffled sounds of the men sleeping. The campfires were no more than smoldering mounds of hot ashes, but they were enough to allow him to see where he was walking.

He was headed for the jeep when another thought hit him. *The safe. They must have information there in the safe.*

He walked up to the jeep and dropped the bag of clothes, then headed toward the command shack. The place was dark. From what he'd seen so far, he was sure it would be deserted.

Opening the screen door, he stepped inside. He reached into his bag, pulled out a small flashlight, and switched it on. He scanned the room carefully until the tiny beam fell on the safe marked AMERICAN BANANA COMPANY. This was something he knew how to do, and he even had the equipment for it. He would never have been able to succeed with a new safe, but with one this old his chances were good.

He set down his bag and pulled out a telescopic rod, which he extended and placed on the combination lock. He secured it with two clamps on each side of the safe and then attached a small electric motor to the rod, adjusting the jaws on the end of the motor to the dial on the combination. He placed electric sensors on the top, bottom, left, and right of the safe door and secured them in place with magnets.

Wires dangled from the motor and the sensors, and he connected them to a twelve-volt battery he had in the bag. Everything looked OK. The electrical current running through the combination and door created an electrical field. The rotation of the tumblers inside the lock caused changes in the current, and any fluctuation would throw a small red switch on the sensing device built into the motor. He slowly turned the combination to the right. The switch bounced when he hit the number fourteen. Turning it to the left, it bounced on number forty-three. Turning right again, twenty-three tripped the switch.

Junior breathed a sigh. He took the sensors and motor off, dropping them back into his bag. Then he removed the clamps and rod. Everything looked in place. He placed the small flashlight in his mouth and pointed it at the combination, quickly working through the numbers: 14-43-23. Cranking the brass handle, the safe opened.

He shined the light inside. Several shelves were filled with stacks of fresh bank notes, mostly fifty- and one-hundred-dollar-bills. There had to be thousands there. Shining the light down, he saw a row of manila file folders. He pulled them out. Some contained names, addresses, and phone numbers. Others had what appeared to be lists of arms and equipment. He put those back inside. He took the remainder of the files and stuffed them into his bag, zipping it up.

He stood up and turned off the flashlight. Picking up his bag, he took the Ruger from his waistband. He was getting out, and no one was going to stop him.

CHAPTER 34

I t was midmorning when they got the tow truck to back up to the swamp. Johnny stood at the water's edge with Frank Bass. Gordon had stayed behind at the hotel with Maria.

"Did you find the photographs?" Johnny asked.

Frank shook his head. "No. We had a few people looking, but we didn't find anything. Did you get a chance to talk to the woman?"

"Yes, we had some long talks. I did get the idea that she wasn't exactly enthusiastic about the chances of American intervention in Cuba."

"Doesn't make sense with her taking them."

The men who operated the tow truck waded into the swamp with their high rubber boots on and hooked a chain to the undercarriage of the submerged Cadillac, yanking it to make sure it was secure.

Frank looked at Johnny. "You know those tag numbers are the same ones we think belonged to your brother and those people he was with. We got descriptions of the men this morning. UXV-1143, a white Cadillac convertible. "Baldassare was a hard case. You don't come into Miami and try to strong-arm Santos Trafficante. Bad move."

"It's all he knew how to do, and, knowing him, he had to do something. He didn't trust me, and there was no reason he should."

"One thing's for sure."

"What's that?"

"He was onto something, and it involved Trafficante and the Cubans here."

"Can we prove anything? If we find the bodies, can we prove these people were responsible?"

"I doubt it." Frank shook his head. "I really doubt they left the bodies in the car. Out here they were probably crock food. People disappear in the Everglades all the time. We never find them."

Johnny stepped back and then walked away as the men operating the tow truck started the engine on their lift. The chains were grinding, and water was pouring off the white Caddy.

Gina, who had been standing alone, stepped over to him and put her arm around him. "I'm sorry. This must be hard for you."

Johnny silently nodded.

"I know you hadn't been close to your brother in some time, but there were childhood memories."

"Yes. He was always so full of life. He played hard, was always the last to come in."

"This whole thing must be a nightmare for you. You had your nice, safe life—and now this."

Johnny looked at her. "In a way I'm glad I left that nice safe life to come here. I was praying about that this morning. My life has always been a little story, one that I could control and one where I knew the ending. But God has a big story. The only problem is, we don't know the ending to God's story. We can't control that. We have to trust the outcome to Him and Him alone. That seems to be the whole issue. Can we trust Him? Do we leave our nice safe lives and allow the bigness of God to sweep us away into what He is doing?"

Gina looked back at the swamp. The rear of the big car was sticking out of the muck, and the men operating the truck continued to reel in the chains that were attached to the undercarriage. "And you see yourself being swept away in all this?"

"My little life is being carried away, but maybe that's OK. Blaise Pascal once wrote, 'The heart has its reasons that reason knows not of.' We all have our personal stories, and sometimes reasons and motivations that not even we are aware of. Often, deep down in our hearts, we have a place that is so well guarded that it has rarely, if ever, been exposed to the light of day. Why did He make me like this? Why did He let this happen?" He looked her in the eye. "Why did He let Karen die? Why did He let me see you again? Those questions form the central core of the deep doubts we all have. Does God really care for me?"

"And what is the answer?"

"I know what the answer is in my head. But my heart is another thing. I think I'm discovering the answer in my heart with every day I've been on this trip, and there are some days, like this one, when I don't like the answer."

It took the men in the tow truck another ten to fifteen minutes before they could haul the white convertible out of the brown water. One of them walked over and opened the passenger door. The water poured out, muck and mud mixed with debris. Johnny walked over with Frank to look it over. He stared into the car and could see several holes punched into the red leather seats.

Frank walked around to the other side of the car. He stooped down and looked it over. Standing up, he signaled for Johnny. "You should see this."

Johnny walked around. There were multiple bullet holes in the driver's side of the car. The patterns were close together.

"I'd say it took machine gun fire. Heavy caliber stuff, too, from the looks of it."

Rocko drove up in the Buick. He had gone back to the camp to find Junior. He got out of the car and walked over to where Johnny was standing with Frank. "Wow," he said, staring at the damage. "Not many people kill like that, not since Capone in Chicago."

"Did you find Junior?" Gina asked. She walked over to where the men were standing.

Rocko shook his head. "No, not a sign of him. People at the camp said they haven't seen him since late last night, and the jeep is gone."

Gina bit her lower lip. The sight of the Cadillac and now the news that Junior was missing seemed to unnerve her. "We've got to find him." She looked out at the sight of the huge swamp in front of them. "If anything happened to him, I'll never forgive myself. He shouldn't have come on this trip. I knew it."

Johnny stepped over to her. "We'll find him. He's probably back at the hotel. We didn't even look for him this morning because we thought he was at the camp. He probably changed his mind about sleeping out here, and I wouldn't blame him one bit."

He looked over at Rocko. "You don't seem worried."

Rocko had busied himself with looking in the glove compartment of the Cadillac. He looked up. "Worried?"

"About Junior," Johnny said.

"Aw, he'll turn up. Don't fret yourselves about him."

"He'd better," Johnny said. He kicked at the dirt. "Those people in that camp have a lot of explaining to do." He then turned and looked at the car. "No one around here has this kind of firepower except those Cuban exiles."

He starting walking back to the Buick with Gina. "I think it's time to call that Cuban we met in New York." He gritted his teeth. "We're not going to get anything out of these people, nothing except grief. Maybe Castro's man has something he can tell us now. I sure have something I can tell him, and frankly I don't care who it hurts. It may not have been our government that's directly responsible for Papa's murder, but they sure had a hand in it."

Once again, he turned around and looked back at the Cadillac. "They sure had a hand in this."

The three of them drove back to the hotel. Johnny was silent. When they got back, he went directly to his room.

When he opened the door, he saw movement out of the corner of his eye. Then he felt a sharp, hammerlike blow to the side of his head. He fell to the floor.

The assailant stepped over him and walked out.

Johnny got to his elbows. His head was swimming, and a dull pain erupted from deep inside. He pushed himself up and got to his feet, stumbling at first, but then steadying himself. He leaned against the door, then pulled it open and staggered outside.

When he stepped into the hall, he saw the elevator doors close. He ran to the stairs. Pushing open the door, he took the stairs in twos and threes. When he hit the ground floor, he shoved the door open with both hands.

The lobby was down the hall, and he knew that with any luck he had beaten the elevator. Now the only problem would be finding the right person who was about to step out of that elevator. He hadn't had much of a look at the man. It could be anyone. If the elevator was crowded, he'd be stuck. He'd have to depend on the man to give himself away.

When the elevator doors opened, he saw three men and a couple with a small child. He could discount the couple right away, along with the first man who stepped out. He was balding and appeared to be in his early sixties.

The second man caught his eye. The man was somewhere in his thirties with dark curly hair and black eyes. He was wearing blue slacks and a white open-collared shirt. He was well built. He looked Johnny in the eye and then rushed out of the elevator and hurried to the door.

Johnny followed him onto the street. The man picked up his pace, and Johnny walked behind him in quick step. Collins Avenue was jammed with midday traffic, and the sidewalks were overflowing.

The man picked up his pace and tried to melt into the crowd. He darted in front of a family and through the swinging doors of the Colony Hotel. Johnny pressed his way pass the people and skirted the edge of the crowd.

In the lobby of the old hotel, Johnny spotted the blue slacks of the man as he ran up a set of side stairs. Johnny hurried for the stairs and took them two at a time. Each floor he passed, Johnny looked at the door to make sure it wasn't closing. When he got to the third floor, he could see the door cracked open. The brass apparatus at the top of the door was in the process of closing it, and Johnny reached out and yanked it open.

He stepped into the hallway and saw the man moving down the hall in front of him. "Hey, hold on just one minute," Johnny shouted.

The man turned around, his face snapping into a frown.

"What were you doing in my room?"

The man stepped toward him softly and then launched into a flying kick, his feet extended and his arms in the air. He hit Johnny while he was in midair, launching him backward down the empty hall.

Johnny landed on the floor and turned over, scrambling to his knees. He pushed himself up with his arms as the man came forward, once again kicking and circling his arms. A kick landed on Johnny's shoulder, tumbling him to the carpet.

The man stood over him and raised a foot to come down on him, but Johnny reached up and grabbed the man by the ankle, twisting it. It sent the man down.

Johnny shot to his feet as the man bounced to his. Johnny was determined not to be taken by surprise again. He put up his left and circled the man.

The man began to twirl his arms, evidently trying to put on a display of his martial arts skills. But Johnny would have none of it. He stepped into the man with a flurry of left jabs that landed on the man's jaw and followed through with a stiff right to the man's midsection. The blow doubled the man over, and Johnny flew into the man's face with a series of left and right crosses that staggered the man backward.

The man landed near the window and Johnny was on him in a flash. He grabbed the man by the shirt and landed a punch directly into the man's chin. The blow rocked the man, and he hung like a rag doll.

Just then the door to the stairway opened and Johnny felt himself being grabbed from behind. Two men held him by the arms as the man he had just administered the beating to blinked his eyes and shook his head. He glared at Johnny and grunted. Then he snarled. "You wops. You are always overmatched."

With that, the man stepped up and began to punch Johnny in the stomach. He landed blow after heavy blow, causing Johnny's knees to buckle. Then he gave Johnny a stiff punch to the face. He reached into his pants pocket and pulled out a switchblade knife. He pressed a silver button on the dark ebony handle, and a silver blade sprang out. "I should have done this to you in your room," he said. "But I was hoping you would follow me."

"Hey, what are you doing?"

Johnny heard the shout from the far end of the hall. The men holding him dropped him to the floor, and the man with the knife followed them down the stairs at a dead run.

CHAPTER 35

Rocko was growing more impatient with every day that passed. He knew what he thought didn't matter, though. Things were pretty much up to Johnny. Johnny was the man in charge on this trip, in spite of knowing nothing and having little to do with the family. Blood was thicker than water. Rocko knew the group wouldn't be able to go back home until Johnny was completely satisfied that every stone had been turned. So far, however, everything they had led back to the Cubans. Maybe that was best. If there were going to be closed doors, better it should be doors closed by the government.

He knocked on Gina's door.

She opened it up. "Come on in. What's this meeting about?"

Rocko stepped into her room and closed the door. He knew Gina thought of herself as a forty-year-old mother, but that didn't make her any less attractive. If anything, her brains made her even more appealing. Not to him, of course, and maybe not to most men, but the woman was a knockout nevertheless. "When I went looking for Junior this morning, I met the Cuban commander."

Gina sighed. "And you think he's going to tell us anything that we don't already know?"

Rocko shrugged. "Not really. It's jest somethin' we gotta do. Arturo, Dom, and Pia are going to want to hear everything, everybody we talked to and everything that was talked about. And what if Baldy is dead? We better not show up with nothing." He shook his head. "But so far we have only hunches. That's about it."

"Maybe, maybe not." Gina smiled. She walked over to her nightstand and picked up her purse, slinging it over her shoulder.

"What do you mean by that?"

"I got a call from John, I mean Junior."

"Where is he?"

"He spent the night here in the hotel. He uncovered something important, but he wouldn't tell me what it was."

Rocko began to pace, mumbling to himself. "He found something?"

"Yes."

"Well, what?" He held out his hand, almost in a plea. "Why won't he tell us?"

"I don't know. Maybe he wants to go over it with Johnny first. It sounded like he had a few things to do before he saw us again, but I couldn't even begin to guess what that was all about."

Rocko shook his head. "I don't like it," he growled. "We got to stick together on this thing, keep everybody on the same page. I don't want any surprises."

"I'm sure he has very good reasons for doing what he's doing. We'll find out in due time."

"We have to have something firm before we report to the family."

"It sounded like he had something firm, something in black and white."

"I think this deal we made with Giancana is going to help us. It's something we got." He pointed to the palm of his hand. "Something in our hand." His mind seemed to drift for a moment. It was a bad habit when he was under pressure, but at least it always drifted into something nice to think about. "Do you have all the paperwork drawn up for that?" He blinked his eyes back to attention.

"I mailed the contracts to him the day before yesterday. We should have them before we go home."

"Good." Rocko rubbed his hands together. "That's something, at least." He looked up at her. "You included my name in the contract, didn't you?"

"Of course. That's part of the bargain you worked out with Giancana, isn't it? You're the casino manager. It's understood, part of the deal."

"Great." He breathed deeply and crossed his arms. "I can tell you, I'm more than a little tired of being the family errand boy. Been doing that for years. It's a kid's job, not something for a grown man."

Gina grinned slightly. "You know Lorenzo never would have gone for this deal, don't you?"

Rocko nodded. "I guess so. Maybe I could have talked sense to him though. You never know."

"He would never have wanted Chicago involved anywhere near Vegas, and he trusted you. He'd want you close to him. He wouldn't want you out on your own."

"That may be true, but with him gone the family shouldn't care. They pick their own men. It's sort of a changing of the old guard. It's something I always knew would happen sooner or later."

Rocko didn't much care for the feeling of not being in control. Lorenzo had always given him a lot of room even if he kept him on a leash. As far as the company business was concerned, people respected him. He had the connections, knew where the bodies were buried. When he stepped into a casino in Vegas, people bent over backward to keep him happy. He liked that. Now, he felt like a glorified baby-sitter. To make matters worse, he hadn't exactly done a great job doing that. Baldassare was dead, and before they got back home, Rocko had the feeling the list of family members who wouldn't be coming home might just be longer.

Gina stepped closer to him and patted him on the back. "Well, this deal ought to see you fixed for life, my friend. Now where is this meeting of ours?"

"I got the thing arranged for someplace close. It's a bar across the tracks."

They went down the elevator and out the lobby. Crossing Collins Avenue was somewhat tricky, but they managed to find a light and blend in with the crowd. They were a strange sight for the streets of Miami. Rocko was wearing pinstripes and wing tips, and Gina was in a dark green skirt with a white blouse. Her sensible black pumps and shoulder bag marked her as a businesswoman.

Rocko kept up a fast pace, winding his way through the crowd. They soon came to the tracks and stopped. A passenger train had pulled into the station minutes before. The depot was a good half-mile to their left. The crossing guard was still blinking as the yellow arm swung up. Rocko could see the porters dashing onto the platforms in the distance, in a hurry to find disembarking passengers. More snowbirds were arriving, people escaping the frigid temperatures even before winter hit. The humidity was no longer a major factor in South Florida; now it was just the sun and the warm weather.

They hurried across the maze of tracks and continued onto the street. Shops were filled with mannequins smiling blankly, sporting swimsuits and terry robes. An ice-cream vendor stood beside his large fridge on wheels. The man serving up the ice cream was pudgy and in his mid-fifties, pretty close to Rocko's age.

Rocko looked at Gina. "You want an ice cream?"

"I think I'll pass," Gina said. "But you go ahead."

Rocko stepped up to the man, ducking under the large, striped umbrella. He held up his index finger. "I'll try one of your raspberry snow cones."

The man smiled. "Sure enough." He scooped down into the box with a silver colored scoop and piled crushed ice into the bottom of a paper cone. Picking up a bottle of colored liquid, he coated the ice on the bottom, then packed the remainder of the cone with more of the frosty snow, cramming and packing it down. When he had the thing mounded with a smooth, curved top, he finished it off with another, more liberal coating of the raspberry mixture. He then handed it to Rocko.

Rocko handed the man a five-dollar bill. "Keep the change."

The man grinned and doffed his white paper hat. "Thanks a bunch, pal. I sure appreciate it."

They walked off, and Rocko bit down on the snow cone.

"Kinda generous, weren't you?"

"I got myself some feeling for working stiffs. Maybe I see myself like that in some ways, just standing by my job without much in the way of thanks, like nobody sees. When a man does a job day-in-day-out, after a while he just disappears. He ain't really a person no more; he's a desk or a telephone, some dang piece of office equipment." He spat out the words.

They turned the corner, and Rocko walked another block before tossing the remainder of his snow cone in the trash and turning into the Voodoo Bar. Rocko opened the glass doors for Gina and followed her inside.

A large, mirrored ball hung in the exposed rafters, spinning slowly and giving off beams of light that cut through the midnight atmosphere. Spears were crossed over the stage at the far wall, and sitting on the stage was a black man sitting cross-legged with a large drum between his knees. He was keeping up a steady rhythm of nonsensical sounds, leaning his head back and allowing his eyes to wander over the rafters, like he was in another world.

Rocko moved to a table in the corner and pulled out a chair for Gina.

"He oughta be along pretty soon," Rocko said. He reached into his pocket and pulled out a cigar and a cutter. Snipping off the end, he planted the cigar between his teeth and struck a match. The black matchbook cover had the bold red logo of the Voodoo Bar on it, complete with dolls that had pins sticking out of them. Rocko raked the match over the blunt end of the cigar and puffed up a small cloud of gray smoke.

Gina leaned across the table and looked into his eyes. "I take it you don't feel very appreciated."

Rocko waved his cigar. "Let's just say I'm always there. When a man is always there, doing what he's always done, what's to notice?" He smiled. "It's the square peg in the round hole that gets pounded on." He reached up and touched his thinning hair. "My head's always been round. I go down in the round holes real nice."

They ordered drinks and waited until Rocko spotted the man who had called himself the Cuban commander. Rocko stood and signaled the man to come over.

Javier Lage walked toward their table. He was tall, almost Rocko's height, but a good fifty pounds lighter. His beard and mustache had that touch of gray that showed maturity and Rocko could tell that the sight of Gina had instantly attracted him.

"Take a seat," Rocko said. "This is Gina Cumo, a friend of the family."

Javier took his seat and smiled at Gina. "Very nice to meet you." His teeth shone brightly, even in the dim light.

"My pleasure, Commander," Gina said.

"Why weren't you around the camp when we came to look the place over?" Rocko asked.

"I was in Cuba, setting up our landing."

"I trust your time there was profitable," Gina said.

The Cuban's eyes gleamed at her and his smile broadened. "Yes, very much so."

"I explained to you this morning why our family is in Florida," Rocko said.

"Yes."

"It would seem that the car we pulled out of the Everglades was one being driven by another member of our family. We found no bodies, though." Rocko leaned forward in his seat. "We did find signs of large-caliber machine gun fire in the car though. The kind of weapons that only your men use down there."

Javier shook his head. "I'm afraid you're mistaken, señor. There are many groups that use automatic weapons in South Florida, paramilitary groups."

"We've also run across people who tell us it was your boys who killed our boss out in California. He was saying no to this Castro thing." Rocko held up both his hands and wiggled them slightly. "One and one is two. We're putting things together." Rocko could see the man's jaws tighten.

"It wasn't us, señor. I can assure you of that."

"We have some contacts with the FBI, people who might be paying you a call. It would help if you told us what you really know."

Gina reached out and patted the Cuban's hand. "I'm sorry," she said. "We don't mean to be pushy. It's just that so much we've uncovered leads only in one direction. Perhaps things have happened that you're not aware of." She smiled. "You said yourself, you travel out of the country a great deal. You're an important man. Surely you can't be expected to know everything."

Rocko could see that Gina's soft-spoken nature was winning the man over a mite. It was hard to argue with a woman that beautiful.

"I would know that. My men have other battles to fight. They don't need this one."

"Then we're wasting your time," Rocko said. "Perhaps the FBI can get better results. They can maybe even find the guns that shot up our man's car."

Javier got to his feet. "Look, I don't like being threatened by the FBI. We are your allies, not hired thugs who can be ordered to kill on command." He looked at Gina, forcing a smile. "I am sorry to have wasted your time. But that is all I have to say."

"You and your men don't take orders from Trafficante?" Rocko raised his voice to drive the question home. Rocko could see the man was unnerved at the mention of Santos Trafficante's name.

Javier blinked his eyes furiously and waved his hand. "No, we do not. We don't commit murder for him or anyone else."

Rocko stood up and pointed his finger. "Trafficante is scratching your back. Don't tell me any different. He's sending people into Cuba to kill Castro. You owe him a lot. If he tells you to jump, you're going to ask how high. I don't think there's any question about that. So don't give me this chest-thumping bull."

Without saying a word, Javier turned and walked out the door, leaving Rocko standing with his finger still out. Gina smiled at him. "I'd say you handled that nicely."

"You're joking, right?"

She nodded. "Yes, I am joking. This guy isn't from the Lower East Side, and it's obvious he doesn't have much to fear from us. With the way you talked to him, it's a wonder he told you anything. Let's hope what Junior has will help. I'm going back to the hotel."

Rocko picked up his drink. He sloshed the ice around in what was left of the amber liquid. "I think I'll just stay right here for a bit, maybe have me another drink."

Gina stepped over to him and put her hand on his shoulder. "Don't be so hard on yourself. You're not a diplomat." She chuckled slightly. "Your diplomacy has always taken on other means."

"Yeah." He looked up at her, his jaw tightening. "I guess seeing Baldy's car this morning did something to me. I'd like to have taken that lousy commander and twisted his neck. Baldy shouldn't have come here, but he didn't trust us to get the job done."

"You know Baldassare. I doubt if he trusted his own face in the mirror."

Gina walked out the door and turned the corner. She was anxious to get back to the hotel. She couldn't let Rocko know because the man seemed to be worried enough already, but Junior had seemed more than a little excited about what he had found at the Cuban camp. Junior wasn't the type of person to get emotional and brag. He was the confident sort. When he had something big, something really big, he would hide it by being cool. He was standoffish when it came to power. He'd wait until other people recognized it and came to him. He never went to them. She liked that about him. It was manly.

The street was getting dark now, with much less in the way of foot traffic. She noticed that many of the shops had already closed for the day. There were several small hotels with buzzing neon signs flashing

in the growing twilight. They were more like flophouses for the dere-
licts on the street than the kind of hotel that catered to the tourists
on Collins Avenue.

She noticed one man who stood in the doorway of the Ajax
Hotel. He was unshaven and had dark skin. Cubans were already
beginning to give her the jitters, and the way this man was looking at
her as she walked toward him didn't help to ease her fears. His eyes
narrowed, and he seemed to stare at her.

She walked past him, and he fell into place behind her. Several
other people were coming in their direction, and Gina almost wished
they wouldn't walk by, not just yet.

When they passed her she picked up her pace, but so did the man.
She heard his steps falling into place behind her. Gina walked to the
end of the block and turned the corner. The man was right behind
her. She could see the ice-cream vendor in the distance, but he was
busy closing up his box and folding his small umbrella. She wished she
was closer or at least that he was paying some attention to her.

Suddenly, the man following her reached out and grabbed her
arm. He clamped one hand over her mouth and his other arm around
her waist, pulling her into him. "Be quiet, señora." He whispered in
her ear. "Very quiet."

She struggled as he dragged her toward an open doorway.
Swinging with her arm, she sent a sharp elbow backward into the
man's midsection. It connected. She could hear the air rush out of the
man.

She then raised her foot and brought her sharp heel directly into
the man's instep. It sent a shock of pain through the man. He yelped
out a squeal and released her.

Gina broke into a dead run down the street but could hear the
man coming up behind her. She reached the ice-cream vendor and,
without saying a word, grabbed his wheeled box, spun it around, and

rammed it into her pursuer. He staggered and fell backward. The vendor looked stunned.

Gina started running again. She knew she had a short lead on the man behind her, but she also knew she'd never be able to maintain it all the way to busy Collins Avenue. She could only hope to run into a cop or somebody else who wasn't as panicked as the ice-cream man.

Lifting her eyes, she saw at once that her biggest problem was the tracks. The yellow crossing guard barriers were down and the red lights flashing. A long train was slowly making its way down the tracks. She could see boxcars and tank cars as far as her eye could see.

She circled the crossing guard, and her skirt was flying as she jumped off the curb and ran for the train. The engine was just ahead of her, and she ran to try to catch it. The engineer was applying his brakes, with steam pouring out the sides of the engine, but even then it was moving too fast. Her pursuer was behind her, his feet digging into the gravel.

When she caught up with the front of the engine, the lights on the tracks sent her into a panic. There would be time for only one try, and she couldn't miss. The heels of her shoes slapped against her feet.

She ran, keeping pace with the engine, her heart pounding. Then all at once, she jumped for the track. One, two steps. She was right in front of the engine. She leaped for the ground on the other side of the train, hitting the hard gravel. She skidded and slid, the rocks biting into her.

PART 3
THE STORM

CHAPTER 36

J ohnny felt a strong arm lift him up from the floor. He looked up and saw Junior. The young man slung Johnny's arm over his shoulder. "Come on. Walk with me. Take one step at a time." They started down the long hall. "We'll go down these back stairs. That's how I came up. I saw you leave the hotel and tried to catch you, but I lost you in the crowd. Who was that man?"

"I have no idea." Johnny rubbed his jaw and then tried to move it with his hand. It felt sore. His whole body ached. "He was in my room when I got back from the Everglades. I chased him down the street, tried to catch him." Johnny's head buzzed. "But I guess he wanted me back here."

"You caught him all right, but he had help."

It was a slow walk back to the Marlin Hotel. Junior let him into his own room and unlocked the door. Junior walked Johnny over to a rattan club chair and eased him into it.

Johnny looked up at him and pressed his hands to his painful ribs. "We looked for you at the camp this morning."

Junior smiled. "Yeah, I got outta there last night. Somebody tried to knife me in my tent. I figured it would be safer back here at the hotel."

"You don't think—"

"Yes, I do." Junior cut him off. "We got a hit out on us."

Johnny looked up at the slowly turning ceiling fan. His mind was drifting. "I think we found Baldy's car in the Everglades. We pulled it out with a tow truck this morning."

"You sure it's his?"

"Pretty much. My friend Frank with the FBI said the license plates matched a car rented at the airport by a man matching Baldassare's description. The car was riddled with machine gun fire, large-caliber stuff."

"Sounds like the Cubans."

Johnny nodded, then put his face in his hands. He had more than sore ribs. His heart grieved for a younger brother he had played with, walked on the beach with, laughed with as a child. Baldassare had come to all Johnny's football games in high school. He would hang around after the games and mix with the other players on the team, always telling them he was Johnny's brother and then carefully adding with a beaming smile, "When I grow up, I'm going to be just like him."

Johnny looked up at Junior. "We didn't find any bodies, just the car. I don't know what I'll tell Mama."

"And if that guy had killed me in my tent last night, you wouldn't have found my body either. I got some things we can use, though, and something very curious. I pulled it out of their safe." Junior cracked a big grin and pointed to the bag on the bed. "Something I learned a while back, how to crack safes. I brought my paraphernalia with me."

Johnny looked up at him. "Why would you bring safecracking equipment on this trip?"

Junior patted the underarm holster he was wearing. "Same reason I brought a gun. I know how to use it and I'm ready if I need to be." He grinned. "The Boy Scout motto: Be prepared. I'm prepared. I guess that makes me a good scout."

Johnny got to his feet and walked over to a rattan credenza that sat under a long mirror. A pitcher of ice water sat there along with several glasses. Johnny poured himself a glass. He sipped it, staring at Junior in the mirror. Junior looked so clean-cut on the outside, like many of the young men Johnny had known in seminary. Of course he was different, much different. The young man's years with the Pera family had turned him into a safecracker and who knew what else. But there was a playfulness about him in the midst of it all, and Johnny found that difficult to deal with.

He turned around and took another drink. "I'm finding this a little hard."

"What?"

"You being a safecracker. I work for a security company. We put people like you in jail. You should be in college, trying to find a career. Why aren't you?"

Junior raised his shoulders slightly and grinned a sheepish smile. "Why should I? I'm doing all right by myself. I like my job. It's exciting. I make good money, go places, drive a Porsche. I don't think I could take sitting around all day in an office, worrying about paying my bills. What do you want me to do, be a schoolteacher?"

"You can do anything you want." He took another drink. "I don't see any future in your being a soldier for the Pera family. You'll wind up just like my brother out there, no grave, nobody will even know where to put the flowers."

"I can take care of myself." Junior tapped the side of his head with his finger. "I'm a thinker. I plan things out."

"Yeah, right. Baldy thought he was a thinker too. Now he's a dead thinker. You're just going to think yourself into an early grave."

"Right now I'm doing just what you're doing." Junior smiled. "Only I'd say I'm doing a little better at it."

Johnny finished his glass of water and set it down. He nodded slightly. "That may be. To be perfectly honest with you, I don't want to be good at this. I don't want to have to think this way for the rest of my life, always looking around corners, afraid someone's going to try to kill me. I don't like doubting people I've known all my life just because they may have some sort of angle, some way to get at me. It's no way to live. I know. I grew up with it."

"So did I. I've been with your family for almost as long as I can remember." Junior's eyes were dark, almost haunting. Looking into them gave Johnny a feeling that was hard to shake. "Of course, you were gone, living your clean life somewhere else."

They heard a sudden pounding on the door. Junior ran to the door and opened it. Gina fell into his arms, breathless. Her dress was torn and dirty. She had broken a heel off one of her shoes. Her arms and elbows were scratched, and blood was oozing out from the caked dirt. Blood and dirt were smeared over her legs. She started to say something, then noticed Johnny. That quieted her even before she started talking.

Johnny jumped to his feet and closed the door as Junior led Gina across the room to the bed. "What happened to you?" Junior asked.

Johnny rushed over to the sink and grabbed a pink towel and washcloth from the towel rack. He ran the water, soaking them. "You'd better call a doctor," Johnny barked. "We'll get her to the hospital."

Junior picked up the phone and started to dial, but Gina grabbed his hand. "No. No doctors and no hospitals." Her voice was stern. She sat down on the bed. "No police either." She gave Johnny a hard glance. "I don't want to start answering questions. There would be too much to explain."

Johnny reached down and took off Gina's shoes, then ripped her nylons away. He began to softly pat her legs with the wet washcloth. "Are you going to tell us what happened?"

Gina nodded. "Yes. A man chased me after Rocko and I had a meeting at some bar with the Cuban commander. The man tried to grab me, but I ran."

"Where's Rocko?" Johnny asked.

"Still at the bar for all I know."

"Why didn't he come back with you?"

Gina grimaced. "I don't know. He wanted to drink."

Johnny looked up at her. "We have a bar here in the hotel." He then handed the blood-and-dirt-soaked washcloth to Junior. "Here, get me another one."

"I think he felt bad because our meeting didn't go so well." She shook her head. "I could have stayed, but the place was so depressing."

Junior came back with the fresh washcloth. "Here, why don't you let me do that?"

Johnny took it out of his hand. "I'll see to it. I've already started here." He began to wipe more of the dirt and blood from Gina's legs and knees.

"I probably just need a warm bath," Gina said. "That and some pants."

"We're going to put a stop to this," Junior said.

Johnny looked up at him. "And how do you propose to do that?"

"I already took care of that. I'm getting us out of Miami to a place where the people with the answers will have to come to us. It's a place called Crab Key. It's in the Keys, has a hotel and a boat dock. You can't get there except by boat. It's a place the Crow used to go when he came down here. He went there to fish, but I know the hotel owner. We can have the whole place to ourselves."

Johnny continued to pat Gina's legs with the wet cloth, then switched to the towel and started in on her arms. "I know the place. But why should the people we need to talk to all come there?"

Junior grinned. "Because I have things they want and need."

"Such as?"

"I have Trafficante's money, the money Baldy stole from him."

Johnny stopped and stared at him. "How did you get that?"

"Simple." Junior grinned. "I called Dom back in California. Dominico knew where Baldy and his men were staying down here. I figured I'd just stay one step ahead of the cops. But Trafficante will want it back even if he has to come to the Keys to get it."

"You've got to get out of this business." Johnny shook his head.

"The Cuban commander will want to get the files I stole from his safe. They contain battle plans, landing sites on Cuba, and the names of Cuban partisans on the island." Junior nodded and smiled. "He'll be dying to come to the Keys, and he'll be quite talkative too."

He glanced at Gina. "And Gina gave me the number of that bookstore in New York. I called and left a message for that Cuban you two met with, told him we knew where Castro would be hit and when. He'll be there."

"And who else did you invite to have a tête-à-tête with you?"

"The CIA man we've heard so much about. You know, the guy in charge of Castro's hit, Cliff Cox."

"And how did you persuade him. Did you tell him you had the secrets to the bomb?" He glanced at Gina. She seemed to be getting more and more uncomfortable with the tone he was taking with Junior.

"Something like that." A big grin spread across Junior's face. "You know that night you were on the balcony with the FBI guy and the Marine?"

"You took Scott's photographs!"

Junior nodded. A cocky look creased the corner of his smile. "Yeah. I figured we could use them. Give us some leverage."

"You're a born thief, aren't you?"

Gina reached out and slapped Johnny across the cheek. "You stop that! He's not a born thief. He was just trying to protect us, something you haven't given much thought to."

The slap stung Johnny, but it shocked him even more. He blinked. "Those are government secrets. People risked their lives for those pictures, including a man I served with in the Marine Corps. What do you expect me to tell him? He wants them for leverage, and the president needs them now."

"Don't get your shorts all in a knot," Junior said. "I got hold of this colonel friend of yours. Gave him the pictures back. He's on his way to Washington with them right now. I just made a bargain with him, that's all."

"What sort of bargain?"

"I told him he could have them back if he promised to tell this Cox fella they were still missing. I told him we needed Cox's honest cooperation, and that was the only way we could get it. I told him that you needed it. He seemed all too happy to help. I really don't think there's a lot of love lost between your buddy and the CIA."

"You have been a busy boy."

Junior smiled. "I told you I should have come on this trip. I found out something else, too, something you may be very interested in."

"What's that?"

A knock at the door stopped their discussion. Junior stepped over and opened the door. Rocko walked into the room. "Hey, we're finally all here," he said, "together." He was puffing on a cigar. His eyes widened when he saw Gina.

"Take that thing out of my room," Gina snarled.

Rocko pulled the cigar out of his lips. His mouth dropped open. "What happened to you?"

Gina slid out of bed and started toward the bathroom. "I'm going to take a hot bath and get into some pants." She waved in Johnny's direction. "Explain it to the man."

Johnny got to his feet and looked at Rocko. "I think he's got some explaining to do to us. Then we're going to have to pack and check out."

"Where are we going?" Rocko asked.

"Crab Key," Junior said.

"We're going someplace else first," Johnny said.

"Where's that?" Junior asked.

"We're going back into that swamp. I can't face my mother unless I try to find Baldy's body."

CHAPTER 37

S cott came out of his meeting at the Pentagon with his brief-case in his hand. The people in the photo lab had done their best with the pictures. The Soviets indeed had the SA-2 missiles in place around the MRBM complexes. Even at the extreme heights flown by U-2 reconnaissance aircraft, the SA-2 was capable of hitting it. It would be a risk, especially if Russian radar picked up the overflights. The only question remaining was the president's resolve to get aerial photos of Russian missile batteries. *Just how determined is he?* Scott wondered.

He got into the backseat of the staff car, and the driver roared off in the direction of the White House. Minutes later they drove into the entrance of the West Wing. A guard opened the door, and Scott bounded out and ran up the stairs.

General Maxwell Taylor was at the top of the stairs to meet him. He held out his hand. "Good to see you, Gordon. The president is anxious to hear your report."

Scott shook the man's hand. There was an air of informality to the greeting, but Scott knew full well it was because of the business at hand. Protocol was often sacrificed when it came to high-level meetings.

He followed the general through the halls of the West Wing to the situation room. "I'm afraid this is a place you're going to have to get used to in the next week or so," Taylor said.

Scott nodded. This was duty he didn't enjoy. He would much prefer to be in command of troops in the field. There was something about the use of power that disillusioned him. Decisions were made, often for the wrong reasons, and resulted in things that nobody could ever know about. History would be written by people who were never involved and would include things that participants had chosen to ignore.

Taylor held the door open and Scott stepped inside. The situation room was normally used as the cabinet room. The brown leather chairs around the long mahogany oval table had the names of the presidential cabinet members on brass plaques embedded into the rear of each chair. Few of them would be present that evening, except for Dean Rusk, the secretary of state, whom Scott recognized right away, and Robert McNamara, the secretary of defense. Scott spotted General Curtis LeMay at once, the Air Force chief of staff. The man was pacing near the far windows, puffing on a black cigar. His coat was unbuttoned, and his belly hung noticeably below his belt. Gordon knew that what the man lacked in form he made up for in brash audacity.

The flag of the United States and the presidential flag stood at the far wall, near LeMay. The walls were a soft cream color with the marble busts of Benjamin Franklin and George Washington in niches flanking the fireplace. Charles Edouard Armand-Dumaresq's portrait of the signing of the Declaration of Independence hung over the fireplace. The president sat in a seat at the middle of the table surrounded by his brother Bobby and Robert McNamara. Vice President Johnson was across the table from the president with his back to the door. Scott was surprised to see him.

"Gentlemen, you all know Colonel Gordon. He's just brought us some photographs he took in Cuba."

The president looked up. "Gordon, good to see you. Have you seen your wife, Jackie, yet?"

Scott shook his head. "No, Mr. President, not yet."

Kennedy smiled. "Then we're in trouble on two fronts."

"Yes sir."

"Well, show us what you have." Kennedy looked at the others in the room. "The colonel was asked to give us an appraisal of the Cuban exile group in Florida, their readiness for combat." He smiled. "Of course he took a little sight-seeing trip to Cuba to get some pictures of Russian missiles there. Right, Colonel?"

"Yes sir. That's right."

He set his briefcase on the table and unzipped it, taking out a portfolio of pictures. "I made the trip with the aid of Cuban partisans led by a woman, a Maria Gonzales."

"A woman?" LeMay blew a cloud of cigar smoke with the question.

"Yes sir. Quite a woman. I saw her kill a Russian sentry with my own eyes."

"Good," LeMay barked. "That's what we need to do to all of them."

"This first photograph is of a Russian medium-range ballistic missile emplacement," Scott stated. "As you undoubtedly know, in Cuba these are strategic weapons capable of reaching Washington."

He passed the photograph to the president, who looked it over and sent it around the table. LeMay looked over McNamara's shoulder. The men took their time looking at the photograph. Dean Rusk picked it up and turned it around. He held it up to the president. "We can't let anyone see these. They were taken from the ground. To show them is to admit that we've been there."

"What's the problem with that?" LeMay asked.

Rusk softened his response. "It's not a problem to be there. Just to admit that we've been there."

"We have planes that can fly over and take pictures, isn't that right, General LeMay?" Bobby asked.

LeMay put his hands on the table and leaned forward. "The U-2 is designed for this job. Essentially, it's a jet-powered glider that can reach up to 60,000 feet and take very good pictures. It has such a unique configuration that there's no chance it can be mistaken for a bomber. It has a miniature electronic intelligence system we call ELINT. It's more advanced that anything we've ever had, capable of collecting data on Soviet radar systems. And we have a camera on board fitted with a 944.7-millimeter lens that can take 4,000 paired photos of a strip of earth 125 miles by 2,174 miles. The planes are on loan from the Air Force to the CIA and piloted by civilian contract pilots." He leaned back and chomped on his wet cigar. "I'd say we could handle this job. We'll get you real pretty pictures."

"I have some good news and bad news for you, General," Scott spoke up.

LeMay glared at him. "Well, what is it, man? Out with it."

"First the good news. Our best information tells us the Russians raise the missiles into firing positions at night and lower them in the daylight hours. Evidently, they are afraid they'll be seen from the ground. But if they are lowered during the day, then I would say you can get excellent pictures. They'll be laid out for your overflights, with nothing to hide them."

LeMay grinned, shifting the cigar in his mouth. "Commies, they're more stupid than I give them credit for. With those people in charge, there's no way they're going to hit a target here, not this far."

"They don't have to miss by much," Bobby added.

"What's the bad news?" the president asked. He sat back in his chair, prepared for the worst.

Scott reached into his portfolio and pulled out another set of photographs. He slid them across the table to the president. "SA-2s, Mr. President. These were the same missiles that shot down Francis Gary Powers over the Soviet Union in 1960. Taiwan has been using the U-2 to fly over Red China. They just lost one to a missile like this last month."

McNamara ran his hand over the side of his head. His hair was already plastered in place. "Mr. President, President Eisenhower authorized a U-2 flight over Cuba on October 27, 1960. Nothing happened."

"There were no SA-2s there in 1960," Scott said.

"I don't want another Francis Gary Powers," Kennedy said. "The Russians had that plane of his on display in Gorky Park. I won't be a part of another Russian exhibition of their marksmanship."

LeMay cleared his throat. "I don't think you have to worry about that, Mr. President. Powers took off from Pakistan. He was supposed to cross Russia and land in Norway, a nine-and-a-half-hour flight covering over three thousand miles. This is going to be a puddle jump by comparison. Powers's plane was fitted with plastic explosives linked to a delayed timing device that he was supposed to initiate prior to ejecting from the aircraft. He was unable to start the mechanism, however, and when he parachuted down, he was captured immediately. For crying out loud, the man even had a poison pill he was supposed to take. He couldn't even do that right."

The vice president had been cleaning his fingernails with a pearl-handled penknife. He seemed almost indifferent to the subject of the meeting, first staring down at his fingernails and then holding them back to admire his workmanship. He looked up at LeMay. "Are you telling us that plane's going to explode right away if he gets shot down?"

"We could fix it that way," LeMay growled. "Nothing to go wrong."

"A kamikaze pilot?" Bobby Kennedy sneered the question.

The president shook his head. "I'm not having any American suicide mission."

"Mr. President," LeMay exploded. "It's such a short flight across that island that if one of them SA-2 missiles was to hit our man, he'd be over the water in no time. Our Navy could pick him up, no mess, no bother. The plane would even go to the bottom if he failed to activate his charges. We ain't talking about nothing here that we can't handle. It's a piece of cake."

"Tell that to Powers's wife," Bobby shot back.

Kennedy looked back at LeMay. "I want Air Force pilots on this mission, no civilians. Am I understood?"

LeMay nodded. "You betcha. My boys would jump at the chance. Do a better job too. They're paid to fly and die."

"I don't want anybody dying," Kennedy added.

Rusk looked at LeMay. "None of us do, General."

"I'll handle it," LeMay said.

The president looked back at Scott. "What about your other business, Colonel? How ready are the Cubans?"

"Mr. President, it's my opinion those people aren't ready to run a cookout, much less an invasion. Their security is appalling. Castro will know when they're supposed to land days before they're even told in Florida. They have no practice with night-firing exercises and nothing to stop tanks. They would need training for that. I think they would be sitting ducks. If you can't make that landing with a Marine Corps division, I wouldn't even bother."

"We could do that, Mr. President," McNamara said. "We have exercises going on in the Caribbean right now. Those men could be ready when the time is right. Of course, if we have a late hurricane down there, the plans could be delayed."

Johnson grunted, once again staring at his nails. "That would be wonderful, a landing during a hurricane."

"What about our Mafia connection?" Bobby asked. "You are aware that our plans call for an invasion when Castro is eliminated?"

"Yes, Mr. Attorney General. I've been briefed on those plans. But Cox is not here to speak for that," Scott said.

"Where is he?" Bobby asked.

"He's taking care of a problem."

"A problem?"

"Yes, it seems one of the Mafia dons was murdered on the West Coast, a man who wasn't going along with the program. His family had their hackles raised, and they're in Florida now trying to dig up the truth."

"What is the truth?" the president asked.

Scott shook his head. "I'm afraid I can't answer that, Mr. President. If I could, I would have told them myself. The guy who's leading the family delegation is a former pastor, a friend of mine who was in the Marines."

The eyes of the men around the table widened. Bobby Kennedy spoke up. "You've got to be kidding, a preacher Marine in a Mafia family?"

Scott shrugged his shoulders and smiled. "Everybody's got to be born somewhere. We can't all be Kennedys."

The president laughed. He looked over at Bobby. "To hear Washington talk, everybody around here is a Kennedy."

CHAPTER 38

J
ohnny and Junior passed the Cuban camp on the edge of the swamp. They kept on driving without bothering to slow down. No doubt they had been seen. No matter how bad the security at the camp was, their Buick had passed several sentries. Johnny had seen the men in his rearview mirror talking on their two-way radios. He only hoped they hadn't recognized that it was Junior who was with him. Much better to have them think it was Frank Bass.

He turned by the pond and drove out onto the causeway. The Everglades were miles of treacherous swamp filled with alligators and deadly snakes. Finding Baldassare's body would be worse than looking for a needle in a haystack.

Johnny had his Walther PPK strapped to his ankle, but this time he had brought the .45 Colt automatic as well. He carried it in a snug underarm holster. The men were both wearing jeans and army boots, which they had bought from a surplus store.

Junior stared out the window as flights of birds took wing at the sight of their car. A flock of flamingos suddenly took off. The birds were beautiful, spreading their shocking pink wings and dangling their legs in midair.

"Quite a sight, isn't it?" Johnny asked.

Junior nodded. "Like nothing I've ever seen before."

"God has a way of painting a picture with real life, and it's nothing like a human being could ever produce."

Junior looked at him. "You have a God thing, don't you?"

Johnny chuckled. "I guess you could say that. There's nothing like death that can change a man's life. When I was in the war, I was sure I was going to die. Scott Gordon, that Marine colonel you met," he glanced at Junior, "He shared the good news of Christ with me. He told me I didn't have to fear death ever again, told me and Frank Bass."

"Is that where you won the Silver Star?"

"Yes. I was just doing my job."

"What did you do?"

Johnny's time in the war was something he never liked talking about. There were too many faces of men he would never see again. It wasn't a time for any man to take glory in. They were all kids then, scared beyond their wildest dreams. "There was a platoon pinned down by a Jap machine gun, my platoon." Johnny reluctantly droned the words. "I had gone to get water. I just did what anybody else would have done."

"Which was what?" Junior was interested now. He turned, his eyes riveted on Johnny.

"I dropped the canteens and took out a couple of grenades. I ran toward the enemy with my tommy gun and then stopped and threw the grenades." He chuckled under his breath. "I was a quarterback, remember."

"Yeah, so I heard."

"Well, those were the best touchdown passes I ever threw, right on the mark."

"I guess you never know when the things you're good at will come in handy."

"No, you never know." He looked at Junior. "That's one of the things that bothers me about you."

"What's that?"

"You strike me as a decent kid, but everything you're learning to be good at takes you outside the law. You take pride in what you do, but there are a lot of proud men behind bars. I wouldn't want that to happen to you."

"You're being a preacher again."

"I suppose I am. Guess that gets in a man's blood and it's hard to stop. I have learned one thing over the years. A man won't change until he wants to change. It took facing death to get me to change. I thought I had the world by the tail in college. I was at Stanford, the star quarterback, a son of wealthy parents, and in love. If anybody had talked to me about Jesus then, I would have listened politely, like you, and walked away thinking how nuts they were. There will come a time for you when you'll want to change."

Junior smiled. "When do you reckon that will happen? I got everything I need right now."

"Maybe it will happen tonight."

"Why should it?"

"If we do find Baldassare's body, you'll be seeing yourself in a few years. He was like you, brash, cocky, not a care in the world. Nobody could tell Baldy anything. You said yourself, if that man in your tent had done his job, your body would be missing too. Maybe God was protecting you. It could be He has something for you to do with your life, something else."

"I think my sap was protecting me, that and some cutlery I hung on the zipper of my tent."

"Think what you want. Me, I'd rather believe it was God. But look, I don't want to press you. You'll make up your own mind in your own time. I look at you and in many ways and I see my son. He's a little younger than you are, but he thinks he's got the world whipped too. People your age believe themselves to be immortal, that nothing can ever touch them, but something always does. It's called life."

They drove past the trees and the small shack on the hill. Rounding the bend in the road, they drove on to the spot where the tow truck had fished the Cadillac out of the swamp. There on a stump was a man fishing. He had a bamboo pole with a line in the water. Johnny pulled the Buick up and turned off the ignition. "I think I know that man."

They both got out of the car. "Jimmy, is that you?"

The man turned his head and grinned a big toothy smile. He was wearing the same Miami Dolphins shirt and red baseball cap. "Yeah, it's me. Come on ahead."

They both walked up close to the man's fishing hole. They could see a string of catfish in the water.

Jimmy looked them over. "Where's that pretty woman you brought before?"

Johnny smiled. "Back at her hotel, I guess."

"You mean her and you ain't together."

"Nope." Johnny stepped back. "This is Junior."

"I'd a thought you had that there woman stowed away or something." He ignored Junior, keeping to his train of thought. "You must be the moral type."

Johnny shrugged his shoulders. "I guess I am at that."

"Well, you better lay hold of that woman afore somebody snatches her away. You'll be sorry fer sure."

Junior looked at him. "Who's he talking about?"

"Maria. We were out here and ran into Jimmy. He's a chef, trained in Paris."

"France?"

Johnny nodded. "The best schools."

"What's he doing out here?"

Jimmy was pulling in his line and listening to them. He twirled the line around the pole and stepped over to them. "I'm on vacation. Been on vacation now for almost ten years. I kinda like it. Nobody bothered me until your daddy here come along, nobody 'cept them blamed Cubans."

"He's not my daddy," Junior said.

Jimmy cocked his head, eyeballing Junior. "He sure looks like your daddy to me, boy." He smiled at Johnny. "Well, what brings you back to my world?"

"That car you pointed out to us the other day. It belonged to my brother. I was hoping to recover his body. It would help my mother if I could bring him back home."

"Yeah, I saw them people in their tow truck." Jimmy shook his head. "You can forget about that body. Old Boss Bino and his folks are probably eating on him right now. Them crocks have a thing about dinner, ya know. They drag whatever it is they catch underwater and store it away like in a refrigerator. Then they go on down and nibble at it from time to time. No telling where that brother of yours is by now."

"I have to look." Johnny eyed the bank along the water. "Could you tell me where I might start?"

Jimmy smiled. "I'll do better than that. I can take you to a spot they might have taken him. It ain't far. We'll have to take you in my pole boat. It's kinda slow going, so we best get started. It's gonna be dark pretty soon, and you don't want to be out here after dark." His smiled broadened into a wide grin. "There be panthers out here after dark."

Jimmy led them around a bend to where his boat was tethered to a rickety dock. He laid his rifle and his string of fish in the bottom of the boat and stepped in. Johnny and Junior followed. Untying the boat, Jimmy picked up the long pole and pushed off. The bottom of the boat was filled with rocks to give it better balance.

They spent the next few minutes gliding over the water lilies and grasses that made up the marshy Everglades. The water was dark, almost a molasses color, with a sheen over the top that caught the dying light of the sun. Large mangrove trees stood at the water's edge, their branches drooping over the water, displaying endless cascades of Spanish moss. Frogs croaked, their throats swelling and then falling with each sound.

"The moss is beautiful," Junior said.

Jimmy smiled. "Witches hair. Ever time I look at them trees I see witches bending over the water and washing their gray hair. Out here a body gets used to pretty things. You got to name them though, or you just might forget."

The water turned a bright shade of green. Slime floating over the surface coated everything it came into contact with. One large 'gator had his nose out of the water. The green slime covered him, sticking to his large protruding mouth and nose. His coal-back eyes trained on them and their boat.

Jimmy pushed the boat straight for the mangrove-covered shore. "'Gator tail is mighty fine eating. I cook it ever which way from Cajun to Chinese."

"Chinese?" Junior asked.

"Sure. Makes an eating fool out of you if you fix it right. I like mine with Kung Pao spices or sweet and sour. I'll have to rustle some up for you."

Junior shook his head, still staring at the large alligator just yards away from them. "No thanks. I'll stick to beef and chicken."

"You don't know what yer missing, boy."

As they got closer to the knees of one of the mangrove trees, Jimmy spotted a curled-up snake. He pointed it out. "Water moccasin. Deadly things, them is. Better fight shy of them. I got no truck with snakes."

Johnny picked up a rock from the bottom of the boat. He slung it in the direction of the snake, hitting it with full force. The thing dropped into the water, slithering below the surface.

Jimmy looked back at him, raising one eyebrow. "You got yourself some kind of an arm there."

"He was a quarterback in college," Junior said.

"I believe it."

Jimmy pushed the boat closer. "Got to be careful now." He grinned. "We're coming up on one 'gator hidey-hole I know of. They're likely to be about, and they won't take too kindly to us stealing their food."

He reached out with the pole, sticking it between the knees of the tree. He pushed and prodded into the dark water. He continued to jam the pole down into the dark water, then pulled it up. "I think I got me something here. It feels soft and has some give to it."

Junior looked over at Johnny. "Doesn't this make you kind of sick? What if it is your brother?"

Johnny shook his head. "It's just a body if it is. There's no soul in it. He's gone, and there's nothing we can do about that."

"I don't get this then. Why bother?"

"This is for Mama, for her sake. If we do find Baldassare, we can take him home for the funeral. Funerals are for the living, not for the dead. I just have to think about Mama, what she would like." He shook his head. "I won't like telling her that her son is out here somewhere in the swamp, part of the food chain."

Jimmy pulled with the pole.

Both Johnny and Junior sat up to watch more closely. A body floated to the surface, or what was left of it. It was just a torso.

Junior sat back and covered his mouth.

"That's Bruno," Johnny said. "I'm sure of that. Bruno was a large man."

"I think there's more where he come from," Jimmy said. "If this one ain't your brother, then maybe he's still down there."

"Let's get on with it," Johnny said. "It ain't pretty, but it's got to be done."

They heard a loud splash in the water. Jimmy swung around and pointed. "That's him," he yelled. "That's Old Boss Bino."

They saw the white alligator swimming right for them. He was huge by alligator standards, perhaps the length of a new car. His tail swished back and forth, moving him steadily and swiftly through the pea-green muck.

Jimmy reached down for his rifle. He picked it up and slammed a round into the chamber. "I hate something powerful to do this. That old boy is practically a god out here in this swamp." Placing the rifle next to his cheek, he took aim and squeezed off a round.

The explosion of the rifle echoed out over the water. The bullet hit the water right in front of the swimming 'gator. Jimmy repeated the procedure two more times, each time with the same near-miss results. Finally, the big alligator turned and swam away, his snowy tail beating at the water.

"That was close," Jimmy said. "I was afeared I was going to have to kill the old boy, and I didn't want to do that."

"I was afraid he was going to kill us," Junior shot back.

Jimmy tied Bruno's corpse to the boat and went back to work with his pole. It took him several minutes before he said, "Got me another one." He looked back at Johnny. "You know the cops would never do this. They wouldn't come out here, and they sure wouldn't know where to look. I lost me a couple of sheep though, and this is where I found them, or what was left of them. 'Gators are creatures of habit, like the rest of us. They put their food where they can find it when they get hungry."

He pushed and pulled with the long pole. Then Johnny could see the body. It was Baldassare. His body was missing a leg, but the head was still intact. "That's my brother."

Jimmy dragged the body closer with his pole. "I don't know what you're going to do with this thing when we get it back to your car, but I'm just going to tie him on to the boat. He's past harm by now. We just have to keep the gators away."

Junior looked at Johnny. His face was almost ashen. "What are we going to do with him?"

"I'll get him to the road and call Frank Bass. The FBI will want an autopsy. There's got to be testing done to see what type of weapon was used." He swallowed hard and sat down. "Then I'll call Mama."

"What about the others?" Junior asked.

Jimmy pointed to a group of gators gathering on the shore. "We stick around and try to find them, and we just might have a war on our hands. I ain't got that much left in the way of ammunition."

They poled their way out of the tree-shadowed area they were in. The sun was setting. Its bright rays, almost orange in color, seemed to blanket the grass and water lilies.

Suddenly, they heard the sound of an engine. It was like the sound of a small airplane. Jimmy swung around and pointed in the distance. "It's an airboat. Them things are powerful noisy. People jest can't take things nice and slow, all the time got to have speed."

As the powerful flat-bottomed boat with the airplane propeller came into better view, they could see the dark shapes of three men on board. One was in the driver's seat and the other two were armed.

"It's them Cubans," Jimmy shouted. He dropped the pole and picked up his rifle.

They then heard the staccato sound of machine gun fire. The bullets cut a swath in the water lilies near the bow of their small boat. They could hear rounds as they sliced the lilies, like a knife going through a head of lettuce.

Jimmy turned around and held his hand up to his face, staring into the setting sun. "Good thing for us that sun's behind us. It'll throw their eyes off a mite." He swung around and held the rifle up to his cheek, taking aim. "But it ain't gonna bother my aim at all."

He squeezed off a round, the rifle slamming into his shoulder. Johnny could see one of the men in the airboat fall. The boat suddenly spun around and cut its engines.

Jimmy looked at them. "I'm gonna make these next shots count, put the fear of the Almighty into them. I only got me three more rounds."

CHAPTER 39

They found the boat tied up at Key Largo the next morning, just as promised. George McDonald was the skipper, and it was just as well. He owned the hotel too. McDonald was a rather rotund man in a flowery shirt that arched over his ample belly. His head was bald except for wisps of gray over his ears that he combed straight back. But you could only see his head when he took off his skipper's cap and rubbed the sweat from the top of his head.

Johnny and Junior loaded the supplies on board the boat. The *Cat-o'-Nine* was a small fishing trawler with an interior cabin and a flying bridge. It rose straight out of the water, and its engines chugged sluggishly.

Junior lifted a box and waited for Johnny. "You got Baldy's body all taken care of?"

Johnny nodded. "Frank took charge of it. It's with the medical examiner's office. He told me it wouldn't be more than a few days, and then we can ship him home."

Junior shook his head. "I don't mind telling you, I was more than a little worried. We were outgunned yesterday."

Johnny picked up a box. "The Cubans didn't know that. It took only a few rounds from Jimmy to convince them we were not going to be so easy."

"Good thing. You reckon they were after us?"

"You bet they were. They weren't trying to disturb Jimmy's fishing. Johnny stopped. "The man whose initial is on that page you showed me from the safe, I think I know who it is."

McDonald stood at the top of the gangplank, watching Johnny and Junior as they brought aboard the last of their luggage. He planted his hands on his hips and grinned. "I'm glad you could come. We get kinda lonely this time of the year, nothing but nuns and kids about, and a few lime farmers."

Johnny put down his bags. He looked out over the water, which was a bright blue. "Why is that? I would think you'd have lots of people."

McDonald untied the lines and threw them onto the dock. "It's kind of late for the Keys. Hurricane season, you know. People get kinda skittish and want to stay locked to land. But I wouldn't worry." He cracked a slight smile. "The Sisters of the Lost are there, and they pray." He laughed.

"Sisters of the Lost?"

McDonald nodded. "It's an orphanage. No telling how many kids there are. They pretty much keep to themselves. You won't have any noise unless you make it yourself."

"We'll be plenty quiet," Johnny said. "Like in church."

"We got us a lighthouse, too, 'course nobody's used it for twenty years or so. The place is a ghost house, nothing left but memories. Every once in a while we catch teenage boys trying to score with a girl." He shrugged. "But it ain't nothing. Crab Key will suit you just fine."

Crab Key was a small island not far from Key Largo. It was no more than a smudge of land from the distance, but as they got closer, they could see a few trees and the towering stone lighthouse. On the small rise behind the dock was the hotel. The three-story structure had wooden turrets and a balcony on the second floor. The wooden steps leading up from the beach were connected to an enormous front porch.

McDonald pointed from the flying bridge. "That's the Queen Hotel. You can get a great view from just about any room I got." He cut back on the engines as the *Cat-o'-Nine* glided toward the small dock.

A nun and several small children were waiting for them on the dock. The children were running to the end of the dock in a sort of race, jumping gaps in the boards, hopping on one foot, then running again. They raced to the end of the precarious series of washed-out wooden planks and whirled their arms around to keep from falling off.

McDonald spun the wheel, easing the boat into a group of truck tires that were nailed to the dock's pilings, and then killed the engine. The boat bounced off the tires, then came to rest beside them, the waves gently rocking. The children began to clap.

McDonald laughed, climbing down from the bridge. "Always nice to come back to applause." He grinned. "Makes a man feel welcome. It's a good feeling, mighty good."

He pushed the gangplank into position and took Gina's hand to help her off. Children surrounded them. "Let me introduce Sister Mary Margaret. She and Sister Janene take care of the orphanage and all these here kids."

The nun was rather portly with a large nose and Ben Franklin glasses that were much too small for her. Her black habit looked hot and her face, while tan and dark, was dripping with perspiration.

She stuck out her hand and smiled. "Welcome to Crab Key."

Gina took the woman's hand. "Looks like you've got your hands full."

There were nine children, all boys. A few reached out and touched Gina's slacks. They were evidently unaccustomed to seeing a woman in pants. Others stared at Rocko. His size was intimidating for many men, and in the children's eyes he must have seemed like a giant. They were mostly dressed in shorts and barefoot.

The nun smiled. "Yes, aren't they wonderful?"

Junior grinned.

Sister Mary Margaret looked down at all the children. "Go up and get our supplies. Captain George will show you which are ours." As the children went up the gangplank, she called out to them. "Don't forget our mail." She smiled at Johnny and the men. "I know you'll like the fishing here. And we will all enjoy whatever it is you catch."

"We ain't here to catch fish, Sister," Rocko said.

Her eyes widened. "Really? There's not much else to do here on Crab Key."

Rocko smiled. "Maybe so, but we're here for a meeting."

"A convention?" she asked.

"Something like that."

"Most men prefer their conventioneering in Miami, lots to do, places to go."

"It's sort of a private party," Johnny added.

"Well, I hope our weather stays nice for you." She glanced at McDonald. "I don't like the look of the waves today, and the radio says there's a hurricane brewing outside the Bahamas."

"It's late in the year for something coming our way," McDonald said. "No doubt it'll turn north, probably hit the Carolinas."

The nun fingered the silver cross around her neck. "It's God's way of causing us to trust Him. Otherwise we would grow too proud." She smiled as the children came back down the gangplank, each of them carrying a box. Some of them were struggling with boxes too heavy for them. "You'll have to come visit us. We love visitors. The other children would enjoy meeting you."

"Can we give you a hand with your things?" Johnny asked.

The nun shook her head. "No, that won't be necessary. The children have to learn that life is a struggle. Nothing worthwhile comes by leisure."

In a matter of minutes Johnny and his party were heading up the steps that led to the hotel. Johnny glanced back at the small parade of children plodding down the beach.

A matronly gray-haired woman opened the screen door that led to the lobby. She was in her late fifties at best, with her hair pulled into a bun. She was wearing a flowered dress that lapped around her bare calves. She had a smudge of makeup applied to her otherwise tan cheeks.

"This is my missus," McDonald said. "Her name is Joyce. She's going to be cooking for you. I hope you like seafood. Too much trouble to bring much else in from the mainland."

As they stepped into the lobby, McDonald raced behind a massive desk that wrapped itself around a wall of slots, each with a key dangling from it. He spun a large book around and took out a long black pen from its holder on the desk. "Here, folks. If we can just get each of you to sign in, we'll see to your room keys."

After going upstairs to room 202, Johnny put his leather suitcase on the lumpy bed and stepped over to the large balcony window. The window had floor-length shutters that folded out onto the mezzanine. It was a simple room with a white rattan chest of drawers, a small writing desk made out of cane, and a wicker rocker, complete with padded seat. There was a small radio on the end table, beside the cane lamp. The bed was lumpy, but the place had a bath.

He had been to this place as a child with his father, the first time he had ever been deep-sea fishing. It was a time when his father could sit back and tell him stories about the family in Naples, Italy, people Johnny had never seen. His father always talked about hard work and the grinding oppression of never knowing where your next meal was coming from. There had always been a sense of self-esteem when his father told the stories of the old country, as if hardship was a matter of pride.

It saddened him to think about his father. The man had come to America and been introduced to life on the streets of New York, a shark tank for an eight-year-old. The streets had taught the man that in order to survive he had to outfight, outthink, and outrun anybody else. His father had climbed to the top of the Mafia. He had succeeded. It had evidently been his conscience that had killed him, a sense of right and wrong. He had refused to participate in a political murder. The irony of that hit Johnny like a hammer.

"Everything OK?"

Johnny turned around at the sound of Gina's voice. "Sure. Come on in."

Gina stepped into the room and walked over to where Johnny was standing. "You seemed to be lost in thought."

"Just thinking about Papa. He brought me here. I was no older than those kids we saw down there."

She put her hand on his arm. "This must be hard for you."

Johnny nodded. "Yes. It hadn't struck me until now."

"And finding your brother's body yesterday on top of that." She shook her head. "I can't imagine that."

Johnny looked at her. "I think I'm feeling more sorry for myself than anything, all those lost opportunities. A man thinks he has his whole life ahead of him and suddenly most of it is gone. Then you think of what you've lost, people you could have been with, people you should have told that you loved them."

"Johnny, your father knew you loved him."

"But he didn't hear it from me, not for twenty years." He pointed to his chest and tapped it gently. "I blame myself for that. I've learned a lot of things about myself on this trip. One of them is that I should never let my pride get in the way of loving people. Life is too short."

Gina faced him and took hold of both of his arms. "It's time to stop blaming yourself. Life happens. People die. Babies are born. The world doesn't revolve around you and what you do or don't do. Other people make choices too. You aren't the only one who gets to decide."

She shook him slightly. "You're conscientious and kind. You care about people. But you still have to be the hero, the guy with the ball. Knock it off. You don't count that much. Just be yourself. I like you. I always have. I love—" She stopped mid sentence and shook her head. "I'll leave it at that."

"You were going to say that you love me." Johnny spoke in a soft voice. "Is that right? Do you love me?"

The sound of an airplane broke the mood. They both looked out the window. Flying low on the horizon was a single-engine floatplane. It was cruising just over the waves, its flaps down.

They heard the sound of footsteps in the hall. Junior stuck his head in the door. "That's Cox's plane. He told me he was going to fly here."

Gina looked at Johnny. "Do you know what you're going to say to the man?" she asked.

Johnny shook his head. "I haven't got a clue."

"You'd better think about it."

Junior stepped closer to them. "I think you should just leave him alone with me for a while. I've been through those files. You should see them, Johnny. There are a few things in there you might need to know."

"All right. I'll take a look at them after dinner."

Junior looked out the window as the plane touched down in the small bay. "You know, if this man is in charge of the family's involvement in this Cuba thing, then he's responsible for your father's death. At least he knows about it. It might mean he's the one who ordered Baldassare's murder, too, maybe even tried to kill us."

He glanced down at Johnny's ankle. "I hope you've got your gun strapped on. You might need it."

CHAPTER 40

Johnny, Gina, and Junior, along with Rocko, all met Cliff Cox as he walked into the lobby. Maria was with him, but she didn't look happy about it. She brightened somewhat when she saw Johnny.

Cox walked over to Johnny and held out his hand. "I'm Cliff Cox. You must be the one I talked to on the phone?"

"That would be me," Junior said, stepping forward and keeping his hands to his side, not making an attempt to shake.

Johnny saw the look of surprise on Cox's face. Junior had no doubt sounded threatening over the phone, unquestionably much older than his years.

Johnny merely nodded. "I'm Johnny Pera. This is Gina Cumo, our attorney. And this is Rocko, a friend of the family."

Cox dropped his hand to his side and smiled. "Your attorney?" A smile creased his lips. "Pleased to meet you." He looked back. "You all know Maria."

Johnny smiled and nodded at Maria. "Yes, we've met. We didn't know she was coming."

Cox smiled sheepishly. "I'm sort of watching her for a while." He glanced back in Maria's direction. "I think she'd much rather be in Cuba right now. We'll just have to keep her entertained, won't we? By the way, Javier Lage couldn't come to this little shindig of yours. But I know everything he does, and I'll get those papers you have."

Johnny walked toward the door. "We were just about to take a tour of the island, maybe visit an orphanage." He looked at Maria. "Would you like to come along?"

"Yes, very much."

Cox put his hand out, as if to stop them. "Just a second. What about my photographs? I'm here to get down to business."

"Our other guests haven't arrived yet," Johnny said. "You'll have to cool your heels like the rest of us. You'll get what you want, provided we get what we want."

They walked down the stairs and onto the beach. The sea was a sapphire blue and the waves appeared to be higher than when they had arrived. The waves curled at the edge of the beach and slammed down on the sand, sending foam and brine surging up to the edge of the grassy bluff the hotel sat on. "Look's like we're going to get our feet wet," Johnny shouted. He was trying to make himself heard over the pounding surf.

They came to the edge of the beach and waited for the next set of waves. Just as the water was retreating, they ran across the open sand. It was soft beneath their feet, and they splashed through the small puddles left by the last set of waves. Just as they got to the bluff, waves came crashing down behind them again.

Gina laughed. "That was close."

"I ain't ready for a swim just yet," Rocko said.

The bluff had a path punctuated by stairs made out of old railroad ties. They were partially buried but offered some footing as they climbed. Johnny fell in beside Maria. "I take it you didn't exactly want to come on this little trip?"

She glanced at him, her lower lip protruding. "I'm wasting my time. I don't trust your CIA, and I certainly don't trust this Cox man."

Johnny nodded. "We haven't exactly brought him here to give him the good citizenship award."

"Why is he here?"

"He undoubtedly knows something about my father's murder."

"Good luck getting him to talk." Maria frowned. "Even if he does, you'd be a fool to believe him."

They got to the steps of the lighthouse. The salty air had long since rusted an old padlock on its faded green door. Johnny circled the tower with Gina, while Rocko and Junior played with the lock and Maria stayed to watch. The lighthouse was a narrow structure made of stone. Windows, many with broken panes, spiraled upward to the top.

"Ought to be a nice view from up there," Gina said.

Johnny smiled at her. "Quite romantic, I'm sure."

Gina glanced back in Maria's direction. "Just be careful who you take up there. Captain George says it's a teenage lover's lane."

Johnny laughed. "I'm well past that now."

She cocked her head, looking at him. "Are you really? I hope not."

"We got it open," Rocko called out to them.

Inside was a broken chair standing precariously on three legs. Steel stairs wound up the inside of the old lighthouse, spiraling only a few feet away from the stone walls. It was dark except for the windows on the sides.

Johnny spotted a light switch almost hidden behind a set of dials. It was attached to a car battery on a shelf. He reached over and turned it on. Several lights came on, bare bulbs hanging at intervals along the winding staircase.

"Hey," Rocko called out from above. "You found the lights."

Johnny yelled up at him. "I wouldn't want you to fall, old man."

Rocko leaned over the railing and stared down at him. The other three were almost a story above them. "Who you calling old? I could whip you on my worst day."

Johnny looked at Gina. "We'd better head up there. We don't want them hurting themselves."

Gina nodded and they started to climb the stairs. She was still limping slightly.

"Your leg still bothering you?"

"I'll be all right. I found some iodine to paint the cuts with."

Johnny made sure they kept the pace slow while they climbed the stairs. He stayed close to Gina, watching her every move. It was a slow, demanding climb. Occasionally they would pass one of the windows. Each one offered a special peek at the water below. The waves crashed onshore, and the swells seemed to be getting bigger with each set. They came to a broom that was on a step. Johnny picked it up and leaned it against the railing.

The top of the stairs had a small landing that led into the room with the searchlight. The handrails there were steel but broken and shaky from years of wear. Johnny pushed them together, and then he and Gina stepped inside. The others were moving from window to window, looking out on the ocean. In the middle of the room was a large steel trestle holding the dead light and its apparatus. The gears were frozen in place like the workings of a huge clock.

Rocko was standing at one of the windows, looking out to sea. He was shaking his head. "I don't like the looks of that sky."

Gina and Johnny walked over to where he was standing. The sky was getting darker in the distance, and clouds were boiling in layers. Whitecaps were on the water as far as they could see.

"It's a storm," Maria said.

Junior looked at them. "I hope this doesn't keep Trafficante away. He's supposed to get here by boat this afternoon."

Rocko grinned. "You ever known a man like Santos Trafficante to stay away from money, especially his money?"

Junior nodded. "I guess you're right."

"Of course I am."

The wooden floor of the small circular room was littered with broken glass, old beer cans, and even older newspapers. A glass-orbed hurricane kerosene lamp stood on a small crate next to what had once been a bed. Now it was nothing but springs set on a broken-down wooden frame. A makeshift bookcase was bolted to the wall next to the bed. It contained copies of paperback books, mostly Louis L'Amour. They were lying on their sides with the titles exposed.

Junior stepped over to them and picked up a copy. He stared at it. "*Hondo*. Guess there's not much to do up here except read."

"Those must have been left here after the lighthouse keeper moved out. Maybe McDonald likes to get away and read."

"Let's go," Johnny said. "If we're going to pay a visit to that orphanage, we'd better get moving."

"You go on to the orphanage without me," Rocko said.

Junior clutched the book in his hands. "I'll go back too. Maybe I'll do some reading."

"I'll just go with Rocko and Junior," Maria said. "You two go on alone."

When Johnny and Gina got outside, the wind was blowing. The clouds nearby were streaked black, brown, and white. The sea was almost a deep green now, but with row after row of whitecapped waves. They headed over the rise while the others went down to the beach.

When they made it over the hill, they could see the layout of the small orphanage. The fruit trees were bending slightly with the wind, their leaves bright and green. One large building had windows with the shutters closed. It was a two-story building that had been painted white with orange trim. Behind it were smaller buildings, each painted in orange and white. They saw the nun they had met at the docks. She was standing beside a long clothesline with three of the children. Sheets and clothes were flapping in the wind, and the four of them were fighting to take them down.

Johnny and Gina hurried down the small hill. "Here, sister, why don't you let me help you?"

He fell into place beside the small children and plucked off the clothespins, one by one, handing the clothes to the little boys at his side.

"Thank you so much," the nun shouted into the wind. "We've got to get these down before that blow hits us." She shook her head. "I don't want to go looking all over Crab Key for sheets and clothes."

When they had filled the large plastic baskets, Johnny and Gina filed in behind the nun and her small entourage and carried the dry garments to the large building.

"You can put them here," the nun said, setting down her own basket on a long metal table. She smoothed her habit and straightened her starched headdress. "It's so nice of you to help us."

"Our pleasure, Sister." Johnny set down his burden and took Gina's. "We just thought we would pay you a visit."

"I'm glad you did." She stared down at her small helpers. "You get back to class. Sister Janene will be missing you."

The children scrambled off, running down the long hallway.

The nun let out a big sigh. "We sometimes have to have help wherever we can find it. Would you like to see our facilities?"

"We'd love to," Gina said.

The nun looked around. "This is our assembly hall and chapel." She pointed to the rows of small chairs. Some were plastic with metal legs. Others were made out of wood and painted a variety of colors. An altar stood on one end with a wooden carving of Jesus on the cross behind it. On either wall basketball hoops were hung. "We worship here and sing." She smiled. "Sometimes we play basketball."

"I can see that," Johnny smiled.

"The kitchen and dining room are through those doors to your left, and down the hall is our school. The dormitories are upstairs."

"Seems like a tidy arrangement," Johnny said.

The nun smiled and nodded. "It is a home to these children and to Sister Janene and myself. God has a home for everyone who will only come to Him."

"That's the problem, isn't it?" Johnny asked. "Getting people to come to Him."

The nun's eyes twinkled. She smiled. "I see you're a spiritual man."

"That he is," Gina chuckled.

"That's good." She spoke with a sigh. "We don't often see men who love God. I think most people see religion as something for women and children. Men are too strong to be meek, but Jesus was a strong man, a carpenter."

Johnny nodded. "And brave."

"The bravest. Come with me. I will show you the children."

She started walking down the hall. "We take turns, Sister Janene and myself. Some days I take care of the cooking and chores while she teaches. Other days I get to teach the children." She shook her head. "She is a godsend. I wouldn't know what to do without her."

She stopped and looked at them. "It will be nice to have you as visitors. Let me explain something to you. The children here all know what visitor's day is about. Nice people from Miami come to take them for a walk. They look them over to see if our children fit into their adoption plans. They almost never do. People want babies. Then they bring the child back and he watches them go away through the window. You see, our children are abandoned. And they are abandoned all over again whenever we have visitors day. The boys at our orphanage have learned to cry at an early age. Now there are no more tears. It is just as well. Jesus will never abandon them."

They both followed her into a large classroom. The nun at the chalkboard was scribbling numbers with a piece of yellow chalk. Unlike Sister Mary Margaret, Sister Janene was thin as a rail. She was young, perhaps in her late twenties, with a long face and pointed chin.

Sister Mary Margaret clapped her hands. It brought every head and every eye swiveling around in their direction. There must have been close to thirty children in their seats, all boys. "Class, I have a special treat for you, two visitors. We have a man here who loves God and his wife."

Johnny cleared his throat softly. "I'm sorry, Sister. Gina is not my wife." He glanced at Gina, whose face now had a soft blush to it. "Actually, she's my attorney."

"Really? How wonderful." She turned back to the class. "Did you hear that children? We have a woman here who is a lawyer." She smiled. "Have any of you ever seen a woman lawyer before?"

"No!" The children all shouted in unison.

"Perhaps you could show them what you can do. Would you like to sing a song?"

"Yes!" Once again, they answered in chorus.

"Fine, then let's sing our special song, 'Jesus Loves the Children of the World.'"

Sister Janene stepped over to her large wooden desk, picked up a small metal pitch pipe, and blew a note. The children then began to sing, "Jesus loves the little children, all the children of the world. Red and yellow, black, and white, they are precious in His sight. Jesus loves the little children of the world."

Johnny felt a nudge at his elbow. Junior was standing there.

"Trafficante's boat is coming in. Thought you might want to get there."

Johnny smiled, looking back at the children. "Did you get a chance to hear them?"

"Yes," Junior smiled. "Very nice."

Sister Mary Margaret turned, taking both Johnny and Gina's hand. "Thank you for coming to see us. New faces are always appreciated." She looked into Junior's eyes. "You know, God makes everyone special. No one is like any other. Our dreams are different, but our souls are all the same, hungry for a home, needing to be loved."

"Thank you, Sister," Johnny said.

The three of them made their way down the hall and out the door. They hurried over the hill and spotted a long speedboat coming into the bay. The chop on the water was causing it to move up and down in the rough sea.

They met Rocko as he was coming out of the hotel.

"I didn't know if you were going to make it," Rocko said.

Johnny looked back at Gina. "You can go back to the hotel, if you like. No reason for you to stand out in this wind."

The three men hurried down to the dock. They arrived just as Trafficante's boat was nudging the tires.

"Nice to see you," Johnny shouted.

"Where's my money?" Trafficante yelled over the sound of the wind.

"It's inside," Junior said. "You'll get it tonight when we all sit down."

Two of Trafficante's men climbed out onto the dock. They lifted three suitcases out of the boat, then reached back for the old man.

Johnny stepped forward. He looked Trafficante in the eye. "This party is just for you, Don Trafficante, nobody else."

Trafficante's eyes darted between the two men at his side. "I don't go nowhere without my people."

"Then you don't come here," Johnny shouted back. "This is a private party. You don't want your money back, that's fine. There's an orphanage here that needs money more than you do." He smiled. "We'll just pass it along to them."

Trafficante put his hands on his hips and looked up at the sky. "You can't expect me to stay here with you people, not tonight. There's a hurricane heading this way, a big one."

"What's the matter?" Johnny asked. "You don't fear the wrath of God, do you?"

"I ain't afraid of nothing," Trafficante growled. He motioned to his men in a sweeping movement with his right hand. "You go back. I'll stay. You just make sure you come back for me late tomorrow. That understood?"

CHAPTER 41

J unior carried Trafficante's bag as the older man waddled up the steps toward the hotel. Johnny held the door for him and followed him inside.

McDonald hurried in from the dining room, a smile on his face. He looked like a dog that had finally uncovered a long forgotten bone. "Hey, great to have you. Joyce is fixing supper now. Ought to be ready in a jiff." He opened the wooden flap that hid the back of the counter and stepped around it, letting it drop with a loud bang. He slammed the guest register open and spun it around. "Just sign in. We'll get you a nice room."

Trafficante eyed the red-painted rafters and the antique lights that hung from the ceiling. One of the lights was blinking, an incessant sputtering flash. "Just make sure it's a dry room," Trafficante muttered. "I want to get outta here tomorrow."

McDonald handed over the pen. "No problem. This little blow will be over tonight. It'll come through here and be gone before you know it."

Trafficante put the pen to the ledger, then looked up at McDonald's grinning face. "Yeah, probably take us with it."

"I'll take his bag up to his room," Junior said.

Johnny nodded. "Thanks." He was certain Trafficante would never thank the man.

The dining room was just off the lobby. Bay windows faced the ocean, several covered with shutters. One shutter banged incessantly, slapping against the window with each gust of wind. A half-dozen small tables were scattered around, but McDonald had unfolded a large one in the middle of the room. It was covered with a damask tablecloth; folded linen napkins stood by each gleaming white plate. Crystal goblets were filled with ice water, and wineglasses made the setting complete. Several bottles of wine were already on the table.

McDonald leaned over an ancient radio. He turned the dial and eased the red needle into place. "It looks like a big one," the broadcaster said, "maybe a category four. Yessiree, friends, you'd better bring the dogs and cats in tonight. Nancy is going to be a real gullywasher. It ought to miss us in Miami, but not by much. Looks to be going through the Keys. Let's hope those folks down in conch country come through this without getting themselves washed away."

Johnny had stopped to listen. "Nancy, that's my daughter's name."

McDonald looked up at him. "Well, you're going to have something to remember her by tonight. Hurricane Nancy is going to hit us. Let's hope she's in a good mood." He turned off the radio and stood up, looking out the window. "I wouldn't want to be out there tonight.

We'll be all right, though." He cast a guarded look in Johnny's direction. "The old Queen Hotel has been through a few of them before."

"Any category fours?" Johnny asked.

"I'm not sure. They never used to categorize these things. Had a big one in 'thirty-five. Lots of folks in the Keys died."

At 6 P.M. the group seated themselves around the table. McDonald circled the room, lighting candles. "Never can tell when we're going to lose power in a storm like this," he laughed. "I want you to see what you're eating. Joyce fixed some swordfish steaks for you tonight. You'll love 'em."

Trafficante reached over and picked up a bottle of red wine. He poured a glass and drank it down, slurping and gulping the glass until it was empty. He then refilled his glass and set the bottle down.

Johnny sat at the end of the table, facing the lobby and the front door. He was flanked by Maria and Gina. Rocko and Trafficante sat with their backs to the bay window. Junior and Cox took the seats closest to the kitchen. There was one empty chair at the opposite end of the table, the one nearest the lobby.

McDonald and his wife brought out the salads. They carefully placed them in front of each guest. "Guess, you got one empty seat."

"Looks like it," Johnny said.

McDonald laughed. "Well, at least he's paid for. He probably got hung up in the storm." He set down the last of the salad plates and went back through the swinging doors into the kitchen.

The group started in on their salads. Cox took one bite and looked in Johnny's direction. "You know those photos you're holding are matters of national security, don't you?"

Johnny nodded. "So I understand." He smiled. "But you won't be going anywhere with them, at least not tonight."

"Nobody's going anywhere tonight," Trafficante mumbled. He shook his head. "How I let you people talk me into coming here is beyond me. Man ain't made to be out in a spot like this, eating let-tuce and drinking bad wine. I got to be crazy."

Trafficante was a man who enjoyed his food. His ample belly was testimony to that.

"Food is food," Rocko said. "I'm thankful for any of it."

Johnny watched as Junior stared out the remaining window. "Something troubling you?" he asked.

"I was thinking about those nuns and kids out there," Junior said. "I hope they're all right."

Rocko grinned. "They got God to protect them, don't they?" He circled his fork in Junior's direction. "You shouldn't worry about them." He let a slight smile crease his lips. "Next thing we know, you'll be turning into Johnny here, a real do-gooder."

The front door to the lobby flew open with a crash. A tall man in a dripping wet trench coat stepped in.

Johnny jumped to his feet. "Felix!" He circled the table in the man's direction. "We didn't think you were going to make it. Here, let me take your coat. You must be drenched."

He closed the front door and took Felix's coat, hanging it on a rack. Then, taking the man by the arm, he led him to the empty place at the table.

Maria jumped to her feet. "What's he doing here?" Her voice was shrill, very caustic.

"You know this man?" Johnny asked.

Felix looked at him. "Maria is my ex-wife."

Maria shook her finger in Felix's direction. "He's a traitor, a com-munist. He had my father killed, and I have sworn to see him dead, him and all like him."

Cox put both hands up. He looked at Maria, wide-eyed. "I didn't have anything to do with this," he said, shaking his head. "I swear."

Rocko laughed. "Well, ain't this going to be a fun evening?"

Johnny abandoned Felix at the vacant chair and circled the table toward Maria. "I'm sorry, Maria. We didn't know you would be here, and we certainly didn't know about any connection you might have had with Felix. I can only apologize for any discomfort."

"I'm not staying in this place, not with him."

Trafficante laughed. "The storm will probably kill us all. You won't have anything to worry about 'cause he'll be dead and so will you."

Gina reached over and took Maria's arm. "I'm sorry, Maria."

"Yeah, sit down and eat up, Missy," Trafficante said. "It'll probably be your last meal. Swordfish steak. We'll be joining them before long."

Maria slowly sat back down. She continued to glare in Felix's direction, every stare filled with hatred.

Johnny took his place. He looked at Felix. "I don't know how you made it."

Felix brushed his mustache aside. "I almost didn't. The boat I was on came close to turning back. If Crab Key hadn't been so close, we would have." He lifted his chin, almost arrogantly. "But my mission here is important. My country is at stake."

"Your country," Maria growled the words. "Don't think it's your country just because they pay you to live in New York." She beat on her chest. "It's my country. I live there. I fight there. I will die there. Not you. You will die here."

Felix smiled. "You are a pawn of the American CIA. They pay you to spy on your own people, your own revolution. You should live in the swamps of Florida with the rest of the malcontents."

Maria got out of her seat and shook her finger at him. "You forget your history. José Marti was driven from Cuba many times. The Spanish had control of our people. He came home to fight them and was killed on the plains of Dos Rios. Now our people's minds have been captured by the Russians, foreigners with strange ideas that keep the people simple, take away their dignity. You have sold your soul to Marx and Lenin, not José Marti. He was one of us."

Trafficante got to his feet and held up his hands. "Look, folks, we're not going to solve Cuba's problems tonight, not in this place. Just sit yourselves down and enjoy your dinner. We're here to deal with another problem. You can solve yours later." He laughed. "I'll even give you the guns and let you both have it out."

"My money's on the woman," Rocko sneered.

McDonald and his wife emerged from the kitchen. They circled the table picking up the salad plates. In a few minutes more, they were back with the main course. It took them several trips before each of the diners was staring at a large hunk of swordfish. Small red potatoes that looked like pebbles pulled out of a stream and French cut beans that smelled of nutmeg completed the dinner.

As they started eating, the noise of the loose shutter grew louder. It banged against the outside of the window. McDonald came out of the kitchen with a hammer in his hand. "'Scuse me, folks. "I'm going to do something I should have done earlier today. I've got some plywood outside, and I'm going to nail it over the windows. Nothing to worry about. I'll take it down tomorrow. No need to get nervous. We'll make it through this thing."

They continued eating. This time they could hear the sound of McDonald's hammer, a constant rapping in the wind.

"Why don't we deal with the matter at hand," Gina said, matter-of-factly. "We finish that and we can find the high ground if we have to."

"There ain't no high ground on this place," Trafficante said. "You best find something that floats."

"We're here," Johnny said, "because all of you have some knowledge of my father's murder. Only one of you knows everything, but you all know something."

Trafficante leaned back in his chair and patted his mouth with his napkin. "I know your papa was a good man, misguided sometimes, maybe, but a good man. I liked him."

Johnny got up from his seat and walked around the table. He stood behind Trafficante. "Why don't we start with you, Felix? You were involved with this, weren't you? Enzo Gatto got you committed, up to your neck."

Felix shook his head. "I had little to do with it. I did get a call from Enzo Gatto. He was worried."

"He was worried about Cuban retribution for these plots against Castro," Johnny added.

"Yes." Felix nodded.

"He thought it might sour the families against the drug trade through Cuba. They might go elsewhere and take you out of it altogether. He told you that you would lose out, that you would get nothing if your country took out one of the heads of the families."

"Yes," Felix agreed. "Gatto said the families had long memories. Enemies stayed enemies. But I told him that something had to happen. I had to show my government that I was doing something about these plots against Fidel or else I would be called home. My usefulness would be over." He balled up his fist and pounded softly on the table. "It was up to me to do something, anything that I could report back to Havana."

"And so you needed Gatto's help. You needed a success story."

"Yes, I did."

"And he needed your promise that your government wouldn't do anything," Johnny said, "that you'd let him handle it."

"Yes."

"So Gatto's responsible," Rocko blurted out. "And he's not here."

Johnny shook his head. "No. Enzo Gatto was just the middleman. It might have been his idea in the first place, but he didn't know who to go after." Johnny looked at Trafficante. "That's where you came in, Santos. You're the one who suggested my father."

"Now hold on a minute," Trafficante blurted out. He put his hands on the table and gripped it.

The shutters shook violently, and the crashing of the surf outside intensified. Suddenly the lights flickered. They flashed on and off and then went out altogether. Now there were just the candles on the table and a tall candelabra next to the window, behind Trafficante and Rocko. Then they also heard a loud crashing of plates in the kitchen.

Johnny held up his hands. "Hold on, everyone. Don't get excited. We have enough light here." He glanced back at the dark lobby. "In fact, I think we have the only light in the place. We're not going anywhere."

He stepped over to the table, beside Junior and Cox, and looked across it to Trafficante. "You did talk it over with Gatto, didn't you?"

Trafficante nodded nervously. His eyes darted around the room. "We kicked around a few ideas. That's all. I turned the thing over to Cox, after I talked to Giancana in Chicago."

"And Sam Giancana told you he had an inside contact that you could work with, didn't he?"

"That Cox could work with." Trafficante's lips were trembling. "Not me."

"But he told you he had someone who owed him a favor, didn't he?"

"He just said he had the wheels all greased. I didn't know who he was talking about."

Johnny looked down at Cox and put his hand on the man's shoulder. "Just be easy, Cox. You didn't know the people involved, did you? They were just names to you, right? Mafia types who probably needed to die anyway. Your little private army could take care of that, couldn't they?"

"I sent men to do a job somebody else wanted done. Santos told me it would make our plans go easier, that we could prevent the Cuban government from taking out its revenge against one of our ambassadors or perhaps even someone higher up in the government. It was a matter of an ounce of prevention, a stitch in time."

"Well, that's it," Rocko said. "Trafficante and Giancana fingered the boss, and Cox and his Cubans pulled it off."

Johnny ignored him. He continued looking down at Cox. "And you had someone right there who could give your men the plans, the timetable for this action."

"Right. Somebody else who wanted the man dead."

Johnny held out his hand in Junior's direction, and Junior reached into his pocket and produced a piece of paper. "I happen to have your plans here. We took it out of the safe at the Cuban camp. It has a map to the road your men took, dates, and times. It's signed with a one-letter initial."

He passed the paper around the table. Each of the people took a good look at the fancy *B* that was initialed at the bottom of the plans.

Rocko looked it over and passed it back to Johnny. "What is that supposed to mean?"

"It's the identity of our inside man, the one who set Papa up, the one he trusted."

Rocko shook his head. "You're not telling me that Baldassare had anything to do with your father's murder, are you?"

Johnny looked across the table at him. "No, Rocko. You're the one who did that. Remember that day Papa was killed? He wanted to be alone with me. You told him he couldn't take me inside because a lot of people in there wanted to see him."

"There were," Rocko blurted out.

"But with the party going on, you wanted to make sure he would be alone with me on the beach. That was the only place left, the place you had instructed your assassins to be."

"Hey, you're forgetting. I almost got killed along with you in Chicago and then had to protect you in New York when you were meeting with this Felix guy."

The windows rattled once again. The high winds were picking up. The sound of the breakers was getting closer.

Johnny smiled confidently. "Yes, let's talk about that. You had words with Giancana before we left there. You no doubt set that up. As far as New York goes, you're forgetting, I took your gun from you. Before I gave it back, I checked the chamber. Three rounds had been fired by you, not two. You said you had returned fire, but in fact you had fired all three shots yourself."

He leaned forward on the table, fixing his eyes on Rocko. "You tried to have us all killed on this trip, didn't you? Junior at the Cuban camp, the guy in my room with the knife, and Gina whom you let go back to the hotel by herself. You fingered all of us. You knew our every move all the time. You could tell them where to find us."

Junior scooted forward in his chair. "You talked me into staying in the camp that night. Said I could learn more if I slept with them, got to know them." He pointed his finger at Rocko. "And I saw you talking to that guy who tried to kill me, that Nasser. You set me up."

Johnny looked at Trafficante, who was seated next to Rocko. "I'm sure you had your buddy Santos here carry it out for you. Those were his boys, his and our government agent's here." His eyes bored into Trafficante. "It was probably your idea to murder Baldassare though, 'cause he took your money."

Johnny crossed his arms and leaned back. "It must be nice for you to have your own private army, isn't it, Santos? You got people to carry out your murders, and they can't be touched, can they? After all, they're on the federal payroll."

"I didn't have anything to do with your father," Trafficante stammered.

"But you did get a call from Rocko here asking for your help with us, didn't you? You knew he was involved up to his eyeballs."

Trafficante nodded.

"Why would I want to do such a thing?" Rocko shouted. "You can't believe this man. That storm out there's got him scared out of his head. He's liable to tell you anything."

Once again, Johnny leaned across the table in Rocko's direction. "You had every reason to do what you did, in your own twisted mind. You had financing from Giancana for a club in Vegas that you could run, a club my father never would have given you. You saw him getting old and figured your usefulness to the family was getting old with him. This was your chance at the brass ring, and you grabbed for it."

Gina nodded. "You felt ignored, didn't you, Rocko? But you never felt ignored in Vegas. You thought if you had your own club, even with someone else's money, that nobody could ever ignore you again." She shook her head. "You opened your heart to me, then sent me out on the street to die."

Johnny reached for the piece of paper and turning it around, shoved it across the table at Rocko. "That's your initial isn't it? B, Rocko Benedeto. It's something like a prayer, isn't it, a benediction. And this is your benediction, old friend. You're finished."

The front door crashed open, and McDonald stumbled into the lobby. He picked himself up and shouted. "We've got walls of water out there, and they're headed right for us. You folks better get yourself upstairs and right now."

With that, Rocko spun around and knocked down the glowing candelabra. He dashed for the door.

Junior jumped to his feet.

Johnny put his hand on his shoulder. "I'll get him."

"Not without me you don't."

CHAPTER 42

With the wind blowing in their faces, Johnny and Junior raced to the hotel door, which was banging wildly. Only traces of the dock were visible through the blowing rain and walls of water coming onshore. The huge waves, some towering over twenty feet, slammed into the dock and spun the little boat around.

Johnny spotted the faint figure of Rocko as he climbed the rise in the direction of the old lighthouse. The man dropped down on all fours, struggling against the wind. Johnny pointed. "There he is."

Rocko scrambled to his feet. He fought hard to keep his balance, then disappeared into the driving rain.

Junior cupped his hands and held them up to Johnny's ear. "Maybe we should just wait for him, wait till this thing blows over." Then, thinking the matter over, he shouted, "No. If there's a way off this place, he'll find it. Let's go get him."

Johnny nodded.

They clamored down the porch, hanging on to the handrails. The fury of the wind pressed them backward, and they struggled to fight it.

They were soaked to the skin by the time they cleared the last steps. They ran in the direction of the bluffs that overlooked the beach. There was a path there that led to the lighthouse. They stumbled and Junior fell flat. Johnny reached down and pulled him up. The waves were crashing against the steep bank. The wind blew biting spray into them, and needles of water pelted them with each step.

Junior grabbed Johnny and shouted. "Is this going to get worse? If it does, it'll take everything and everyone off this island."

Johnny pointed in the direction of the stone lighthouse. He shouted, jabbing his finger in the air for emphasis. "Everyone, but him."

The rain was blinding, stabbing at their eyes and faces like millions of tiny spears. Bits of sand were mixed with the rain, and the combination of sand, wind, and seawater felt almost solid.

At the top of the rise, they could see the dark outline of the orphanage to their left. The lighthouse was straight ahead. The orphanage buildings were still standing, but the wind was blowing shingles off the roof like cards in a mixer.

Junior grabbed Johnny's arm. "Should we go down there and check on them first?"

Johnny nodded. "Yeah, maybe we should."

They ran down the hill, the wind at their backs. It pushed them along like so much debris caught up in the storm. They could hardly keep their feet under them. The wind spun them around and sent them to the wet ground with a skidding thud. They scrambled to their feet, slipping and sliding on the wet grass.

When they got to the steel handrails that led up to the main door, they hung on for dear life. The wind roared at their backs, propelling them face first into the door.

It took both of them to pull the door open. They squeezed a small crack through the narrow opening, and the door slammed behind them.

They could hear children singing. "Go tell it on the mountain, over the hills and everywhere. Go tell it on the mountain, that Jesus Christ is born."

Running down the hallway, they came to the classroom. The nuns had already nailed plywood over the windows. The room was dark except for a few candles on the desk at the front of the room. The children were seated in rows with the nuns standing between them. They had tied two ropes connecting the children, and one nun in the middle of each line, like an anchor.

Sister Mary Margaret held up her hand to stop the children's singing. "Here are our gentlemen guests again, children." Her soft eyes peered out at them from her tiny glasses. "You are most welcome here," she said. "Can we help you?"

Johnny shook his head. "No, Sister. We were wondering if we could help you. Are you all right?"

"Mercy, yes." She held up her hands. "The Lord is our shepherd, we shall not want. Do not worry about us. Even though we walk through the valley of the shadow of death, we will fear no evil, for He is with us."

She looked at the children. "Isn't that right children?"

They all answered with a resounding "Yes."

"And we have nothing to fear, do we children?"

"No." The children slowly shook their heads.

The nun smiled at them. "So you see, all is well here. We have nothing to fear. God is with us."

Junior spoke up. "Sister, we've seen what's outside. If I were you, I'd get the children upstairs. The water will be in here in no time."

Sister Mary Margaret looked at Sister Janene. "Perhaps they are right. Maybe we should go upstairs."

The other nun nodded rapidly.

"All right children." She clapped her hands. "Let's get to our feet and go upstairs, just like we showed you."

The children all stood up and began to march in place.

"All right, children, good, very good. Now let's march." In single file they moved to the door, first the group connected to Sister Janene. Mary Margaret's group continued to march in place until the other group was safely through the door. "Now let's go, children," she said. "March."

"Are you sure you wouldn't be safer at the hotel?" Johnny asked. "We could help you get there."

"Mercy, no," she shook her head. "This is God's special place. He will protect us."

Johnny and Junior watched the long chain go up the stairs.

"She might be right," Junior said.

Johnny shook his head. "I don't think she knows what's coming."

"Neither do we."

They walked to the assembly hall the nun had called their chapel and stood by the door. They could hear the fearsome wind outside. Junior looked at Johnny. "Is this what you meant by facing death?"

Johnny nodded. "Yes." He put his arm on Junior's shoulder. "I gotta tell you though, boy, if I'm going to face it again, I'm just glad it's with you."

Junior smiled. "Are you praying?"

"You bet your bottom dollar I am."

Putting their shoulders to the door, they shoved with all their might. The door resisted but cracked open enough so they could squeeze through.

The wind met them head-on. They sank to their knees and grappled for the metal handrails, crawling as they went. They could feel more sand mixed with the water now. Finally finding the ground, they stumbled forward. The rise in the bluff would offer them some protection, but already they could see the waves crashing against the top of that. For all Johnny knew, the lower floors of the lighthouse might already be underwater.

They swerved as they tried to run, fighting the wind. Occasionally, they would slam into each other. Then they would bounce off and continue to run, squat, drop, and stumble again in the direction of the faint outline of the stone lighthouse.

When they got to the path that led from the bluff to the old lighthouse, they could see the waves washing across it. The bluff and the path had been a good twenty to thirty feet above the beach. Now the whole key seemed to be awash with the fearsome sea.

Johnny took Junior's hand. He waited until he saw a set of breakers hit the bluff, then tugged. Both men started to run ankle deep in the surge and up to their calves and legs through retreating water.

Johnny could see the outline of the steps and the door that led to the stone tower. He pointed out to sea. A large twenty-foot dome of water was moving swiftly over the surface of the ocean, carrying away everything in its path. He screamed, "We have to get to the door before that thing hits."

Both men moved with deliberate steps toward the tower, leaning forward against the wind and struggling with the water snarling at their legs and trying to carry them out.

Johnny fell, and Junior stopped to help him up, wrapping his arms around Johnny and wresting him to his feet. They lunged for the cold steps, their fingers grasping at the wet concrete. On hands and knees they crawled up the steps, and, finally, Johnny yanked the door open.

The door slammed shut behind them, and they could hear the rush of water cover the steps. It washed in the bottom of the door, sending a river over the cold floor.

The place was dark, like a tomb. The spiraling staircase towered above them, winding up into the lighthouse. The surf crashing against the stones echoed in the tower. Faint light, along with a shower of seawater, filtered in from the broken windows. Water trickled along the steel stairway, forming tributaries that cascaded down from stair to stair.

"We know you're here, Rocko," Johnny shouted into the darkness.

They waited for a moment, but heard nothing.

"You might as well give up," Johnny shouted. "We have the evidence, all the evidence we need to convict you."

Suddenly, they could hear the echo of laughter, a gravelly, rolling laugh that carried down the stairs. "That evidence and all those people will be washed away tomorrow. And you'll be with it. I'm glad you're here, Johnny boy. It'll save me the trouble of looking for your body." He laughed again, a rumbling, menacing sound. "I won't even have to take you back to your mama, just be there for the grieving. They'll believe me, their precious, long-lost son, finally lost for good. She won't even have to cry. She's cried enough tears over you. That's long gone now."

"You think everyone will be gone but you?" Johnny yelled.

"I know they will. You forget. I've got a great view from up here. I know what's coming. Nobody's getting off this place but me."

"I don't understand you," Johnny called out. "It's over. Believe me. Give up. I've always thought of you as family."

"I am family," Rocko called out. "But you left your family a long time ago. We get old. We're shoved aside. Sometimes a man's just got to look out for himself."

"But Papa trusted you."

"Yeah, and I feel bad about that. He wanted me close, too close. He was suffocating me. I hated to do it, and I'm gonna hate to kill you too."

Johnny turned and looked for the dials he had seen earlier. He felt the walls with his fingers, finally finding the switch. He whispered in Junior's direction, "These interior lights are on batteries. Let's shed a little light on the subject."

He flipped the switch, and the small bulbs that had lit the stairs came on, casting a series of shadows over the rock walls. They could see the water coming from the windows now, tentacles of seawater creeping down the walls and onto the floor. Together with the water seeping under the door, a large puddle was rising around their ankles. One large wave rattled the door.

"Let's go," Johnny said. "Follow me."

The two men climbed the stairs. The water rippled over their shoe tops with each step. There was no stopping it, and there was no stopping the muffled roar of the waves outside the stone structure. It beat against the stone tower with great fury.

"Come on up, Johnny," the low voice sounded from the tower. "Be the hero. You've always been the hero, haven't you?" More gurgling laughter rumbled down the length of the tower. "You just forgot one thing. I'm armed. You're the Boy Scout here, not me."

Junior patted his underarm. His face went blank. He wasn't carrying a weapon.

Johnny reached down and unsnapped the PPK from his ankle holster. He had been wading through seawater, and he could only hope the pistol still worked. He gripped the black handle. The Germans always made good guns. That gave him some confidence. "Don't be so sure of that, Rocko," he yelled up into the staircase. "You forget, you've taught me a lot on this trip, never to trust anyone and never to come to a gunfight armed with a knife. I learn my lessons. I'm a good student."

"Come ahead, Boy Scout. I'm waiting for you."

They continued the slow climb up the stairs. Johnny peered up into the dark spots the lights weren't getting to. He was beginning to feel sorry he'd thrown the switch. He was sure now that Rocko could see more of them than they could of him. The one thing Rocko didn't know was that Junior was with him.

Johnny turned back to Junior. "You wait here for a minute," he whispered. "Give me the chance to get to him first."

Junior shook his head. "No chance." He spoke in a low tone. "You got the only gun."

"But he doesn't know you're here. It'll be better this way. Trust me."

Junior took a deep breath, sucking in the air with his nose, then blowing it out. "All right. But I won't let you get too far."

All of a sudden, a huge wave hit the lighthouse. It exploded through a couple of the broken windows, sending a shower of glass mixed with seawater onto Johnny and Junior.

Johnny reached up and wiped his face with his left hand. He slung the water away, shaking his fingers. He gripped the little automatic and headed up the stairs. The loops of steel that made up the meandering staircase made it difficult to see. It also made Johnny an easy target. He knew that. Rocko could find a good spot and wait for him to come into view. Johnny knew he had to be careful. He also knew that Junior was right about one thing. He had the only gun. If Rocko managed to kill him, he would also find and kill Junior.

He crouched low and wound his way up the stairs.

"You coming, Johnny?" Rocko shouted. "It's better this way. A bullet's better than drowning. I figure I'm doing you a favor."

This is good, Johnny thought. He wiped the water away from his eyes. *If I can only keep him talking, then I'll know better about where he is. But how? How do I keep him talking without giving myself away?*

He crouched low and kept the little automatic pointed up toward where Rocko must be waiting. There would be no time. Everything would happen in a split second.

Then he saw the broom he had moved earlier. He picked it up. He would make another forward pass, something that might catch Rocko off guard. He could barely see the open door of the dark upper room now. Rocko must be there, waiting.

He transferred the gun to his left hand and held the broom like a spear. Taking another few steps, he leaned back and heaved the thing.

The broom hit the landing above him. Shots thundered, three of them. He could see the plumes of flame stabbing out of the dark room. Rocko's .45 made a resounding noise in the close confines of the tower, so much so that the man would never be able to hear Johnny's footsteps.

Then he heard the man laugh again. "A broom. Is that the best you can do? I can say this for you, you ain't well armed."

Suddenly, Johnny saw him. Rocko stepped into the doorway, apparently in an attempt to crow over his imagined conquest. Johnny aimed low and fired. He heard a yelp of pain as Rocko disappeared once again into the room.

Johnny took the last of the stairs running. Johnny didn't know how badly Rocko had been hit, but he wasn't about to wait until the man recovered. He burst into the room and ran straight at the darkened figure who was still backing up. They both landed on the bare springs of the bed, the .45 tumbling out of Rocko's hand.

Johnny landed a couple of punches to Rocko's face. They had little effect because the big man was much too close.

Rocko gripped him around the neck and head, turning him over. "So, you did have a gun."

He grabbed Johnny's hand, the one with the gun, and shook it. The small automatic came free, bouncing and then sliding across the wooden floor. "Too bad it was just a kiddie gun," Rocko growled.

He got to his feet, dragging Johnny upright. He sent a blow to the side of Johnny's head, stunning him. Johnny's head was buzzing.

The man was enormous. Johnny was feeling the effect of being out of his weight class. Rocko sent a couple of blows into his stomach that doubled Johnny in pain.

"You like boxing," Rocko said. "I'm going to show you some close-in fighting."

Johnny tried to shield himself from the man's punches, but several of them landed cleanly. Rocko kept hitting him, sending him backward toward the large window.

"Hey, big man." Junior stepped into the dark room. He motioned with his hands. "Why don't you try me on for size?"

Rocko looked over to the door. He grinned. "I didn't know you'd come. It'll be a pleasure. I always kill the children first, 'cause they run."

He dropped Johnny to the floor like so much dirty laundry, then ran for Junior. The man never missed a step. After Junior landed a punch with little effect, Rocko hit him with a powerful blow to the chin. Johnny could see Junior's knees buckle. Rocko then shoved him out onto the landing. "Now we see how you handle a fall, a big fall."

Grabbing Junior, Rocko jerked him over to the railing.

Johnny crawled in their direction. He got to his knees and stumbled up.

Rocko bent Junior over the rail. He lifted him to send him over the rail, grabbing the young man's arm and leg.

Johnny laid his hands on Rocko's wet shirt and spun him around. He pulled him forward, away from Junior.

"You again." Rocko pushed him to the floor of the steel landing. "You want more?"

Johnny was starting to get to his feet when the big man came charging at him. Johnny rolled forward, into his legs.

Rocko spun out of the way and landed hard on the steel railing. The broken section Johnny had fixed came loose. Rocko's eyes widened. He grasped for the wet steel and stumbled backward off the platform.

Johnny jumped to his feet. He ran over to where the man was hanging on to the loose piece of railing.

Rocko reached out his hand, and Johnny grabbed it. Rocko's lips quivered as he hung in midair. His eyes looked deep in to Johnny's. "I'm sorry, kid. Don't think too bad about me."

Then the grip slipped. Johnny watched as Rocko fell down the tower, flipping over and over before landing at the watery bottom. Johnny laid his head down on the stub of the steel rail.

The stone tower shuddered suddenly as an enormous wave crashed up against it. The water was rising.

CHAPTER 43

Maria was the last to leave the dining room. She stepped into the lobby in time to see the others who had been at dinner retreating upstairs. She circled the big counter and opened the wooden hatch. It came down behind her with a bang. Then she started going through the drawers. Some of them were filled with papers and envelopes. One drawer was overflowing with receipts, bits of paper, and string.

She slid open the long drawer under the cash register and there she saw what she was looking for, a revolver. She pulled it out and stuffed it behind her belt. Most businesses in America kept a handgun near the cash register. The Queen Hotel was no exception. As implausible as it might seem on Crab Key, McDonald was like the rest of the Yankees. He trusted no one.

She continued her search through the files until she came to a small slot that contained a beat-up flashlight. She picked it up and shook it, then turned it on. The beam was faint, but it was light. It worked.

She made her way out from behind the big counter, slamming the hatch behind her. She could hear the pounding surf outside the door. It would be only a matter of minutes before the entire downstairs was flooded. It didn't give her much time. This wasn't exactly the place she wanted to die, but if she could do it while killing an enemy of Cuba, it would be worth it.

She climbed the stairs into the dark hall above. She began to shake the brass knobs on the doors, one after another. One of the doors opened, and she poked her head inside. Cox and Trafficante were standing in the room. Maria shone the light on their faces—both men looked frozen with fear.

"Maria? Is that you," Cox asked. He was trembling.

"Si." She slammed the door and backed out into the hall. A *perfect way for the men to die*, she thought. *Two murderers together.*

She moved down the hall, shaking each doorknob. A second door flew open. Gina was standing in the middle of the room.

"Maria?" She asked.

"Yes." Maria stepped into the room. The doors and shutters that led out onto the balcony were buckling and slamming against one another. Maria stepped past Gina and looked out at the foaming surf beneath the hotel. "Señora, I think you should climb outside, onto the roof."

"The roof?"

"Si, the water will sweep away this hotel, but the roof floats. You get out and hang on. I will help you."

Gina nodded. "All right."

Maria opened the shutters and took the bolt out of the banging doors. The doors flew open with great fury, smashing the glass as the doors hit the walls. The wind was coming into the room now. It roared past them like a runaway freight train, ripping the pictures off the walls and sending them flying.

Maria grabbed the doorframe with her left hand and reached out for Gina with her right. "Take my hand," she screamed.

Gina leaned into the wind, bracing herself against the onslaught of wind and seawater that was rushing through the room. Her fingers felt for Maria's and then, touching them, hung on.

Maria pulled Gina forward. Both of them fought to get out onto the balcony. They didn't have much time, and Maria knew it.

When Gina was past her, Maria slipped in behind her and pushed. It took them time, but soon they were out on the balcony.

Maria shouted into Gina's ear. "Step in my hands and push yourself to the roof. The wind will keep you next to the wall. Don't worry about falling."

Gina nodded.

Maria bent down and laced her fingers together. Gina stepped up and hoisted herself to the side of the building. She could reach the roof. Her fingers clung to the wooden gutters on the top. Maria was right. The wind did plaster Gina onto the hotel. Gina began scrambling with her feet, trying to inch her way into position. She pushed herself up and swung over the top.

She then leaned back down and offered Maria her hand. "Here. Take my hand," she screamed.

Maria shook her head. "No. There's something I have to do first."

Making her way back to the doorway, the wind slammed her against the banging doors. It bounced her into the room, and she tumbled onto the bed and then over it, flipping and landing on her back on the other side of the bed. She felt for the revolver behind her belt. It was gone. *Where was it?*

She switched on the flashlight and crawled over the carpet on her hands and knees, feeling for the cold steel of the revolver. The wind was moving the tables now, and she could feel even the bed shifting. The noise of the surf was growing more intense. Soon the downstairs would be awash and the whole building might very well collapse.

Then her hand touched it, the revolver. She picked it up and stuffed it behind her belt. She stumbled to her feet and slammed against the door. Squeezing around it, she entered the hallway. She braced herself and once again moved down the hall.

She pushed open another door and saw him. Felix was huddled down behind the bed, his back to her. Maria pulled out the revolver and cocked it. "Get on your feet, you coward," she shouted.

The man looked back at her and held up his hands. "No," he yelled.

"Yes, on your feet." She shook the gun. "Or I'll kill you right where you are."

Felix tottered to his feet, holding on to the bedpost. "Now you're going to be a murderer too," he shouted.

"No." She waggled the gun in the direction of the balcony window. "We're going to see how much you love your country." She grinned. "I'm going to give you a chance to swim to Cuba. You love it so much and you love your Marxist revolution. Swim to it," she shouted.

He rounded the bed as she stepped forward. He held up his hands. "You can't do this."

Maria marched forward. "Yes I can and I will. Today is the day you die." She shook the gun. "You will be judged, but why should you worry? You're a Marxist. There is no God in your world."

He backed up to the bolted doors of the balcony.

Maria stepped forward and then froze. There outside the window was a thirty-foot dome of water heading straight for the hotel.

Johnny and Junior spent the night in the tower. When the eye of the storm passed overhead, the water was still covering the entrance to the old lighthouse. There had been no way to get out. The water level inside the tower itself had been well above their heads, rising to the midway point of the staircase. The remainder of the storm that followed the eye hit them during the wee hours of the morning. It was close to midday before they could wade to the door.

Both men put their shoulders to the door and pressed hard. It gave with great effort, and they squeezed outside.

The sky was a bright robin's-egg blue, with seagulls sweeping in lazy loops. There was almost no wind, just a gentle ripple that tugged at their hair.

They started across what was left of the path that led to the bluffs overlooking the beach. Most of the hillside was washed away, and the sand from the beach was piled high. It would be some time before the beach regained its normal shape.

When they got to the top of the bluff, they could see a line of children seated in front of what had once been their dormitory and school. In the midst of them was Sister Janene. To the left was the hotel, or what was left of it. The roof had collapsed, and the *Cat-o'-Nine* was now resting in what had once been the hotel lobby.

Junior bit his lower lip. "Do you think anyone got out of the hotel?"

"I don't know. Let's go see to the sister."

They walked over to where the nun was seated with the children on the ground. The young woman seemed stunned, and she stared off into the sea beyond.

Johnny bent down and put his hand on her shoulder. "Are you all right, Sister?"

Her far-off look never changed.

"Where's Sister Mary Margaret?" Johnny asked.

One of the little boys raised his arm and pointed to a spot behind the debris that had been their home. His finger shook. "Sh-sh-she's over there."

Johnny stood up straight. "We better go take a look."

They started for the wreckage of the school. Wood, corrugated metal, and furniture were heaped on what was left of a concrete foundation. Books were strewn everywhere, along with rulers and samples of the children's artwork.

When they rounded the mass of destruction, they saw her. The old nun was lying on the ground, still tied to her string of children. They seemed peaceful, at rest and content.

Johnny and Junior walked over to them. Junior began to cry. Johnny put his arm around him. "Don't worry about her, son. She's with the Lord, with the Lord and her children." He swallowed hard, staring at the children. "And the children will never be abandoned again."

"Why?" Junior shook his head and wiped his eyes. "I don't understand it. Why'd it have to be her? And why kids? What did they ever do?"

"The statistics on death are remarkable. One hundred percent of people die. The real questions are, how do we live our lives? Whom do we touch? Do we please God? This nun died doing what she loved, loving and protecting her children. That's the lesson she would have wanted us to learn."

"What lesson?"

"God put us here to love people, not drive fancy cars and live in big houses. We won't be remembered for those things, but she'll be remembered for this. Her life counted. It made a difference."

Junior looked over at the debris that had once been the hotel. He left Johnny and started to run toward it. Johnny followed.

When he caught up to him, Junior was tossing large planks of wood aside. "Hello," he called out. "Is there anybody here?"

"John? John? Is that you?"

They heard a voice from behind the wreckage of the hotel. It was Gina. Junior dropped the piece of plywood he was holding and ran to the sound of the voice. "Mom!" he called out. "Is that you, Mom?"

Gina stepped out from behind the crumbled hotel and opened her arms. Junior picked her up and held her, kissing her cheeks. "Mother. You don't know how glad I am to see you." He kissed her again. "I didn't know what had happened to you. If I'd known it was going to be this bad, I wouldn't have gone."

She put her hands though his hair. "I'm glad you did. You're safe. I made it through all right." She glanced at Johnny. "Thanks to Maria."

"Where is she?" Johnny asked.

Gina shook her head. "Gone. They're all gone. She helped me get to the roof but then left. I think she was so intent on killing that ex-husband of hers that she couldn't think about anything else. Hatred is a terrible thing."

Johnny stepped closer to them. "Did I hear right? You're Junior's mother?"

Gina smiled, then looked at Junior. She put her arm around him and then fastened her eyes on Johnny. "Yes, you heard right. He's your son. I didn't want to tell you without first talking to him. Figured it would then be up to him. I didn't even tell him the whole story, just that you and I were once boyfriend and girlfriend. But I named him

John, after you. I started calling him Junior, because he was." She smiled.

"Johnny never knew what happened." She turned to Johnny. "Your parents never said a word about it. They sent me away and took care of me, then sent me to college and law school." She looked back at Junior. "As you know, they raised you like a grandson. That's because you were."

"Why?" Junior asked. "Why didn't they ever say anything?"

Gina smiled. "You know how people are. They didn't like my family. I suppose in a way they thought it wasn't good enough to be a part of theirs. Johnny would have made it right if he'd known about it, but he didn't know."

"Didn't Junior ever ask about his father?" Johnny asked.

"Of course he did. I always told him his father had gone off to war, which was true."

Junior glanced at Johnny and then Gina. "I knew something. The way you two look at each other. It had to be more than you were letting on."

Johnny reached over and tousled Junior's curly hair. "The kid's got his mother's brains. I think people can sense things even when it isn't being talked about."

He took Junior's hand. "I suppose at some level I always wondered if Gina had my baby. She just disappeared, vanished. I never said much. Thought she never wanted to see me again. My letters were all returned. But I would see a boy in a schoolyard and picture you. I'd see a little girl all dressed up with dark curly hair and imagine her to be mine. I told my wife, Karen, about it before we married. I was ashamed. She understood. She told me I was just a boy, not a bad boy, just a boy."

Johnny put his hand on his shoulder. "Can you ever forgive me, John?"

MORRO BAY, CALIFORNIA
MONDAY, OCTOBER 22

CHAPTER 44

The black limousine pulled up to the beach house gates, and the motor on the iron gate churned, cranking open the steel enclosure. The brass lion heads parted, and the big Lincoln rumbled down the drive.

Johnny knew that Mitch and Nancy would be overjoyed to see him, but he also knew that he had unfinished business. He wanted to check on Isabella, and then there was the matter of his mother. She had lost a husband and a son in only a matter of weeks. He wondered if having him come back could ever make a difference.

They pulled up to the entrance, and Junior was the first one out. The driver tossed him the keys, and he opened the trunk and carried two of their bags inside, his and his mother's. Gina put her hand on Johnny's. "I guess this whole thing isn't over for you yet."

Johnny shook his head. "No, I'm afraid not. Wish I could say I was lovable enough to pass muster. But what are you going to do with a kid who runs away from home?"

"You'll be fine." She patted his hand.

They slid out of the car, and Johnny took his bag. He breathed deeply. The salt smell of the ocean always had a special effect on him. It made him think of happier times. When they got inside, most of the family were gathered around the television set in the great room. Some sat on chairs, hunched over to get a better view. Others paced nervously. They were watching a broadcast from the United Nations. The American ambassador, Adlai Stevenson, was smiling at the Soviet delegate and showing photographs of Russian missiles in Cuba.

Arturo waved the two of them over. "Look at this," he said. "The Russians have rockets in Cuba. They could even hit California with those things. Can you believe it?"

Johnny set down his bag. "I think I've seen enough of Cuba to last me a lifetime." He followed Gina into the kitchen.

The counter was covered with fresh vegetables on the cutting boards. Anna beat a batch of dough in an oversize metal bowl, her muscled arms churning madly.

Gina walked up to her and put her arms around her waist. Anna turned around, smiling.

"We're back, Mother."

Anna's smile quickly turned sour when she saw Johnny standing at the door.

"Mother, everything's out now. Junior knows that Johnny's his father."

"It's about time," the old woman blurted out. "He should have known a long time ago."

Gina smiled. "He's smart, Mother. I think he knew already." She glanced back at Johnny. "He said he could see something between us."

"But there's nothing there now?" Anna was concerned. She dropped her eyebrows when she asked Gina the question. Johnny didn't much blame her. Her daughter had lived in shame and her grandson without a father. It was only right that she should blame him.

"But it's not his fault, Mother. He didn't know. His parents never told him and his letters to me were returned. So I won't have you blaming him."

Johnny stepped forward. "It's all right, Gina. I understand. Your mother's had a lot of years faulting me for what happened to you. It's going to take her some time."

He looked at Anna. "I can only say that I'm very sorry for the pain and the shame I must have cost you. What we did was wrong, only I didn't know it then. Gina and I were in love, and I didn't think about anything else. I was young." He shook his head. "And kind of stupid. I can only ask for your forgiveness."

He saw her face begin to soften. "I know that God is sovereign. Nothing catches Him by surprise. Think about what life would be like without John. He's a fine young man. I'm only sorry I haven't been around to help raise him. But you have done a wonderful job, you and Gina here."

Gina smiled at him.

"I'd better go find Mitch and Nancy, maybe introduce them to their brother." He scratched his head, shaking it. "It's going to be a shock to them, like it was to me."

Johnny spent the next hour with his kids in the guest house, all three of them. There was a nervousness in John Jr., but Nancy and Mitch helped with that. Both of them could laugh about having him as a brother. They made Junior feel comfortable. They asked him many questions about his life and told him all about their own lives—school, romances, dreams, and hopes.

When Johnny got up to go, Junior stood up too. "Can I have a word with you?" he asked.

"Sure. Walk with me."

Junior turned to Mitch and Nancy. "I'll be right back. I just need to talk to your father for a few minutes."

"Your father too," Nancy said.

"Oh, yeah, right." Junior smiled and nodded.

They walked out of the guesthouse and down the walk. "I just wanted to talk to you about what we discussed."

"What's that?"

"You know, about my life, God and all."

Johnny gave a sheepish grin. "Oh yes." They continued walking.

"I've been thinking about what you said, about me finding God. I don't know what that means yet, but I'd sure like to look. I keep thinking about that nun, Sister Mary Margaret, and those children. Made me and what I'm doing seem kind of small."

Johnny stopped and faced him. "You know, John, you can be anything you want to be. The world is open to you. The only question is what you are on the inside. How you make your money follows that."

Junior nodded. "Yes, I'm sure of that. Can we talk about this later? I'd like to get back to Mitch and Nancy. We've got a lot of catching up to do."

Johnny watched him walk away. He had hope for the man. At least there was an openness there. *God, I've got a lot of catching up to do with this family,* he prayed. *Help me to do it, to make things right. You've always taught me that there's no fix I can ever get into that true humility can't deliver me from. I need that now, humility.*

He walked back into the house and up the stairs to Isabella's room, knocking on the door.

"Come in."

He opened the door and stepped into her room. Isabella was in jeans, dressed in a paint smock with blotches of color all over it. She was working on a new painting, something she had never done before, impressionist. Johnny stepped over behind her. "That's new, isn't it?"

She laughed. "Yes. I figured I'd do something more like me. Thought I'd create"—she leaned back to admire her work—"just a touch of confusion."

"It does look like you, Sis." Johnny laughed. "The strokes are everywhere." He put his thumbs together and framed the painting with his hands. "Just like you. Can't exactly tell what it's going to turn out to be."

"Have you talked to Mama, yet?"

"Not yet."

"Kinda scared, huh?"

Johnny chuckled. "Maybe a little, I guess."

"Well, don't be. No matter what kind of noise she makes, she still loves you. Oh sure, she would have picked a different career for you and a different church, but she loves you all the same. You were always the golden boy, remember?"

Johnny nodded. "Probably makes her disappointment that much worse."

"Well, I believe in you."

Johnny reached out and embraced her, wrapping his arms around her. "Isabella, I believe in you too. I know you've had a lot of discouragement in life, but you'll always be that same sweet little girl who used to bring me her finger paintings. You were so alive. That's still in you."

"And I'm looking forward to getting to know you better, Johnny." Her eyes twinkled. "You got smarts. I need that."

Johnny held her back. "OK, Sis, deal. You come see us in San Francisco. Maybe we'll show some of your work in the galleries up there." He glanced at her painting. "Like the one you're doing now."

When he left Isabella, he walked slowly to his mother's room. He was a big boy now, a grown man. Still, there was something about facing a mother's disapproval that didn't sit well with him. He also had to remember not to sound too moralizing. His mother would never take well to a sermon on forgiveness. He was odd as far as she was concerned, out of place. His mother liked things tidy, all her dolls in a row and each dressed in their finest. Johnny hadn't been that way in his mom's mind in years.

He knocked lightly on her door.

"Come in."

Johnny opened the door and stepped inside. His mother was sitting in her favorite chair, the one that looked out on the beach behind the house. For some reason he felt it hard to speak. He just stood there.

"Come over here, Johnny. I know it's you."

Johnny smiled. Mothers always seemed to have eyes in the back of their heads, and his was no exception. He walked toward her. "Mama, I just thought I'd come and tell you about our trip."

She turned and looked at him. Tears were welling in her eyes. "I already heard. Junior came up and talked to me. So did Gina. They told me everything."

Johnny hung his head. "I'm sorry about Baldassare. I didn't even know he was down there."

Pia ripped a tissue out of a box that was sitting next to her. She dabbed her eyes with it. "You wouldn't have been able to stop him. He wouldn't have listened." She looked up at him with tears forming in her eyes. "Junior told me what you went through to find his body, how dangerous it was for you and how you did it for me."

Johnny said nothing.

She held out her hand for him. "I'm touched you would think of me."

Johnny took her hand. "I always think about you, Mama. I only hope you can forgive me for staying away from you for so long."

"You thought I disapproved of you, and I did. I am stubborn, and so are you."

Johnny smiled and nodded.

"Gina told me about how you found out her little secret."

"Yes, Mama."

"And Junior didn't seem too taken aback by it when I talked with him. I suppose he finally feels like some missing piece of the puzzle is back where it belongs."

"I never knew about this until Papa told me the day he died."

"It was for the best."

"Yes, Mama, I suppose it was. I loved Karen and our years together, and we have two wonderful kids. I wouldn't have missed that for the world."

"We all wind up missing out on something because of our mistakes. I missed out on you. You weren't part of our family."

"I am now, Mama."

She squeezed his hand.

There was a knock at the door, and Gina stepped in. When she saw them, she stopped in her tracks. "I'm sorry. I didn't mean to interrupt. You two probably need to talk."

Pia dropped Johnny's hand and waved Gina closer. "No, it's all right." She looked up at Johnny. "I think we've said everything that needed saying." She smiled. "But you two probably have a lot to talk over."

Johnny and Gina exchanged glances. The thought frightened him. He knew there was still chemistry between them. A man would have to be blind to miss that. Even Junior had caught it.

"I'm sure Johnny and I will be getting together for coffee when we get back to the Bay Area." Gina smiled. "I have to go over his father's trust with him."

"There is one thing there I would like to discuss." He looked at his mother. "On Crab Key there's a Catholic orphanage, the Sisters of the Lost. They were wiped out during the hurricane, and one of the nuns was killed. I would like to give part of my trust, whatever it takes, to help them rebuild."

Pia smiled. Her face brightened. "You would do that, a Catholic orphanage?"

"Of course. They're doing good work. I think Papa would be pleased."

Once again, Pia took his hand. "I'm sure of it, and I'm pleased."

WASHINGTON, D.C.
SUNDAY, OCTOBER 28

CHAPTER 45

A gentle rain fell on the lawn overlooking the Washington Monument. The attorney general had his customary Secret Service agents. Sam and Wendell were both in their mid-thirties, veterans of the Secret Service. Sam was tall and lanky, a deadly serious look about him as his eyes scanned the passersby. Wendell was the "people person." At least he would smile. He checked his watch.

"Yes, I know," Bobby said. "He's late. Probably trying to convince me of how important he is with the people at the Kremlin. No doubt he's going to hand me his latest wire from Mother Russia."

"Do you think he knows?" Wendell asked.

"About how far behind they are? I doubt it. The Russians only tell people who need to know. What better thing to tell a born liar than nothing. But we know. That's what counts. We tried for years to launch satellites that could tell us about Russian missile operations. Last year we finally got Corona up. When we recovered it, it showed us much more than all our U-2 flights combined."

Bobby nodded, rocking on the balls of his feet. "They're busy beavers all right, but what we saw was at the most only six ICBM sites. They're way behind, and if Gromyko doesn't know it, his bosses do."

"What about the missiles in Cuba?"

"That was their sucker punch. It's those things we have to worry about."

"What about the blockade?"

"That'll stop them from putting new missiles in, but it doesn't help us with the problem of what to do about what they've already got." He smiled at Wendell and wiped his nose. He'd picked up a cold. "That's why we're here. We're going to give them what we don't need and pull the teeth out of the tiger."

"Let's hope it works. The wife is getting kinda nervous these days."

"Yeah," Kennedy nodded. "Everybody is. The papers are full of it. Everybody's trying to guess who wins World War III. Truth is, nobody does. Now if we can just convince Khrushchev."

Suddenly, they saw him. Soviet Foreign Minister Andrei Gromyko was well built and in his fifties with a full head of dark hair and a quick smile. He walked along the sidewalk in their direction, trailed by two men who were obvious KGB agents. He wore a suit and a long, carefully tailored dark coat.

Wendell drifted into the background, and Bobby stuck out his hand. "Good to see you, Andrei."

Gromyko shook his hand. "My pleasure, Mr. Attorney General."

Gromyko's guards circled the meeting spot, only a few yards away. "So are we ready to talk?"

Gromyko nodded. "Of course. My government is reasonable. We are always ready to talk." His English was precise, although the heavily rolled r's of his Russian accent put a comical emphasis on *reasonable*.

"And are they equally ready to remove those missiles?"

"Those missiles are protecting our allies."

Bobby looked him in the eye. "Those missiles are endangering your country. They're putting us on the brink of war."

"Mr. Attorney General, if we were to remove our weapons because of your bullying, what would the Warsaw Pact nations think? They would have no confidence in us." He nudged Kennedy slightly with his fingers. "They would see us as being intimidated."

"They would see you as being wise. They might even trust you. Those countries who are in your orbit depend on you. If you are in a nuclear war, so are they."

"If we withdraw our weapons, then you will invade. You've tried that once already." He shook his head. "No, I am afraid our missiles must stay where they are. Cuba is a friend."

Bobby clasped his hands behind his back and started to pace. Gromyko pulled up his coat collar. The rain was starting to get to him.

Bobby suddenly stopped. "Suppose we strike a bargain?"

"What sort of bargain?"

"Suppose we promise not to invade and in return you withdraw your missiles. Of course we would have to have inspections."

"No inspections." Gromyko shook his head.

"We have to inspect to see if what you're telling us is true."

"And you will allow us to inspect your exile bases in Florida?"

"Don't be silly," Bobby smiled.

"Then you must understand why we cannot give in to your demands."

"OK. I'll give you another deal. We will remove our Jupiter missiles from Turkey and we'll inspect."

"No inspection." Gromyko shook his dead.

"But you will remove your missiles?"

"I will have to contact Moscow."

"OK, that's the deal. We take our Jupiter missiles out of Turkey and you take your missiles out of Cuba. The only thing is, you've got to start taking them out right away. We'll have to wait a few months before we take the Jupiters out of Turkey. We don't want these things to appear to be linked together."

Gromyko held up a finger. "But we must have your assurance that you will not get involved militarily in an attempt to invade or destabilize Cuba. Are we agreed?"

Bobby nodded. "Agreed."

Gromyko stuck out his hand. "OK, I'll contact Moscow and we'll make the arrangements."

"Fine, Andrei." Kennedy shook his hand. "We have a deal."

Bobby watched him walk off. Sam and Wendell stepped up to his side.

"Everything go OK?" Wendell asked.

Bobby nodded. "I think we have a deal. You can tell your wife to put away the dried food."

They started to walk back toward the car. "You know, I still get worried about this Cuba business," Sam said. Sam was the quiet, thoughtful type. His long face just made that natural for him to pull off.

"Well, it looks like we have that taken care of," Bobby shot back.

Sam shook his head. "No, not the missiles. I knew we could get through that."

"What then?"

"Castro. We keep trying to assassinate the man. From everything I've studied about Castro, I can tell you that he's not going to stand for it. And with the Russians pulling their missiles out, he's going to get even more desperate."

"What do you think he's going to do?"

They continued to walk. Sam staring at the ground. "I think he's going to retaliate, and in a big way."

Bobby looked at him. "Now how's he going to do that?"

"Castro may try to kill the president."